THE BOOK OF J.

AN ERIN SOLOMON MYSTERY

THE BOOK OF J.

AN ERIN SOLOMON MYSTERY

JEN BLOOD

Adian Press
Maine

Second Edition
ISBN: 978-0-9904076-9-0

Adian Press
934 River Rd. #1
Cushing, Maine 04563
www.adianpress.com

Publisher: Adian Press
Cover Design: damonza.com
Author's Photograph: Amy Wilton Photography

For Mom,
Who has read, re-read, edited,
and weighed in on every word
since Erin Solomon first began whispering in my ear.
I couldn't imagine this series without you.

1

WITH ONLY SLIGHT VARIATIONS, the dream remains the same: A Maine forest deep in the night, rain pouring down. I stand in the shadow of a pyramid that shouldn't be here—an ancient ruin that dwarfs the tall evergreens around me.

My father stands at the foot of the pyramid. His lips are moving, but I can't hear a word he says. He has a gun in his hand. Around him, there are bodies—dozens of them. People I knew from the Payson Church, burned but still recognizable. A woman who used to do the baking for the church sits on the ground, crying. Half the flesh of her face is burned away, one eye socket empty. Joe Ashmont is there. Matt Perkins, wailing like a lunatic. Max Richards. Bonnie Saucier, a bloody J. carved into her pale, naked breast. Everyone is dead—there's no question of that, but they are more real, more animated, than any live thing I've ever seen.

"Is this what you wanted?" my father asks me. He's younger than he was in that jungle in Coba—about the age I remember him from my childhood. The age I am now. "You did this. Is it what you wanted?"

My father raises the gun. I try to get up, but those masses—the writhing, rotting dead—are coming for me. I'm frozen. Terrified. My father points the gun.

The barrel touches his temple.

A second before the gun went off, something shattered beside me. I sat bolt upright in bed, my heart galloping. A gust of icy wind blew into the dark room and sent the curtains flying. I tried to figure out where my father was. Where the bodies were...

Where the hell I was.

I reached for Diggs beside me. His spot was empty.

A wriggling mass of fuzzy curls tried to escape my grasp. Einstein.

"Easy, buddy," I said. The sound of my own voice eased me back toward the real world.

I was in the Payson boarding home, I reminded myself. Shards of glass, strewn across the floor from a broken window behind me, sparkled in the moonlight. I could make out the peeling wallpaper and ancient furniture. Einstein whined, still trying to get away from me. After nine months without him, I wasn't keen to let the mutt go—forget the fact that his paws would be cut to ribbons if I did. As would mine.

"Diggs!" I shouted. No answer.

I reached for a battery-powered lantern on the nightstand, and turned it on. It did little but cast eerie shadows. I hung my legs over the side of the bed, mindful of the evil dead that could be lurking underneath, waiting to grab my ankles and devour my toes. While I searched for my slippers with one hand, I held tight to Einstein's collar with the other.

My first coherent thought was that J.—the organization that Diggs and I had been running from for the past several months—had found us. We'd been stateside for twenty-four hours, maybe less, though, and we'd been careful. Unless they were psychic, I couldn't see how the hell they could have found us.

Jesus, I really hoped they weren't psychic.

I finally found my slippers, shoved my feet inside, and sat up. I was gradually getting acclimated to the real world again—the one without ghosts and zombies and my father, all casting blame.

My eyes settled on the rotting doorframe, my heart still pounding too hard...

In an instant, reality fell away all over again.

A dark-haired girl, no more than nine, stood at the door. She wore glasses. The left lens was broken.

"How many lies do you believe?" she said in a whisper—the tone Allie Tate, my childhood best friend, had always used when we were talking about something important.

The problem was that Allie Tate, like so many others from Payson Isle, had been dead for twenty-five years. My mind blurred. Was I still dreaming? The wind howled and the curtains blew; Diggs remained missing. My father was nowhere to be seen.

Allie stayed where she was.

Which meant she was either a ghost, or I was losing my mind. I voted for the latter. Panic rose and bloomed in my chest. Outside the room, something crashed into the door. Allie didn't budge.

"You're dead," I whispered back.

She didn't say anything. Behind the broken eyeglass lens, blood ran from her left eyebrow. She wore a pink dress that was torn in the front.

"How many lies?" she said again.

The door burst open. Einstein flew from my arms and scooted out of the room. Allie vanished.

Diggs stood in the doorway in jeans and a jersey, breathing hard. He looked as terrified as I felt. "Are you all right? What the hell happened?"

Fifteen minutes later, I sat at a picnic table in the old Payson meeting room. A fire was raging in the fireplace, but it didn't do much to warm the cavernous room. The walls had been stripped of the artwork members of the Payson Church had done—no more satin crosses or faded paintings of Jesus and his flock; no sign of the terrifying artwork Reverend Isaac Payson himself had done of Christ, crucifixions, and burning Romans. Nothing had been put up in their place, however.

I'd signed Payson Isle over to Jamie Flint before Diggs and I left the States nine months before, and Jamie had definitely left her mark on a good part of the island since relocating her business there. She trained search-and-rescue dogs—reputedly some of the best in the world—and ran a search-and-rescue business of her own, which meant the island was now home to kennels and training grounds, dog runs and dog trails. She may have been using the rest of the land well, but I got the sense Jamie didn't know what the hell to do with the Payson House.

Diggs returned bearing antiseptic and cotton balls, interrupting my thoughts. He still looked freaked out. Personally, I had yet to stop shaking.

"You okay?" he asked for the tenth time.

"Yeah. I think so."

He dabbed a cut at my temple I hadn't even realized I'd gotten. "It was probably just a gust that tore a tree limb off. Jamie said the wind's been bad out here this winter. I'm sure it was nothing."

"Probably so," I agreed. I stared into the flames. *How many lies do you believe?*

"Hey," Diggs said after a second or two. He tipped my

chin up so I looked him in the eye. "We can leave if you want. Catch the first plane out, and go back where women glow and men plunder. Just say the word."

We'd been over this before—a few times, actually. "No," I said. "We're here for a reason. I'm not going back now, just because of a little wind and a ghostly apparition."

He raised his eyebrows at me. It seemed impossible that seventy-two hours ago we'd been in Australia, both of us sun-kissed and moderately relaxed. What the hell had I been thinking?

"I'm sorry, a what?" he said.

"Forget it. It was a joke." He frowned. "Okay, not my best material. I'm bleeding from the head here—cut me some slack. Are Monty and Carl checking the island? What the hell time is it, anyway? Our first night here, and I'm already getting people out of bed in the middle of the deep dark."

He smiled at me inexplicably. "I think they'll get over it. It's not really that deep dark."

"What do you mean? What the hell time is it?'

"Six." I stared at him, still confused. "At night."

We'd taken off from the Albany Airport in Western Australia at ten till seven p.m. on December 26, and from there were scheduled to get into Portland, Maine, at just past eleven p.m. on the 27th. Four layovers and three flight delays later, we landed in Portland at seven a.m. this morning—the 28th. By the time we got a rental and drove the two hours to Littlehope, then hopped a boat for the hour-long ride out to Payson Isle, it was almost noon. We had barely managed a coherent hello to Jamie before Diggs and I both passed out in the room she had waiting for us.

"I thought it was later," I said. "Or earlier."

"It'll take a day or two to get re-acclimated," Diggs said. "You'll get there."

Diggs didn't look like he needed any time at all to get re-acclimated; the man thrives on long hours in planes, trains, and lobster boats. He'd trimmed his hair and shaved his beard in order to fit the fake ID Cameron had given us, but he still looked good. I'd had to dye my hair brown again—which Diggs is not a fan of. All things considered, he'd definitely fared the trip better than me so far.

"Right. You never answered my question—where are Monty and Carl?"

"They're just taking a look around, to make sure we've got nothing to worry about. They'll be back shortly." The idea of the two men out there alone didn't sit well with me, even if it was only six at night. And the window had broken because of the wind. And the creepy ghost girl was all in my head—obviously. I saw the look on Diggs' face at my uneasiness.

"I'm fine," I said before he could press it.

"You're shaking and white and you look like you're about to toss your cookies on my favorite t-shirt. You're not fine. What's going on?"

"You mean besides the bedroom window exploding all over me while I was dead asleep?"

I could tell he knew I was deflecting, but a second later Monty burst through the door, and that put an end to the conversation for the moment.

"No one on the island but us," he said. "Must've been the wind, princess. It blows like a whore at Mardi Gras out here most nights."

"So I've heard," I said. "About the wind...not the Mardi Gras whores."

"Strictly going by word of mouth, you understand," he said. He winked at me.

Monty worked for Jamie Flint. He was southern, about fiive-foot-eight, with dark, burnished skin and the body of a man who clearly knew his way around the gym. The first time we'd met was during that whole horrific chain of events that led to my father's death in Coba the winter before. Despite the circumstances, I'd liked him immediately. Diggs wasn't quite so keen on him, but I think that mostly had to do with how quick Monty was with a double entendre—and the fact that many of those double entendres seemed to revolve around me. Personally, I thought it was kind of cute.

Carl came through the door next, closing it quickly behind him to shut out the elements. Carl was taller, thinner, darker, and much, much quieter than Monty. Originally from Nigeria, he had enough of an accent that I had to focus to understand him, but ther was something about his wide, dark eyes that made me think of the phrase, 'Still waters run deep.' Right now, that stillness was reassuring.

"We didn't see anything, but it appears the winds are quite still, for now," he said, his words clipped and precise. "Seas will be high and the winds gusting for the next two days, until the storm hits. But I don't believe we're seeing that effect yet."

"All it would've taken was a good stiff wind, though," Monty said. "Half the trees out here have dead wood we'll need to trim once spring comes. I'm sure that's all it was."

"Right," I said. "Thanks for checking, though."

"Do they know yet when the storm's supposed to get here?" Diggs said.

"Too early to say," Monty said. "It's been a cold goddamn winter, but this'll be the first major snow. Whole state is on the alert. I thought you Mainers were supposed to be tougher than this."

"It's just because it's the first one of the season," I said. "Give it another couple of storms, and nobody will think twice. They're still saying New Year's Eve?"

"That's when it should be worst," Monty agreed.

Of course.

Jamie came down the stairs next, a graying German shepherd by her side. Jamie was blond and lean, with a dancer's body, a pierced nose, and a faint Georgian accent that just added to the charm. As usual, she seemed totally Zen about the mayhem I'd brought to her door.

"It's all set up there," she said. She joined us at the table. Einstein greeted the shepherd—Phantom was her name—with enthusiasm that Phantom didn't really return before both dogs settled in front of the fire. "If you want to switch bedrooms, though, it's no problem. There's another one made up farther down the hall."

I did some mental calculations. The room Diggs and I had been sleeping in was my old bedroom—the room the other young girls in the Payson Church had shared when I was a kid. Which made the room Jamie was talking about most likely the one where my father used to lay his weary head.

"That's all right," I said. Like my father didn't already haunt me enough these days. "The one we're in is fine. I think I'm done with sleep for now, anyway." I looked at Diggs for confirmation, not sure whether our plans had changed while I'd been in Dreamland. "You still want to head for Littlehope before it gets any later?"

"You two are still fugitives, right?" Monty asked. "I mean, that hasn't changed in the last few minutes. You really think heading out into the world is the best idea right now?"

"That's why we waited till dark," I said. Diggs and I had been on the run from both the FBI and the fine folks with Project J. ever since we'd left on a wing and a prayer last April. The Feds wanted us for questioning, ostensibly on suspicion of consorting with terrorists since shit tended to blow up at an alarming rate around us. J. just wanted us dead. "We'll go into town, do what needs doing, and be back later tonight."

"That actually brings up a good point," Jamie said. "I know this is your island, so obviously you're free to come and go as you please, but I'd love to know just exactly what brought you two back now."

"A, it's your island now—I gave it to you," I began. "And B… Diggs and I aren't ready to share B with you yet. We just need a place to rest our heads that's out of sight—otherwise, you're out of this."

"But—" Monty began.

"That's nonnegotiable," Diggs said. "We're just gathering information. If we have any reason to think things will get dangerous, we'll let you know."

Monty put up a little more of a stink, but Jamie and Carl seemed content with our lack of an explanation. Jamie's son, Bear, came in a minute later and effectively ended the whole debate. He had a white pit bull with him. Phantom couldn't have cared less who was around as long as Jamie was there, but the pit bull greeted Einstein like they'd been separated for years instead of just a few hours.

"I got the dogs in for the night," Bear said. He was seventeen, with short dark hair and a big, sturdy build. He didn't talk much, but there was something about Bear that made me think he knew things. Deep Things. Dark Things.

The kind of kid who probably got a lot of shit from the guys in his class, while the girls were lined up ten deep. "Is everything straightened out here?"

"It is," I said. "The consensus is that it was just the wind. Sorry if I disrupted the routine."

"No disruption," he said. He looked at me strangely, a little too intent. When he realized I'd caught on, he shifted his gaze. "We would've been wrapping up soon anyway. Dinner almost up?" He directed the question at Carl, who nodded.

"I was waiting for everything to settle," Carl said. "It won't be long. Urenna is in the kitchen, if you would like to help her." He said the name like he was saying a prayer—Er-Renna, a smile coming to his lips with the name.

I saw a hint of a blush before Bear nodded and excused himself. Whoever Urenna was, my guess was that she'd inspired those pink cheeks. The kid headed for the kitchen with both my mutt and the pit bull on his heels. Phantom didn't move from her place by the fire.

"You will stay for dinner?" Carl said. "You must be hungry."

I was starved, actually. As much as I wanted to get started on the nightmare Diggs and I were about to take on in Littlehope, I figured sustenance before the fact would be a good idea. Sustenance, and a shower, not necessarily in that order. Then we could set out to save the world. Even superheroes have to keep their priorities straight.

"That sounds good," I said. "Thanks. Though before I break bread, if there's any chance I could scrub some of this travel dirt off me, I think we'd all be a little happier."

"Diggs knows where the showers are," Jamie said. She and Diggs shared a secret smile I wasn't crazy about. "He can show you."

Diggs grinned back at her. Cute. "I'll tell you now though, kid," he said to me. "You're not gonna like it."

Sun showers are open-air showers using rainwater warmed by the sun. In Australia, Diggs and I took them all the time. They're great: good for the environment and the wallet, they're the perfect way to wash the salt off or cool down after a long day. As I said—they're great in Australia. Taking a sun shower in Maine in December is the kind of thing they'd come up with at Guantanamo Bay.

A half-moon hung overhead, the stars still not quite visible in the early evening sky. A wooden partition staked into the frozen ground was the only thing that protected me from the prying eyes of the world around. I stripped naked, pulled a string, and screamed when ice-cold water rained down on me.

"Told you it was cold," Diggs said from the other side of the partition. I let loose with an impressive litany of expletives while I lathered up and rinsed off, my teeth chattering, nipples tighter than pebbles, goose bumps on my goose bumps.

He came round the wooden partition with a fluffy towel and wrapped it around me while I shivered. "Refreshing, right?" he said.

"Fuck you," I said. "Why would anyone do that to themselves?"

He rubbed the towel up and down my arms while I pulled a clean pair of underpants, long johns, and jeans up my still-damp legs. Diggs eyed my frozen, naked breasts for just a second before I shot him a withering glare and grabbed a clean sweatshirt—one of his, of course—from the pile.

"Sex in the freezing cold isn't sexy," I said.

"I'm not arguing," he said. "It's not great for the ego, either. Shrinkage is too much of a factor."

He took the sweatshirt from me and pulled it over my head. He kept hold of the fabric afterward and pulled me closer. I looked up at him.

"We should go in," I said.

"We will."

Instead, he leaned down and kissed me. His mouth tasted like cinnamon and ice water—in a good way—but my hair was literally freezing and I was still shivering. I kissed him back anyway. It's easy to forget the elements when you lock lips with a man like Diggs.

"I don't like this business where I can't just ravage you whenever I feel like it," he said when we parted. I tried to come up with a pithy response, but my brain was partially frozen. He laughed. "All right, come on. Back inside. You want me to carry you?"

"I think I'll make it." We started back to the house. With Diggs' hand in mine, I scanned the night in search of Allie Tate or Mitch Cameron or any of the nameless, faceless monsters who wanted Diggs and me dead. All I saw were trees, frozen ground, and darkness.

"Have you heard anything from Juarez yet?" Diggs asked me when we were almost to the front doorstep.

"No. He's still MIA. I asked Jamie earlier—she hasn't heard any word, either."

Diggs squeezed my hand. "I don't like it. If we're doing this, I'd feel a lot better about it if he was with us."

"I'll keep trying," I said.

We hadn't heard from Jack Juarez for about four months, when we risked a phone call from Tasmania because we'd heard through the grapevine that he wasn't doing so well.

According to our sources, he'd been suspended from the FBI after the whole shit-storm in Mexico, and was getting more and more obsessed with unlocking memories of his childhood that he was convinced would lead him to the men who'd murdered his wife six years ago.

The fact that Jack had fallen completely off the radar since then had been keeping both Diggs and me up at night, worrying about what could have happened.

Diggs stopped walking a few feet from the front door. The walk and the six layers of clothes were starting to work their magic, and I'd warmed up marginally; I could even feel my toes. I looked at Diggs.

"Why are we not moving?"

"I just want to make sure you're sure," he said. "Because if we start doing this tonight…"

"I know," I said. "J. could find out. They could find *us.* But I can't sit back anymore—we've talked about this."

"We talked about it when we were ten thousand miles from all this shit. It's different when we're just a boat ride away from possible catastrophe."

"I told you, I can do it alone." That earned a glare. Diggs isn't a big fan of that argument. "I'm not saying that to guilt you into something—you know that. But I can't let any more time pass, knowing J. is out there. That they're continuing to kill, and I'm not doing a damned thing about it."

The number of times we'd had the exact same argument must have been approaching triple digits. Diggs looked as tired of it as I was. He nodded.

"Yeah, I know. I just wanted to make sure you hadn't changed your mind. If that's the case, let's grab some grub and get to work." He draped his arm around my shoulders and drew me closer. "You'll give me a shout if you come to your senses?"

"You'll be the first to know."

Having dinner with Jamie and her clan, I couldn't shake the feeling that we were suiting up for some kind of cable reality show. In addition to Monty, Carl, Jamie, Bear, and the dogs, we had Urenna—Carl's daughter, a gorgeous, dark-skinned teen probably close to Bear's age, with a quick smile and intelligent eyes,—Diggs and me, and three heavily tattooed women who worked with the dogs. I recognized one of them—Cheyenne—from the year before, but the others weren't familiar.

We sat around the picnic tables with the fire roaring, the smell of Indian spices thick in the air as Carl and Urenna served up some kind of potato vegetarian thing and a thick lentil stew that tasted better than pretty much anything I'd tasted in the past nine months. The dogs sprawled in front of the fire while the crew debriefed their day. There was a lot of laughter mixed in with talk of the business and the dogs and the dog business. Before long, I found myself drifting.

I thought of Allie again, and tried to remember community dinners with my father and other members of the Payson Church. We would have sat right here for a lot of those dinners. There would have been a prayer to kick things off—Isaac Payson at the head of the table, our heads bowed. *Close your eyes,* Allie hissed at me. *He'll catch you otherwise.* I jerked my head up sharply at the voice—one real enough that it could have come from anyone seated at the table around me. Allie was nowhere to be found, though.

I realized Bear was watching me with the intensity of a serial creeper. He looked away when our eyes met.

I tried to get back to my memories of the Payson Church. Everything surrounding my childhood was hazy—especially anything having to do with Allie Tate. We'd been best friends growing up. It was only last year that I'd remembered the truth about her death, or at least flashes of it. Allie had died a couple of years before the Payson fire, killed by Isaac himself. Or at least that's what I thought had happened—the whole incident was fractured, coming to me in fits and starts that sometimes made no sense at all. The only things I knew for sure were that Allie hadn't died in the fire, Isaac had been responsible for her death, and my father had used some kind of J.-created psychological warfare to erase the memory from my mind—the way he'd apparently erased anything else that might have been deemed disturbing about Isaac Payson and the congregation he led out here.

"Solomon," Diggs said.

I looked up, snapping back to reality. "Yeah—sorry. Daydreaming..."

"We should probably get going."

"Right." Only Jamie, Bear, Carl, and Urenna remained at the table with Diggs and me. "Do you need help with cleanup?" I asked them. "Diggs slings a dishcloth like a pro."

"That's all right," Urenna said. Unlike her father, she had no accent. "Bear and I can do it." She looked at Bear. "Right?"

"Sure, no problem," he agreed. I got the feeling she could have suggested they dip themselves in honey and roll in a nest of fire ants and he would have had the same response. They got up. Urenna took a few dishes; Bear took a few more. On his way into the kitchen, though, I sensed him watching me again.

When he came back for the last of the dishes a minute later, Carl, Jamie, and Diggs were talking. Bear came round to my side of the table. I handed him my plate. He hesitated before he took it.

"She won't hurt you, you know," he said.

That cold chill I'd felt earlier came gusting back. "Who won't?"

He just smiled at that. "You don't have to worry about her. Whoever blew out that window, it wasn't the girl."

The others at the table had fallen silent. Diggs looked at me curiously.

"Go on in and help Urenna, please," Jamie said to Bear. I wasn't sure whether there was a warning in her voice or I was hearing things. And seeing things—apparently, things that Bear also heard and saw. This just got better and better.

Diggs continued to watch me after Bear was gone. "What was that about?"

"Uh…nothing, really," I said. I shook my head and forced some certainty into my quaking voice. "Seriously, it was nothing." I got up from the table. "We should really get going before it gets any later."

"Right," Diggs said, still watching. Still wary. I went upstairs to grab my gear and hoped to God I didn't run into any other ghostly visions along the way.

2

THE SEAS WERE QUIET and the sky was dark when Diggs and I set out at a little psat seven that night. Diggs hadn't asked me again about my exchange with Bear, but I knew that didn't mean he'd forgotten about it—just that he was biding his time before he brought it up again. We drove a little fishing boat of Jamie's with *Flint K-9* written on the sides. Diggs and I were both dressed in deep blue, flannel-lined overalls with Jamie's logo emblazoned on the front. Matching baseball hats pulled the ensemble together. When I was a kid envisioning my future life of intrigue, I'd imagined disguises with a little more *va-va-voom.* These would do in a pinch, though.

It was eight o'clock by the time we reached town. Littlehope is a working fishing village of just under fifteen hundred people, many of whom still make their living on the sea. That means even in December, there are usually still a few boats in the harbor. Thanks to the impending storm, however, it looked like even the heartiest Mainers had pulled up anchor and dry docked until the weather cleared.

Diggs pulled up to the wharf and tied the boat off while I grabbed our backpacks. It was cold by Australian standards, but not by Maine's—above freezing was my guess, though probably only by a couple of degrees. The air tasted clean. Salty. I'd never been a fan of Littlehope when I was growing up, but I was finally starting to see the charm. It was less charming given J.'s propensity for trying to kill everyone we cared about whenever we hit town, of course, but for the normals out there who just hit Route 97 intent on a summer of fishing and cold beer, I could definitely understand the appeal.

We transferred our gear from the boat to the Taurus Diggs had rented—under an assumed name, of course—in Portland, and hit the road.

It was weird being back. Diggs drove slowly through town while I took it all in. Nothing had really changed—Wallace's General Store was right where we'd left it, though it looked like they'd gotten a new sign up front, maybe added a few lobster buoys to the clusters that hung from the sides of the building. There was a single light on in my mother's medical clinic, and I wondered if Maya—Kat's former girlfriend—was still working there. I hadn't talked to her since we'd left; hadn't talked to Kat for nearly as long. I wasn't sure which of the two I missed more, but the fact that it was even a debate spoke to the changes in my worldview over the past year.

I set thoughts of family and near-family aside, and took in the rest of the scene. Someone had written "Don't" at the top of the STOP sign on the corner, and "Dancing" below it. It looked like it had been that way for a while. A cluster of reporters stood smoking outside the *Downeast Daily Tribune*, where Diggs and I used to spend our days. I caught Diggs watching them. Not far down the street, a few pickups were parked in the lot at Bennett's Lobster Shanty.

There was a dusting of hardened snow on the ground, but not much more than that. Around town, houses were still lit with Christmas lights and inflatable Santas.

"Have you missed it?" I asked Diggs. The *Trib* was in the rearview by the time he answered me.

"In some ways. I've missed the people. Wallace's pizza. Trivia and pool nights at the Shanty. Late nights riding a deadline at the *Trib.*"

I was surprised. We hadn't talked much about Littlehope while we were gone. "That would be a yes, then." He still didn't look so sure. "It's not a crime if you have, you know. I won't hold it against you. I never really belonged here—you did. People look at me and all they see is the creepy sole survivor of the Payson fire. Daughter of the town drunk. They look at you, and they see the favorite son."

He glanced at me, though I couldn't see his expression in the darkness. "I don't think you have a clue what people see when they look at you, kid."

His intensity got me flustered, which is usually what Diggs' intensity does—either that or it turns me on. Either way, it's not helpful. I changed the subject.

"So, where are we headed first? I know you want to check out your place, but it's getting late—if we're gonna talk to this guy, it's probably better we don't do it in the middle of the night, right?"

"That's my thought," he agreed.

Mention of the mission changed things between us—the air got heavier, the silence thicker. I persevered.

"And your source is sure this is the guy, right? It's definitely his social security number on the list?"

"He hasn't been wrong yet, has he?"

He hadn't.

Mitch Cameron had compiled the list I was referring to, though we'd gotten it in as roundabout way as possible when Diggs pried a computer chip from the cold dead hand of a professor in Kentucky. Cameron was a former J. operative who had recently been proven to be a possible/probable ally—though I totally wasn't ready to write his name in ink on the good guys' jerseys just yet. The list itself was a coded series of entries with the details of J. operations dating all the way back to 1951. Every entry included geographic coordinates, the social security number of the J. operative working the mission, the month and year the mission took place, and the J. team leader overseeing the whole thing. When you forgot about the part where every entry represented weird mental manipulation and gruesome death, decoding the thing was actually kind of fun. The fact that the list included things like Jonestown, the Manson family killings, the Oklahoma City bombing, Ruby Ridge, and Columbine, made it a lot harder to forget that, though.

What was worse was the fact that the list wasn't just about the past—the dates extended all the way to 2018, four years from now. While we'd been in Australia, Diggs and I had watched from half a world away as several of J.'s plans became reality. It's not like we didn't try to do something, but there were some issues that made it next to impossible to sound anything but completely freaking nuts every time we tried to bring the cops in on things.

For one thing, the coordinates were anything but specific, giving only the whole degree in latitude and longitude—which meant we were looking at about three thousand square miles, minimum, in which each mysterious event could take place. We didn't have a day, either, just the month. The only hard fact we had in the entries was the social security number of the J. operative. That alone was indisputable. And even that had its issues.

But, the social security numbers—one in particular—were precisely why we were back in Littlehope now.

About ten minutes outside town, Diggs turned left onto a darkened, dirt fire road. He stopped the car, put it in park, and turned off the lights no more than fifty feet in.

"What are you doing?" I asked.

"I just wanted to check, one more time," he said.

"Jesus, Diggs. I'm sure. I'm absolutely, positively, one hundred percent clear on this."

"Because I could drive us out of here right now. Head back to Portland. We could catch the first flight out of Maine, and not look back. Go back to Australia—or go somewhere else. The Caribbean, maybe. Dance all night, make love while the sun rises the next morning…"

"We did that once, Diggs. It's not like we've spent the past nine months dancing and screwing."

"We did our fair share, though," he said. "Maybe not the dancing…" My cheeks warmed. Diggs turned toward me, more serious now. "This isn't your fault. Whatever J.'s doing—it's not up to you to stop them."

"Remind me again what the next entry is on that list," I said, because I was so not having this argument again. "When does it take place?"

He didn't answer. I waited him out until he finally relented. "April."

"Four months from now," I said. "And what are the coordinates, again?"

Another second of hesitation. He cleared his throat. "I don't remember."

"Bullshit. Forty-three north, sixty-nine west." The

numbers were branded on my brain. "Which lands us right here—right along the coast of Maine. And this guy we're about to see is the one who'll pull the trigger when the time comes; the social security number on that list led us to his front door. We've got it in black and white." I shook my head. "There's no way I'm running from that. And you're not the man I thought you were, if you could."

"If it meant keeping you safe—keeping us together and breathing? Trust me, Sol. I could run."

He was full of shit, but I wasn't going to fight him on it. We'd both watched people die over the past nine months: a bombing in Vancouver; a school shooting in Texas; a mother in Nebraska who poisoned her three kids before shooting her husband and then slitting her own wrists... Diggs might not have said anything about it, but I wasn't the only one who lost something every time one of J.'s forecasted events made headlines.

"I told you before," I said. "I'm doing this. All we'll do is take a look around. See what we can figure out, and go from there."

"Right. Go from there." I expected him to get sulky, but after a second he took a deep breath, exhaled slowly, and rallied. "All right. We're here; we're apparently doing this, so let's get on with it. Prepare to meet Mike Reynolds—meth cooker, meth smoker, modern militia enthusiast, and proponent of a greener tomorrow. You ready for this?"

I leaned across the console, grabbed him by his shirtfront, and pulled him in for a quick kiss. "You know I love you, right?"

He held me there when I tried to get away. Diggs isn't really a big fan of quick...anything. "You'd better, woman," he said when we parted. He pulled back, but didn't go far.

"We do this my way, right? Let me take the lead. He's got kids in there—we figure out how many there are. Where they are. What Mike's state of mind is. If I give the signal, we leave. No questions asked, no starting something."

"I know," I agreed. I started to go for the door, but he pulled me back.

"I'm serious," he said.

I looked at him. For the past nine months, it had been just the two of us—twenty-four/seven, he'd been there for my moods, my nightmares, every twist and turn. There had been parts of these past months that had been damned near idyllic. Others, however…not so much. I knew it had taken its toll, his constant worry over my well-being. I held his gaze. "I know, Diggs. You've more than met me halfway here… We do it your way."

We rolled into Mike Reynolds' compound without incident two minutes later. It was everything Diggs had promised when we'd first talked about this—and so much more. Think *Breaking Bad* meets *The Dukes of Hazard*, without the sophistication. Three trailers were situated on a barren plot of land surrounded by half-dead evergreens, like even the trees were too depressed to survive this place. A pile of Hefty bags had been torn open by dogs or wildlife, the garbage strewn across the yard. Two rusted pickups with the hoods popped open were up on cement blocks off to the side of the driveway. A skinny mutt on a chain watched us warily as we drove up.

Diggs stopped at a rickety gate held together with fishing line. "It hasn't gotten any better with time," he said, "but this is it."

He handed me an earbud. I put it in my ear, my adrenaline

already running higher, while he put a tiny microphone in his collar. It was the same set we'd used in Coba—a parting gift from the worst night of my life.

Diggs got out of the car and walked around the shitty fishing-line fence. When he was about ten feet from me, I heard his voice in my ear.

"You with me, kid?" I flashed the car lights once, then doused them. "Good to know. Wait till my signal, then come on in and take a look around."

"Got it," I said, even though he couldn't hear me.

He got closer and continued narrating, speaking quietly. "There are two kids and a woman—the girlfriend, I think, same one he's had for a while—in the trailer on the right. Middle trailer's got cardboard on the windows. I'd say that's the meth kitchen." He paused. I heard a dog start barking. "One dog. Skinny mutt—chained, so I think we're safe there."

Three floodlights came on, one from each of the trailers. "Jesus," Diggs said in my ear. My heart tripped a few beats faster. "It won't be easy hiding out here with it lit up like this. Take it easy, huh? Stick to the trees."

He got quiet again. The barking dog continued without much enthusiasm. I squinted, trying to get a good read on what was happening. I could make out Diggs' silhouette as he got closer.

"Shit," he whispered. "Okay, Sol. Showtime. Mike's on his way out. Don't do anything rash—stick with the plan."

I got out of the car and shut the door softly, still listening for whatever was happening with Diggs. I went around the gate and ignored the multitude of No Trespassing signs, but not without serious reservations. Keeping low to the ground, I headed toward the back of the trailers. I paused beside one of the rusted pickups when I heard Diggs speak again.

"Hey, Mike—it's good to see you, man. It's Diggs, from the *Trib.*"

I peered out from around the truck. Diggs stood in the glare of the floodlights, his hands raised. A smaller man strode toward him. I wasn't as concerned about the man as I was what he carried with him—a shotgun, held loose by his side.

"Easy, kid," Diggs murmured to me under his breath, like he was right there with me. My hand curled around the Ruger in my jacket pocket, despite his reassurance. Mike Reynolds kept coming toward him.

"I was back in town," Diggs continued, talking to Mike. He sounded completely relaxed. "I just figured I'd swing by and say hi. Last time we talked you said you were getting those windmills, right? I was curious how that worked out."

To my profound relief, the man set the gun down and leaned it against the trailer before he moved any closer to Diggs. I took an overdue breath. The distinct smell of pot filled the air, thick enough that I was willing to bet I'd have a contact high before we got out of here. Not that that would be a bad thing—as I saw it, right now getting stoned was one of the better ways this whole thing could turn out.

"How you been, man?" Mike said. His voice was surprisingly clear—I'd expected the low rasp of a lifetime smoker, but he sounded like he hadn't left puberty behind all that long ago. For the first time, he became something other than a social security number, a tool J. would use to take more lives.

"I haven't seen you in, like…shit, I don't know how long," Mike continued. "Come on in. I'll get Eddie to make us something—you remember her, right? We got married, not long ago. Jesus, you look good. You still on the wagon?"

He didn't wait for Diggs' response before he continued, the words coming in a manic rush. "Yeah, I can tell you are. You got that look about you, you know? You look really good. I keep saying it, you know? Gotta stop smoking. Get my shit together. But there's a hell of a lot going on right now. When things slow down a little… Then, maybe. There'll be time for all that later, maybe. I'm working on something big right now, though."

Diggs asked him what that was, but I reminded myself that I had a job of my own to do. I got down low again and ran along the perimeter until I was behind the farthest trailer.

It was darker back here, but there was enough residual light from the floodlihgts out front that I could make out the basics: a dumpster, a good-sized shed, and a windmill that didn't look remotely functional. It smelled like dog shit and trash and pot. I slunk closer, focused on the shed. The door was cracked, light spilling out from inside.

Diggs asked Mike about the mysterious 'big things' he kept talking about. I could hear the man's distrust when he answered.

"You know, it's not like I'm not glad to see you," Mike said. "But you come here out of the blue, right? And what am I supposed to think, man? Where've you been, anyway?"

I crept closer, careful to keep to the shadows around the shed. There was a clatter inside, like someone had dropped something light—or several somethings. I pressed my back against the shed and held my breath.

"I was in Australia, actually," Diggs said to Mike. "My girlfriend and me. We had a little trouble with the law…you know how it goes."

"Yeah, man—definitely," Mike agreed. He sounded

more relaxed at mention of Diggs' legal troubles. Common ground.

The shed was quiet now. Off toward the trees, I thought I saw a shadow moving in the darkness—definitely more humanoid than animal. I closed my eyes for a second and tried to still my racing heart. I thought of the good old days, when I just watched this kind of thing on TV. I refocused on the shed.

The light went out inside. The door creaked, as whoever was in there exited. I wet my lips. Muted my ear piece, so the sound of Diggs' voice didn't give me away. I moved forward, just an inch. Then another. I eased myself toward the corner of the shed so I could see whoever was coming out. The door clicked shut. I heard someone fumbling with a lock.

I peered around the corner.

At exactly that moment, the person at the door looked up. He met my gaze. He held a bow and arrow in his hand—like Katniss used. The difference was that this bow and arrow was roughly the same size as its owner.

The kid frowned when he saw me. He held the bow tighter. I caught the look he cast toward the trailer, though, and realized something:

I'd caught him just as much as he'd caught me.

"Hey," I whispered.

"Who are you?" he whispered back.

"Don't worry," I said. "You weren't supposed to be in there, right? It's no big deal—I wouldn't rat you out."

"What are you doing here? You're not supposed to be back here."

"Neither are you though, right?" I said. That stumped him. His frown deepened. He had curly dark hair and a round face. I doubted he was more than eight years old, maybe ten. "What were you doing in there?"

Silence. I'm not great with kids—if he was a dog, we'd be golden right now. I nodded toward the bow and arrow, grasping at straws. "That's pretty cool. Can you really shoot?"

Pride softened his face. "Damn right I can. That's why I went in the shed." He had dark eyes and that low, raspy kind of voice Disney always uses for cartoon puppies. "Mike's got all this ammo in there—I saw a show where you can light your arrows on fire, you know? I thought maybe I'd find something in there. How cool would that be, right? Just, like...shooting fire."

"That would be cool," I agreed. Or terrifying, take your pick. "What else has he got in there?"

"Aidan!" A woman shouted from out front. The kid flinched at her voice. "It's bedtime, get the hell in here!"

"You're Aidan?" I guessed.

"I've gotta go," he said. "You better hide, though. You get caught out here, and Mike'll skin you alive."

He ran for the trailer, bow and arrow still in hand. It sounded like things were getting tense between Mike and Diggs again, so I headed back toward the woods. The shed was locked now anyway, but I had a good idea what I would have found in there.

None of it was good.

Ten minutes later, Diggs and I met back at the car. I'd already been there for five minutes, listening through the microphone as Mike explained to Diggs all the horrible ways we could have been killed in Australia. "They got crocodiles that can bite a man in two—right through the gut," he said. Diggs had sounded appropriately horrified, and finally extricated himself from the conversation.

"What'd you find out?" he asked as he slid into the driver's seat.

"I met one of the kids—" Diggs glanced at me as he started the car. "Don't worry—he had more to lose than I did if Mike caught him. But he was going into a shed back there. He told me the thing's filled with ammo. Did you get any idea what he's got planned?"

"No clue, but something's definitely up. He said he's been working with some people. Didn't say who, didn't say what they were working on. Just that he was tired of being pushed around."

"That doesn't sound good."

"No. That was pretty much my thought, too." He paused, thinking. "Did you know there are ten thousand different kinds of spiders in Australia?"

"You really think those are the kinds of facts you should start spouting if you ever want me to go back there?"

"Probably not," he agreed. "Listen, do you mind if we swing by my place now? I just want to check things out. Make sure it's still standing."

I agreed with a nod, already too far back on the J. track to give it much thought. "If J. has been working with Mike, how long do you think they've been at it?" I asked. "Their old M.O. was to get in touch with these guys when they were just wayward kids—do you think they've had him in their sights that long?"

"I don't know," Diggs said. "It's possible. Between your father and Isaac Payson, we know they had people from the organization around here."

I fell silent, lost in thought. J. had started as Project J-932, an offshoot of MK Ultra—the conspiracy theorist's wet dream come true that ran experiments on human subjects around the U.S. until it was shut down in the mid-1970s. J-932 started by doing mind control experiments on young boys around the country—boys with shitty home lives and no advocates to keep them from falling into the wrong hands. Their alumni included Jim Jones, Timothy McVeigh, a serial killer by the name of Max Richards…and my father. And now, Mike Reynolds.

After MK Ultra went dark, J. continued for another few years in the secret annals of the U.S. government. It was shut down officially in 1979, after Jim Jones spearheaded the mass suicide in Guyana in November of '78. After that, Dexter Mandrake—the founder of J-932—found his own funding, and continued his work in the private sector.

Mandrake was killed in the '90s, but J. continued to thrive under new leadership after that. The problem, as I saw it, was that we had no clue who that new leadership might be. Their M.O. was still preying on the mentally unstable, though they were an equal-opportunity organization now; almost as many women were featured on Cameron's list as men now. I still didn't understand exactly how they did what they did—how they pushed these people to kill time and time again—but whatever their technique, it had proven damned effective so far. If they were pushing Mike in that direction, I wasn't sure how much faith I had that we could stop him.

Diggs pulled up in front of his house a few minutes later and stopped the car. "You're quiet," he said.

"Thinking."

"About?"

"Nothing new—just more J. stuff. What do you think Mike has planned?"

"Not a clue," he said promptly. "Nothing good. I want

to keep talking to him, though—we did all right tonight. He got jumpy a couple of times, but I've dealt with worse than him before. He's not a bad guy. If there's something we can do…"

"Like save him?" I said. "Diggs…"

He held up his hand. "I know, I know. Stupid idea. It's not even like he's a good guy… I just hate the idea of one more body, you know?"

"Yeah. I know."

He leaned across the console and kissed me. "I know you do. Come on. Let's go in and think about something else for a while. Maybe we can see if my bed still works."

"You think it might have gotten rusty while you were gone?"

"It's a possibility. We've been gone a long time." He got out without further discussion. I knew we were supposed to be doing other things, but I had to admit the idea of having a house to ourselves again for an hour or two was appealing.

When we reached the front door, Diggs got out his keys. Since he'd had the electricity shut off months ago, the porch light naturally didn't come on. I got out my flashlight and shined it on the door while he fumbled with the lock. The encroaching darkness and the profound quiet kind of murdered my libido; instead, my spidey sense kicked into gear. It didn't get any better when Diggs finally fit the key to the lock and the door opened before he could turn it.

He drew his gun. "Hang back a second, okay?"

"Sure," I said, then followed him right in. He glared at me over his shoulder, but he didn't look at all surprised.

I scanned the room with my flashlight, shining the light into the darkest corners. There was no sign that anyone was here but us now—but someone had definitely paid a visit before. And not a friendly one.

"Shit," Diggs said under his breath, once he'd gotten the full effect.

My sentiments exactly.

The entire place had been trashed: cupboard doors pulled off their hinges, furniture slashed, pillows unstuffed, graffiti on the walls.

"Vandals?" I asked.

"In Littlehope?" He moved past me and up the stairs, to his bedroom in the loft. I followed at a more sedate pace, all the while looking back over my shoulder in case the bad guys had lingered.

When he reached the loft, he went straight to a bank of built-in dressers along one wall. The drawers had all been pulled out, clothes strewn in all directions. Apparently the hoodlums weren't keen on vintage concert tees, because they'd all been left behind. Diggs knelt in front of the dresser and reached all the way to the back with one hand, holding the flashlight in the other.

"Goddamn it," he murmured.

"What are you looking for?" I asked.

"Nothing," he said. "Forget it." He straightened, utterly disconsolate.

"Did you have a fortune in gold doubloons hidden back there you never told me about?" No answer. "Your porn stash? Jimmy Hoffa's remains?"

"Let it go, Solomon," he said. I frowned. I'm not known for letting things go.

"That My Little Pony collection you could never explain to the women who came before me?"

"Seriously, woman…" It was a tone that brooked no argument.

"Okay, fine. Moving on then—for now. Do you have any idea who this could have been?"

"Not really, no."

I followed him back down the ladder to the main level and stood there for a few seconds, trying to make sense of the destruction. The graffiti on the wall wasn't enlightening. In fact, it was the weirdest graffiti I'd ever seen from hoodlums.

Which made me worry that hoodlums hadn't done this at all.

MURDERER was written—not spray painted, but written in what looked like permanent black ink—in large letters across one wall. Slightly below it were the words, *A FUGITIVE AND A VAGABOND SHALT THOU BE.* I watched Diggs, waiting to see if he got the significance.

" '...and I shall be a fugitive and a vagabond in the earth; and it shall come to pass, that every one that findeth me shall slay me...'" he quoted. "The story of Cain and Abel."

"Nice to know growing up a preacher's son wasn't totally wasted on you," I said. "You think whoever did this is talking about your brother?"

Diggs' brother died diving into the local quarry when he and Diggs were just kids—a freak accident that Diggs still blames himself for to this day. Unfortunately, his parents never did anything to relieve him of the idea that it was all his fault.

"I can't think of anything else that makes sense," he said. He went radio silent and stared into the darkness. After a couple of endless minutes of that, he turned to me. "If it's all right, I'd kind of like to check in on my father before we head back. Maybe he knows something about this."

I made a face—not a good one. Papa Diggs was a miserable son of a bitch who'd made Diggs' life a living hell for the bulk of his formative years; I wasn't exactly a fan. But after watching my own father put a bullet in his skull before my eyes, I figured at least one of us should have a shot at resolving our daddy issues.

"Yeah, of course. You think he might know something about this?"

"I doubt it, but it couldn't hurt to ask. And I haven't talked to him in a while… I just want to make sure he's okay."

"Sure," I agreed. Something roiling in my gut told me this would be a bad move—some sixth sense that suggested this was a path we'd be better off leaving alone right now.

Unfortunately, I ignored the feeling.

3

DIGGS GOT QUIETER the closer we got to his dad's church. I heard him take a deep breath as we pulled into the parking lot, psyching himself up. I tried the same, but I needed more than oxygen to steel myself for a visit with Reverend Diggins. A shot of JD and a bag of Hershey's Minis might do the trick, but even that was doubtful. Still, Diggs had been nothing but supportive while I'd lugged around my considerable baggage for the past year—it was about time I was able to return the favor.

The church was a big whitewashed building with a white picket fence around it. the substantial parking lot was cracked and definitely in need of re-tarring. There wasn't a soul in sight, and no cars in the lot. The only sign of life was a light in the basement where Reverend Diggins kept his office.

Diggs parked at the back of the lot, and we both got out. Though it was dark outside, I still felt exposed the second we were out in open air. It had been different at the Reynolds place and over at Diggs' house, both of which were tucked away from prying eyes. This was in the center of town, streetlights lit. I looked around, chilled to the bone. I saw no sign of J., the cops, or any creepy specters from my past sent to scare the crap out of me. It struck me as sad that I was more freaked out heading into a church than I'd been while lurking in the shadows of a drug dealer's compound. Understandable given my past, but still sad.

I glanced at Diggs, and realized he was much worse off than I was. I bumped against him as we walked. "Your collection of personally penned *Baywatch* fanfiction?" I said.

He stopped and looked at me. "What?"

"The thing that got stolen. I'm just trying to figure out what could possibly be so shameful that you wouldn't tell me. I mean…I know all your secrets, Diggs. Come on."

"God, you're a pain in the ass… I'll tell you another time, okay? Just not tonight."

"But another time."

"And another place."

I let that sink in. We got moving again. "Hey, Diggs," I said.

"Yes, dear heart?" he said, the words syrupy sweet and dripping with sarcasm.

"You okay?"

He glanced at me. I caught just a slip of a smile. "I'm not sure. We'll find out in a minute, right?"

Indeed.

The back door to the church wasn't locked, which wasn't that surprising. Time was marching on, sure, but Littlehope was still a tiny coastal town in one of the safest states in the country. What could anyone possibly have to worry about around here?

If they only knew.

Diggs didn't turn on the light when we went inside, but there was enough illumination from the intermittent runway/night lights in the hallway to guide us. When we reached the stairs, he turned to me.

"When we get to his office, do you mind hanging back?" He looked nervous.

"Whatever you want."

"Thanks." He didn't seem comforted. I kicked his shin lightly before we started moving again. "Ow. What was that for?"

"Breathe," I said. "He's your dad. And if he's a prick to you, I'll kick his ass. Okay?"

That, at least, earned a smile. "Fair enough."

We set out again. When we reached Daddy Diggs' office door, Diggs hesitated. I gave him a little push.

"You're freaking me out," I said. "Just go already. I'll be right here."

He straightened his shirt, rubbed his sweaty palms on the legs of his jeans, and took another deep breath before he eventually tapped lightly on the wood. A second of silence followed. Then:

"Come," Reverend Diggins called from behind the door. Even the single word came out a command.

Diggs glanced at me, visibly steeled himself, and opened the door. I moved close enough to see inside without being seen. Diggs didn't look like he cared. Or even noticed.

Reverend Diggins looked older than he had the last time I'd seen him—much older. A lifetime older, his thin shoulders stooped, his sparse white hair even sparser. The past couple of years apparently hadn't done him any favors. The old man looked up at sight of Diggs. A shadow I couldn't read crossed his face.

"Daniel," he said. He stood.

"Hey, Dad," Diggs said. Neither of them raced across

the worn carpet for a heartfelt father-son hug.

"What are you doing here?" the reverend said. The prick definitely didn't look overjoyed.

"I just wanted to check in on you," Diggs said. He stood stiffly in the doorway, hands at his sides. "I was in town. Wanted to say hello."

"The police are looking for you," the reverend said. "They've been to see me more than once."

"Sorry about that. Whatever they're saying we did, we didn't do. I'm sorry if they scared you."

"I wasn't frightened, it was just an annoyance." The reverend hesitated. I could almost see him replaying the tape in his head. "You said 'we'?" He leaned forward, following Diggs' eye to the door. "Ah, yes. Miss Solomon." He raised his voice so it was clear I was officially part of the conversation now. "Don't lurk in the hallway like a common criminal—come in, please."

I didn't wait for Diggs to nod me in before I joined them, forcing Diggs deeper into the room. "How's it going, Reverend?"

"Fine, Miss Solomon. And for you? I don't suppose if I ask where the two of you have been…"

"Overseas, the last few months," Diggs said. "Australia."

Reverend Diggins nodded, half to himself. "I've never been. I took your mother to Europe when we were young. She wanted to go to New Zealand, though. We never had the money. Or the time." He came to, as if he'd drifted to some distant world. "The police are looking for you," he said again.

"I'm sorry they bothered you," Diggs said. "We'll figure it out—if you wouldn't say anything about me coming here, I'd really appreciate it."

"Of course."

Diggs hesitated. The reverend didn't move. Time slowed to a warm, sticky crawl.

"We also wanted to check with you about something else," I said, since no one else was jumping in. "We stopped at Diggs' house earlier, and someone had broken in. The place was trashed, graffiti on the walls, and whoever was there stole something..." I looked at Diggs expectantly, since he still hadn't shared with me exactly what that something was.

"That's right," Diggs said. "They stole something I'd really like back. I wondered if you'd heard anything about that?"

The reverend frowned deeply. Backlit by a soft lightbulb, I was reminded again of Mr. Burns on *The Simpsons.* I squelched a bubble of hysterical laughter. It occurred to me that I needed sleep. Badly.

"I haven't heard a thing," the reverend said. "It's probably the friends you keep. That's always been your problem—the associations a man makes speak volumes about him. Joshua has always..." He trailed off.

I looked at Diggs to see if he was following this. Joshua was Diggs' brother—the one who died almost thirty years ago.

"Dad, Josh is—"

"I know what your brother is," the reverend said.

Diggs glanced at me, his brow furrowed with concern. Clearly he'd expected hostile, not crazy. It's hard to anticipate the curveballs in Littlehope, though. He dug his hands into his pockets awkwardly. "Well, if you hear anything about the break-in, I'd appreciate you letting me know. I really would like to find what was taken."

Once again, he made no mention of what that mysterious something was.

The reverend said something under his breath that I couldn't quite make out.

"What was that?" I said.

"Nothing," the reverend said. He spoke over my head, directing the comment to Diggs. "You shouldn't have just left your house to rot. Run away like that. Your brother—" Diggs and I waited for him to finish the thought. Instead, he changed tacks again. "How long are you here?"

"We're not sure," Diggs said. The latest exchange seemed to give him more courage than he'd had before. He still wasn't the Diggs I knew, but he was inching closer. "Look, since I've got you here, I have some questions I'd love to run by you, and I'm not sure when we'll have the chance to talk again. Do you have a few minutes?"

Reverend Diggins looked at his watch uneasily for a second before he nodded. "Only a few. I need to get back."

As far as I knew, the reverend had lived alone since his wife had died and Diggs left town more than fifteen years ago—when Diggs was building his house a few years ago, he always stayed with friends. I wondered what the hell the old man had waiting for him that was so pressing he couldn't spare a few minutes to talk to his only surviving son. I stayed quiet rather than asking, though. And people say I have no restraint.

"I won't keep you long," Diggs assured him.

"Of course. That's fine. What do you need from me?"

"Like I said, just some answers," Diggs said.

We all sat—Reverend Diggins behind his desk, Diggs and me in plush leather chairs in front. Diggs pulled his chair closer to mine. I resisted the urge to pull farther away. Daddy Diggs had that effect on me, like he was seeing every ungodly thing Diggs and I had done to each other over the years. Silece as uncomfortable as damp wool fell between us. The reverend stared impassively at Diggs. The look on his face was...disturbing—there was no other word for it. A combination of fear and loathing so raw, so intense, that I kind of wanted to clock the son of a bitch.

Number one in my rule book of life?

Don't fuck with my dog.

Number two?

Don't fuck with Diggs.

Number three has to do with chocolate.

Right now, I was most concerned with rule number two.

"What did you have to do with the Payson Church?" Diggs finally asked. I tensed. So did the reverend. This was definitely not something I'd been prepared to discuss now.

"I'm not trying to make trouble," Diggs said. "But with everything that's happened in the past two years, with the deaths of Matt Perkins and Joe Ashmont, what we've learned about the island and the night of the fire… I'd just like to know." He was completely earnest, no trace of malice in his tone.

"It was years ago," the reverend said. "I've already told you what I know."

"In the days before the fire, though," Diggs pressed. "How much contact did you have with Isaac Payson? What did you know about him?"

"I knew nothing of him—had virtually no association with the man," the reverend said. "What I did know, I can't recall now."

"Just think about it for a second," Diggs pushed. Still earnest, quiet—nothing like the take-charge man I knew in every other situation we'd ever been in. His father changed him, though; he was twelve years old all over again, still trying to figure out a way to get what he needed without pissing off the old man. "Concentrate. Think back."

"I told you—I don't recall."

"You must remember something about the place, though," I said. "Something about the church, or Isaac Payson…"

"You were the one who lived there," he said to me coolly. "I have no idea. Your father came to me for help. I never would have had anything to do with them otherwise."

"What did he say to you that night?" I asked.

This was a piece of hte puzzle that still didn't make a lot of sense to me: shortly before the night the Payson Church of Tomorrow and most of its members went up in flames on Payson Isle, my father had allegedly come to the reverend for help getting a woman named Rebecca Ashmont away from the island. The story was that Dad was afraid Rebecca was putting the church at risk by tempting Reverend Payson in ungodly ways.

Of course, the fact that I now had a vague memory of Payson murdering my BFF pretty much shot that story to hell—clearly, the man had bigger skeletons in his closet than one oversexed member of the congregation with unholy designs on him. What made Rebecca Ashmont such a threat?

"When my father came to you," I persisted, "what was the plan? What were you supposed to do about Rebecca Ashmont?"

"That was more than twenty years ago—I don't recall the details. Your father came to me with concerns. I told him that I would do what I could to help him get the woman away from the church," he said. "Clearly, that never happened. Rebecca's husband called late that night and told me to forget it. That I was to leave her alone."

"And you never had any interaction with Isaac Payson?" I said. "Before the fire, you never had any idea what he was doing out there."

The reverend shook his head. "I already told you: I had no association with the man."

Diggs didn't say anything, but I could tell Rebecca Ashmont's name had triggered something for him. Since Daddy Diggs had consorted with Rebecca when she was a member of his congregation, his reaction was understandable. If possible, the tension got even thicker.

The reverend's gaze shifted from Diggs to me. "Miss Solomon, I wonder if I might speak with my son alone for a few moments."

"I'd rather stay, if it's all the same to you," I said.

"It's not all the same—"

"Whatever you have to say, you can say it in front of her," Diggs said.

The reverend stood and walked to his bookshelf. I noticed a limp that he hadn't had the last time I was in town. He turned to face us again once he was across the room, like he was drawing strength from the dusty old tomes behind him.

"I'd like to know what it is she's pulled you into," he said to Diggs. "I know her parents had secrets… That whatever happened on Payson Isle had roots in evil beyond anything I've ever touched."

"That's a load of crap and you know it," Diggs said, taking me by surprise. He said it quietly enough, but there was no mistaking the shift in tone.

"Excuse me?" his father said.

"You're going to tell me they were any more un-Christian than Jesup Barnel? That the things they did in the Payson

Church were any more wrong than what that man did to me in Kentucky?"

When Diggs was twelve, shortly after his little brother died, Reverend Diggins sent him to a Fundamentalist Kentucky preacher with a unique approach to the word of God. While Diggs was there, the preacher—Jesup Barnel—performed an elaborate, crazy-as-hell backwoods exorcism on him, at the reverend's request. I'd seen a videotape of the whole thing—the highlights of which included branding Diggs with an iron cross and basically waterboarding him until he renounced Satan. Diggs was still a little bitter about the whole thing. Not without justification.

"Don't take that tone with me," Reverend Diggins said. "You drop out of sight for months at a time with no explanation, the police roust me searching for you, and then you return with your little protégé once more under your arm…" He said protégé like he would have said whore, if he hadn't known it would push Diggs too far. As it was, Diggs flinched. He stood.

"This was a mistake," he said to me. "Come on."

"Hang on," I said. I turned my attention to Daddy Diggs. "Look, I don't know what you've got shoved up your ass, but Diggs came here because he was genuinely concerned. Obviously, something happened while we were gone. You look like you've been sick…"

The reverend stiffened at the something-up-his-ass comment. He looked at me coolly. "I had a stroke six months ago—not that it's any of your business. Clearly, the year has had its ups and downs."

"Oh," I said lamely. "Well…see, there you go. We didn't know."

"No. You wouldn't," he said.

I waited for Diggs to jump in. When he did, I really wished he hadn't. "I'd like to get back to what we were talking about before," he said. "About Rebecca Ashmont. Remind me again: how did you know Rebecca?"

"Diggs," I warned.

He didn't even look at me. "Just a second, please. Come on, Dad. You told Erin once, right? Admitted to her what there'd been between you and Joe Ashmont's wife?"

"Leave," the reverend said. He remained standing with his books. His voice was even, but there was fire behind it.

"Why? Is this something you forgot about over the years, too?" Diggs asked. He advanced on the old man. The earnest son desperate for his father's approval was gone; the man I saw now was infinitely more familiar, since it was the one I'd seen in countless interviews over the years—the man who got answers no matter what. I knew the shift didn't bode well for the reverend. "The fact that you were banging Rebecca Ashmont while Mom did your laundry and cooked your dinners and took your beatings—"

"Enough!" the reverend shouted, the dragon awoken. "You will not come into my church and speak to me that way."

"I'll speak to you however I damned well please," Diggs said. "You lost the ability to beat me into submission a long time ago."

If the reverend felt any regret for the way he'd treated Diggs in the past, he showed no sign of that now. His eyes, a deep brown that looked nothing like his son's clear blue ones, burned darker. "Get out. I didn't invite you here. Don't come back."

The old man was physically withered now, a good head shorter and at least fifty pounds lighter than Diggs. Diggs stayed where he was, his body taut. I thought of the little boy he'd been; the things the reverend had done to him—the lashes on his back, the crucifix on his chest. I put my hand on Diggs' arm.

"Come on. Let's go."

Reverend Diggins turned his back on us both. "Your mother was right," he said. I willed the son of a bitch to shut up, trying to steer Diggs out before the old man delivered his killing blow. "Losing Joshua was my punishment. God took the wrong son. He left me with a bastard child with the devil in his heart. Get out," the reverend said again. He sank into his chair, his strength gone. "I don't want to see you again."

Diggs didn't move. I took his arm and pulled him toward the door, none too gently.

He remained silent even after we'd gotten back in the car. It was past eleven now. The moon was high overhead, the air cold enough that I could see my breath. I cranked the heat and waited for Diggs to get us out of there.

"Family, right?" I said finally. "The gift that keeps on giving." He didn't crack a smile. I hesitated before I broached the next subject, knowing it wouldn't be popular. "Listen, do you think there's a chance he could call the cops on us? That Fed who shot Einstein is still out there somewhere."

"Trent Willett? He shot you too, Solomon," Diggs reminded me. "I don't think my father would call him, though. I mean…" He stopped and gave it some thought. "Damn it. We shouldn't have come. Maybe I can try talking to him again."

I could just imagine how well that would go over. "Why don't we head back to the island for now? You're probably right: he won't say anything. But right now, you're practically dead on your feet. You got even less sleep than I did today—we can figure out the next step tomorrow."

"Just a second," he said. He put the car in drive. "I want to stop somewhere first."

"Somewhere where?"

"I just want to check something out at my old house."

"Your old house, as in your father's current house?" I shook my head. "No way. Not tonight—we're not breaking into your father's place."

"It wouldn't be breaking in," he said. "Look, something's not right with him. The way he reacted when you mentioned the Paysons, the way he looked at me… I just want to look around. See if I can figure some things out."

The back door to the church opened. We were parked far enough back that the reverend didn't appear to notice us, but close enough to get a good look at him when he came out. Reverend Diggins stepped out, searched the lot briefly, and locked the door behind him. He struck out, cane in one hand, briefcase in the other.

"So breaking into his place is out for now," I said. Diggs put the car back in park, focused on his father's every move.

The reverend didn't have a car with him. Instead, he picked his way painfully across the parking lot, then crossed the empty road to the sidewalk on the opposite side. A woman walking her dog in the yard waved to him.

"Let's go back to the island," I said.

"Yeah," Diggs said after another second or two. He nodded reluctantly. "I think you're right, for now. There's nothing else we can do tonight."

He put the car in gear. We'd barely inched forward when I heard the scream of an engine at full throttle as another car tore over the hill. It was a dark color, either deep blue or black, but I couldn't tell anything beyond that in the darkness. The car barely cleared a twist in the road before it righted itself. I froze. The other driver sped forward.

Headed directly for the reverend.

4

FROM THERE, it all happened in a split second. The woman walking her dog screamed in the instant before it happened. The reverend turned to face the car speeding toward him. Diggs reached for his door handle.

The car struck with a screech of tires and a sickening thud. Diggs' father rolled up over the hood and flew ten, maybe fifteen feet. At first impact, Diggs was out of our car and in motion. I was out at the same time—though not for the same reason. On the street, the woman who'd been out with her dog raced to the reverend's side, screaming the whole time. Another half-dozen doors opened along the street.

"Stop," I said to Diggs. He tried to get past me but I pushed him back, my hands on his chest. "We can't go out there. This could be J.—this could be their way of luring us out in the open. They've got this, Diggs."

I kept my hands on his chest, and slowly pushed him back. He stood in the darkened parking lot breathing hard, shaking. I didn't take my eyes from his face. Behind me, I could hear sirens. The woman who'd seen it happen had stopped screaming, but she was crying loudly. A man shouted over the chaos.

"We need to get out of here," I said, trying to get through to him. "Diggs—look at me. We have to go."

Eventually, he nodded.

I got in the driver's seat this time. Diggs slid into the passenger's seat without complaint, his complexion paled to ghost white.

"Go," he said, hoarse.

We left before the cops or paramedics arrived, listening to the sirens as we got into the boat and I guided us out of the harbor. Diggs didn't say a word, the whole time.

Despite the cold, he stood outside the pilothouse for most of the ride. His gloved hands gripped the steel railing as he leaned into the icy sea spray. My stomach rolled, that split second of impact replaying itself over and over in my mind. Shaking myself, I got out my cell phone and called Jamie. She answered immediately.

"Everything all right?" she said.

"Not really." I swallowed past a fresh wave of nausea. "There was an accident on the mainland—or, not an accident. Definitely not an accident. Diggs' father was hit by a car."

Jamie sort of gasped. "What do you need?"

"I just need to know if he made it. If you can check in with the hospital, use whatever sources you might have…"

"Of course. You're on your way back now?"

"Yeah. We'll be there in about forty-five minutes. Thanks."

I hung up.

The seas were choppier than they'd been earlier, the night darker. I kept our speed low and my eyes on the instruments as I navigated out of the harbor and back to open ocean. We were back in the inlet just off Payson Isle before Diggs finally came back in. He was shivering violently. I wasn't sure how much of that was cold and how much of it was shock, but either way it wasn't great.

"He could be okay," he said, after I'd stopped the boat and he'd secured us at the dock. They were the first words he'd spoken for the entire trip. "He's tough—it looked bad, but we don't know..."

He looked at me, waiting for me to give him hope. I couldn't do it, though. Jamie would tell us for sure, but the way that car hit...the force of the impact... He might have been tough, but I was sure Diggs' father hadn't survived this.

"We'll know for sure soon," I said. I resisted the urge to look away. "I'm sorry, Diggs."

He stared out into the night. I've seen Diggs do distant over the years; have seen him check out in any number of circumstances when things got tough. I'd never seen him like this, though.

I set my hand at his back when we were on solid land again and propelled him forward.

"We'll get them," I said. There was no question in my mind that, somehow or other, J. was to blame for this. "We're taking them down this time."

Diggs didn't say a word.

It was almost midnight when we walked through the door of the Payson boarding house. Einstein whirled at my feet with a completely inappropriate grin, while Jamie's dogs were much more sedate. Jamie met us at the entrance to the meeting room. Monty and Carl were seated at the table, though no one else was in sight. She shook her head subtly when our eyes met. I took Diggs' arm. He shook me off.

"They just left him there," he said numbly.

"You should sit down," I said to him.

"I'm fine."

"Will you get us some tea?" I said to Jamie. "And a blanket?"

She nodded. She went for the kitchen, while Monty stood and went in the other direction—presumably for the blanket, though he may have just been fleeing the drama. Carl followed Jamie into the kitchen, leaving us alone.

Instead of sitting, Diggs scratched the back of his neck with a shaking hand and began to pace the room.

"We need to figure out what this means. Why would J. try to kill him? You saw how he reacted when we were talking about the Paysons. If he knew something about Isaac Payson or your father, maybe he had information that could have helped us. We need to get into his house. The old bastard always locks the place tighter than a drum, but I'm sure I can find a way in—"

"Diggs," I said. He just kept going. I grabbed his arm on his third pass by me. He looked at me, surprised.

"What?"

"Sit down."

"I don't need—"

"Daniel Jacob Diggins, sit your ass on that bench."

He sat, albeit reluctantly. "I'm fine. I want to go to the hospital tomorrow, though. I'll be careful, but I don't want him to be alone—"

"Diggs," I interrupted. The name stuck in my throat. "You saw that car hit. He didn't survive that—there was no way. He's dead, Diggs."

He just stared at me. I waited for tears. Denial. Anger. Instead, comprehension gradually took hold. He nodded after a while. "Oh. Okay. I..." He shook his head. Jamie came in with the tea and handed it to Diggs. "Thank you," he said. He held the steaming mug, but didn't take a sip. Jamie looked at me.

"I think we'll all head to bed now. But if you need anything…"

"Thanks," I said. "I really appreciate it."

Instead of leaving, she hesitated. "Tomorrow, I think we should talk."

Diggs stared silently at his tea. Monty returned with the blanket and handed it to me. It spoke to gravity of the sitaution that he didn't make any comments about the two of us breaking it in first.

"Yeah," I said, returning to Jamie's suggestion. "That's probably a good idea."

When we were alone once more, I wrapped the blanket around Diggs' shoulders. He was still shivering, though not as much. The fifty-yard stare hadn't gotten any better, though.

"I'm fine, Sol. I don't need to be babied," he said as I moved away from him. He wet his lips. "I hated the man, okay? That's the reality. And he hated me. He always did." A flicker of emotion broke through the cool blue. He stood abruptly. "We can't afford to get derailed by this—you were right when you said this could have been J.'s way of drawing us out. We still have to stop Mike Reynolds."

"We do," I agreed. "And we'll do that…in the morning. Right now, you need sleep."

"I'm not tired."

"I'm not arguing," I said evenly. "This isn't your girlfriend speaking, this is a medical professional. Sort of. Come on."

He considered resisting before he finally shook his head. "Can I at least go use the john first?"

"I can go with you."

"You're not taking me to the bathroom, Sol." I set my jaw. He read me for a second before he tipped his head and fixed me in his gaze. "Worried I'll score an eight ball between here and the outhouse?"

I hesitated. IN the past, Diggs has been known to turn to chemical support when times get rough. It didn't get much tougher than tonight. "I'm worried that you've been sober for five years now," I said, choosing my words carefully, "and I don't want that to get flushed down the drain after everything you've been through to get here."

"Me staying clean isn't your responsibility—it's not on you. That's up to me."

"I grew up with a mean drunk, Diggs. Trust me, I know what's my responsibility and what's not. I'm not saying your recovery's suddenly on my shoulders, for crying out loud. I'm saying, you just had a shitty night and right now you shouldn't be alone. You're really gonna fight me on that?"

I tipped my chin up and held his gaze. A flicker of a smile touched his lips. He shook his head.

"Fine. But, seriously—give me twenty minutes to go to the outhouse, alone. I'll meet you upstairs."

Against my better judgment, I agreed. There's no question that growing up with Kat has colored my attitude toward addiction, but there's a fine line between being supportive and being an untrusting ass. I pride myself on staying on the right side of that line at least seven times out of ten.

After he'd gone, I went upstairs and walked the long, dark hallway to the bedroom that had been mine twenty-five years ago. There was a gas furnace to heat the house, but it was still pretty damn chilly. I thought of the…whatever it was, that I'd seen earlier that night. Allie Tate. I don't believe in ghosts, and Diggs *definitely* doesn't believe in them. If Allie had appeared to me—via the power of my subconscious, presumably—then there was a reason for it. My brain was trying to tell me something; I just wasn't smart enough to figure out what.

I went into the room, using a flashlight to light the path to the lantern beside the bed. I turned the light on, and extinguished my flashlight. A sliver of cold air made it through the plastic at the broken window, and I shivered as I stripped down to my base layer of underclothes: long johns and a long-sleeved t-shirt. There was no way more than five minutes had passed since Diggs had gone out, and I was already thinking it was a terrible idea. I got into bed anyway. Einstein hopped up beside me and promptly burrowed under the blankets. I thought of Allie Tate again, standing at the door with a bashed-in skull and broken glasses.

"If you want to talk tonight," I said out loud, "do me a favor, Al? Either do it now, or wait till morning."

I lay back in bed. Closed my eyes. Allie made no appearance. Einstein snuggled closer in my arms. The image of Diggs' father flying through the air ran through my mind, that sickening thud playing on a loop in my ears. *The bastard child...*

I was sorry for the way Reverend Diggins died. Sorry for his pain, his suffering, any fear he might have felt. I was sorry for the mess he'd left behind, while Diggs tried to sort through their muddled relationship over the years. I couldn't say I was sorry the son of a bitch was gone, though.

Half an hour had passed and I was debating the wisdom of organizing a search party when Diggs finally came to bed. I'd left the light on, but pretended I was asleep—trying to give him some space to do whatever it was he needed to do.

He got into bed and gently set Einstein at the end of the bed. He got under the covers beside me and pulled me close, my back to his front, his arms wrapped around me and his face at my neck.

"I know you're awake," he whispered.

"No, I'm not," I whispered back. He didn't say anything. Seconds passed. Then a minute. And a minute more. "Are you okay?"

A long pause followed. Finally, he took a deep, shuddering breath before he said anything. "I'm not sure. I don't think so."

I rolled over. He'd had to cut his hair before we left Australia, since we were going back to being other people. It wasn't buzz-cut short this time, but it was still a lot shorter than he'd had it when we were living the dream as beach bums. Now, I ran my hand through the close-cropped curls that remained. In the moonlight, he looked tired. Worn down. Sadder than I could remember seeing him since his mother's death.

"What can I do?" I asked.

"I'm not sure. Nothing, probably—beyond what you're doing. Keep being a pain in the ass. Don't give up on me."

"I'm pretty sure you never have to worry about either of those."

He leaned in and kissed me. It started out slow, quiet, but built fast—as it tends to do with Diggs and me. I draped my leg up over his thigh and pressed closer; I could already feel him hard, more than ready.

Before things took their natural course, though, he pulled back. "I… Not tonight, okay? Do you mind if we just sleep, tonight?"

Two words I never thought I'd hear from Diggs: *Not tonight.*

"Yeah," I said. "Of course, not a problem. Whatever you need."

He rolled away from me.

I lay awake for a long time that night, trying to convince myself we shouldn't just pack everything up then and there and head back to Australia.

•

At six o'clock the next morning, Einstein reacquainted me with the new schedule he'd adopted thanks to life with Jamie and Bear. I cracked one eye open and groaned when he pawed my chest.

"Seriously, dog? You're delusional if you think we're getting up now."

He whined and pawed my nose. Wagged his tail. Whined some more, giving me a little play bow for good measure. Despite the fact that it was still dark outside, I could hear activity downstairs. The kicker that finally ousted me was the realization that Diggs was no longer beside me. I felt the pillow; it was cold. Wherever he was, he'd been there for a while. The events of the night before came rushing back.

"Right," I said to Einstein. "What the hell. Let's be morning people."

I staggered down the stairs to find the rest of the team of *Flint K-9* already in action. Coffee brewed. Dogs paced underfoot—in addition to Einstein, Phantom, and Casper the pit bull, a little curly-haired moppet dog and two brindle mutts had joined us. Much to my relief, Diggs was already in the mix. I took stock from a distance. He looked like hell—clearly hadn't slept, his eyes rimmed with red. Though he was putting up a good front, I could see the residual shock of last night tinged with that first weight of grief. Despite all that, he put a mug of coffee in my hand before I had to ask.

"How are you doing?" I said. The others continued to banter and joke around us. I wondered how many of them even knew what had happened.

"I'm breathing," he said. "I don't really want to talk beyond that."

I got it. I wouldn't have before this year, but now it made perfect sense to me. I let it drop and moved on. "Okay. Next question, then: why are we up?"

"We like to kick off every day by running the dogs," Jamie answered. I got the feeling she'd been keeping an eye on Diggs in my absence. Rather than the green-eyed monster who used to share my skin, I just found myself grateful that I wasn't the only one who had his back right now. "Sorry if we woke you," she continued. "Einstein probably heard us. He's used to being front and center."

"Super," I said.

"Care to join us?" Jamie asked.

I looked at Diggs. He already hs his running clothes on. "You're going?"

"I thought it might clear my head. You up for it?"

Once upon a time, the whole idea would have been my definition of torture: get up before it's light outside, harness everyone you know, and run around an ice-cold island until you drop. The past year had given me a new perspective on torture, though. This? This wasn't even close.

"Sure," I said. I could see the surprise in Diggs' eyes. "What the hell."

Ten minutes later, Diggs and I headed off with the rest of the team. A dozen dogs—including Einstein, who whirled in excitement the second we hit the trail—led the charge, with Bear and Urenna not far behind. Jamie and Carl followed, while Monty entertained-slash-annoyed the women on the team. Diggs and I kept to the rear, more for a shot at privacy than because we didn't think we could keep pace.

Diggs remained silent, distant, while we raced over lichen-covered granite and a carpet of rust-colored pine needles, the air crisp and clean and lightly salted. I'd liked Australia, but it never felt quite like home. For one thing, it was hotter than the sun half the time; Maine-bred girls don't deal well with that kind of crap. A little cold air first thing in the morning was damned appealing now.

As we covered more ground, I was surprised at how familiar some of the trails on the island were—haunted passages I'd traveled as a kid, back when my father was my world and I had no clue how screwed up that world would eventually become. About twenty minutes in, we reached a grove of spruce at the top of an incline, the ocean deep blue off the cliffs below. There was a giant rock at the top of the incline, split through the center and laid open with a sliver of a path between.

If you make it through the Crack, you live forever, Allie Tate whispered to me. She stood between the two rocks just as I'd seen her a few hours before—glasses broken, dress torn. Blood trailed down her forehead.

I tripped on a tree root and went sailing, then leapt to my feet before Diggs could get to me.

"Okay, you really need to stop doing that," I said out loud. Because now I was talking to dead people. Excellent.

Forever, Allie whispered again.

The Crack. We'd come here as kids, I remembered suddenly. Vivid and immediate, I saw the lot of us trekking through the undergrowth of this very path. A lean, dark-haired boy was in the lead. Will Colby.

If you get stuck in the Crack, you die there, I remembered him saying. He was a hard kid. Cruel. A troublemaker. My father never liked him—never wanted me around him. *Make it through the Crack and you'll find all our secrets.*

We live forever if we make it through, Allie said again.

"Sol," Diggs said. His hand was on my arm, eyes uneasy. "Hey—you okay?"

I nodded. My palms were sweating, my heart racing. None of it had a thing to do with the morning run. "Yeah," I said. "I'm fine. Come on—we're losing them."

I took off before he could question me further. I'd forgotten about those treks up here as a kid. I'd forgotten so much of my childhood, though, that it was getting hard to keep track.

It was seven-thirty and breakfast was up by the time we got back to the house. Considering everything that had happened, my appetite was slim to nil but I dug into the food with as much gusto as I could muster. Between mandatory morning runs, dead dads, and rampaging ghosts, I figured I could use the nourishment. To my relief, Diggs plowed through a full plate of food before he pushed it away and leaned back.

As had been the case before, the meal ended with only Diggs, me, Monty, Carl, and Jamie still at the table. I got the feeling that wasn't an accident. I finished off the last of my coffee and set the cup down.

"Let me guess," I said to Jamie. "This is the part where you kindly ask what the hell's going on."

"In so many words," she said. She said it with a smile, but she was tough about it—not the kind of woman you messed with. "I'd like to know, first and foremost, if there's a possibility that we could be in danger out here. I'm not worried about myself, but I have a son, a whole team, and a dozen dogs I'm responsible for. If something could happen…"

"I know," I said. "You're right. We didn't come here with the intention of pulling you into anything—we still aren't. Whatever happened last night with Diggs' father… We never saw that coming. Neither of us is sure how it relates to what we're doing here."

"Which is what, exactly?" Monty said. "No offense, princess, but tight lips are only good for one thing, and this ain't it. In case you've forgotten, Carl and I weren't just with you last year because we're so damn pretty. If you need a hand…"

"I think the better thing for us to do at this point," Diggs said, "is to just move along. We could stay at my place on the mainland. Like Solomon said, we didn't expect things to escalate—and we especially didn't expect it to happen this fast. We'll get out of here—"

"Hang on a minute," Jamie said. "That's not what I'm saying. But I'd at least like some idea of what we're facing, before I make a decision one way or another."

Diggs looked at me, his question clear. Did we tell them? I was still reeling after what had happened to his father the night before; the state of Diggs' house; Mike Reynolds and his shed full of ammunition. Juarez still seemed to be off the radar, and I wasn't ready yet to call Cameron in on this—mostly because I wasn't completely convinced yet that we could trust him.

So, what were we supposed to do?

"We already know some of this shit from last year,"

Monty said.

"We were in that jungle with you when your father passed," Carl said. Somehow, the quiet strength behind his words lent weight to the conversation. "We would like to help you. *I* would like to help you, if I can."

I looked at Diggs again. He shook his head. "It's your call," he said.

Another five seconds passed, while I thought about it. All those bodies, piling up in my dreams with no end in sight. Diggs and I had come back here to try and stop J., but the truth of the matter was that we didn't have a clue how to do that.

"Will you go get the file?" I finally asked.

He nodded grimly. I wasn"t sure, but I thought he looked relieved at my decision. We'd both been carrying this alone for way too long.

While Diggs went for the folder, I briefed them on what we knew about the organization to date, including the whole spiel about J-932, MK Ultra, Jim Jones, and my own father. Diggs returned from our room a minute later with a manila folder filled with loose-leaf pages, and tossed the folder in the center of the table without looking at me. When Jamie made no move, Monty reached for it. He opened the folder, took a few seconds to peruse the pages, and set it back down.

"Heavy," he said. "What the hell does it mean?"

"It's a code," Diggs said.

We explained the breakdown: coordinates; social security number; month and year; and the initials of the J. team leader who had overseen each operation.

"Okay," Monty said. "So…maybe I'm not seeing the whole picture here, but this seems pretty straightforward. You don't have the exact location, you don't have the exact date, and you don't know whose initials are at the end of these entries a lot of the time, right?"

"That's the gist," I said.

"But you've got the social security number. Which means that's where you go—you get the son of a bitch who's about to go nuts, and you put him on ice. Call the cops. Call the Feds. Hell, I don't know, call local action news. Just get the asshole off the street for that month."

Diggs looked at me. I nodded. If we were telling them, we might as well tell them everything.

"You're right," he said. "That's the one thing we do know for sure. There's a problem, though. Over the past several months, the J. operatives on this list have been dropping dead left and right."

"How's that a problem?" Monty said. "You ask me, that's the *solution* to your problem."

It wasn't incredibly PC, but Diggs and I had actually been arguing the same point for a while now. "That's one way of looking at it," I said. "The problem comes from the fact that something happens anyway—even if the operative is dead. There's still some kind of incident within the coordinates during the time frame on the list. People still die."

"So J. has…" Carl hesitated, searching for the word. "An alternate? A contingency plan? That *is* a problem."

"It is," I said. Diggs had gotten quiet again, staring at the list in front of him. "We did what we could to stop them from a distance, but this is the kind of thing people get put in padded cells for."

"Besides which," Diggs added, "every time we tried to warn anyone, J. managed to track us down."

"This next J. extravaganza pulled us out of retirement, though. It's all fun and games till a super-secret formerly government-sanctioned gang of mad scientists targets your hometown."

Diggs didn't even crack a smile. "You were the one who decided to come out of retirement, actually. If I'd had my way, we'd still be as far from here as we could get."

"And it would have eaten at both of us until we couldn't stand it or each other anymore," I returned evenly. "You know there was no choice in this."

"You do realize how all this sounds, don't you?" Monty said.

"Like we should be wearing tinfoil hats?" I said. "Yeah, we've been over it. J.'s ever-growing body count makes it seem a little less nuts."

Jamie had been quiet through most of this, but now she pulled a copy of the list toward her and looked it over. "Other than this, do you have any evidence at all to back up what you're talking about? Other than Mitch Cameron and his daughter, you don't have a single name of the people behind this. And you're hoping Cameron and his daughter are on our side now…"

"Cameron is," I said. "I mean—I think he is. He saved our asses. Saved my mother. Jenny—his daughter—is a wild card at this point. So…no. Right now, we don't have any evidence, and we don't have any names. That's where we start. Up till this point, everyone we've met who was involved with the project—on either side—is dead."

"Except Cameron and Jenny," Diggs added.

"Right. Except for them."

He paused. "Wait. What about Hank Gendreau? Do we know where he is now?"

About a year and a half ago, Hank Gendreau had been in prison for murdering his teenage daughter when he got in touch with me to tell me he wasn't the killer. It was that investigation that had led me to my father's past—ultimately exonerating Hank for the crime, while simultaneously putting Diggs and me on J.'s scent for the first time.

"The last I heard, he was out of prison and back in Black Falls," I said. "We can try to get in touch, but I doubt he knows anything about this stuff."

"The prison is just down the road, though," Diggs argued. "We could maybe talk to a warden or two there—see if Hank ever mentioned anything to them."

I weighed the idea, but it still seemed like a waste of time to me.

"You said someone is killing these operatives before they have an opportunity to complete their missions," Carl said. "Correct?" I nodded. "Do you have any idea who might be doing that? It would seem you both have the same objective, wouldn't it?"

This was something else Diggs and I had given a lot of thought to. "We only know a few people who have access to the list and want J. gone enough to kill," I said. I thought of Juarez, still off the reservation while he tried to track down his childhood. Tried to track down the people who'd raped and murdered his wife. Juarez, trained former military, former Special Agent with the FBI…

"We don't know who it is," Diggs summarized. "But we've got some ideas. As far as I'm concerned, Cameron's daughter is at the top of the list."

"Agreed," I said.

"But you don't know how to get in touch with her?" Monty said.

"I don't have her on speed dial, no."

"So…" Monty scratched his head. "If you don't mind my asking, what the hell was your plan when you came here? You were just gonna come in, ask some questions, maybe talk to this fella about to go off his rocker and see if you could get him to check in with a shrink before April?"

Diggs bristled at his tone. "We didn't know what we were going to do, all right? We came back, figured we'd talk to Mike Reynolds—the guy J. is using right now—and try to get some information from him. And…somehow, we'd stop what's supposed to happen in a few months."

Carl looked at him, his gaze steady. "And then?" he asked.

Diggs took a breath. He looked at me. "And then, we'd get ready for J. when they came for Solomon and me."

"And you're certain that's what they would do?" Carl said. "If they knew what you had done, they would come for you."

"They're sure," Monty said with a nod. He studied Diggs frankly, quieter now. "You don't mind me saying, that's a crap plan. You're in over your head, brother." There was no malice in his tone.

Diggs laughed humorlessly. "You think?" He ran a hand through his short hair. I thought about how much lighter he'd seemed when we were living away from here. I lay my hand on his arm; it was like petting a caged tiger. And not a happy one.

"So what can we do?" Jamie asked.

"Now that Diggs' father's dead?" I said. "Nothing—*especially* not you. If Monty and Clar feel like signing up for this, that's one thing. But you said it already: you've got a son and a team and an island of hounds who rely on you. I'm not bringing you into this. Diggs and I will clear out."

"It's your island," she argued.

"Stop saying that. It's not my damn island. I gave it to you."

She smiled at that—actually smiled, with teeth and everything. "Erin, you can't just write a bill of sale on a piece of paper, charge me a dollar, and say the island isn't yours anymore."

"Why not? People do that all the time on TV. I don't want the goddamn place."

"Well, right now the goddamn place is yours," she returned. She didn't seem at all impressed with my tough talk. "There's a training coming up in Northern Maine—I'd originally declined the invitation, because we've been busy out here trying to get set up. I'll call my brother and tell him we're on board. We'll be gone tomorrow morning." She looked at Monty and Carl. "If you guys want to stay, you're welcome to do so."

"You can't pack up a dozen dogs and a dozen people and just…leave," I said.

"We can, actually," Jamie said. She didn't even seem fazed at the thought. "We do it pretty regularly, as a matter of fact. I'll talk to Bear and Urenna, and they'll get everything arranged."

"What if things run long here?" I argued. "J. doesn't even have anything planned until April. You're saying you'll just vacate indefinitely?"

"We won't need to," she said. The smile disappeared—no more white teeth, no more lit eyes. She studied me for a few seconds. "You've set this in motion now. From here, it won't be long."

Diggs glanced at me to see if I had any idea what she was talking about. I didn't have a clue—all I knew was that Jamie and her creepy kid were starting to freak me out.

"So, we've got a plan, then," Monty said. "Jamie and the rest of the ranch heads for the hills. Meanwhile, the four of us will figure out how to get a handle on this Mike Reynolds. Then, as I see it, we need to start figuring out who the next person in line might be—whoever J. would use if Mikey boy gets taken out of play."

"And how, exactly, are we supposed to do that?" I asked. "It's one thing if we have a social security number like we do with Mike. Without it, what are we supposed to do? Call a town meeting and ask for a show of hands for anyone who's had unexplained homicidal urges lately?"

"These behaviors don't come out of nowhere," Diggs said. "You know that. J.'s operatives are people with a history of mental illness, violence, depression. We look for patterns of abuse, arrest records…whatever. No one's completely surprised when someone J. chose snaps—the world's usually been expecting it for a long time."

"So we just need a list of all the people who fit those criteria in Littlehope," I said. "Great. In a town of hard-drinking fishermen whose favorite pastime is beating the piss out of each other, that should be a short list."

"I'll go to the town office this afternoon," Monty volunteered. "The old guy who works there loves to talk—I'll see what I can get from him."

"Good idea," Diggs said. "I'll make a list myself, maybe check in with a couple of sources."

"Aren't we supposed to be working under the radar?" I said.

"I'll do it quietly, dearest." He gave me his most angelic smile.

"See that you do."

"We should get started with the day," Carl said. "There's much to be done." He eyed Diggs for a second before he spoke to me. "Is there anything else I can do for you, before we get things under way?"

"I don't think so," I said. Diggs had lightened marginally, but he was still understandably quiet and broody, and Monty was already preparing to saddle up while Jamie got the rest of the island mobilized. I was grateful, suddenly, to have a cool head like Carl on the team.

More than that, though, I was grateful to have a team at all.

5

GIVEN LAST NIGHT'S EVENTS in Littlehope, we decided it was definitely in Diggs' and my best interest to steer clear of the mainland until the sun had set again. I was starting to understand how vampires felt. Diggs went out with Carl and Monty to get a feel for the island and figure out how best to keep things secure at the house if things ramped up with J. over the next few days, weeks, or months. He'd said very little after the meeting, but it was hard to miss his exhaustion. I was worried about him—and quickly realizing how good it might feel to *not* be worried all the time.

I was beyond ready for this thing to be over.

While Diggs and the guys cruised the island, I placed my standard ad for Cameron on Craigslist, under Missed Connections:

Red Riding Hood is thinking about you again. It's been too long.

That's it. The Red Riding Hood bit felt creepy to me, but it was Cameron's idea. He's not the kind of man you argue with, especially about spy stuff. From there, all I could do was wait for him to contact me. It usually only took a few hours, but that felt like an eternity today.

Diggs was still busy when noon came around, the rest of the crew busy prepping to leave come morning. It was just Einstein and me in the house while I waited for Cameron's e-mail. I'd been listening to the weather radio for most of the morning. The whole state was gearing up for the coming storm, due to hit in two days—on New Year's Eve, of course. Most celebrations were tentative at best at this point, though in Maine you don't know for sure how bad a storm will be until you're already buried in powder. So far, though, the bullets for the blizzard were impressive: two feet of snow along the coast, gusting winds up to fifty miles an hour, and seas at ten to fifteen feet. Meteorologists warned that predictions could change in the next twenty-four hours, but every computer model they had said pretty much the same thing—batten down the hatches and stay the hell inside for the duration.

The perfect way to ring in the new year in Maine.

When I couldn't stand watching my inbox or listening to dire forecasts any more, I snagged Einstein, shrugged on a second layer and my winter jacket, and headed out to see what the rest of the world was up to.

I found Diggs working on stabilizing a barn-in-progress with Monty and Cheyenne, to make sure the thing didn't blow over while the others were away. They looked like they had it all under control, so I struck out in search of Jamie.

A warm front was moving through the state, the air almost balmy compared to what it had been. The sky was clear and cloud-free. Chickadees sang. Squirrels skittered. Einstein trotted along beside me like he didn't have a care in the world, while we followed the same path I'd traveled with the others that morning. The smells of pine and salt were strong in the air, and every so often I'd catch a flash of crimson in the trees when a cardinal would settle on a low branch. It was a great day to be alive; it was a shame I was too caught up in the thought of one dead girl to give it much notice.

I consciously followed the path to the place where Allie Tate had appeared from nowhere, spouting cryptic allegories I didn't understand. *Make it through the Crack and you live forever.* What the hell did that even mean?

I slowed at the place where I'd seen her during the run—the Crack. All I saw now were cold forest and a big hunk of granite sliced down the middle. A headache daggered in at my temples as I tried to push past the mental brick wall my father had put there when I was a kid.

Before I ever got close to knocking that wall down, I heard dogs barking farther down the trail. Einstein woofed back and looked at me hopefully. I looked back at the Crack. It was definitely still empty.

"Sure," I said to Stein. "Let's go see what the others are up to. Maybe Allie's hanging with Bear now."

Einstein grinned like a fool, his tail wagging, with no idea that I'd gone completely nuts. Or maybe he had an idea, and he just didn't care. That's what I love about dogs—they never judge.

In the valley where the Payson barn/chapel once stood, Jamie had cleared out the underbrush and replaced the rubble of the burned-out structure with an indoor/outdoor training facility for the dogs. It was the only thing actually finished on the island. That was where I found her that afternoon.

The building consisted of a covered arena that was maybe 60 x 120 square feet, with a padded floor, and obstacles and equipment set up about halfway across the arena. A dozen dogs of varying sizes and breeds sat patiently at the other end when I came in. Bear stood just behind the dogs, Jamie waiting at the equipment.

Einstein whined beside me. One of the dogs—a shepherd mix with a mottled coat who looked younger than the others—looked over.

"Sorry," I said. "Didn't mean to interrupt."

"We're due for a break anyway," Jamie said. "Just give us ten minutes. You can let Stein join in if you want. He loves this part."

That was news to me. I started to walk him over on the leash, but Bear shook his head. "You can just let him go. After nine months with us, he knows the drill."

I unclipped his leash. Einstein trotted over without bothering to greet the other dogs, and sat at attention at the end of the line. Bear tossede him a treat, which he caught in mid-air before he sat again. I stood there, gobsmacked, while Jamie put the dogs through their paces. They ran through basic stuff like sit and stay, which the dogs did in perfect synchrony, then moved on to individual tracking routines. When Einstein's turn came, he stood with wagging tail and waited eagerly for the command.

"Find it, Stein!" Bear said, after what seemed an unnecessarily long wait. Einstein took off running, snuffling the air and the ground for only about two seconds before he caught the scent. A stuffed duck was hidden beneath an orange cone on the other side of the arena. Einstein sniffed the cone once, whimpered, and lay down, his gaze expectant on Bear.

Apparently, Einstein was a damn genius.

When they were done, Jamie and Bear released the dogs with a single command and all dozen of them stood, tails wagging, and trotted outside to a fenced enclosure.

The exception was Phantom, Jamie's shepherd. Gray at the muzzle and slightly lame at the hips, she came over and settled at Jamie's feet without so much as a glance at me.

"That was incredible," I said to Jamie. "Seriously. I had Stein for four years before you got hold of him, and the best I ever did was teach him not to eat frozen dog crap."

"He's a natural," she said. "Bear's the one who did most of the work with him, though."

"Whoever did the work, you've done a great job," I said. I looked at Bear, who smiled shyly. He wore jeans and a t-shirt despite the cold weather. Standing out here like this, it was the first time I actually realized how big he was. At seventeen, he topped six feet, his shoulders broad, his gait a lope that was more wolf than bear. "I really appreciate you two taking him into the fold like this. With everything else you've got going on, it couldn't have been easy."

"One more dog in this place is nothing," Bear said. "Besides, he was fun. He's smart, and he has a great nose. He missed you, though."

Watching Einstein wrestle with the other dogs, I wasn't so sure about that. Rather than appear pathetically insecure about my dog's loyalty, however, I let the subject drop. I had other fish to fry right now.

"So…" I began, in the least subtle subject shift so far today, "the other night, with that whole window-shattering thing…" Bear didn't look at all surprised, though he did look a little uncomfortable. He waited for me to finish. "You mentioned seeing a girl?"

He glanced at Jamie, like he wasn't sure whether or not he should answer the question. She nodded, silent.

"Phantom saw her first," he said. "When we first came out here, last spring. Mom and I came out with Carl and a couple of the dogs, to check the place out. I was walking through the woods, and Phantom caught the scent."

"The scent of…what?" I asked. Skepticism definitely made it into my tone. "A ghost?"

He looked embarrassed, which really hadn't been my intention. Before Jamie could intervene, the dogs all shifted focus to the path leading in to the center. A couple of them woofed. All of them wagged. Seconds later, Urenna emerged from the brush and trotted toward us, out of breath. There was a light sheen of sweat on her forehead.

"I thought you were meeting me back at the house," she said to Bear with mock severity. "Instead, I come out here and find you slacking as usual."

I expected him to be flustered, but he just grinned at her. "You know you've been looking for an excuse to get out of that house. I was just trying to help you out."

"Always so considerate," she said. She battered her long, thick eyelashes at him. Their eyes locked. Jamie cleared her throat, and Urenna refocused and dropped the flirty banter. "I was able to get us a block of rooms at the lodge for tomorrow through Wednesday. The core dogs are okay to stay with us, and the others will be kenneled at the center."

"Good. Thank you," Jamie said.

"I got an itinerary," Urenna added. "It looks like fun, actually. They've got a workshop on scenting with small dogs that I thought would be perfect for Pru and Dobby."

"That's great," Bear said. "A whole class for people who can't handle real dogs." His gaze sparked when he said it. Urenna arched an eyebrow, but she didn't take the bait.

"There's another session I know my dad will have a good time with—a whole training on rehabbing retired military dogs to use in search and rescue. He'll be psyched."

"I think your father may actually sit this one out," Jamie said, glancing at me. "He's staying behind to keep an eye on things here." I caught a flicker of uneasiness before Urenna shut it down. "He didn't tell you?"

"He's been busy out at the building site—I didn't want to bother him," she said. She frowned. "Okay. Well, I guess that's one less head to worry about feeding while we're there, right?"

The news had taken the wind out of her sails for some reason. Bear clearly caught her mood, and nodded toward the house. "Speaking of grub, we should get back—it's my turn to cook tonight."

"Which means it's my turn to keep watch and make sure you don't accidentally poison us."

"Funny." He shifted focus to Jamie. "We can get the dogs rounded up and in for the afternoon if you want. You want to keep Stein back?"

"Yeah," I said, already feeling guilty for ruining my dog's fun. "If you don't mind."

"Leave Phantom and Casper, too," Jamie added. "Phantom's getting too old to traipse all over the place, and Stein and Casper can wear each other out. The rest of them can go, though."

"Got it," Bear said. Urenna lingered for a second before she seemed to sense that we had other business to tend to.

"I'll just get started," she said.

"I'll be right there," Bear said. He waited until she was out of earshot before he spoke again. It took him a couple of seconds to work up the courage this time. "The little girl—the one I keep seeing. You knew her, then? You were there when she was killed."

My innards went ten degrees colder. "I'm not exactly sure. There's a lot of stuff I don't remember."

"You will," he said. "I saw her again last night. She doesn't… I mean, it's not like she sits there and talks to me or something. But I get the sense it's important—you remembering."

"She told you that. My dead best friend."

"Sort of. Like I said, she doesn't talk—I just get impressions from her."

All righty then. He turned again before I could follow up with another question, and left us. Jamie waited until he and Urenna were rounding up the dogs before she returned her attention to me. She pulled out a couple of chairs at the edge of the arena, and we sat. The sun was still out, though it had gotten chillier as the afternoon wore on.

"Interesting kid," I said.

"You don't know the half of it. I know what he was talking about is a little out there, but try to keep an open mind."

"I'm doing my best. Have you seen the girl Bear has seen?"

"No. She's apparently taken a liking to him, though." If Jamie was skeptical, she didn't show it.

"He's mentioned her to you before the other night?"

"There are a few here that he's mentioned. She's the one who visits him most regularly, though. I think she might have a little crush."

"On your son."

She opened a metal container, drank from it, and closed it again before she answered, smiling. "That's right."

"The ghost of my nine-year-old best friend, who's been dead for twenty-five years."

"It's just a theory."

A bat-shit crazy one, but who was I to judge. I studied

her for a few seconds, trying to figure out where to go from there. Jamie was about my age—maybe a year or two older, but I couldn't imagine she was more than thirty-five. That meant she would have been a teenager when she had Bear, her giant, soulful psychic son.

"Aren't you scared, living out here on this island of ghosts?" I finally asked. To my surprise, she didn't answer right away. I caught the hesitation in her eyes. "You are. Why the hell are you staying, if you're afraid of this place?"

"I'm not afraid," she said. I'd offended her—which is a talent of mine. "I'm just…cautious. This is an incredible opportunity for us. This island came at a critical time, just when the business was really starting to grow. I never would have had the funds for a setup like this myself."

"Do you think you're in danger here?"

Another second or two of thought passed before she met my eye. "I think we have more to fear from the living than the dead. My biggest concern, to be honest, is that I don't think the living are done with this island yet."

"Meaning J. and his people," I guessed.

"There's something about this place that makes me think they still have business here. That worries me much more than a little girl who died a tragic death, who takes comfort in the little bit of attention my son gives her every now and then."

Einstein and Casper reached us in a tumble of white paws, still half chasing each other when Stein butted his head against my thigh.

"We should get going," Jamie said, standing. Phantom got up with her. "I've still got a lot to tie up if we're clearing out tomorrow."

I got up with her. As we headed out, I thought yet again

of Allie Tate. Whether she was actually a ghost—and I was absolutely, positively not prepared to concede that point—or just a niggling part of my subconscious trying to get me to remember, I had a feeling I'd be seeing more of her before long.

•

I still hadn't heard from Cameron by the time the sun was down that night. Of course, it was technically only four-thirty, so I figured that was understandable. We stuck with the plan anyway. This time, Diggs and I walked down to the boat with Monty and Carl alongside, the four of us traveling in silence for most of the trek. The trees were stripped of leaves, the moon half full, the air cold enough to freeze the tips of my nose and the ends of my fingers and toes.

Maine without either snow or foliage is a weird place—the world a landscape in browns and grays, the kind of monochromatic palette you'd expect in limbo, waiting for the final judgment to be handed down. It can be beautiful in a stark, dismal kind of way, but at the moment I really wasn't seeing the beauty. Right now, with Diggs' father dead, Payson Isle about to be abandoned once more, and J. still running free, it was just depressing.

When we reached the mainland, the four of us got into a black van Monty had parked at the wharf. Monty started the engine and got us on the road, while Diggs gave him directions back to Mike Reynolds' place. Diggs had gotten quieter as the day dragged on. He was still in shock over what had happened the night before, I knew—it would be a while before that faded and he transitioned into grief. Now, he sat silent on the other end of the bench seat, our bodies close but not touching, his jaw set and his expression dark. No one does brooding quite like Diggs.

This time when we went to Mike's place, Diggs and I made the decision to go in together. The reasoning was that I'd get a chance to talk to Mike myself that way, and maybe glean some insights Diggs hadn't.

We got there while the kids were running around the front yard with the dog. Aidan had surrendered his bow and arrow, but I doubted he'd done so willingly. Now, he was chasing another little boy—younger than him by a couple of years, probably—and a little girl who was barely walking. He made machine-gun noises and swooped after the other kids with a plastic airplane, dive bombing them and the dog while they all shrieked and whooped and hollered. They made a hell of a racket, but it looked like they were having fun—even the dog, who was loose in the yard now.

All the fun stopped the second Diggs and I came into sight, though. Diggs had instructed Monty and Carl to stay out of sight with the van, in case Mike got twitchy and thought he was being invaded. I was grateful for his foresight when I saw how the kids reacted.

The younger boy and girl came to a screeching halt a few feet from us. The girl took one look at me and burst into tears, which made both Aidan and the dog come running.

"What are you doing back here?" Aidan demanded. The dog got in between us and the kids, suddenly not looking nearly as harmless as he had the night before. "You're not supposed to creep around here."

"We're not creeping," Diggs said. "You remember me, right? Diggs—I ran your picture after that ballgame a couple of years ago. You scored the final run after you guys went into extra innings. You played a mean game that day."

Aidan softened marginally. The little girl was still wailing, while the younger brother just gaped at us. "Take her in," Aidan said to his brother. "Tell Mum somebody's here."

Before the y could move, Mike's wife emerged from the house. She had to be at least ten years older than Mike, thin as a menthol smoke, and just as unappetizing. She stood in the doorway of the farthest trailer to the right in baggy sweats and slippers, her hair pulled back in a ponytail.

"What the hell's going on?" she demanded at sight of us. I expected her shotgun to come out next, but instead she just bellowed over her shoulder for Mike. In the meantime, Aidan had successfully shooed his siblings, but he and the dog remained with us, stubbornly watchful.

"You here to tell Mike where I was last night?" he asked me when the other kids were gone.

"I told you I wouldn't rat you out," I said. "I don't go back on my word. What about you?"

"I didn't say anything. It's none of his business, right?"

"Thanks," I said. "We're here to talk to Mike now, but since you're here, I thought maybe you could answer a question or two."

Aidan frowned. "Nope." Unequivocal.

"It wouldn't take long," Diggs said.

The kid's frown deepened. Diggs had been trying to get on his good side, but something had clearly gone wrong. He glared at my man for a second, silent, before he shifted focus back to me. "You can tell him, I don't talk to reporters. Got my name and my picture in there that one time, and I caught deep shit for it. I don't talk to reporters since then."

He said it like he was a veteran at navigating press conferences and paparazzi. Diggs glanced at me, then back at the kid.

"I got a release from your folks about that, Aidan. You shouldn't have gotten in trouble."

"I didn't then," Aidan said impatiently. He crossed his arms over his thin chest and glared. "But a couple months ago, Mike found the clipping. Just about had an attack—I got the shit kicked out of me. He almost went after my brother, too. The government's always trying to track you, you know that? And you get your picture in the paper, and they got you there forever. They know where you are—they got a record of you from then on out, Mike says. So I don't talk to reporters no more."

"Okay," Diggs said. He looked at Aidan seriously, his regret obvious. "I'm really sorry about that."

Aidan considered the apology for a few seconds before he shrugged. "It's all right. You probably didn't know—not everybody does."

The trailer door opened behind him, and Aidan flinched. I watched as Mike Reynolds took the front steps, his jaw set, and made straight for the kid. I felt Diggs tense beside me.

"Your mother told you to get inside," Mike said. He didn't even acknowledge Diggs and me—the world was a pinpoint at the moment, and Aidan was seated at the tip. Mike got lower, until he was face to face with the kid, grabbed hold of his thin arm and pointed back to the trailer. "What'd we tell you about not listening to what she says? You don't get two warnings, you don't get five seconds. You do it now."

"I'm going," Aidan said. Mike didn't let him go. Diggs stepped up.

"He was talking to us," he said.

Mike dropped Aidan's arm and twisted his head to look up at Diggs, hovering above him. If it weren't for the look on

Diggs' face, the moment might have been comical. I knew Diggs well enough to know he didn't see the humor. Mike straightened.

"Go on inside," he said to Aidan.

The kid didn't argue, but ran for the door at top speed. That left Mike with Diggs and me. Now that the kids were safely out of sight, the dog slunk off to a dilapidated doghouse in the yard. Even he seemed afraid to look Mike in the eye.

Personally, I didn't see what the big deal was. The guy was a head shorter than Diggs, with a patch of red hair, a goatee, and a bunch of tattoos that twined up his scrawny arms. He wore jeans that hung too low, and a dirty Gap t-shirt a size too small.

"I don't remember you saying you was coming back here today," he said to Diggs. He eyed him warily, his gaze shifting to me and then back again. "And you never said you'd bring somebody else out here. You pull something like that, and it doesn't feel like you're respecting me. Doesn't feel like you're respecting our friendship."

"I wanted to talk to you," Diggs said. He didn't bother trying to infuse an ounce of friendliness into his tone this time. "Did you hear anything about what happened last night? With my father?"

"The reverend?" Mike said. He blinked slowly. I watched as he ground to a halt and tried to switch gears. "He got hit, right? I heard he got hit."

Inside the trailer, Mike's wife was screaming at the kids. I saw the blue light of a TV come on. Magically, everyone went quiet. Mike scratched his neck nervously, digging in hard enough to draw blood. "I don't know anything but that, though," he continued when Diggs didn't say anything.

"I don't know anything else about it."

"So you don't have any idea who might have wanted my father dead?"

Mike glanced back toward the trailer. He shifted from his left foot to his right, still digging into his neck. "I'm supposed to get in there for dinner," he said. "Eddie hates it when I miss dinner. I'm sorry about your dad, man, but I didn't have anything to do with that. If they went after him, it didn't have nothing to do with me."

Diggs followed up without giving him time to backtrack, his voice sharp. "What do you mean by that? If who went after him?"

Mike took a step back, his hands up. This time when he glanced backward, his focus went to the tree line. I followed his gaze. It was too dark to see much of anything, but I could have sworn I saw movement over there. Mike shook his head.

"I don't know anything. Now get off my property. You don't respect my bounds, we can't be friends no more. It's not like you got some magic ticket that'll make me talk. Nobody's got that magic ticket but me."

Eddie appeared in the door again, just about ripping the flimsy metal screen off its hinges. This time, she had the shotgun with her.

"Supper's getting cold. Get in here," she said to Mike. I wasn't sure whether the shotgun was for us or him, but I had no intention of sticking around to find out. I touched Diggs' arm.

"We should go," I said.

He nodded, but didn't move. He glanced at Eddie and her shotgun fleetingly before he closed the distance between him and Mike. He wrapped his hand around Mike's throat.

I thought of the thin stream of blood there a second ago, and cringed. If we survived this at all, Hep-C could be a very real concern.

"When did you start beating on your kids, Mike?" he asked. His voice was low—very Eastwood. Diggs can be tough, but he's never been the Eastwood type. It wasn't even kind of a turn-on, right now. "I thought you were better than that. You remember how much you hated getting the shit kicked out of you? I thought we got this straight."

"I don't beat on my kids," he said.

Diggs tightened his grip. Miake started to turn an unhealthy shade of puce. I grabbed Diggs' arm, while Eddie strode toward us with her shotgun raised.

"You want to try again?" Diggs said.

"Aidan? That little asshole ain't even mine. I'm teaching him the way the world works," Mike gasped the words through his rapidly shrinking vocal chords.

"Let him go," Eddie said. She leveled the gun at Diggs. I pulled on his arm, preparing to kick him somewhere that might jolt him out of the sudden testosterone surge.

"If you touch him again," Diggs said, "I'll have someone come for you. I don't know what kind of shit you're into right now, what kind of plans you have, but you lay a hand on the kids again and I've got twenty guys I can call who'll end you."

He finally let Mike go seconds before he turned purple. He turned his back on Eddie without acknowledging her, and strode away. I had to run to catch up. Once we were presumably out of shotgun range, I grabbed his arm.

"You've got twenty guys you can call who'll end him?" I said. "Since when? What the hell was that? We were going in soft—asking questions. That was *not* going in soft."

He didn't answer. Fury rolled from his shoulders, his hands clenched tight. I held onto his arm until he wheeled, and took a step back. "Give me a minute," he said.

The violence still lingered in his voice. I've known Diggs a long time—he'd be more likely to show up in a mankini at the next Republican convention than hurt me. It wasn't that I was afraid of him in that moment; it was more like he was suddenly afraid of himself, this unexpected fury he'd tapped into. I gave him his space while he pulled himself back. The two of us walked back to Monty's van in silence.

We got back in the van a minute alter, and I gave Monty and Carl an abbreviated version of what we'd learned. Diggs remained locked in silence, a million miles away beside me.

"So you think this guy had something to do with what happened last night?" Monty asked when we were on the road again.

"He knew something," I said. "Unfortunately, Diggs tried a new interview tactic that wasn't that effective. I'm not sure how well we'll do with him from here on out."

"It's too late anyway," Diggs said. I looked at him in surprise. His voice was cooler, more measured now that he'd gotten the beginnings of a grip. "Whatever's going on, they've got Mike now—J., or whoever it is. Everything Aidan said: Mike losing it, worrying about the government tracking him… Short of getting him checked in somewhere, there's no reasoning with him now. I don't see that happening."

Personally, I hadn't considered that a possibility from the start. Knowing that Diggs had been holding out hope up till now was sobering. "Okay. So, we know that much now," I said. "What's next?"

"We stick to the plan," he said.

I grimaced. At the moment, I wasn't a big fan of the plan.

Ten minutes later, we pulled up in front of the old Victorian home that had been Diggs' childhood home. The expansive front lawn was dead, and two rock gardens were overgrown with wilted flowers and dried leaves. A huge oak tree in the front yard stood sentinel over the scene. The white picket fence needed painting.

"Park down the street," Diggs said. "I'll be back in a few minutes."

"*We'll* be back in a few minutes," I corrected him. He glanced at me. I couldn't make out his expression in the darkness, but I could feel the tension radiating from him.

"It won't take long," he said.

"Then it'll take even less time with two of us," I returned. Before he could argue any further, I opened the door and hopped out. Monty and Carl remained in the van as Diggs and I walked down the silent side street. It was barely seven o'clock and the neighborhood was already quiet, Christmas lights lit and windows shuttered.

When I was a teenager, I climbed Diggs' trellis and snuck in his window the night of his mother's funeral. It was the first night we slept together, the two of us curled up together in the twin bed he'd had since he was a little boy. Emphasis on "slept"—there was no hanky panky between us in those days. Back then, I was still the student, he the reluctant mentor, our relationship on the cusp of something it would take us both years to admit.

Now, Diggs strode ahead of me, the tension still thick between us after whatever the hell had just happened with Mike Reynolds. We both carried flashlights, though at the moment only mine was lit. It was dark, the old granite stones leading to the back door slick and cracked. Directly in front of the rear entrance was a hulking old birdbath that Diggs had to bodily heft to the side. Dead climbing vines clung to the side of the house, tangled and brown. I pulled a notification from UPS from the door and shined my light on it. According to the paper, delivery had been attempted five of the past seven days unsuccessfully; the package was being returned. Meanwhile, Diggs reached onto the sill above the door and retrieved a key.

"Some things never change," he muttered.

Diggs turned on his light, opened the door, and went in without another word. I followed.

As soon as we were through the door, I paused. Something was very, very wrong. Like, flashing-neon-sign wrong. The back door opened onto a small mudroom that I remembered as immaculate, just like the rest of the reverend's life. Now, it smelled like rotten garbage and looked like a hurricane had hit it. Diggs walked ahead of me, his own light bouncing along the walls and over the floor. The house was freezing.

"What was that you were saying about things never changing?" I said.

The mudroom led to a cramped living room—more cramped now, as it appeared the reverend had raided the local antique shop and added every piece of broken furniture they'd had in stock. My flashlight beam bounced from corner to corner, taking everything in. Half the furniture was stacked directly in front of the door. If the mudroom smelled like rotten garbage, it was nothing compared with the rest of the house.

"What happened here?" I asked.

Diggs shook his head, silent. He went to a corner lamp and tried to turn it on. Nothing happened. "I think the electricity's been shut off."

"I feel like that's a really good cue for us to leave."

"Go ahead. I just want to look around."

He continued moving through the house, past the living room and into the dining room and kitchen. Of course, I followed.

The dining room table was piled high with newspapers, most of them torn apart. I moved closer and trained my light on the pages. Whole articles had been highlighted, stories circled in red. Several yellowed articles had been taped to the wall in the dining room, which was apparently where the reverend had done the bulk of his "work." Half a dozen half-empty plates of food were stacked off to one side beside several candles burned down to their wicks.

"What the hell is going on?" I said, staring at the mess.

Reverend Diggins was the most meticulous man I'd ever met—OCD was his middle name. Diggs paused at sight of a picture on the corner of the table. It showed him and his brother as boys, his brother pudgy, dark-haired, while Diggs had been blond and lean. They both wore swim trunks, their chests bare, hair wet. There was another picture of the whole family, Diggs' little brother barely more than a baby, Diggs only three or four.

Even in that shot, Diggs' mother held Josh while his father looked on, Diggs standing apart from them both. His hand clutched the corner of his mother's skirt; it was the only connection he had to the rest of the family unit.

Diggs lingered at the picture for a second before he pushed it away and moved on. The kitchen smelled like more rotten food. It appeared the electricity had been out for at least a few days, most of the scant contents in the refrigerator spoiled now. Diggs gave it only a cursory look before he made for the stairs to the second floor. I debated playing the voice of reason and insisting we leave, but Diggs wasn't the only one who wanted to know what the hell was going on here.

When we were upstairs, Diggs passed the door I knew led to his own old bedroom, and went straight for his father's room instead. I decided maybe it was best to give him some space, and went to his room instead. I had to put my full weight against it before the door finally gave. My heart jackhammered in my ears. I stood in the doorway, paralyzed as I ran my light through the room.

"Sol!" Diggs called. I shut the door quickly and whirled around.

"Jesus," I said. "Take it easy, huh? No yelling in this place."

"You should see this."

I followed him to his father's room and stopped dead. "Shit," I heard myself say.

"I think we just found J.'s contingency plan," Diggs said.

6

I DIDN'T SAY ANYTHING. I couldn't. Both flashlights trained on his father's bed now, I took inventory. It was covered with weapons: three rifles, an oversized spool of copper wire, a bag of fertilizer… I started to go in, but Diggs grabbed my arm before I could.

"Stay out. He could have wired the place—we should get out of here."

"How would your father have known how to wire… anything?"

"I don't know, but I'd rather not find out the hard way if he did. I just want to check one more thing."

He started toward his old room. I stepped in front of the door before he could open it. "I already checked. There's nothing there."

"I want to grab a couple of things," he said. He looked at me curiously, shining the light over my face. He set his jaw at my expression. "Step aside."

I didn't move. "There's nothing you need to see in there."

"Damn it, Solomon." He took me by the shoulders and bodily moved me. I didn't bother fighting him any further, but I wished like hell I could stop him. He opened the door.

And stood there, much as I had.

Unlike the rest of the house, the room was immaculate. The bed made neatly, the curtains pulled. This was no longer Diggs' room, though. He stepped inside, running his flashlight from corner to corner. The high school trophies, music posters, everything that had littered the place the last time I was here, were gone. Instead, the room was designed for a much younger boy: *Star Wars* bedspread and curtains, a framed photo of Diggs' mother with a dark-haired baby I knew was Josh. Other photos of Josh plastered the walls. Children's books lined the bookshelves. A Crayola lamp was on the nightstand, a case of Matchbox cars on the floor.

Diggs just stood there for a few seconds, staring. I ran my flashlight over the photos, searching for any sign of Diggs in them. Thre was none. The same photo I'd seen downstairs—Josh in Mrs. Diggins' arms, the reverend beside her—was framed here. Diggs had been cut out.

I took his hand. To my surprise, he let me. "I think your family might be gaining on mine for the title of Most Dysfunction in a Single Household," I said.

He laughed. It sounded faintly hysterical. "Yeah. Lucky me."

We left the room, and closed the door.

We were back downstairs in the dining room, still in a daze, when headlights lit the house as someone's car swung into the driveway. Diggs froze. As did I.

"Who do you think it is?" I whispered.

"No idea," he said, but I knew we were both thinking the same thing. If J. had killed Diggs' father, or used him, or…whatever, maybe they were back for something they'd left behind.

Whoever was driving the car out front killed the engine.

The headlights went out. A car door slammed. Diggs and I ducked back against the wall with a perfect view of the driveway. A man in full winter gear got out of a king-cab pickup.

"What do you want to do?" I asked. "Can you tell who it is?"

"Not a clue. You have your gun?"

The Ruger was in my purse—which was in the van. "I didn't think I'd need it here."

He drew his Glock. When Jack Juarez did that, it was damn sexy; when Diggs did it, it scared the hell out of me. Not that he wasn't a good shot, but it still looked wrong somehow. "Stay here," he said.

"Don't be an idiot," I said. "At least wait until we know who it is."

"And how are we supposed to figure that out?"

Right on cue, headlights flashed on the street again. Brakes screeched. Another car door slammed. The mysterious man in the driveway looked up.

"Hey!" I heard Monty shout outside. "I lost my dog. You haven't seen a little beagle around, have you? Answers to Snoopy. I've been looking everywhere for the little shit."

The man in the driveway looked toward the house once, then started walking toward the road. When he turned, I caught a glimpse of a full beard and a baseball hat pulled low. I didn't get a good look at his face, but the voice was enough to identify the man.

"Where'd you lose him?" he asked Monty. Diggs and I seemed to take a breath at the same time.

"Jed, right?" I said.

"I'm pretty sure. He's probably here to check up on the place—he used to do a lot of yard work for my father."

Jed Colby was a local mechanic who, as far as I'd known up till now, had little to do with Reverend Diggins or the Episcopal Church. He did, however, have something to do with the Payson Church: his sister-in-law died in the Payson fire. His nephew was none other than Will Colby, the kid who'd just joined Allie Tate in haunting the visions of my past.

"He'd be someone good to talk to," I said.

"Agreed." Diggs holstered his gun. "Will you make the call?"

"Yeah. No problem."

He returned to the dining room table to look through his father's prodigious piles of paperwork. Meanwhile, I could hear Jed and Monty shouting for Snoopy outside. I punched in Monty's number.

"You found that damn hound yet, woman?" Monty answered.

"Nice work saving our asses," I said.

"Anytime, baby girl. What's the word?"

"The guy's a friend of ours—you can actually let him go. We'd like to talk to him."

"You sure?" He lowered his voice. "Maybe we should have a talk about what staying under the radar actually means. Because as far as I can tell, you and your boy toy are doing the exact opposite."

"We'll be all right," I promised.

"I hope so. You people are gonna make me go gray before my time."

He hung up without waiting for a response. A second later, I heard him say something off-color to Jed about his wayward hound and his wife's little pussy. Jed laughed. I groaned.

Another few seconds of suspense followed before the back door opened. Diggs and I had decided there wasn't really a way to do this without scaring the holy hell out of poor Jed, so we just stood out in the open in the dining room, waiting.

Much to my surprise, however, before he came in, Jed stopped in the mudroom. He fumbled with something for a minute or so, and every light in the house magically came on.

"Crazy old loon," I heard him mutter. He started slinging trash bags out the back door, while Diggs and I continued to wait.

Eventually, he made his way to the dining room. By then, we were seated at the table going through Daddy Diggs' files.

"Jesus Christ," Jed said when he came through the door. He clutched his chest. "Are you trying to give me a heart attack? What the hell are you doing? Have you just been sitting here in the dark?"

"I thought the electricity had been shut off," Diggs said.

Jed frowned. "No, not yet. Your dad would turn everything on at once, though, and end up blowing a fuse. Half the time, he couldn't pull it together enough to flip the breaker and get things back on again. I'd usually check on him, but Gracie and me took the kids up north for Christmas. We just got back, and I heard the news."

He looked around the room again, and shook his head. "It's a crazy world out there."

"Do you have any idea who it could have been?" Diggs asked. "Reports are saying it was a black or navy-blue sedan that hit him. Does that sound familiar?"

Jed went to the table and started picking up dirty dishes.

There were a lot of them, most caked with dried food. Diggs and I followed suit, then followed him into the kitchen. He cleared out the sink, got some dish liquid from the cupboard, and started the water going.

"You don't have to do that," Diggs said.

"I've been doing it for the better part of the past six months," Jed said. "It won't hurt me to do it one more time."

Diggs opened kitchen drawers randomly until he found the dish towels. It looked like this was a two-man job and they had it well in hand, so I cleared some space on the sideboard, washed it down, and hopped up there to get out of their way.

"So you were coming in to see Reverend Diggins since the stroke?" I asked.

"I was, yeah."

"You never answered my question: do you have any idea who might have run him down?"

"You hadn't talked to him in a while, I guess."

"We saw him the night he was killed," Diggs said. "I didn't even know about the stroke until then."

"To be honest, the stroke was kind of the least of his problems, if you ask me. And as for who was behind the wheel…after what he's been up to the last few months, it could have been a few people." He hesitated, unwilling to say whatever had just crossed his mind.

"Including me?" Diggs said.

Jed shrugged. "It's not like I'm judging. My dad was my best friend, right up till the end—the guy I'd most like to have a drink with after a long day, the guy I still work my ass off to be. I know it wasn't the same with you and the reverend."

"I didn't kill my father, Jed," Diggs said.

"That's good," Jed said. "But like I said, I'm not judging.

I saw him more than most this past year, and I got to know that firsthand."

"Do you have any idea what was going on with him?" I asked. I looked around Daddy Diggs' hovel. "I mean, clearly something was up."

"You could say that," Jed agreed.

"So spit it out already, Jed," Diggs said.

"Some accusations were made."

"Accusations about what? Jesus, Jed, give it up. You said it yourself: there was no love lost between us, it's not like you'll shock me. What did he do?"

He let some water out of the sink, squirted more dish liquid in, and added fresh hot water. When that was done and a new wave of bubbles were bubbling, he looked at Diggs. "He was accused of sleeping with one of the members of his church." He shifted uncomfortably. "A *young* member."

"How young?" Diggs asked, expressionless.

"You know Jake and Alice Smith? Jake runs the Littlehope Lobster Trap place—distributes his traps all over the East Coast. It's their girl. Laurie. She's eighteen—barely."

I thought of the reverend's words when we met in the church last night. *Clearly, the year has had its ups and downs.* He wasn't kidding.

"After that," Jed continued, "the shit hit the fan fast. Most everyone left the church, even though Laurie wouldn't press charges. So obviously it wasn't business as usual. After the stroke, though…that's when Gracie and me really got worried. She had me start checking on him."

"Why? Was she worried for the reverend, or someone else?" I asked.

"Both," Jed said. "He'd walk around town at night talking to himself, or else talking to someone it seemed like he saw. I was at the grocery store a few months ago—a couple months after the stroke, I think—and saw him go to the backseat and lean in…" He shifted again. "It looked like he was buckling someone in back there. I got nervous, knowing what had happened with Laurie, so I went over."

"And?" I asked.

"There was no one there. The reverend got weird, though. Said he needed to get home, he was late for dinner. The way he was acting, it was clear something was going on. I asked him who he had with him, even though the car was definitely empty."

"What did he say?" Diggs asked. He'd stopped drying, clean dishes now crowded in the strainer. He had a stranglehold on the dishrag.

Jed hesitated again. He scrubbed a hand along his jaw. "Josh," he said. "He said him and Josh were making dinner for your mum. I asked him then, if he'd heard from you lately. If maybe you might be coming soon."

Silence fell in the room, heavy as a wool blanket.

"And he didn't know who I was," Diggs guessed. Jed looked torn.

"No—he did," he said. "But he got…agitated, as soon as I mentioned your name. I ended up having to take him to the psychiatric crisis unit over to PenBay. They kept him for a few days. Got him hydrated, gave him some food, and that seemed to help a little. But he wouldn't stay, and once he was making sense again they couldn't hold him. They had to let him go."

"What did he say?" Diggs asked.

"Diggs—" I said. He held up his hand, his eyes never leaving Jed. Jed turned a woeful gaze toward me.

"He wasn't in his right mind, Diggs."

"What did he say, damn it? It could be important."

Jed finally met Diggs' eye. "He said you weren't his son. That you'd never been his son. That you were sent there to hurt him—that if you had the chance, you would rip him limb from limb." He studied Diggs' reaction, sad now. "He said you were the punishment he'd earned for his sins. Those were the words he used."

It was like Diggs sort of...shrank, before my eyes. He took a step back. Jed turned to me. "I told you, he was out of his mind."

Diggs set the dishtowel down and went into the dining room. I followed, Jed behind me.

In the cluttered room, my gaze returned to the articles Diggs' father had taped to the dining room wall. I'd been too preoccupied with whether or not Diggs was going to lose it to pay much attention before, but looking more closely now I noticed a definite theme: "Father Saves Son from Burning Building"; "Father and Son Die in Fatal Accident"; "Boy Drowns in Bath, Father Charged with Negligence"; Father and Son Survive Deadly Plane Crash."

Story after story about fathers and sons and the tragedies that befell them, all over the world. I tried to imagine what kind of connection the reverend had made in his twisted mind; what he had decided happened. Did he really think Josh was still alive? And Diggs was…what? That Diggs had died instead, or that he'd never existed at all? And how had any of that led to the arsenal upstairs and whatever he'd been planning before his death?

"Listen," I said, when it became clear that Diggs had checked out of the conversation, "have you been through the rest of the house recently? Noticed anything strange about the reverend's behavior? People he was maybe spending time with?"

"Other than the Smith girl?" he said. "Not really—after they split, or…whatever, he was pretty much a loner. And he never wanted me going upstairs, so I respected that. I helped out with the chores down here and around the yard. Figured since Diggs wasn't around, he'd appreciate knowing someone was looking out for the old man."

"Thanks," I said. I hesitated. "I know this is a weird request, but we'd really appreciate it if you didn't mention seeing us tonight. Just for now. We've got some things we need to sort out."

"No problem," Jed agreed. "You know I'm not exactly on speed dial with the sheriff's office, so it don't make any difference to me."

"Thanks," I said. "Just one more question, and we'll let you get out of here. Do you know anything about Mike Reynolds?"

"Other than he's bat-shit crazy?" he asked. "Not much, no. I steer clear of that whole bunch up there on the ridge."

"Do you know if he had anything to do with my father?" Diggs asked.

Jed started to shake his head, then stopped. "They did get into it a few months ago, come to think of it. I don't know what it was about, but him and the old man had a fight in the parking lot at Wallace's. Something about a girl, I think."

"The Smith girl?" I asked.

Jed shrugged. "Hell if I know. Any girl the two of them were fighting over, I figured they could keep."

Diggs strolled back over to the window, so I finished things up with Jed and thanked him for keeping an eye on the place. As he was leaving, though, I stopped him one more time.

"We just checked out Diggs' house yesterday, and somebody trashed the place. Any idea who might have done that? He's missing something he'd really like to find."

Yet again, the poor guy looked uncomfortable. He glanced toward Diggs, then lowered his voice when he spoke.

"If you're missing something, there's two places I'd check: here, and Laurie Smith's place."

"You think Reverend Diggins trashed his place?" I asked. Diggs hadn't turned aroun~~d, but I~~ could tell from his posture that he'd heard.

"I told you," Jed said. "He was nuts. And Laurie's not playing with a whole deck, either."

"Okay. Thanks a lot," I said. I scribbled the number of my Tracfone on a scrap of paper and handed it to him. "If you think of anything else, or you see someone nosing around over here, I'd really appreciate it if you'd give me a call."

"Will do. Take care of yourselves," Jed said. "I don't know what in hell's going on, but it seems like you've stepped in something big. Be careful."

I promised him we would. After he was gone, Diggs returned to the table and sat down beside me. He leaned down and rested his head on the table—which was sad, but also disgusting given Daddy Diggs' cleaning habits lately. I rubbed his back.

"Sorry," I said.

"About which thing?" he asked without looking up. "The fact that my father was banging a barely eighteen-year-old or the fact that he thought I was a demon sent to make his life a living hell? Or that he apparently thought my dead little brother was living with him?"

"All of the above," I said. "This begs a pretty big question, though. If it's possible your father really was J.'s number-two guy for the mission in April, why the hell would they kill him?"

Diggs considered the question. He really was off his game—I would have thought he would have gotten here before me. I had mercy and put the pieces together for him myself. "What if the person who ran your father down wasn't someone from J.? What if instead it's the same one who's been killing the other J. operatives these last few months?"

"Why would they start with the alternate instead of the go-to guy on the list?" he asked.

"Killing the go-to guy hasn't worked for them," I pointed out. "They kill the guy, but J.'s plans still come through. But maybe they figure if they take out the alternate *and* Mike Reynolds..."

"Which means Reynolds is next," Diggs said.

I got up, my mind already in overdrive. "We have to get over there."

Diggs didn't budge.

"Why aren't you moving? Whoever is doing this could be about to off Reynolds as we speak."

He didn't say a thing. Didn't move.

"What the hell is wrong with you?" I said. "If he dies—"

"If he dies, what?" Diggs said. His voice was cool enough to drop the temperature in the room. "You heard what he said tonight. Saw the way he lives. Who knows what he'll do to those kids, or what he's got planned for this town. We can catch him, or someone else can just take him out."

"That's a great plan if we're now following the *Sociopath's Guide to the Universe.* If it's all the same to you, I'm not ready to resort to that yet. Besides which, what if he has information?"

I started for the door without waiting for his response.

"You're just going to leave without me?" he called after me.

"Unless you get your ass in gear, yeah. Come on."

I forced myself not to look back, but I won't deny it was a relief when I heard him open and close the door behind me.

7

"CHANGE OF PLAN," I said when we climbed into Monty's van a couple minutes later. "And thanks again for coming to the rescue. I knew you guys would come in handy."

Monty shifted his driver's seat, currently reclined, to the locked-and-upright position. He cast a lazy glance over his shoulder at me. "Always glad to be of service. If there's anything else I can do you for…"

"There is," I interrupted before he got too far down that path. "We've got a problem."

"Whoever killed my father is most likely about to try and take out Mike Reynolds," Diggs said, with considerably less urgency. "Solomon here is of the opinion that we need to stop them."

"Based on the story you told about what just went down over there, why the hell would we want to do that?" Monty said.

Diggs raised his eyebrows at me. "See?" he whispered.

"Just take us to Reynolds' place, would you?" I said. "At the very least, we can try to get the kids out of there so they don't get caught in the crossfire. Or does your newfound brand of vigilante justice mean we just leave them to die, too?"

"Do you have a plan for how you would like to do that?" Carl asked. "Men like Mike Reynolds aren't the type to simply relinquish their families."

"Just drive," I said. "I'll think of something on the way."

Monty put the van in gear.

It was barely nine o'clock when we rolled up at the Reynolds' place. It felt like midnight. The dog started barking before we reached the gate, and all three floodlights came on. Monty's stealthy black van might as well have been painted lime green in the glare. The front door of one of the trailers opened, and Mike Reynolds appeared. Even from a distance, I could see the shotgun in his hands.

"Get out of here!" he shouted, already moving. Our headlights illuminated him as he ran headlong toward us, shotgun up. "I've had it—get off my property!"

I was guessing after his run-in with Diggs earlier that night, Mike would not be inclined to talk things out this time. Monty put the van in reverse, pulled a U-turn on the narrow road, and sped away.

"What if we call the cops?" I asked as we drove off. "Tell them we have evidence suggesting Reynolds' kids are in danger. You saw the conditions there. It's not like anything we said would be unfounded."

Diggs didn't say anything. When we were safely out of shotgun range, Monty pulled over. He turned in his seat so he could look at Diggs and me.

"What do you want to do?" he asked. I waited for Diggs to weigh in.

"You heard Jed—there were other people who probably wanted my father dead," he said. "Who's to say any of this has to do with J. at all? And even if it does, we don't know they're going to make a move on Mike tonight. With four months to go, it's just as likely they'd spread out the carnage a little."

"I never like to be the voice of reason," Monty said, "but did you see that guy just now? That's a man already on the verge—he's got Kamikaze eyes. Something's going on. And I don't think it's gonna wait four months."

"So what if we take Erin's suggestion," Carl said, "and call the police?"

Diggs and I looked at each other, and I knew we were both thinking the same thing. "You call the police in now, and what might be nothing definitely turns into something. Tonight," he said.

"Do you know his girlfriend?" I asked Diggs.

"Eddie Stoocher," he said. "Tweaker—maybe more hardcore than Mike. She won't be the voice of reason in this, I can promise you that."

No one said anything for a stretch, time closing in on us.

"Perhaps our smartest move right now is to go back to the island," Carl said. "We can discuss this in safety there."

I set my jaw. Diggs looked like he knew what was coming.

"No," he said before I could even tell him my plan.

"Just hear me out," I said.

"*No,*" he repeated.

"No, what?" Monty asked.

"No, we're not going back to the Reynolds' place," Diggs said. "Absolutely, positively—"

"I've spent the past year thinking about all the kids who died in this," I said. "Back in Kentucky. Out on Raven's Ledge. All the J. ops we couldn't do a damn thing about while we were hiding out on the other side of the world..."

"None of which were your fault," he said.

"That song's starting to get awfully old, you know it?" I said. "Let's just go over there and keep an eye out. Just for a while, and make sure everything's copasetic."

"And if it's not?" Diggs said.

"Then, we could call the police," Carl suggested.

"Exactly," I said. "If it looks like something's about to get hinky, we make an anonymous call to Sheriff Finnegan."

"And what do you think Reynolds will do, the second he sees the cops headed his way?" Diggs said. I didn't answer. "You saw how close to the edge he was yesterday, and it looks like he's crept even closer tonight. We've got four months before this thing is supposed to unfold. You really want to push him over now?"

"All I'm saying is, we keep watch. If you don't want to, I'll do it alone. I'm sick of sitting by and letting shit like this happen."

Diggs' jaw tightened. He scratched his neck, which is one of those tics he gets when he's trying not to strangle me.

Monty looked back over his shoulder at us. His gaze landed only briefly on me before he settled on Diggs.

"What do you want to do?"

Diggs frowned. Thought. Scratched his neck again.

And sighed.

"All right," he said. "Fine. We keep an eye out."

Four hours later, we were still keeping an eye out. It was one a.m., and pitch black. Carl was asleep. Monty was reading. Diggs had dropped into a deep, impenetrable silence. The only light coming from any of the trailers was from a TV in the trailer farthest to the right—the one it appeared Reynolds and his family lived in.

Diggs sat up suddenly.

"Okay," I said. "So—you're right. Nothing's happening."

"Ssh—hang on," he said. He peered out the van window into the darkness. I joined him.

"What are we looking at?" I asked.

"Just a second. I thought I saw something." A few seconds passed.

And a few more.

Nothing.

"What's the verdict?" Monty said from the front. "Because I've gotta tell you, this isn't the most fun I've ever had in this van. I'm ready to head back."

"Give it five more minutes," Diggs said. "I'm going to take a walk around."

"You're what?" I said.

"I'll be fine."

How many times had we said that in the past two years? I just raised my eyebrows at him. Shook my head.

"Either I'm coming or one of the guys is," I said. "But you're not going alone."

"Fine," he said. "Monty, you up for a moonlit stroll?"

"Not the company I'd choose, but I guess I could do worse," Monty said.

"What do you want us to do?" Carl asked. Despite having been dead asleep no more than two minutes ago, he sounded fully awake now.

"Just wait here," Diggs said. "We'll call in the sheriff if we see anything."

"Be careful," I said.

He nodded. A gust of cold air swept into the van when he opened the door. He and Monty slipped into the night.

Carl and I remained in the van in silence. I'm not good

at being left behind—I never have been. But I forced myself to stay where I was this time, a splinter of dread needling under my skin. I watched every indecipherable shadow in the darkness for what felt like an hour.

We were parked in the trees, off the Reynolds property but within view of the trailers. The compound was surrounded by forest on three sides. We were off to the left.

Then, just off to the right, I thought I saw a flash of light—either a flashlight or something metallic catching the moonlight.

"Did you see that?" I whispered to Carl.

"Could have been Diggs or Monty," he said.

Except they'd taken off in the other direction.

I saw the flash again; definitely not a flashlight. Something metallic. A signal? I was still following the movement, pulse up now, when the door to the van opened. I swallowed a completely girlie scream, but may have whimpered instead.

"Someone's out there," Diggs and I said at the same time.

He didn't even smile, his body tensed. "Something's definitely happening—someone was out by the bunker."

"Did they see you?" I asked.

"I don't think so. Unfortunately, I couldn't really see them, either."

"*Now* do we call the police?" Carl asked.

"Make the call," Diggs said grimly. "But tell them if they do come out here, to be careful. They know Reynolds, without a doubt—they should already have an idea what they're walking into."

I saw the same flash of light once more, this time closer to the trailer. Carl was already on the phone with 911. I pointed the flash out to Diggs.

"We should go back there," I said. "If something's about to happen, maybe we can just get the kids out."

"How do you plan on doing that?" Diggs asked. I hadn't thought that far ahead.

Meanwhile, Carl was trying to report suspicious activity at the Reynolds place without actually giving them reason to send in the cavalry. So far, he just sounded nuts.

"We talked to Aidan," I argued with Diggs. "He'll come with us. I'm telling you, I can get them to follow us out." He wasn't buying it. I shook my head, aware of the seconds ticking past. "Forget it, we're wasting time. Let's just go."

At just shy of two a.m., Diggs and I circled around to the trailer where all the activity seemed to be centered, at the far right of the compound. We waited, crouched in the darkness and the bitter cold, for something to happen.

Behind us, the woods were deep black and filled with shadows. I got the uneasy feeling of eyes watching us. Clouds hid the moon overhead. Reynolds' backyard smelled like garbage and spent ammo, and I was pretty sure I was crouching in dog shit.

The blue glow of the TV set still lit the darkness. I tried to figure out what Reynolds was watching inside, but I couln't get a good view. We hadn't had a lot of TV time in Australia.

Out front, the dog started barking again. I heard the front door to the trailer open, and Reynolds screamed at him to shut up.

While he was out there, I saw the flash of light one more time.

Diggs pushed me down an instant later, when a gunshot cracked the night wide open. A second shot followed. The barking got higher pitched, frenzied. My cell phone buzzed in my pocket.

I glanced at the text from Monty:

U ok? Reynolds is hit.

I texted back that we were fine, but didn't go into details. Lights came on in the trailer. I could hear a kid crying. Eddie—Mike Reynolds' wife—screamed.

Another gunshot sounded. A window in the trailer shattered. I heard Eddie swearing, screaming at the kids. I waited for her to call 911—the most logical solution in this scenario. She didn't. Then, I heard Reynolds' voice.

"I told you they were coming for us," he said. "I told you, didn't I? You said I was paranoid. Paranoi-this, you stupid bitch. They've been watching, all this time. Get the kids in the back. Take the shotgun."

Another floodlight came on—this one in the backyard. Diggs and I hit the ground as Reynolds opened the backdoor.

"You think you can pin me down, you bitch? Bitch! I go, and everybody goes. That's on you."

He shot wildly into the night. He wasn't working with a pea shooter, either—a barrage of rifle fire, machine-gun-style, sprayed the ground just inches from where Diggs and I lay. Sparks flew when a bullet hit Reynolds' bunker.

A single shot came from the woods behind us.

Reynolds dove back into the trailer.

"He'll kill everyone," I whispered to Diggs. If I'd been crouching in dog shit before, I was laying in it now. It's amazing how little something like that matters in the middle of a fire fight. "We need to get the kids out of there."

"Would you stop saying that and come up with a plan, please," Diggs whispered back. Far in the distance, I heard sirens.

Reynolds heard them, too. "Goddamn it—they're coming. They're coming." It sounded like he was half crying. Fully crazed. "Eddie, you cover the back," he screamed. "I got the front."

Another kid joined the first, crying.

"You kids stay in the bedroom," Eddie shouted. "And shut them up, Aidan. Everything's gonna be fine."

Except it clearly wasn't.

Another single gunshot came from the woods. It didn't hit the trailer this time, though—it hit the bunker behind Diggs and me.

And then another.

The cops might be able to talk Mike and Eddie into coming into town, but that's not what the sniper was after.

The sniper just wanted them dead.

I texted Monty. *We need distraction out front.*

K was the only response I got.

Seconds later, I heard Monty's van roll up the road toward us again. He had Guns n' Roses' *Appetite for Destruction* playing loud enough to blow the speakers. Another gunshot hit the storage shed, tearing through the metal sheeting.

"Shit," Diggs said. "We have to get away from this thing."

Out front, I saw the glare of high beams as the van got closer. Heard Reynolds swearing up a storm inside the trailer. The poor dog was going crazy, barking his head off.

"Let's go," I said.

Reynolds headed out the front door, no doubt with his AK-57 at the ready. At the same time, Diggs and I stayed low and raced closer in toward the back of the trailer. Miraculously, no shots came while we were en route.

A second later, I realized why.

One more shot fired—out front this time. I heard Reynolds scream. Monty's van backed up, and I heard him drive off, the music receding. Another text came in.

Reynolds dead. Where r u????

"Mike!" Eddie screamed. I could hear her crying. Frantic.

There was a gunshot inside the house.

Stillness fell.

I went cold. Diggs hand was wrapped tight around my wrist.

Behind us, one more shot tore through the side of the storage shed.

I heard the *whoosh* of flames.

"We have to get those kids," I said. I shook myself back to life.

The dog was in a frenzy now, his barking deep and ferocious. The kids had stopped crying, though. I didn't want to know why.

Everything inched toward slow motion.

I heard sirens in the distance.

An instant later, the shed blew.

I pushed myself off the ground and into the trailer, propelled by adrenaline and pure terror.

Inside, Eddie was dead. She lay in the narrow hallway, her head half blown off. I flashed back to my father, just for an instant, before Diggs pushed me past her body. We ran down a dark, claustrophobic hallway, slamming doors open along the way.

"Aidan!" I called. "You need to come with me. Come on out. Get the other kids, we need to get out of here!"

At the third and final door I came to, I paused. I could see flashing lights and hear sirens out front. The gunfire had stopped, but there was a fire blazing in Mike's storage shed, flames spreading fast.

"Aidan?" I said, more quietly this time. Diggs was behind me. I pushed the door open with my foot, more slowly than I had the others, my hands raised.

The boy sat cowering in the corner, his brother and sister

behind him. His bow and arrow were aimed right at me.

"Hey," I said. I tried to keep my voice steady. "Please, Aidan—we're not here to hurt you guys. But there's a fire outside. I need to get you out of here."

"Mum said not to move," he said roughly. The toddler was still crying, cradled in the younger brother's arms. "Shut up, goddamn it," Aidan said to the kids. He kept his eyes on me. "Get out of here. I'm taking care of 'em."

"Please," I said.

Outside, another gun went off. An instant later, a second explosion rocked the ground beneath us. Something loud and very, very big smashed against the side of the trailer. I almost fell over at the impact. I steadied myself. I could see the kid shaking, fighting to stay in control.

"We need to go," Diggs said, his voice riding a razor's edge of panic.

"Let us go, Aid," the other boy said. He was crying too, now. "Come on."

"I'm supposed to keep watch," Aidan said.

"You've done a good job," I said. "A really good job. You're supposed to keep them safe, right? The best way to do that is to come with me."

I saw Diggs out of the corner of my eye, but he kept his distance. I took a breath. Focused on Aidan.

"Will you come?" I said.

Another second passed.

Finally, he nodded.

Before his chin had finished the nod, I was in there. Diggs grabbed the toddler, while I took both boys' small, sticky hands. We charged out of the room and herded the kids past their mother, dead on the floor. Outside, sparks flew high in the night sky, the shed ablaze.

As soon as we were clear of the fire and ostensibly out of harm's way, Monty appeared.

"Cops are here—you've gotta go. I'll make sure the kids get taken care of. Go!"

I glanced at Aidan, his brother's hand still in mine. "You guys will be okay," I said. "You're safe now. I promise."

It took a second before the younger boy let go of me. Diggs surrendered the toddler to Monty, the kid's face purple from crying, her hands fisted in Diggs' shirtfront. Monty pulled her free.

"Take the van—it's up the road." He handed me the keys. "Carl's at the dock waiting. I'll catch up."

"You sure?" I said.

"Go, damn it!" he shouted, losing his customary cool.

We went.

8

MONTY JOINED US about ten minutes after Diggs and I reached the wharf, all three of us breathless.

"I got the kids in the arms of the nearest fireman, and got out of there," Monty said. Meanwhile, Carl shepherded everyone on board and got the boat untied and headed out of the harbor. "I figure the less we tie the island, Jamie, or you guys in to this thing, the better. They were all okay, though. All three kids—not a scratch on 'em. Scared shitless, but they'll be all right."

"And Mike Reynolds?" I asked.

"Dead," Monty said. "He came at me, would've taken out the van, but somebody got him first. What about the woman?"

"Killed herself," Diggs said. "Inside the trailer."

"You think whoever did this was the same person who killed your father?" Monty asked him.

"I don't know. But it doesn't make a lot of sense otherwise."

Carl ate up the distance to the island at a hell of a clip, freezing salt spray drenching the deck. The four of us huddled in the pilothouse and tried to keep warm. Diggs got quiet again. I watched him for a few seconds, taking stock. He had a cut on his forehead and crescents as dark as bruises under his eyes. His face was stained with soot.

Monty followed my gaze, but said nothing. He went over to talk to Carl, leaving Diggs and I with the barest illusion of privacy in cramped quarters.

"You think we made a mistake going in like that?" I asked. I thought of Mike Reynolds and Eddie Stoocher, now dead.

"I think you saved three kids' lives tonight," he said.

"If we'd called the cops earlier, maybe Mike and his wife would still be alive, too."

"I don't think so," he said. "I think what happened tonight would have happened whether we were there or not. The only difference from where I'm standing is the fact that those kids are still breathing." He wrapped his arm around my shoulders and kissed my forehead. "So…I guess maybe we could put that in the win column for a change."

"Maybe so," I agreed. The adrenaline was gradually receding, but my heart still hammered in my chest. If this was a win, I wasn't sure I could handle a loss next time out.

•

That night, after everyone was briefed on all the horrors of the evening, Diggs and I headed to bed with Einstein. Both Diggs and I were exhausted, sore, and freaked out; Einstein, on the other hand, seemed to be holding up well. We barely spoke when we climbed under the covers, and I ended up cuddling with Einstein while Diggs kept as far to the other side of the bed as possible without physically sleeping on the floor.

It was almost four a.m. by the time I dozed off. When I woke later, it was to a freezing cold, pitch-black room and a notably absent Diggs. According to my cell phone, it was only five o'clock. I forced myself to some semblance of wakefulness, roused Einstein, and got up. All the while, I was going over the story. Mike Reynolds was dead. Reverend Diggins was dead. And someone who supposedly had the same objective we did—to shut down J.—was running around loose, killing off J. operatives at an impressive rate.

I pulled on two pairs of wool socks, and thought of Jack Juarez. If I could get in touch with him, he would have contacts he could tap; information he might be able to give us. Cameron still hadn't responded to my message, which seemed like a bad sign. I thought of the mysterious missing…something, in Diggs' house. Something he couldn't tell me about. My mind immediately went to the worst places: a last-resort drug stash he'd been hanging onto in case things got unbearable; photo albums from one of his previous marriages, proving that one of them had actually been the love of his life… I wasn't sure what else it could be. I knew there were plenty of things he'd done and never told me about over the years. Hell, up until I'd called him on it in Kentucky, it felt like I spent most of my time playing connect-the-dots with his past.

I got up at quarter past five and went downstairs. The meeting room was empty, as was the kitchen. Lacking any better ideas, I went outside with Einstein. December in Maine is the darkest month—the sun rises at seven, sets by four in the afternoon. That morning, it was still dark out, the sky a deep midnight blue. It was cold, too, the smell of snow in the air.

I found Diggs at the old greenhouse—the one my

father used to tend for Isaac Payson. It was a place I hadn't wanted to visit, for fear of all those ghosts of Christmas past. Surprisingly, I didn't find any there.

The greenhouse was made of stone, glass, and steel. The glass and steel panes had long since shattered and Jamie's people must have hauled them off. It felt like ancient ruins now, Diggs alone on a granite bench inside the structure. At sight of him sitting there, blank-faced and solitary, it wasn't hard to forget my own worries.

I went in and sat beside him on the icy stone bench. Einstein looked at both of us anxiously, snuffled a bit, and settled at my feet. Cold soaked through my ski pants. I took Diggs' hand. It was freezing.

"What are you doing out here?" I said.

"Thinking." He was shivering. "Freezing my ass off." I wrapped my arms around him. He leaned into my much-smaller frame and rested his head awkwardly on my shoulder.

"Come to bed. Nobody should be up this early. Or out in this kind of cold."

He kissed my neck. Even his lips were cold. "I want to leave," he said after a while.

"Then let's go –"

"Not the greenhouse. Littlehope, I mean. Just leave it behind like we did before. Never look back. This place is cursed."

I wrapped my arms more tightly around him. He wore a knit cap and a parka, but somewhere under them, I could still feel him in there. "We never would have met, without Littlehope," I said.

He didn't say anything, but I could feel him thinking, those wheels forever turning.

"I'm sorry," he said.

"For what?" Another long silence. Foreboding built. "Diggs?"

He pulled back abruptly. The end of his nose was red with the cold, his eyes glassy from lack of sleep. "I'm sorry I'm not…more."

"More what? Jesus, Diggs. You keep me safe, keep me sane, keep me sated… If you were any more, I'd have to build a fucking shrine." I touched his stubbled cheek with a gloved hand. "You couldn't have saved your dad. Whatever happened with him, it wasn't your fault. You didn't do this. *They* did this."

How many times had he given me the same speech, in the wee hours of Australian dawn? I watched for signs I might be getting through. All I saw was a storm brewing in troubled blue eyes.

"You know I love you, right?" I said. "More than coffee. Almost as much as chocolate. Anything you need to say…"

"I know," he said. He was still distant, but he pulled himself back with some effort. Forehead furrowed. He met my eye suddenly. "Me, too. Always. I'm just… I'm a little blindsided, God knows why. It's not like I thought my old man was back here waiting for me to come home, crossing off the days."

"You just didn't think he'd gone completely round the bend," I guessed.

"Yeah. I definitely didn't see that coming." He paused again, building to something. I waited him out. With Diggs, it's really the only way to get to anything. "Why do you think he said that stuff to Jed? About me not being his son, I mean?"

"He was sick, Diggs," I said. "And he was a mean son of a bitch. I'm sorry, but you know that better than anyone."

His eyes drifted. I couldn't get a bead on him—what he was thinking, what was eating him up so much. Diggs has never been much for sharing, but it seemed like we'd gotten past that in the last year.

"Diggs—"

"He called me a bastard."

I waited for more. Since I had no doubt the reverend had called Diggs far worse in his day, I wasn't sure of the significance. "He was out of his mind, Diggs."

"No. He called me *bastard.* My father didn't just toss curses around. He knew the meaning. Why would he say that? Use that particular word? 'All I have left is a bastard son who stole everything that was real.'"

I winced. How often had those words echoed in his mind over the past twenty-four hours? "He wasn't thinking."

"No, he wasn't. I think that's why he let himself say it—something he'd been wanting to say to me for a long time. I don't look like him, Sol. I never did. You look at old pictures of the family, and you can see the resemblance to my mother…."

"Your parents were married for a couple of years before they had you," I argued. "I mean, it's not like there was a shotgun wedding and you came along six months later. Your dad was a preacher—"

"A preacher who beat the shit out of his wife. A preacher who's already admitted to sleeping with other members of his church. Who's to say my mother didn't pay him back for that with a little something of her own on the side?"

"You don't think he would have told you before now? Why wouldn't he say something—especially after your mom was gone?"

"I don't know." He shook his head, lowering his gaze to the ground.

My chest tightened. Kat had inflicted plenty of damage on me over the years, but I was pretty sure it didn't hold a candle to anything Diggs' father had done to him. And at least with Kat, I knew by now that she cared about me—loved me, in her way. And always had.

I stood and turned to face Diggs, since my thighs were going numb anyway. I lifted his chin and forced him to look at me. "Whether you were his or not, the shit he did, the shit he said… That was him, not you. You're a good man, Diggs. I'll kick the ass of anyone who says differently—including you. Okay?"

His mouth twitched, a hint of a smile playing there. I leaned in and kissed him. He pulled me to him, hard, arms wrapped around me and his head on my chest.

"Now take me to bed before I freeze to death in this hellhole."

"Yes, ma'am," he mumbled into my boob. Einstein got up and put his paw on Diggs' knee. All for one, one for all.

We walked back to the house hand in hand with Stein on our heels as the sun rose on the horizon, ghosts converging in the shadows behind us.

We were almost back when we heard the first explosion—a concussion across the water that seemed to rock the very air we were breathing. Diggs' hand tightened in mine.

"What the hell could anyone possibly blow up now?" I asked.

He pulled me with him as we broke into a reluctant lope back to the boarding house. We were on the front doorstep when a second explosion went off in the distance.

I heard a phone ring inside the house. When I opened the door, it seemed like everyone was in action—half-asleep action, but action nonetheless. As soon as we came through the door, Monty held up a hand for us to be quiet. He didn't look amused, for a change. Jamie was on the phone.

"What about casualties?" she said into the receiver.

Carl, Bear, and Urenna had also gathered.

"Thank you," Jamie said. "We'll be there with the dogs within the hour." She hung up.

"What's going on?" I asked.

"I was on the line with Sheriff Finnegan about bringing the dogs over to search for weapons when there was another explosion at the Reynolds place. They thought they had it contained, but apparently the meth lab just went up."

"Do they know what happened?" I asked.

"They don't have details yet," Jamie said. "Emergency crews were still out there—everyone's accounted for at this point, but now they want me to bring a couple dogs back and see if we can sniff out anything on the property."

"I thought you were leaving this morning," I said.

"So did I." She shrugged. "It's all right—we'll just head out after we wrap up there. It doesn't sound like this will take long. Skies are supposed to stay clear, seas pretty steady for the next twenty-four hours. We'll be fine."

"What can we do?" I asked, my attention on Jamie. She was already in emergency mode, an impressive sight, issuing calm directives to her team.

"Stay here," she said to me, like it was obvious. "You're supposed to be hiding out, remember? For now, the best thing you can do is stay put."

"We can help with the search," I insisted. "I'm an EMT."

"Bear, load the boat," she said calmly. "We'll want Casper and Belle. Phantom stays behind today."

When Bear and Urenna were gone, Jamie returned her attention to Diggs and me.

"Stay here," she said again. "Seriously. They have EMTs on the mainland. We've got this. We have a job to do—I can't spend my time worrying about what you two are up to. In the meantime, figure out what the hell is going on, and find a way to stop it."

"Can you keep us in the loop, at least?" Diggs asked. He eyed me warily, but I eyed him right back. Historically, neither of us have been the best at staying put.

"I will," Jamie promised. "As soon as I'm safely able to give you a call, I will."

"Okay," I said, nodding. "Go. Be careful."

9

Earlier that morning…

IT WAS COLDER than he remembered Maine being—but then, Jack Juarez had always made a point to avoid the state in the heart of winter. The months he'd spent in South America didn't helped matters. His blood had thinned, his body grown used to soaring temperatures and light fabrics. Still, he'd known for some time that this would be where he'd end up: in Littlehope, in the heart of winter. Still chasing J., intent on stopping whatever it was they had planned for the fishing village.

He hadn't reached out to Jamie for months. Had yet to contact Diggs or Erin. He'd been watching, though. Tracking their movement. They were surprisingly stealthy now; he was impressed. Erin looked good—a fact he reflected on with no bitterness. They'd spent time in the sun, by the look of them both. Diggs had mentioned Australia before; Jack felt sure that's where they had been.

None of those things were at the forefront of his mind when they'd appeared from nowhere last night, of course, suddenly at the heart of things when he knew everything was about to go to hell. They'd gotten out safely—even gotten

Reynolds' kids out with them—but it had been by the skin of their teeth. Afterward, he'd watched them go. Stayed behind in the woods, watching the place burn. Searching for any sign that J. might come back here, now that Reynolds was dead—maybe reclaim their weapons, wipe their tracks.

So far, though, no one had shown.

Chilled, he pulled his wool jacket around himself more tightly. He'd lost weight, he knew. Forgotten to shave for…a few days. He wasn't sure how many. He peered up over the hill, watching the emergency crews as they cleared debris and made sure the fire was out.

It was almost six a.m., the sky the kind of deep, dark blue he could remember from Crayola boxes as a child. Half remember. Truthfully, those early memories were more like flashes of films he'd watched years ago than events he'd actually been part of.

He wasn't entirely sure what he was waiting for. What he expected to see. With Reverend Diggins and Mike Reynolds dead, though, he had no idea where else to go.

An ambulance had taken Reynolds' and his wife's bodies away late that night. The children were already gone. Someone had come and taken the dog as well, unscathed. As far as Jack was concerned, everyone was better off now. He didn't know when he'd started thinking that way.

Reynolds had been a thin man with red hair and pasty-white skin, wiry and bursting with kinetic energy. Jack had bumped into him—purposely, of course—at the town store the afternoon before. Reynolds had muttered something about spic faggots taking over his town, then looked away when Jack asked what he'd said. The man had mumbled more curses but no apologies, and left his purchases on the counter without paying. Then, he tore out of the parking lot in a jacked-up pickup, tires spinning with a prolonged scream before he finally left.

Since then, Jack had been camped out in the woods here in order to keep an eye on things. Determine exactly what it was he was dealing with. There were three children: a toddler, one barely school age, and a boy who was likely eight or nine. Reynolds' wife was a woman he called Eddie; she, like him, was an addict. The two of them spent most of their time screaming at the kids, the rest of the time screaming at each other.

Not anymore, though.

Jack's eyes drifted shut. He forced them back open. One of the trailers and the bunker were unrecognizable now, while the two trailers that remained on the lot were scarred and soot-stained. Two fire trucks, a few police cars, and half a dozen pickups belonging to men on the volunteer fire department, remained on the scene.

A navy-blue sedan rolled up to the gate.

Jack tensed. He sat up and watched as a pretty blond woman got out of the driver's side. The sheriff met her at the gate. They conferred for a minute or more. The sheriff pointed back toward town, apparently giving directions. The woman nodded. She started to get back in her seat, then stopped and got out again. Called to the sheriff. He returned to her side, annoyance clear in his expression.

Jack crept closer, but he still couldn't hear what they were saying. He wasn't surprised at the woman behind the wheel—he'd been following her for some time. He just didn't know why Jenny Cameron would be here now. She'd already done the damage: Reynolds was dead.

Jack watched her scan the scene, eyes taking in everything at once while Sheriff Finnegan no doubt explained to her why she couldn't be there. Jack saw her gaze light on the smoldering bunker, then shift from that to the trailers. Uneasiness rose in his chest. She said goodbye to the sheriff one more time, got in her car, and drove away.

Jack had forgotten the cold, completely consumed by the moment. There was something wrong, something indefinable. He scanned the stark horizon behind the trailers. Snow hadn't fallen yet, but winter had definitely taken hold—the trees were bare, the grass long since dead. The sun rose on the horizon, the color doing little to lighten Reynolds' compound. Even the evergreens on this property seemed leached of the will to live.

Jack's eyes held on a spot opposite him, behind a thatch of scrubby pine trees. He saw a flash of light: the glint of steel reflecting off something in the distance. Sheriff Finnegan was talking with one of his deputies, both of them looking in the direction Jenny Cameron had gone. Jack sat up, focused on that glint of light. The world held its breath.

The sheriff took another step toward one of the remaining trailers.

Another flash of light in the darkness.

Jenny wasn't done yet.

Mind the dark spots, Jackie, Jack heard someone whisper to him. He pushed the voice away.

"Sheriff!" he shouted.

Sheriff Finnegan turned, scanning the tree line. Jack stood with his hands up.

The shot that sounded came from everywhere, and nowhere.

It echoed through the clearing, a crack like thunder. The sheriff went down flat—not hit, just taking cover. Jack waited to feel pain, half expecting that he'd be the one to leak blood. There was none, though. Time hung suspended for a split second. Then, a second shot came from that same source; he saw another flash just across from him.

It was too late before Jack realized Jenny wasn't aiming for a person.

One more shot was all it took: a spark flew off the first trailer when the bullet crushed through aluminum siding. The middle trailer. A whoosh of air, and the spark ignited. A third shot sounded—this one aimed at the first trailer. Jack got down low and watched, powerless, as the building went up in a Hollywood-worthy explosion that left him momentarily deaf. Stunned. One of the aid workers who'd been going through debris flew through the air. The trailer that had exploded was consumed in flames within seconds, aluminum siding and pieces of the building, both interior and exterior, strewn in all directions.

The middle trailer hadn't exploded, but fire leaked from the roof and Jack knew it was just a matter of time. The sheriff got back on his feet, looking baffled and shaken.

For the second time in a matter of hours, the world was in flames.

10

JACK WAS AWARE OF MOVEMENT around him. Flames. Smoke. Burning in his chest so powerful he thought he'd never get another full breath. And someone familiar, standing over him. He stared up, aware of the cold at his back, the heat on his face. He'd gone toward the explosion instead of away from it, which in retrospect probably hadn't been his best idea.

"Jack?"

Jamie Flint stood there, brow furrowed, concern clear in pale-blue eyes. "Can you hear me? The paramedics will be over in a minute." He read her lips more than actually heard the words. He sat up, ignoring her protests.

In the distance, he watched Jamie's son lead a dog toward the only trailer still standing. The fires were mostly out, but the damage was already done.

Jamie made him sit down on the ground, gesturing to an EMT. He thought of Erin and Diggs. Hoped they hadn't been foolish enough to come here again.

"They're supposed to be hiding," he said out loud. His throat was raw; the words came out strangled. Jamie handed him water.

"I need to go back to work," she said to him. She was crouched in front of him, studying him. "Stay here, okay? I'll be back. Let the EMT take a look at you. I'll be back as soon as I can."

He watched her go. She wore a heavy blue jacket, an orange vest over it. She joined Bear, the two of them communicating more with gesture, unspoken glances, than actual words—the same way they communicated with the dogs. Jack closed his burning eyes.

Mind the dark spots, Jackie.

Arm straight out, son. Wait till you find your target. Line it up. One hand—I don't want to see the other one. That's a sign of weakness. You're stronger than that.

But it's heavy.

You're strong. You'll get stronger, the more you do this. Find your target.

Got it. She's moving.

It, Jackie. A target isn't a being. It. This is your job. This is how you'll survive—the way you'll keep us safe. Now: find it again.

Got it.

Good boy. Now, fire.

"Sir? You should go to the hospital to be checked out," a man said, close to him.

He opened his eyes, his head pounding. Magically, the chaos had receded around him. Some emergency vehicles remained. Smoke still hung heavy in the air, but the flames had vanished. He wondered how long he'd been sitting there.

"I don't need to go to the hospital."

"There were a lot of fumes here—we need to check your lungs, make sure you're okay. Some of these things are slow-acting. You could have inhaled something, and it would take a while before the symptoms manifested."

"I don't need a hospital," he repeated.

"I'll take him," Jamie said. Her pale cheek was smudged with soot. She had a white dog with her—a pit bull. As a child, Jack had been afraid of dogs. Especially dogs like this. He knew this dog, though. They'd met before, when Erin was lost. Then again out on Raven's Ledge. Casper.

He held out his hand casually. The dog sniffed it, tail wagging, then butted his head against Jack's knee. Jack scratched behind the dog's ears.

"I don't need to go to the hospital," he said for the third time.

"I do," Jamie said simply. "You want to ride with me, or with them?"

He stood dutifully, then wavered once his feet were under him. "With you."

"That's what I thought."

Jamie told Bear and the others to leave, she'd follow when they were finished. The men Jack remembered from Coba—Monty and Carl—nodded at him. Smiled. They'd been here last night, as well. Jamie told them not to say anything about Jack being in town. To wait until they got back, let it be a surprise. When they were gone, Jamie led him to an SUV with two large, empty dog crates in the back. *Flint K-9 Training* was advertised on the sides and windows.

"It doesn't smell great," Jamie said. "Sorry. One of the hazards of traveling with dogs."

Jack got in without a word. It didn't smell bad. He thought of the police car he'd ridden in in Nicaragua. This smelled much better than that. Jamie pulled out and got on the main road, away from the dissipating smoke and the emergency vehicles. He stared out the window, watching Littlehope as they drove past. It hadn't changed, really.

Not since he first started coming here as a teenager—it was always the same here.

Littlehope was behind them when Jamie touched his arm. His ears were still ringing. He turned and realized she'd been talking to him.

"Jack?"

"Sorry—what was that?"

"How long have you been in town?"

"Not long. A few days, maybe." Something flashed in her eyes—hurt, he thought. "I meant to call," he added. It was a lie. He hadn't meant to call at all.

He realized then that it hadn't been hurt. It was worry.

"Did you know Diggs and Erin are here?" she asked.

He nodded briefly. His head hurt. He was dizzy, ears ringing, world too small. His hand tightened on the door handle.

At the hospital, the doctor checked his breathing. His lungs. Asked if he had insurance, eyeing his tattered clothes. His insurance was gone with his job; he paid his bill in full from a roll of hundred-dollar bills he carried in his jacket pocket. Jamie sat in the waiting room the whole time. She stood when he came back out. The doctor approached her. They knew each other—greeted one another with a familiar smile. They kept their voices too low for him to hear.

The doctor was a small man, wiry and lean. A runner, probably. The way he looked at Jamie, Jack knew the man wanted to know her better. Had probably asked her out before. He wondered if she had accepted. She smiled at the man, but didn't reciprocate when the doctor touched her arm.

They approached Jack together, warily, as if approaching a wild animal. Jamie smiled. Again, a smile meant for a wild thing.

"Were you in an accident before today, Jack?" she asked.

The doctor stood by patiently and let her take the lead. Jack thought of Nicaragua. A car speeding toward him, lights bright.

"Car accident," he said.

"Did you see a doctor?" the doctor asked.

Jack shook his head. "I was fine—just walked away. I didn't want to be any trouble."

"Jack, you have two broken ribs," Jamie said. "How long ago was this?"

He had to think. "A month, maybe."

She looked at the doctor for confirmation. Jack chafed but forced himself to remain still. Seated patiently in his chair, he waited for them to grant him permission to go. He was a grown man, for Christ's sake.

"Based on the way they've healed—or haven't, as the case may be," the doctor said, "a month makes sense. Were you hurt anywhere else?" he asked Jack. "If you suffered a blow to the head…"

"I didn't," Jack said. He stood. "I was in Nicaragua, and a car hit me—backed into me, trapping me in an alley. There was no blow to the head. I didn't lose consciousness. I was awake. Aware, through all of it. And now, unless there's a reason to keep me here that you haven't told me about, I'd like to go."

"Of course," the doctor said. He looked unhappy. "But if you find you're having any trouble at all breathing… If you experience lightheadedness, feel any burning in your chest, please come back immediately."

"We will," he heard Jamie promise as he walked away.

•

Jamie kept sneaking glances at him as she drove them back to Littlehope, but she said very little. They made polite chitchat, talked about the most inane aspects of both their lives... Eventually, Jack leaned his head against the cool glass of the window and let the car's movement lull him to sleep.

He remained quiet on the boat ride over to Payson Isle, aware the whole while of Jamie watching him. Finally, when the island was in sight, he summoned the courage to go to her. She stood in the pilothouse of a small fishing boat, *Flint K-9* emblazoned on the side, eyes intent on the horizon. Jack stood next to her, noting her steady hand on the wheel, her level of focus.

"Everyone has a past, Jack," she said without looking at him.

He laughed briefly, without humor. "Not everyone has a past like mine, though."

"We all have secrets. Some of us darker than others. It doesn't change who you are now."

A well of grief rose in his throat unexpectedly. He thought of Lucia. The woman he'd vowed to love, honor, protect. Brave Lucia, who died alone. Terrified. Men on her, taking her. She died crying out for the husband who never saved her.

These were the things he'd learned in Nicaragua.

"And who is that?" he asked. "Who am I now?" His eyes strayed to Jamie—took in the delicate, feminine bearing, the proud line of her spine. A woman who knew who she was; what she was here for. She looked at him fully, a sad smile on pretty lips.

"You're a good man, Jack. You can't save everyone. You couldn't have saved her. They wouldn't have let you."

Reality blurred to a haze around him. He didn't ask how she knew, but it didn't surprise him that she did. Knowledge seemed innate, with her. He remained on his feet, but he turned away. Saw something on Jamie's face as he did so—regret. Loneliness, that thing that stared him down in the mirror every night. She'd expected his reaction, he realized—the turning away. The pain. She stood at the wheel alone, an island with her eyes forever on the horizon.

For the first time in...how long, he wondered, he felt something nudge itself past his own grief. "Everyone has secrets, hmm?" he said to her.

"Everyone," she said.

"So, what are your secrets, Jamie Flint?"

The woman who never faltered, who knew herself and her role, the woman with her eyes on the horizon, wavered—if only for a moment. He saw her throat move when she swallowed. "My secrets are my own," she said.

He nodded, holding her gaze. He had a sudden, undeniable desire to touch her—to reach out, draw her closer. There was too much happening, though. Too many questions, too much uncertainty. Too much death, on every side.

He remained beside her, though. Stood there, their bodies not touching, as the island grew closer, the shadows darker. And before he knew how it happened, he was back on Payson Isle again.

11

TWO HOURS LATER, we learned the whole Reynolds hillside had been evacuated. Two more explosions had rocked the town before emergency crews were able to get it under control. Jamie had called and given us a brief overview of events: no fatalities beyond Reynolds and his girlfriend the night before; the kids were with social services now, the dog in foster care with the local humane society. One of Jamie's dogs had sniffed out another cache of weapons in a smaller, underground bunker. Jamie finished up by telling me that the rest of the crew was safely on the way to Caribou for the SAR training, but she would be coming back with Monty and Carl, for now.

And she had a surprise for us, when she got back.

I didn't know if I was up for any more surprises.

"This means the primary and secondary J. assassins are dead," I said. Diggs and I were in the meeting room, currently alone on the island. "We need to figure out who's killing these people."

"Two names spring to mind."

"Cameron and Jenny."

"Exactly." He hesitated. "Though there is one other

person… He's seen the list. Definitely has a grudge against J. And the last I knew, he wasn't exactly the man we once knew."

"It's not Jack Juarez," I said immediately.

"You don't know that. You have no idea what's going on in his head right now. You can't say for sure—"

"The hell I can't. I'm telling you, no matter how much he might want to stop J., he wouldn't put three little kids' lives at risk. I don't care how shitty life has gotten for him in the last nine months, there's no way he's changed that much."

It took about two seconds longer than it should have before Diggs agreed. "Okay—let's just say you're right for now: it's not Jack. So. Cameron or Jenny. Or your mom."

"Kat isn't killing people, either." At least I hoped to hell she wasn't. "Anyway, what matters now is what we're supposed to do next. And what J. will do next, if their top killers are out of the game."

"Do you have any brilliant theories?"

"Maybe they'll just skip Maine now," I said. "They'll cut their losses and move on to the next big event."

"Sure. That could happen." Right. He tapped his knuckles on the table and gazed out the window for a few seconds. He was building to something—gearing himself up. Which meant I probably wouldn't like it.

"What's on your mind?" I prompted when he didn't say anything.

"A lot." He tapped his knuckles a little longer, until I finally grabbed his hand to stop him. He looked up. "Have you remembered anything else about when you were here as a kid? I know you don't like to talk about it, but maybe it could be important. Anything about your father?"

"I've told you before—nothing that makes sense." I

thought of Allie Tate and her broken glasses; the way she continued to pop up and scare the crap out of me. That had to mean something, right? Other than that I was losing my mind, ideally. Diggs stared me down. "What?" I asked.

"What did you see the night we first got here? When the window broke? Or *who*, might be the better question. I'm not blind—I could tell whatever Bear said spooked you."

"I don't believe in ghosts, Diggs. And you sure as hell don't."

"Yeah, but I believe in the subconscious. I don't know what's going on with Jamie's kid—maybe he really sees dead people. Maybe he just wants to think he does. But I do know you, and if someone appeared to you, it meant something. That's the way this shit works."

The closeness we'd had that morning out at the greenhouse had cooled, and I wasn't sure exactly why. Diggs had stayed apart from me since that time, something dark that felt a lot like violence bubbling just below the surface of his carefully crafted façade. I still knew I had nothing to fear from him—there was never any doubt of that. But considering the way he'd reacted to Mike Reynolds last night, right now I wasn't sure how well anyone else would fare if they got in his way.

"I know that's the way it works," I said. I thought of Allie again. My head began to throb. I took a breath. We were supposed to be doing the honesty thing. "Fine, you want to know what I saw? I saw the girl Isaac Payson killed when I was a kid. I keep seeing her."

Diggs softened incrementally. He didn't look like he doubted me, or thought I was going nuts—which was reassuring, since I wasn't nearly as confident. "Does she say anything?"

"'How many lies do you believe,'" I said. "And then…

something about a crack. 'Make it through the Crack and you live forever.'"

"Does that mean anything to you?"

My head pounded so hard it felt like blood was about to burst from my eardrums. I tried to push past it and focus on the words, but that just made it worse. I shook my head. When I looked at Diggs, his frustration was clear.

"I'm sorry—I'm trying," I said. "But I don't know. I've been thinking about it, trust me. Hell, it's pretty much *all* I've been thinking about. But I don't know how many lies I believe, and the Crack Allie is talking about is this old rock with a crack through the center, that we used to dare each other to go through sometimes. I don't know how getting through it equates to living forever. I don't know what she's talking about."

"Just think about it," he said. "Why would it be this girl appearing to you? What lies is she talking about? And maybe it's not literally living forever. It could be figurative. Just concentrate, for Christ's sake."

"I'm concentrating!" I shouted at him. The pain in my skull was ready to drop me, but I held my ground. "I'm thinking. I'm trying to remember. It's not working, all right? I see her in my dreams, I see her in doorways, I see her out in the woods, and I don't know what the fuck she wants from me."

Diggs ran a hand over his scalp. Frustration simmered between us.

"I'm going for a walk," I said. "I'll try to sort my head then. Maybe give you a chance to cool down."

"I don't need a chance to cool down," he said.

"Say that to me without your teeth clenched and fire in your eyes, and maybe I'll believe you."

"I'll come with you."

I shook my head without looking at him. "No—I'll be fine. Stay here. I won't be long. I'll be careful."

I took Einstein with me. The door slammed behind us when I left the old house. From there, silence prevailed.

I broke into a run on the island trail, Einstein keeping pace beside me. The terrain was uneven underfoot and I'm hardly the most graceful person on the planet, but I kept moving.

How many lies do you believe? Allie Tate asked me again. I stopped dead. She stood just ahead on the trail, immovable. Einstein whined, eyes fixed on me.

"You're not real," I said. "You died—years ago."

"Why won't you tell him what happened?"

I waited until my breath had evened before I answered. Becuase if you're going to have a conversation with a ghost, God knows you should be calm for it. "I should have helped you," I said.

"You remember that day?"

"A little… Not really. Just impressions." Before I could say anything more, the memories struck in a blinding series of flashes—as real, as visceral, as a physical assault.

Allie on the ground. Payson on top of her. Body crumpled, leg bent at an awkward angle. Her eyes catch mine. I can't scream. Can't call out. Not until it's too late—not until her eyes are clouded and I know she's gone. That he did that. And I didn't stop him.

I run.

"I'll make her forget," my father says—whispering the words, a desperate plea. Isaac is so angry. "I'll make her love you again. She won't be afraid. She'll never be afraid of you again."

My father on his knees as Isaac lays the whip into his back.

Women kneel in the greenhouse. Isaac stands above them. He is naked.

I'm walking in the woods. I know Allie is gone. Instead of my best friend, I'm with a boy. Will—Will Colby.

"He's evil," Will says. "I don't care what you say."

"Isaac loves us," I say. Will stops, serious the way only kids can be.

"I love you," he says. He's eleven years old. I just turned eight. "Isaac will kill us all. You'll see. He's a bad man, Erin."

"Isaac loves us," my father says. "There's something wrong with Will. He doesn't believe. You believe, don't you, Erin? You just need to forget the dark spots. Move beyond them." Over and over in the night.

No sleep, for those days.

No food.

"We're bleeding the darkness from you," my father says. "The way they did for me. You love this place. You love Isaac. Isaac loves you. He would never hurt us."

I'm so tired, my stomach empty. The room is dark and closed off—I don't know how long I've been here.

"I do," I say. "I love Isaac. I love Payson Isle."

"And you love me, don't you?" my father says. There's something sad and frightened and lonely in the words. "You still love me, Bean?"

"I do, Daddy. I still love you."

"Allie's okay. You don't have to look for her anymore—she's right here. You see her?"

And I do, then—in the dark and the cold, my stomach shriveled from hunger, mouth parched. She sits beside me with her thick glasses and her pretty dress, hair braided the way it always has been.

"She's okay?" I say.

"She's okay," my father says. "And Isaac loves us. Will is wrong—he's a mean-spirited boy. He has the devil in him. You won't listen to him again. You understand me, Bean? Isaac loves us."

"Please let me out," I say. My voice quavers, tears in them now.

"You believe? Say it again, Erin. Isaac loves us."

"He hurts people."

My father stands suddenly, and I can see his anger. "Isaac loves us. I can't let you go until you believe that. You have to believe," he says. He crouches down beside me once more. Cups my cheek in his hand. "You have to believe me, Erin."

He stands, even when I call out for him. Opens the door. I see light outside. Someone is waiting. Isaac. My father closes the door.

He leaves me in the dark.

I was still standing on the path when the world rushed back, realization with it. I'd remembered the bit about Isaac killing Allie when I was in Mexico last year; had known that the child I remembered that last year on Payson Isle wasn't real. I just didn't know the details—and had no idea what my father's role had been in all of it. My stomach curdled; a seismic ache rocked my temples. All of it had been lies. Will Colby—the boy I remembered as cruel and hateful—had tried to warn me. We had been friends.

My father was the real monster, protecting Isaac every step of the way.

How many lies do you believe?

"Erin?"

I whirled, nearly coming out of my skin. When I saw who it was, I almost lost it all over again. "Are you really here?" I said.

Mitch Cameron smiled. He seemed to find nothing strange in the question. "It seemed like you could use a hand." He studied me for a second when I just stood there, still shaken, tears falling. "You're remembering."

I nodded, brushing ineffectually at my eyes. "Yeah. I've gotta tell you, I can think of better ways to spend my time."

"Yes," he said. "I imagine you can."

"How long have you been here?" I asked after a few seconds, gradually forcing myself back to reason. Whatever had happened in the past, however shitty it seemed now, it couldn't be undone. But maybe we could do something about the future.

"Not long," Cameron said. "A few hours."

"Did you hear what happened to Diggs' father?"

"I did." Any trace of a smile vanished. "I told you two not to come back here."

"You've seen the list; you know what's coming next. You really think we could have stayed away?"

"J. will think the same thing, if they don't already. You're playing directly into their hands."

"You said you've only been here for a few hours," I said. "So does that mean you weren't the one to kill Reverend Diggins, then?" He didn't look surprised at the suggestion, though he shook his head.

"No. It wasn't me."

"But you know who did," I pressed, reading him. "Don't you?"

He didn't say anything. What Diggs had said about my mom ran through my mind briefly before I chased it away. Kat wouldn't do this.

"Jenny?" I said.

He wouldn't look at me. "She left again, a couple of

months ago. She didn't say where she was going—just that she was going to stop them, once and for all."

"And taking J. down means killing anyone who might kill for them?"

"To her?" he said. "It's possible." Probable was more like it. Jenny had been working with J. since she was a toddler, as far as I could tell. Bred to be a psycho, in other words. Of course, I wasn't so sure I didn't fit into that category myself these days.

"But you don't think killing their operatives will stop them," I said. "This isn't the right approach?"

"Not now. The people who kill for J. now—the operatives on those lists—are just puppets, most of them brainwashed with no idea who or what they're really killing for. It was different before."

"Before what?" I asked.

"When Mandrake was in charge. Then, those doing the killing were closely tied to the organization."

"Like you," I said. In addition to his initials, I suspected that it was Cameron's social security number on at least half a dozen of the entries on the list we'd decrypted, including the fire on Payson Isle. "So that changed with new management?" He nodded. That brought me back to the question that had been fueling Diggs and me for the past year. "So, who exactly is this new management? Who runs J. now?"

"I don't know," he said without a moment's hesitation.

My eyebrows shot up. "Seriously? You've worked for them your whole life. How could you not know?"

"After Mandrake was killed, everything changed. Secrecy was paramount. Triggers were selected outside the project, and trained for one mission only. Operatives had little contact with one another, and no contact at all with the highest echelon of the organization."

"So how the hell are we supposed to stop them, if even you don't know who we're trying to stop?"

He leveled a long, heated stare at me before he dropped his gaze. "You've forgotten—*you're* not supposed to stop them. You're supposed to leave that to me."

"Okay. Well, then how the hell are *you* supposed to stop them if you don't know who you're trying to stop?"

"I haven't figured that out yet," he said reluctantly. "Come on, let's go back to the house. I'm curious to hear what kind of plan you've come up with."

I didn't tell him that, so far, we didn't really have a plan so much as the blind belief that some action was better than no action at all. A belief that, thus far, hadn't proven completely accurate.

We started down the trail, retracing my steps back to the house with Cameron beside me. He actually looked good—better than what I'd seen from him in the past, anyway. He was still on the thin side, but his face had lost that drawn look. Life running from J. agreed with him.

"Have you heard anything from Kat?" I asked. "Is she here, too?"

"I convinced her to stay put."

I paused to look at him. "So you're still in touch, then."

"Yes."

Was that a blush on Mitch Cameron's face? "Are you two together?"

"That's none of your business. If it were, though, I would tell you that Katherine remains devoted to Maya…despite the distance."

"And the fact that Maya doesn't know if Kat's alive or dead."

"Your mother has never been the most rational woman."

Maya was a world-class neurosurgeon who had been my mother's girlfriend before our whole world got up-ended last year. As far as I knew, she still had no idea what had happened to any of us when we all vanished after Cameron's daughter blew Kat's house up. Dating anyone in my family should come with hazard pay.

"You two are close, though. Friends," I said. "How's she doing?"

He smiled, just faintly. "You mean is she still drinking?"

"Yeah. That's what I mean."

"The last I knew, no. Again, not that it's your business. She stopped while we were running last year. To my knowledge, she hasn't had a drink since before Coba."

"If anything was going to drive you back to the bottle, I guess it'd be knowing your ex blew his brains out in front of your kid." It was meant to come out pithy—instead, I just sounded overly dramatic and a little nuts. "Sorry. Forget I said that."

"She was more concerned about you, actually," Cameron said. "*Is* more concerned about you."

Strangely enough, that didn't seem implausible. If all the other memories of my childhood were just fantasy, who knew what Kat's role had actually been in those years. Sure, she'd beaten the tar out of me more than once—it was hard to just sweep that under the rug. As far as I knew, though, at least she'd been honest with me.

Cameron and I reached the path up to the boarding house, and stopped. Or Cameron stopped, rather. I turned when I realized he wasn't beside me anymore.

"Are you coming?"

He frowned. Almost shivered. "I hate this place."

"Have you been here a lot? I mean…besides the obvious." When he'd set the Payson Church on fire with thirty-plus people inside.

"A few times."

"When?"

The front door opened behind me before he could answer. I turned. Diggs stood there, looking wary.

"Looks like you picked up a friend," he said.

"You know me and strays," I said.

"Hello, Diggs." Cameron walked up the path to join him.

"You got Solomon's message, I see," Diggs said.

"I did. I thought I'd come see what kind of trouble you two have gotten yourselves into this time."

"Just trying to save the world," Diggs said. "And failing miserably. Same old shtick." He opened the door and stood aside so we could enter.

"Considering your track record," Cameron said, "have you considered getting a new act?"

12

WITH NO ONE TO TRIP OVER in the boarding house, we set up camp in the meeting room again. Diggs sat beside me, casting an uneasy glance my way every so often. Despite our fight earlier, he kept no physical distance between us. I could still feel the frustration that radiated from him, though.

"Our big question is whether something will still happen if the operative J. had in place and the secondary operative were both taken out of play," I asked after the niceties—however brief—were out of the way. I directed the question at Cameron, and tried not to reflect on the fact that phrases like "primary and secondary operatives" and "taken out of play" were now part of everyday conversation.

"Losing those two individuals won't have an impact on the final mission," he said without hesitation. Another theory shot to hell. "As team leaders, we were trained to come up with contingencies if something happened and the trigger was somehow disabled."

"The trigger was disabled?" Diggs repeated. "These are people you're talking about." He stood and walked away. "They're not weapons. It was my fucking *father* who got run down the other night, Cameron. You screw with people's heads, and you turn them into killers. Let's tell it like it is."

Cameron didn't say anything. It wasn't like he could argue the point. Considering what he'd done for the organization over the years, the number of lives he'd taken, Mitch Cameron knew all too well about J.'s methods.

"We're all agreed here," I said. "J. does horrible things. But now the most important thing we can do is stop them before it happens here. So, how do we find the other 'triggers'? Or whatever you want to call them," I added, in deference to Diggs.

I looked at Cameron. He hesitated.

"We can't let this town lose more than it already has," I said when no one answered. "First Payson Isle back in 1990, then the shit-storm I brought here pursuing this whole thing a couple of years ago… Diggs' father. The Reynolds. The least I can do is try to save this friggin' cesspool now. How do we stop it?"

"I don't know," Cameron said. Definitely not what I was hoping for.

"Well, think," Diggs said. "The primary and secondary 'triggers' have been decommissioned. What happens next? They haven't programmed half the town, right? How many potential psychotic assassins do we have floating around a town with less than fifteen hundred people in it?"

"I told you," Cameron said. He didn't sound quite as patient as he had before. "I don't know."

Diggs sighed, that frustration once more at its tipping point, and leaned across the table to push J's list toward Cameron.

"Explain this to me," he said. "Your initials—MC—are everywhere on this thing. The social security number belongs to the guy who actually does the killing, right? We figured that much out: November 1978, that social belongs to Jim

Jones. Oklahoma City, 1995—that's Tim McVeigh's social. So this entry here—August, 1990… That's you?"

Cameron stared at the list for a moment before he shook his head, never meeting my gaze. "No. That's not me."

"But you were the one who set the fire…right?" I said. "I mean—you did it. That's what you've said all along."

"I did. That wasn't the original plan, but I was the one who lit the match. Everything happened too quickly. I went in. Did what needed to be done."

"Setting fire to a building with more than thirty people in it," Diggs clarified.

Cameron looked at him coolly. "Yes."

"If the social security number doesn't belong to you, who does it belong to then?" Diggs pressed. "It shows up a few times here."

"You weren't able to trace it?"

"No," I said. "We tried to find out, but kept running into brick walls. There are a few socials that are like that. We've had someone working with us on it, but even he can't get the names."

Again, Cameron went quiet. He wouldn't look at me. That heavy, awful ball of dread that seemed to be nesting in my intestines lately set up camp once more.

"Does it belong to my father?" I said. "All those other entries, after the fire on Payson Isle—my father was responsible for all those?" We'd looked into every atrocity, until we knew the details cold: ritual killings, mass shootings, unexplained disappearances, fires… We just didn't know who every perpetrator had been.

But now it looked like we'd found one more.

"If you look at the dates for that operative," Cameron said, "you'll note that he wasn't active between 1979 and

1990. When he was on Payson Isle, your father truly had severed ties with J. We caught up to him when Rebecca Ashmont began asking questions, though. Dexter Mandrake gave the order. I spoke with your father shortly before the fire. He was meant to be the trigger."

"But he backed out," I said.

"He ran," Cameron agreed. "I was the team leader. It was my job to see that it was carried out."

"So the team leader—we were right, that's what the initials at the end of each entry stand for, then," Diggs said.

"That's right."

"The initials at the end of the entry for Littlehope in April," I said. "They're LW. That's the person in charge of the whole thing? If this guy's triggers are disabled, he's the one who has to make sure the plan is carried out?"

"In essence," Cameron said.

"Half the things that happen over the next five years have those initials attached," Diggs said. "Dozens of locations around the world… Dozens of different social security numbers, all representing human beings about to go off like time bombs. So who the hell is this LW?"

"I don't know," Cameron said. "There are tiers within the project, varying levels of responsibility. At the top is the project leader: Dexter Mandrake initially, before he was replaced."

"By whom?" Diggs asked.

Cameron looked away, clearly pained.

"You can't seriously have no idea," I said. "You must at least have a theory. For Christ's sake, Cameron—just give us *something,* would you? The only thing I can think is that you're still protecting them." He had no response for that, but it was clear from the way his eyes hardened that the words had an impact. "Will you please just say?" I finally prompted.

He stood and pushed back from the table. "Honest to god, sometimes you remind me so much of your mother it's maddening. I'm not protecting them, you idiots, I'm protecting you. Which is what I've been trying to do for the past year, and you're making it damned near impossible. An all-expenses-paid life in Australia, and what do you do? Turn around and come back here."

"Forgive me for having a conscience," I said. "And stop trying to protect us—I don't want protection. I want these assholes to go down, once and for all. I'll keep going at it with or without your help, so why don't you just tell us what you know already." He still didn't say anything. "You really don't have a clue who the head of the project is?"

There was no hesitation when he nodded this time. "No, I honestly don't."

"And the team leaders?" He looked away. "Cameron? Stop lying to us—you have to know this. Who are the team leaders?"

He turned around, paced for a second or two, and then returned to the table. He sat down so roughly he almost up-ended the bench.

"Fine. You really want in on this? Then we do it my way. No more running off half-cocked, no more half-assed plans that put everyone in jeopardy."

I looked at Diggs for confirmation. He nodded infinitesimally.

"We're in," I said.

Cameron took a deep breath, nodded, and pulled the list toward him.

"There have been ten team leaders that I know of over

the years—represented by the initials on this list. Dexter Mandrake, Jeff Anderson, Chris Marlin, Jim Jones, Max Richards, Lilah Waters, Susan Stargill, Isaac Payson, Ben Cutler, and me."

"Hang on—Isaac Payson was one of the team leaders?" I said.

"Before he left in '76." Cameron pointed to about a dozen scattered entries with the initials IP at the end. "He was very effective in his time. I was just coming up, so I worked under him a few times."

"And how many of those team leaders you listed are still with the organization?" I asked.

Cameron hesitated. When he finally spoke, I couldn't shake the feeling that he was holding something back. "Jeff, Lilah, and Ben, to the best of my knowledge. It's possible some of the newer recruits have been promoted in the past couple of years and I never heard about it, though. The organization is very insular now—at J., it's rare for the right hand to know what the left hand is doing."

"Or to even know there is a left hand," Diggs said dryly.

"I know Jenny was slated to become a team leader last year," Cameron continued. "And Lee—the big man who was killed in Coba. The two of them were high up in the organization. Obviously, J. has taken a few hits since you came on the scene."

"Well, I guess that's something," I said. "So—Max Richards was a team leader, too?" Max Richards was the lunatic who'd nearly killed Diggs and me up in Northern Maine, after tracking and killing young girls for forty years.

"He was at one time," Cameron confirmed. "But the organization got rid of him when we realized what he was doing. He continued to run his experiments supposedly in

J.'s name, but he'd been cut off from the project for years."

I thought of the J. that had been carved into the chests of Richards' victims for all those years.

"When we met him, Max called himself J," I said. "That's how his second-in-command—Will Rainier—referred to him. Rainier was with the organization?"

"He was one of the early subjects in Maine," Cameron confirmed. "They weren't happy to learn of any of Max's activities. And when Adam contacted me to say Max and Rainier had you in their sights, it was clear what I needed to do."

I remembered being in the woods with Rainier's belt looped around my neck; the things he'd said he would do to me while Diggs watched. I suppressed a shiver, and moved on when the memory of Rainier's voice got to be too much.

"Okay," I said. "But Max Richards is dead. And you say you know of three team leaders now, for sure. Do you have any idea how to find them?"

"No. Everyone within the organization is adept at keeping a low profile."

Sure they were. That's like Diabolics 101. "We can't find the team leaders, and we don't have a clue who the head of the project is anymore. Where does that leave us?"

Cameron studied me. "To be honest, I was hoping you might have some ideas."

"Me?" I said. "How the hell would I know? My father didn't have anything to do with J. when I was growing up, remember? And even if he did, he wiped my memory. I don't remember a thing."

"But you're starting to," Diggs pointed out.

"There are a few things, sure, but they're fuzzy," I said. "They don't make sense. I definitely don't know the political infrastructure of your psychotic organization."

"You said there are a few things," Cameron said. "What are they?"

"I told you—they're fuzzy."

"It doesn't matter if they're fuzzy," Diggs pressed. "What are the impressions you get?"

"I don't know," I said. "I don't know what they are, I don't know what they seem like. They're just...things." Things I wasn't ready to talk about, with anyone.

"What happens when you try to remember?" Cameron asked.

"Uh—I can't do it. Jesus, am I speaking a foreign language?"

"No," he said patiently. "Physically, what happens? Are you experiencing any pain?"

"Headaches," Diggs said. I'd been trying to keep the migraines I'd been getting over the past year under wraps, figuring it was just a side effect of near-constant terror and emotional anguish. "She hasn't said anything," he continued, "but they get bad."

"Is that true?"

I met Diggs' gaze before I looked away. "Yeah," I said. "Nothing big. But when I push too hard, things get a little jagged in there."

"Why is she getting them?" Diggs asked. "Is this something they did?"

"No—this isn't a sci-fi movie," Cameron said. He smiled at me. "Your brain won't implode if you start remembering." That, at least, was a relief. "But your father buried the memories deep in your subconscious, and I expect there are a lot of painful associations that go with them. The effort of dredging that up can manifest in physical symptoms. Intense ones, I suspect."

Another legacy to thank dear old Dad for: migraines that could potentially melt my brain. Thanks, Pop.

"You should have said something," Diggs said to me. "I wouldn't have pushed so hard before."

"You heard Cameron," I said. "It's not like my brain will implode."

"No," Cameron said. "But that physical distress can be severe. We'll take our time with it. I'll help you work through the memories."

I scoffed. "Take our time? People are dropping dead left and right. I'm done taking my time. What are we supposed to do? How do we stop it?"

Before anyone could address that question or come up with any semblance of a concrete plan, Einstein catapulted into the room barking like a banshee. My heart kicked up into my esophagus and remained lodged there until I heard Monty in the kitchen.

"We come in peace," he shouted as he came through the kitchen door. I heard Einstein's nails on the wood floors as he scrambled back into the meeting room, Monty close behind him. Monty took in the picture of me with Diggs and Cameron in a glance before he nodded toward the door. "Looks like the party's finally getting started." He shifted his focus to me. "We could use a hand, princess, if you don't mind."

I shot a look at Diggs before I nodded and followed Monty out again. Cameron and Diggs weren't far behind me, Einstein in the lead.

We were just past the path to the greenhouse when I stopped. Jamie was to one side of the trail, squatting on the balls of her feet beside a dark-haired man seated on a tree stump, his head lowered as they talked quietly. His hair was nearly to his shoulders, dark and lank. He looked up.

Holy shit.

I picked up my pace.

"What's going on?" I said.

Jack Juarez looked up, smiling weakly. "I'm fine—I just got dizzy, that's all. Wanted to take a break."

I crouched beside Jamie and took Jack's hand, my fingers slipping to the side of his wrist. His pulse raced. If he was a hummingbird, he'd be doing great. He had a full beard, his shoulders thin beneath a wool coat that wasn't nearly warm enough for the weather. While Diggs and I had immersed ourselves in the land down under, Juarez had apparently gone full-on hobo.

"He just got dizzy?" I asked Jamie, sensing there was more to the story.

"He was at the Reynolds' place when the meth lab exploded this morning. He breathed in some of the fumes… then refused to stay at the hospital."

"My lungs don't hurt," Jack said. "I just got dizzy—I'm not nauseous. My head's clear. I just… I think I just forgot to eat."

"For how long?" I asked.

Hesitation. Maybe a hint of embarrassment. "I'm not sure. A few days. I bought a sandwich at the Co-op on Tuesday."

Today was Saturday.

"Let's start by getting you some food, then," I said. I stood. Diggs had reached us by then. He extended a hand for Jack.

"Jesus, Juarez," Diggs said. "We would have come back eventually. You didn't have to go on a hunger strike."

Jack leaned against him on the way up the path to the

house. They talked too quietly for me to hear the words, though I heard Jack laugh at one point before we reached the door.

We got inside and went straight back to the meeting room, while Carl and Jamie went to the kitchen to round up some food. Jack sat heavily at the picnic table, his face gone gray.

"You heard about the Reynolds family," he said. He looked at me, then Diggs.

"Yeah," I said. "Any idea who might have attacked their place?"

"Not me," he said. He wasn't looking at me, but Diggs. Diggs smiled at him.

"We figured that. Or Solomon did, actually. But I didn't fight her too much on it."

Cameron sat down next to me wordlessly. Jack went killer quiet across from me.

"It's okay," I said. "He's with us now."

"Excellent," Jack said, his eyes cool. "And now that you've bought that, there's a bridge in Brooklyn I'm selling at a great price."

"We haven't forgotten who he is," Diggs said.

"I have no illusions about your views of who I am and what I've done," Cameron said. "But we don't have time for me to prove myself. Things are moving more quickly than I expected—thanks in no small part, I suspect, to my daughter. Have you seen her?"

"She was at the site last night, and again just before the second explosions," Jack confirmed. "Seems she's on a mission."

"She's being pretty damned sloppy about it," I said. "Collateral damage isn't a big concern of hers, I guess."

"J. taught us that the goal is paramount; whatever it takes, we get the job done."

"Even if kids could have died," Diggs said. "Even if half the people J. is using don't have a clue what's going on—what they're part of."

"She's trying to stop them," Cameron said. "I don't know what her strategy is, but I have no doubt she has one. If I had to guess, I'd say she's simply trying to force their hand—make it so that they have no choice but to take some kind of action against her."

"So she's luring them out of hiding," I said. "You think that could work?"

Cameron shrugged. "Two of their triggers are decommissioned, and this next mission is an important one. They won't just let that go."

I thought back to the entry on the list. "The initials attached to the Maine mission are LW—Lilah Waters, you said? So there's a possibility she could show up here."

"Back up," Diggs said before Cameron could answer. "Why is Maine so important? Do you have any idea what their target is?"

Cameron shook his head. "I'm not certain."

I searched his face. A niggling unease crawled under my skin, but he didn't look away. He would know how to lie, though; of any of us, Mitch Cameron would be able to make us believe anything he wanted us to believe. At the thought, I suppressed the urge to kick him out and bolt all the doors and windows.

"You didn't answer my question," I said. "Do you think Lilah Waters might come here?"

"It's a strong possibility," he confirmed.

I noticed that Jack was still watching Cameron, his

expression unreadable. Cameron noticed, too.

"What have you been remembering?" Cameron asked him.

Jack shook his head, eyes never leaving Cameron's. "Nothing."

Unlike Cameron, Jack was always a crap liar.

"So, the explosion…" I prompted. "You were there?"

He broke the stalemate with Cameron to refocus on Diggs and me. "I'd been watching the Reynolds place for a couple of days—knew it was the next likely target." He glanced at Diggs. "I'm sorry about your father. I wasn't there in time to stop it."

"Thanks," Diggs said. "So does that mean you just got to town? Or you've been here a while?"

"I've been here for a couple of weeks," Jack admitted. "I just didn't want anyone to know, for now. Wanted to see what was happening."

Jamie came in then with a bowl of the chicken soup from the night before, a hunk of homemade bread with it.

"Take it slow," I said to Jack as Jamie set the food in front of him. "Between the whole meth buzz and this new diet of yours, it'll go right through you if you don't pace yourself."

He got half the soup down and all the bread before he pushed the bowl away. His eyelids kept drooping. He'd stopped talking a while ago.

"Maybe it would be best if you got some shuteye for now," Diggs suggested. "We can go over the rest of your story later."

Jack nodded gratefully, then asked if I would show him to a room. I agreed with a glance at Diggs. The ex-and-the-current-boyfriend thing should have been awkward, but not much ever seemed awkward between Diggs and Juarez. Half the time, I got the feeling they'd toss me out of the life raft first if it came down to it. Or, more likely, just jump out together.

I took Jack up to a room that used to be reserved for the single women in the church. The place had been stripped down, the single beds once there now replaced with one double bed with an antique wood frame. Rose-patterned wallpaper, patchy and faded, still clung to the walls.

"Do you have any clothes?" I asked.

"Back on the mainland. I left my duffel in my car."

"That's all right. Diggs can loan you something, hang on."

I went across the hall and grabbed a pair of sweats and a jersey. They'd be loose on Juarez right now, but at least they'd keep him warm. When I returned to his room, he was still seated on the bed staring into space. I handed him the clothes.

"You okay?" I said. To the man who'd lost a good thirty pounds in the past nine months and been blown up in a meth lab this morning.

"I'm glad to see you," he said rather than answering. "You look good. You and Diggs both—despite everything. I'm happy for you."

I sat down beside him. "Jack, what the hell happened? The last time I talked to you, you were on suspension—"

"Which, in the Bureau, is code for fired." He paused. "It was all right, though—it was what I needed. A wake-up call. As soon as it registered what had happened, all that I still needed to understand about who I am and where I came from, I let it go. The Bureau's in the past. There were other things that had to be addressed."

"Such as?"

"I went to Nicaragua," he said.

Nicaragua. Where six years ago, three men raped and murdered his wife—something he'd just learned, thanks to Diggs and me, had been orchestrated by J.

"Did you find anything?" I rested my hand at the small of his back. He didn't move—toward me or away. Just sat there, frozen.

"I saw where she died," he said. There was no inflection in his voice. "I'd seen before, of course. I was there before. The men who did it are dead. I never got the chance to question them; they were killed by the police before I even reached the country. I think now, though, that it was probably J. who took them out."

He wet his lips. Massaged the back of his neck for a second before he continued. "This LW—you said the name is Lilah Waters?"

"That's what Cameron said. You know the name?"

"No. Just the initials."

I nodded. He didn't have to elaborate—I already knew. LW were the initials of the team leader who'd overseen his wife's murder, too. Apparently, Lilah Waters was a busy bee.

"I spoke with a nun this time, when I was away," Jack continued. "A woman who knew Lucia; worked with her. I spoke with others who knew her. No one could tell me anything. No one ever heard of J. No one knew why someone would want to kill my wife."

He stopped, his gaze fixed on the ground. "She was pregnant, you know. We'd been fighting—I told her she should come home. Seven months pregnant. They would have known. The men who attacked her. She was showing. It was part of the reason she believed she was safe. 'No one hurts a pregnant woman, Jack,' she told me."

"Jack—"

"They killed her because of me. And I don't even know why. Were they trying to send a message? Trying to prove something? Trigger something? What was killing her like that supposed to accomplish? Have I done what they expected me to, all this time? Everything I do now, I wonder: is this what J. had planned all along?"

I stood to face him and lay my hand on his cheek, which was more bearded than I'd ever seen it. Even with the mountain man look going, he was a handsome guy. He looked at me with those dark eyes, and I felt like I was seeing clear through to his soul. It wasn't an easy sight.

"We'll figure this out, Jack. I still don't know how the hell we're going to do it, but we're taking these sons of bitches down. Whatever they think they had planned, they don't know who they're messing with." I ruffled his greasy hair and kissed his forehead. "Change into the clean clothes, huh? You smell like a grizzly bear. Then try to get some sleep—we'll talk more later."

"Right," he said with a nod. When I started to go, he stopped me with a hand on my arm. "Erin. What do you know about Cameron?"

"Not much. That he worked for J. Knew my father. Was a handler for J. for the better part of forty years before he went rogue. I'm pretty sure that of all of us, no one wants to take them down more than he does."

"You trust him?" Jack asked.

I considered the question for only a moment before I shook my head. "No. I wish I did, but…no. There's something he's not telling us. And he said it himself: J. teaches that the ends always justify the means. He wants to take them down—I'm not sure what he would do if any of us got in the way of that." I looked him in the eye. There was a vaguely mad glint there. "Why? Did you find something out?"

"No. But…I think I remember him. Or something about him." He closed his eyes, his hand going to his temple. I thought of the conversation with Diggs and Cameron earlier. If I was having those killer headaches, I wondered if Jack could have the same side effect.

"It's okay," I said. "Don't worry about it right now, all right? Just relax. Get some sleep. We'll be right here when you wake up."

•

"Did you find out anything else?" Diggs asked the second I closed the door behind me. He'd been lurking in the hallway, which had become an unfortunate habit of his.

"Jesus, Diggs. Wear a bell, would you?"

"Sorry." He didn't look sorry at all.

"Yeah, right," I said. "But… No, nothing much. He went to Nicaragua apparently. Did you know his wife was pregnant when they killed her? Seven months along."

Diggs' brow furrowed. "Christ," he said.

"We have to stop them," I said. "It's like they have a meeting every year to figure out how they can be a little more evil than they were the year before. The horror stories never end."

"I don't know how Juarez held it together this long. I mean, you're a pain in the ass, but if something happened to you—"

"It won't," I said. I looked him square in the eye. "Don't

even start thinking that way. If we start worrying about all we have to lose, we'll never do this. We have to stay focused."

"Trust me, I'm doing my damnedest. It isn't easy, though. Did he say anything else?"

"No," I said. "No big revelations yet."

We went downstairs. Cameron and the rest of the gang were still in the meeting room. I glanced at the wall clock and realized half the day had passed. It was past three o'clock.

"Is there somewhere we could talk privately?" Cameron asked before we'd had time to get settled. I glanced at Diggs. He nodded readily.

"After we're done," Cameron said, directing the statement at Carl and Monty, "I'd like to go over whatever security you have in place for the island. We should beef that up as quickly as possible, just in case."

"That brings up an excellent point, actually," I said. Jamie was seated at the table with Carl and Monty. She looked at me like she knew exactly what was coming. "I thought you were headed up north with the rest of your crew."

"I'll join them soon," she said. "I didn't expect to find Jack out there this morning—I just want to make sure he's all right. I'll leave tomorrow."

"What about the storm?" I said.

"It's not coming in until afternoon—I'll be fine. Trust me, I've driven in worse."

I didn't argue, mostly because Jamie didn't seem like the kind of person who responded well to arguments. She nodded toward the other room.

"The kitchen's empty, if you want to talk in there." A dismissal if ever I'd heard one. Maybe I still technically owned the island, but she was getting pretty damned comfortable running the place.

Einstein preceded us into the kitchen and headed straight for the fridge. He sat down expectantly and looked at me. Then at the fridge. Then at me. Subtle.

On the top shelf were stacks of glass containers, neatly labeled. *Chicken liver. Peanut butter carob. Banana blueberry. Duck hearts.* Presumably, treats for the dogs—though the banana blueberry didn't look bad. I took out a couple of heart-shaped cookies and gave them to Einstein, while Diggs and Cameron settled at a small table by the window. Outside, it was already getting dark. The temperature had dropped today, and the winds were already picking up.

I sat beside Diggs, facing off against Cameron. "Okay. So, what's with the urgency? I mean, apart from the obvious?"

"Did Jack say what he's remembering?" Cameron said. If possible, he looked more intense now than he had since he'd found me in the woods.

"No," I said. "We didn't talk much about it."

"So he said nothing about me?"

"No," I lied, thinking of Jack's warning. "Why should he?"

I saw a trace of very uncharacteristic uncertainty.

"Cameron—" Diggs started, when Cameron still didn't speak.

"Jack and I have some…history," he finally said. "Before he was taken from J.—before his memory was wiped and he was placed with the nuns in Miami."

"You knew him as a kid? How?"

He shifted to look out the window when he spoke again, avoiding both Diggs and me. "I was the one who wiped his memory. I was the one who took him from the project in the first place."

13

JACK HAD HEARD IT SAID that people only dreamed in black and white, but he'd never found that to be true. His dreams were always rich in color—tropical jungles in vivid shades of green, vibrant splashes of yellows and reds. The jungle he saw now was familiar; he visited it often in his sleep. When he awoke, however, he could never remember how he knew the place.

Above his head, monkeys scream. Swing from branch to branch. Colorful birds screech at him. *Watch your step, Jackie. Dad's watching,* a voice cautions. He looks up. He is holding someone's hand—a woman's. He can't see her face, the sun blinding him.

They continue to walk. He wants to stop; he is tired. Hungry. The jungle gets darker and darker.

"Where are we going?" he asks the woman.

"They're asking for us. Everyone's waiting, Jackie. They're waiting for us."

She is crying. He knows the woman—her hand holds comfort, soothes him. He doesn't want her to cry.

"It's all right," he says. She kneels in front of him. There are other people now, murmuring nearby. Crying. A man's voice, shouting.

Who wants to go with their child has a right to go with their child. I think it's humane. I want to go—I want to see you go, though. They can take me and do what they want—whatever they want to do. I want to see you go. I don't want to see you go through this hell no more. No more.

"Don't cry, mama," Jack says.

"I'm sorry," she says to him. "I can't let them take you. I won't let them steal you. Dad will lead the way. He always has."

Jack looks up. Two men stand by the trees. He can't see their faces. They have guns—big guns. And military clothes, green that blend with the jungle around them.

"We need to go," one man says. The woman sobs. She stands, and picks Jack up in her arms. They lead the way up a trail while monkeys scream overhead.

It's never been done before, you say. It's been done by every tribe in history. Every tribe facing annihilation. All the Indians of the Amazon are doing it right now. They refuse to bring any babies into the world. They kill every child that comes into the world. Because they don't want to live in this kind of a world.

The voice is louder now. It strikes terror in Jack's heart, and he struggles in his mother's arms. "Go back, mama. I want to go back. Not there. I don't want to go there."

She holds him tighter, her tears warm on his skin. She keeps moving, taking them closer. Something terrible is about to happen. Jack can feel it—his chest full to bursting, the air around crushing him. He tries to get away. She won't move.

"Ssh—Jack. You're okay. It's a dream, Jack. Just a dream."

He woke in a cold sweat, the sheets drenched. His body rung out, heart racing. It was dark in the room, nothing but a spear of moonlight coming in through the glass. Jamie sat at the edge of the bed. She didn't touch him—just eyed him closely, her voice even. He sat up, pulling the blanket with him. The room was cold.

"You've been out for a few hours. The others are together, rigging some security and checking out the island."

He pushed his lank hair from his eyes. Embarrassed, suddenly, at all of this: his appearance, his behavior… Coming to this woman's place and sweating all over her sheets.

Jamie watched him as though she read his every thought. She smiled—a sad smile. She had a hundred variations of it, he thought.

"I'm glad you're here, Jack. Trust me, I always tell people when they're not welcome."

"What time is it?"

"Just past eight."

He'd been asleep for nearly five hours, then. Not quite enough rest to say he was fully caught up, but it was a start. He scratched his chin, and paused at the beard that had grown there. He had great sympathy for Rip Van Winkle, suddenly.

"Do you have showers out here?" he asked.

"We do, but they're all outside. It'll be cold."

"That's all right. Anything would be good."

She led him outside. It was freezing, his breath coming in plumes of white in the arctic chill. The shower was behind a wooden partition, the water just a hair warmer than the air. His testicles threatened to climb back inside his body, but Jack lathered himself thoroughly and rinsed himself clean. Jamie had gotten him another change of clothes, and left them on a bench just outside the partition. Shivering, he pulled them on. Wool socks, fleece-lined jeans, cotton undershirt, two layers of outerwear above that. They weren't Diggs' clothes, he realized--these were too close to his size. Bear's, maybe?

When he was finished, Jamie was still waiting for him. Her arms were crossed over her chest, teeth chattering slightly. The German shepherd that was usually with her was gone. It seemed odd to see her without the dog.

"You didn't have to stay," he said. "You're freezing."

"I'm all right. It's dark out here. Cold. You shouldn't have to be alone."

"Thank you."

She nodded. He thought he saw a flush of pink to her cheeks in the beam of the flashlight, but couldn't tell whether it was from embarrassment or cold.

"I don't suppose you know anyone out here who cuts hair, do you?" he asked.

"I could probably hook you up."

He smiled. That would be good."

They walked back to the house in silence, without touching. Jamie had kissed his cheek once—in Coba, just before they all went to war. That night, he had been too consumed with the knowledge of what J. had done to Lucia to even notice. Now, though, he recalled how soft her lips had been. How cool.

He and Erin had been apart nearly a year now. He'd taken no one to his bed since that time. Not because he was in mourning for the relationship—theirs was never a love affair, he knew now. He cared for her. Enjoyed her, when they were together. But it was hard to give yourself completely to a woman so clearly in love with someone else. Harder still when the ghost of the woman you'd loved refused to make room in your heart for anyone else.

He missed the companionship, though. And the sex, he could admit. He did miss the sex.

Jamie glanced at him—reading his mind again, he was sure. This time, he was the one who blushed. She looked away without a word.

She led him to the meeting room. When Erin brought him here the first time, nearly two years ago, there had been a painting over the fireplace mantle. It had been painted by Isaac Payson, she'd told him. He wondered where it was now.

"Have a seat," Jamie said. "I'll be right back."

He did so, and looked around when Jamie had left the room. There were three full backpacks piled against the wall, several leashes draped over them.

"You're leaving?" he asked when she returned.

"We decided it would be best," she said. She had scissors and a towel with her. "The rest of the crew's already gone with the dogs. I had a few things to wrap up here."

"Like giving me a haircut?"

"Desperate times call for desperate measures."

"I didn't realize my hair was that desperate."

She laughed—a good laugh. Rich, strong. Utterly without self-consciousness. "Have you looked in the mirror lately? Yes, Jack—your hair's definitely desperate."

Jamie cut his hair the way she seemed to do everything: with practiced ease and an air of competence he suspected some men found intimidating. He'd never minded a strong woman, though. Her hands were cool on his skin as she brushed away the strands of hair that fell to his shoulders. When she was nearly finished, she crouched in front of him, her face close to his. She studied him, forehead furrowed in concentration as she eyed her handiwork.

"There," she said. "I think it's even, at least." Her breath was minty, as though she'd brushed her teeth in the not-so-distant past. He smelled no hint of coffee. "That should do, until you can get someone else to tidy things up."

Their eyes held for a moment. When his gaze drifted to her lips, she backed away.

"Now, let's do something about that beard," she said. She straightened. The moment ended.

By nine-thirty that night, Jack was clean-shaven, trimmed, and fed. The team—Erin, Diggs, Monty, Carl, Cameron, and Einstein—returned shortly thereafter, and Erin whistled at Jack as soon as she saw him.

"Wow. Did the makeover fairy visit while you were sleeping?" she asked.

"Close. Jamie."

"She did a good job." She smiled. "Good to see you again, Jack."

"It's good to be seen," he admitted. "And now, if it's all the same to you, I'd like to talk about tomorrow."

"Good idea," Diggs said. He and Erin exchanged a glance that Jack couldn't read—which wasn't uncommon for the two of them. Diggs wet his lips and frowned, clearly uncomfortable. "First, though, I was hoping maybe we could take a walk. Before we get down to plotting and planning for tomorrow, I mean."

"You don't think it's a little dark? And cold?" Jack said.

"It'll do you good," Diggs said. He slapped him on the back lightly. "Come on. A night hike through the woods. Just the thing to cure what ails you."

Uneasy now, Jack dutifully added a layer of clothing and took a headlamp Diggs gave him. Then, he headed out the door after Diggs, close on his heels as they took to the trail.

It didn't take long to fall back into the rhythm of movement, focused on where his feet landed, the way his body moved. The two men hiked over a pass of slick granite; up a steep hill littered with apples fallen from trees that lined the path. It smelled like cider just on the edge of turning. The light of the headlamps was jarring, pale white, and made Jack think of extended Steadicam shots in horror films. Moonlight lit their way, casting everything in a pale blue glow. The air was bracingly cold—he breathed in deeply, his lungs still tight from the morning tragedy.

Diggs pushed him hard until they were on the other side of the island, close to the cabins the Payson church members once inhabited. Only then did Diggs slow, waiting for Jack to catch him. Diggs was barely winded, a healthy glow on ruddy cheeks. Jack stopped, his own breath coming hard.

"You all right?" Diggs asked.

"Yeah," Jack nodded. "I told you, I haven't been to the gym much."

"Give it a week, you'll be back making me look like a slouch again." He took a long swig of water, then handed the bottle to Jack and nodded toward a weathered wooden stoop in front of one of the little cabins. "Sit a sec, would you?"

"Is this the part where you tell me what all those significant glances from Erin were about just now?"

"That woman's got to work on her poker face. Sorry about that."

"Don't be sorry, just tell me what the hell's going on." He sat beside Diggs on the doorstep, both men removing their headlamps. Jack kept his lit and set it beside him so they could still see, and sat far enough from Diggs that he could look the man in the eye. The foreboding built when Diggs hesitated. Jack studied him. None of them looked their best these days. "Diggs," he prompted.

"You've been remembering some things about your past, right?" Diggs said at last. "They don't necessarily make sense, but you're still remembering."

"Flashes, yes. As you said, though—they don't make a lot of sense."

"Is there anything about a jungle? Maybe from when you were a little kid?"

Jack thought immediately of the dream he'd had just that afternoon. He tensed. "What do you know, Diggs?"

Diggs paused for another agonizing moment before he continued. "You know that the high-ups at J. were involved with Jonestown. That Erin's father was there—and so was Cameron. Jim Jones was part of the operation."

His stomach turned, heart stilled in mid-beat. "I remember."

"The day that it all went down, Cameron went in afterward. When most everyone was already gone."

I don't want to see you go through this hell no more. No more. Jack heard the man's voice in his head again.

"All right," Jack said. "What does that have to do with me?" He already knew, though. *Dad's waiting for us, Jackie. He's watching.* He knew what it meant. A dagger's edge pierced his temple.

"Easy," Diggs said, his voice even. "Don't try to remember, okay? I'm going to fill in the blanks for you."

Jack nodded, mute.

"You were a year old—living with your mother at Jonestown. You'd been there since the beginning. Before that, Cameron says you were born in the church when they were in California." Diggs paused. Wet his lips. "Your mother took a fatal dose of Jones' so-called Kool-Aid… You didn't drink yours, though. Cameron found you. He took you—hid you from the rest of J."

"I don't understand. Why would he do that?"

"I don't know," Diggs admitted. "The man's motives usually elude me. But I think maybe he'd just seen too much killing that day. He liked you—had been around you before, I guess. That's what he told us, anyway."

"So he took me, and hid me from J." Jack turned the idea over. The other images came to him. *Hold the gun steady, Jackie. It's us or them.*

"What about the years in between?" he asked. "You said I was a year old. I don't remember anything until I woke up in that hospital at thirteen."

"Cameron took you to a family."

"What family?"

"I don't know. Cameron wouldn't say. He placed you with them, but something happened. I don't know what from there."

"Cameron told you all this," Jack said. Jonestown. His mother had died there. It came back in a rush, a wall of water that nearly pulled him under. *I don't know who fired the shot. I don't know who killed the congressman. But as far as I am concerned, I killed him.* Jim Jones. Jack had been there for all of it. His mother, weeping. Holding him too tightly. People shouting. Crying, all around him. The paper cup; the sickly sweet, warm liquid. They fell, one by one. His mother, holding him even as she sank to the ground.

"Jack," Diggs said, pulling him from the memory. "Listen to me, okay? I lost my father to these people. I sleep beside Solomon every night, and I see her wake from dreams she won't talk about—dreams that are ripping her apart from the inside out. Shit she won't let me close to went down because of these people. I know what J. has done. We'll get them, all right?"

Jack nodded. His headache was worse now; the moonlight that made its way through the trees felt like it would crack his skull. The shock was already wearing off, though, anger settling in its place. The throb in his head receded. He glanced at Diggs. "What else did Cameron say?"

"Not a lot. When we get back, he wants us all to sit down. He'll give you whatever else he can then."

"He wanted you to get me primed, though," Jack guessed. The anger swelled, climbing higher.

"No. He was going to talk to you. I asked him to let me." Diggs gripped his shoulder. The look on his face suggested he knew exactly what Jack was thinking. "You're pissed. I get that—if someone had done to Solomon what these people did to your wife, I…I don't know what I would have done. Chances are good I wouldn't be around to tell the story, because I would have offed myself and taken everyone I could have with me. You're a better man than that. We will get these guys—"

"Cameron *is* these guys. He worked alongside them for how many years?"

Diggs paused. He dropped his hand from Jack's shoulder. He considered the statement, and nodded after a time. "You're right. The things he's done for the organization… There's no coming back from that. He's got a lot of blood on his hands. But without him, we don't get the rest of J. Mitch Cameron is the key to this, Jack."

"I still don't trust him."

"I don't think you should—I don't think any of us should. But I don't see a way around working with him, for now. And the one thing I am sure of is that he wants to take

J. down—and if you can hang on without losing your shit, he'll make sure you find the son of a bitch behind your wife's death. And they'll pay for what they did."

It took some time before Jack finally nodded. The anger didn't disappear, but it dissipated enough that he could get a full breath again. See clearly.

They would find the men who killed Lucia. They would find the people behind all the other deaths. The men who had convinced his mother to take her own life in that jungle… The men who stole his history.

And he would kill them, one by one.

14

WHILE DIGGS TOOK JACK out into the woods to tell him an origin story to rival the darkest DC superhero, I took Einstein out for his evening constitutional and the followed Cameron into a little alcove he'd commandeered next to the meeting room. There were a couple of flat-screen computer monitors set up on a card table, each monitor showing half a dozen different views of the island.

"Where the hell did you get equipment?" I asked him. "Cameras, computers...whatever you need to make cameras and computers work?"

"Always come prepared," he said. "I usually carry equipment with me—I thought it would probably come in handy here."

"So you just carry ten thousand dollars work of surveillance tech in your boat with you."

"It cost slightly more than that, but...yes." He shrugged. "I told you: I come prepared."

"Right. Where is everyone, anyway?"

"The shorter man—Monty, isn't it?—went upstairs to get some sleep. The others are there." He nodded to the monitors, and I saw Carl and Jamie go into a small, newly constructed building out near the greenhouse. In the weird green glow of the night-vision cameras, I saw Carl laugh at something Jamie had said before he shut the door behind him and they both vanished.

Interesting.

Cameron settled at the controls, his eyes on everything at once.

I stepped closer and surveyed the monitors. Another of the windows showed the old Payson village, the collection of little cabins on the other side of the island. Two blurry figures sat together on the steps of one.

"They've been gone for a while," Cameron said.

"They've got a lot to talk about."

"They do," he agreed. He'd gone quiet. Grim. Cameron's default. "I should have talked to him myself."

"If you had, I'm pretty sure you'd be dead by now, and we'd be cleaning your blood off the walls and trying to figure out how the hell to take down J. without you. This is better. Diggs can talk to him… Explain things a little better. Let Jack get his head around it, before you swoop in and give him the rest of his life story."

"I can't give him the rest," Cameron said. "I only know pieces."

"You know more than anyone else he's ever known, though. For a guy whose first thirteen years is a big question mark, that's powerful information." I studied the other monitors, and went over everything I knew and everything I didn't know, about my father and J-932 and Mitch Cameron and… There was a hell of a lot I didn't know.

"You're thinking very loudly," Cameron said.

"Sorry. I have a question, though."

He met my eye. Half amused, half concerned. "When do you *not* have a question?"

"Right." I shrugged, conceding the point. "It's what I do. But this one… I've been going over it for a while. And I was hoping maybe you could clear something up for me."

"What?"

"After Payson Isle," I said, "somehow or other, Kat got information that kept me safe for the better part of my life. But…" I stopped. That image I couldn't shake, the one that was forever tattooed on my brain, returned: my father, lifting the gun to his head. The look in his eyes. "My father wasn't a strong man. I mean—not strong like you." He started to speak, but I shook my head. "It's all right. He was what he was. But I can't figure out how he had the guts or the ingenuity needed to get all that information on J., that would ensure we were safe. It doesn't add up for me."

Cameron just looked at me with deep, sorrowful eyes. "What are you asking?" he said.

I held his gaze. "I'm asking how you saved us. And… why, maybe."

AUGUST 29, 1990
Littlehope, Maine

SHE IS THE MOST BEAUTIFUL WOMAN he's ever seen, without question. Coal-black hair, porcelain skin, a hint of fire in clear green eyes. Cameron goes into the clinic a week after the fire. His hand is burned from setting the blaze. His mind is still muddy. He can't get the sound of children's screams, the scent of burning flesh, out of his mind.

Mandrake is trying to get him to come back.

Something keeps him in Littlehope, though.

The medical clinic where Katherine works is small, cramped. Understaffed, considering the amount of work they do throughout the region. But he manages to get an appointment anyway, though he has no insurance. No address.

Katherine leads him to an exam room in the back of the old building. A child—tiny, with red hair and haunted green eyes—follows them into the room. Adam's daughter. He remembers her from the island, the day of the fire. Recalls the terror in her eyes when she looked back at him. The way she ran. She is older than Jenny, he thinks. Older, but not as robust. His mind recoils at the thought of his own daughter, waiting for him to come home.

"She needs to be here?" Cameron asks.

"She's in training," Katherine says. She winks at him, then turns her back on the child and focuses her full attention on him. "Unwrap the bandage. Let's see what you've got under there."

She turns to the child again. "The first thing you do is find out what's wrong. Ask questions. Look at the injury. Use the two together to get the whole story, but remember that people will lie. The science is what's reliable. The medicine."

She takes Cameron's hand when it is unwrapped. Her hands are cool. Steady. His burns are infected, blisters oozing noxious yellow pus. The girl shrinks from it, pale.

"I don't want to see that," she says.

"It's all right," Katherine says. There is no softness to her words. "It's just the same as you or me—just sick, now. It's our job to restore health. How did this happen?" she asks him.

Cameron falters. "Please get her to leave the room."

Katherine looks at him for a few seconds. Studies his face. "No. She stays—"

"I can go," Erin says. "I don't want to be here, anyway."

"You'll stay," Katherine snaps. "You'll learn this. Go sit over there."

Erin sets her jaw, her own eyes reflecting the same fire Cameron has seen in her mother's. She takes hold of her mother's lab coat and physically pulls her away. "He was at the fire!" she says. She hisses the words at her mother, barely looking at Cameron now. She's on the verge of tears. "He's what I told you. He's the hooded man."

It is Katherine who pales this time. "Go wait in the office."

Erin holds fast to her sleeve. "You should come too. Don't stay with him. Please—just stay with me. I'll help you with your work—"

Katherine crouches in front of the girl. "Erin. Go in the office, now. I'm going to be fine. I won't leave you. I'll be right here."

The girl nods reluctantly and then, agonizingly slowly, goes to the door. When she's shut it behind her, Katherine turns to him again.

"What's your name?" she asks.

"Cameron," he says. He should kill them, he realizes. Already, he is thinking of the plan—that's what he does. What his mind defaults to, at all times. He will strangle the woman. Get the little girl alone, and snap her neck. They saw him. They know.

His head feels light, the space shrinking inside his chest.

"Let me look at your hand," Katherine says.

She takes his hand in hers. It isn't as though he's never been touched—he's thirty-five years old. Has been with many women, before his wife. And he and Susan don't lack for sexual attraction. This, though… Katherine touches him, and paths inside his mind suddenly line up. She makes sense to him, and he doesn't know why.

"It's infected," she tells him. "Badly. You'll need antibiotics. And you have to keep this clean. Change the bandage regularly. Do you have someone who can help you with that?"

"Adam told you about us," he whispers. He can't get his heart back. Can't make himself focus.

"Cameron—do you have someone to take care of you? To help you with your hand."

"No," he says quietly. "It's just me."

"Then come here. At the end of the day—wait till the others are gone. Don't let Erin see you again. You can do that?"

He hesitates. He is supposed to return to the team. To his family. They're waiting for him. There is a plan he's supposed to follow through with.

He thinks of the screams. The smell of people burned alive. The look in the child's eyes. The woman who thought he was an angel. Adam.

"Yes," he says. "I can do that. I'll come back tomorrow."

"Good. I'll see you then."

A week later, his hand is nearly healed. He waits outside, hidden in the trees, until the last worker at the clinic is gone. He goes to the back door, and opens it a crack. Katherine is talking to the little girl. Erin. He will strangle the woman. Snap the little girl's neck. Or poison them both, perhaps. Make them go to sleep. No blood. No flames. He doesn't want them to be hurt. Or frightened.

"I just want to go home," he hears Erin say. She is crying. "You stay here all the time—why can't I see Dad? He's probably afraid. Probably he misses his friends. He misses me."

"Damn it, Erin—listen to me. It's just us now, okay?" Katherine hisses the words. Cameron feels the desperation in them. "Your dad's gone. He won't ever be like he was, okay? Whatever he told you about that island, it was lies. And now it's all gone. This is our life now. So sit down, and give me a few minutes. We'll go home when I can."

They fight for a few more seconds. Cameron hears the sound of a hand slapping bare flesh—a sound he knows well. Erin stops crying. He waits by the back door. Trembling.

He will strangle the woman.

Snap the girl's neck.

It's another five minutes before Katherine comes to the door. She's been crying; she brushes the tears away impatiently and leads him inside. She is young, he realizes—younger than him by a few years. Carrying too much.

He will strangle her. Bring her peace.

Go into the lobby, where Erin will be alone.

So easy.

"You have any kids?" Katherine asks him when they are in the exam room. He blinks uncertainly. She smiles past the tears that still cloud her eyes. "It's a simple question, Cam. You either do or you don't. Unless you're the kind of guy who's been nailing bimbos from shore to shore without a raincoat. In which case, maybe you really don't know."

"No," he lies. The word comes out small. He clears his throat. "I don't have any children."

"Maybe someday, right?" she says. She motions to his hand. He unwraps it obligingly, and holds it out to her like an offering. He wants to give her something, he realizes suddenly. She won't take payment from him, and he doesn't understand why. Maybe because his money is tainted.

He searches the room—he forgot to bring anything with him. It's his last day here, and he has nothing to wrap around her neck.

He doesn't want to use his hands. Her neck is small. Delicate. He thinks of the marks he would leave behind, and his stomach turns.

"I never wanted kids," Katherine says conversationally, as she puts ointment on his burns and rewraps his hand. "I knew I'd be shit at it. My mom died when I was a baby, you know. And my dad—it was always just us. He could be a little…hard. I'd be doomed—dead mom, and a dad who beats the crap out of you. Talk about shitty genes."

"Genetics aren't everything," Cameron says. Dr. Mandrake taught him that. "The human mind is powerful. You visualize your goal, and work to achieve it. Genetics is secondary to free will. Secondary even to environmental conditioning, I think."

He could use her stethoscope. The string that hangs from the drapes. Or hold her close, and wrap his arm around her neck until she stops gasping for air.

His chest tightens.

"It's a nice thought," Katherine says. He looks at her blankly. She smiles at him again. She is lonely; he can see that. Lonely, and frightened. But not frightened of him, he thinks. It makes no sense, but he believes it is true.

"You're a good listener, you know that?" she says. "Figures. The first guy I feel like I can talk to since my ex, and you're…" She stops.

They haven't talked about that. He knows that she knows who he is. What he did. And she knows that he knows that she knows, like some demented situational comedy. But they haven't talked about it.

"Adam told you about us," he says. Unlike days earlier when he broached the subject, he says it with a full voice this time.

"Yes," she says. So simple. Will she close her eyes, or will he have to close them for her afterward? He doesn't want her to look at him, when it is done.

"Then why aren't you afraid of me? You know what I did. What I've done."

She looks away. He can see the pulse in her neck. Can smell faint perfume, and beneath it an even fainter note of perspiration. There are circles beneath her eyes; though he finds her beautiful, her face is drawn now, almost gaunt.

"You are afraid," he whispers.

She meets his eye. Stands taller, her back straight. "I've never been so scared in my life, as I've been this week. I keep waiting for you to just…do it…"

"You don't need to be afraid," he says. He doesn't

know why he says it. Where the words come from. A plan somersaults through his mind. He could strangle her now. Snap the girl's neck. Drag them into the woods. Burn the clinic down. Stab them both. Poison them. Drown them in the swimming hole down the lane. So many ways to kill. "I won't hurt you."

He is more surprised than she is, when the words come out.

"Adam said you have no choice."

"I have a choice," he says. The thoughts quiet in his head. They can live. He will let them live. "But I'll have to help you, or they'll send someone else to do the job I couldn't."

•

"So you were the one who gave Kat the dirt on J.," I said. We were still seated in the surveillance cave. Neither of us had moved much since Cameron began the story.

"I gave her what I could. What I knew would keep you and her safe."

I thought about the story for a few minutes, trying to remember the terrified little kid that I had been. "So you watched out for us, over the years."

"I tried," he said. "I had my own life to live. But I did what I could. Tried to keep you away from J., whenever possible." He grimaced. "If I'd realized how difficult that would prove, I might never have intervened all those years ago."

"You're saying Kat and I haven't been worth the effort?"

He smiled at me shyly, lowering his gaze. "No. I would never say that."

With story time over and an impending awkward silence

descending, I pushed aside the other countless questions that I had and moved on to other concerns. I studied the security monitors in front of us. Jack and Diggs had moved on; everything else looked clear.

"Still no sign of trouble," I said.

"Not yet."

"How likely do you think it is that J. will come out here?"

"It depends on whether or not they know we're here."

"They might not. Maybe we're stealthier than you think. Just because we weren't trained in guerrilla warfare doesn't mean we can't stay under the radar."

He didn't look convinced. I hesitated. I'd been considering a plan for a while now—one I knew Cameron wouldn't love, and Diggs would outright hate. Still… Sitting around waiting for more shit to go wrong was doing no one any good.

"Listen, there was something else I wanted to talk to you about. I have an idea."

His eyes were unquestionably pained. "Does that ever end well for anyone? Your ideas, I mean?"

"Not usually," I admitted. "But it's doing even less good just rattling around in my brain. You have a second?"

He sighed. "I could probably spare a few more."

Cameron was more receptive to my idea than I'd expected. By the time we had a rough plan hatched, Diggs and Jack were back. Cameron and I watched them come up the path, Cameron tenser with every step they took. I knew he was a stone-cold killer who'd taken out God only knew how many people… Despite that, I still felt kind of bad for the guy.

He stood as soon as Jack strode through the front door. "Do you want to talk to Diggs while I speak with Juarez?" he asked me.

"Cameron!" I heard Jack call from the other room. Not a happy call.

"Maybe we should stick together on—"

Jack interrupted before I could get the rest of the thought out. He strode through the door, slamming it open so hard it cracked against the wall. Einstein, who'd been resting peacefully at my side, skittered to his feet.

"Jack," I said. I stood in front of Cameron. Diggs was beside Jack, a restraining hand on his arm.

"Get the hell out of the way, Erin," Jack said.

"Not if you're going to murder Cameron, I'm not," I said.

"Why shouldn't I?" he demanded. "Do you have any idea what he's done for this organization?" His usually handsome face was dark with something that went far beyond simple anger.

"It's all right, Erin," Cameron said. He brushed a surprisingly gentle hand across my shoulder and pushed me aside. "There's no excuse for what I've done in my life. Certainly no redemption. I accepted that long ago."

He stepped around me. Jack stood there for a split second, he and Cameron face to face. He wavered.

"What did you do to me?" Jack asked. His voice shook. "What the hell did your people do?"

"I'm sorry," Cameron said. He sounded it, too. "I tried… I did try, with you. And I got you away from them, eventually."

"Tell me what happened."

And Cameron did.

It started in Guyana—or before Guyana, actually, since Jack was born in the People's Temple in San Francisco. Cameron was part of everything, back then. Working with Jim Jones; working with Project J. When Jones moved his congregation to the remote village in Guyana that would eventually become known as Jonestown, Jack's mother was there.

"What was her name?" Jack asked.

Cameron hesitated. Looked pained. "Sonya," he said finally. "She was Mexican. Beautiful—and very sweet. She'd gotten pregnant. Her family threw her out. So, she joined the church."

"Mexican. Not Cuban," Jack said.

"Your father was Cuban—or that's what Sonya said," Cameron explained. "I don't know who he was. I'm sorry. Sonya didn't talk about him much. She was very devoted to the church, though. And Jim."

"Jim Jones," Jack clarified. "I don't understand something, though: the memories I have of that place are so clear. I remember talking to my mother, hearing Jones' voice… If I was only a year old, how is that possible?"

"Things get muddied when a person's memories are erased," Cameron said. "They're often more vivid when they do return, shaded with impressions you may have had at the time, things you heard later. You probably heard Jones' death tapes at some point when you were older, and they've become enmeshed with your true memories of that day."

Jack considered the answer before he nodded for Cameron to keep going.

The story went on: Sonya was there for that fateful November when everything spun out of control. She drank the poison. Jack didn't. Cameron found him. Barely a year old, crying, crawling among the dead.

And he hid him.

"So why don't I remember anything?" Jack demanded. "If you saved me from J., why do I have no memory of the family you placed me with?"

Cameron didn't answer for a moment. I could almost see the whole thing replaying, scene by scene, in his head. "Because they didn't keep you for long. I left you with a family in Guyana, intending to either return for you when it was safe or just let you stay with them. They were good people."

"What happened to them?" I asked. What appeared to be genuine pain flashed in Cameron's eyes.

"They were killed. J. found out—the organization had already started work with you, Jack. You were important to the project; one of the first subjects they were able to work with virtually since birth. J. found the family I'd left you with, and slaughtered them."

Silence fell in the room. We were seated by then, four of us in the small room, so close our knees touched. Einstein had curled himself up an dwas lying directly under my chair, his chin on my foot. Despite everything, it felt really good to have my damn dog back. Every so often, I'd glance up to look at the monitors of the island. They were empty—every one of them. No sign of anyone out there.

"So J. took me again," Jack said. His voice had gone flat. "Who raised me after that? I get flashes of moments: a woman teaching me to shoot. To kill. Holding a gun as big as my arm. I couldn't have been more than six or seven."

"Dexter Mandrake," Cameron said.

"Dexter Mandrake—the head of the project?" I said.

"That's right," Cameron said. "Mandrake wanted to see

what he could accomplish with unlimited access to a subject. Up to that point, the boys he worked with lived elsewhere—were raised by someone else."

Jack sat there for a second, taking it all in. "What happened when I was thirteen?" he asked.

"I don't know that much," Cameron said. "There was someone else who wanted to take over the Project—I do know that. We hadn't been part of the U.S. government for more than a decade, but Mandrake still adhered to the old protocols. We had systems in place. Misguided as he might have been, he believed he was doing the right thing. Was convinced the work he did was important."

"But this guy who took over—he didn't believe that?" Diggs asked.

"I don't think so," Cameron said. "I don't know who took over, what his name was, what his motivation is."

"And this man killed Mandrake?" I prompted.

"He ordered it," Cameron said. He paused. "It was another execution—another slaughter. They went in, killed the family." He stopped at the look on my face.

"How was Jack saved that time, then?"

"I didn't work for Mandrake or J. anymore. I'd distanced myself, after Payson Isle." I thought of the story he'd just told me. What he'd gone through after he set the fire on the island; how he'd saved Kat and me. I kept quiet, and let him continue. "I was still following the Project, though. Watching Mandrake, just to keep tabs… It's difficult to explain. I'd checked out of my life to a large degree by then. I thought if I could understand Mandrake better, then I might be able to understand myself, the things I'd done."

"So you were there the night these people attacked?" Diggs asked. Jack had gotten quiet.

"I was," Cameron confirmed. "I saw them come in, and I managed to take out two of the team members." There was something he wasn't telling us, something that had happened that night that he either wouldn't or couldn't share. "I could only get to Jack, though. Everyone else was killed."

"You saved me. Again," Jack said.

Cameron nodded. "After that, I wiped your memory using a technique I'd learned when I was with the military. I placed you with the nuns in Miami, where I hoped you would be safe. Where you'd be able to live a normal life."

"But there's still something I don't understand," I said. "If you got him away from J., how did he end up here in Littlehope—just a few miles from my father…who, by then, was working for J. again, right?"

"Coincidence," Cameron said. Everyone in the room just stared at him. He shrugged. "It happens. It had nothing to do with J. They had no idea who you were at that point."

"That's bullshit," Jack said. I've gotta say, I was with him on that. "Then how did they figure out who I was? Because clearly they did. My wife…"

"Shit," Diggs said before I could ask the question. All eyes turned to him. He nodded to the TV monitors. "We've got company."

I followed his gaze. In the greenish-white glare of the night-vision camera lens, a single figure strode along one of the paths, an automatic rifle in her hand. She was young. Pretty. Trim.

And crazy as hell.

My blood curdled.

"What the hell's your daughter doing here?" I asked Cameron.

He stood. "Stay here. I'll take care of it."

"How, exactly?" I asked.

"I'll talk to her." I just stared at him. "She's my daughter, Erin."

Right. In the real world, that was supposed to mean something. This was J., though. With them, it seemed family just meant one more pawn in their endless mind games.

"If she's the one who killed my father—" Diggs said.

"I'll take care of it," Cameron repeated, more firmly this time. We all got up and followed him into the meeting room, Einstein scrambling after us. Monty was at the table with a bowl of cereal, reading. He looked up when we came out.

"We've got company on the island," I told him. He set his book aside with a nod, while I turned to Cameron. "What do you want us to do?"

"Stay here," Cameron said without a second thought.

"Forget it," Jack said. "How many people have you killed over the years? Slaughtered in their sleep? How do we know this isn't a setup? I'm coming with you."

"I don't negotiate when it comes to my daughter," Cameron said. "Stay here," he repeated.

This time, Jack didn't argue.

15

OF COURSE, the second Cameron was out of there, I was ready to saddle up.

"Someone should stay and watch the monitors," Jack said.

I looked at Monty. "Do you mind?"

"I was thinking this would be a good job for you, actually," Diggs said.

"Like that would happen in this lifetime. Now come on, or we'll lose him. Are you okay staying back?" I asked Monty again.

"Do I mind not going out in the wind and the ball-numbing cold to chase some hot bitch who's probably here to kill us?" He crunched on a spoonful of Cheerios and pretended to ponder. "That's a tough one."

I pulled on my boots. Einstein whimpered, tail wagging. The dog has a keen nose for adventure. "Sorry, buddy—not this time. You mind watching him, too?" I asked Monty.

"The dog and the TV—got it."

Thirty seconds later, Diggs, Jack, and I were all out in the cold again. It stole my breath and burned my lungs, the night too cloudy for stars. Nine months away from this, and it was possible I'd forgotten how to appreciate the charm of nights like this. Given the circumstances, summer would be a hell of a lot easier to handle right now.

Cameron was already out of sight, but thanks to the cameras, we knew where Jenny was—and, presumably, that's the direction he was headed. We walked in silence, single file with Jack in the lead and Diggs behind me. Dead leaves on the path meant our footsteps were hardly silent, but we did the best we could. I couldn't imagine that Cameron really thought we'd stay behind, anyway.

Beyond our own breathing and the occasional, hollow hoot of an owl in the darkness, the night was quiet. After we'd walked for ten minutes or so, Jack stopped and held up his fist—which I knew from years of devoted primetime viewing meant we should stop, too.

He was the only one with a flashlight—a headlamp that he turned off now, so we were all plunged into darkness. I waited for Allie to show up, but we were on the other side of the island from the Crack where I'd seen her before.

I listened while we remained huddled together on the path. At first, I heard nothing but the faint murmur of voices; after a second or two, I could distinguish between Jenny's murmur and Cameron's, but I couldn't make out their words. I peered over Jack's shoulder. I could just make out the beam of a flashlight off to the side of the path, through thick brush and naked white birch trees.

"...you need to stop," I heard Cameron say. "This isn't the way—"

Jenny cut him off, too low to hear.

"Stay here," Jack whispered to me. "I'm going closer."

Diggs and I nodded. He crept forward without turning on the flashlight. He made it no more than a few steps before a branch cracked beneath his feet—it sounded like cannon fire in the stillness. Jenny and Cameron both went quiet. Then:

"Don't go," Cameron said. "Damn it—stay here. You don't need to do this, Jenny."

She didn't answer. I could hear her retreat in the night, no worry any longer about being heard. Before any of us could take off in pursuit, Cameron appeared on the path.

He wasn't happy.

"I'm not arguing with you about it anymore," he said as we returned to the house. The door slammed behind him, and we were in the meeting room yet again. Einstein raced to greet us while Cameron continued with his dressing down. "Any operation needs a chain of command to be successful."

"You're not commanding anything," Jack said. His voice was so far from the cool, reasonable Jack Juarez I once knew, it was barely recognizable. "And you sure as hell aren't commanding us. It's not our fault she ran."

"You sounded like a herd of elephants—of course it's your fault she ran," Cameron insisted. He strode past us to the alcove. "Did you see her go?" he asked Monty.

"A boat left maybe two minutes ago," I heard him say. A couple of chairs scraped across the floor, and he appeared in the doorway. He joined us in the meeting room, Carl and Jamie behind him. "It was hidden in an inlet on the western shore. You got any idea what she was doing here?"

"Either looking for me or looking for Erin," Cameron said. "What was she doing when you saw her?"

"Just wandering around, as far as I could tell—at least, that's what she was doing until you got to her. Didn't look like she was looking for a person, though. No offense, but you guys ain't that hard to find. It looked more like she was searching for some*thing* than some*one.*"

I tried to read Cameron's expression at this information, but he was just as impenetrable as ever. "Either way, there's nothing we can do about it now. The good news is that I don't believe she meant any of us any harm. She wants J. taken down just as much as any of us now."

"That would be comforting if it weren't for all the people she's mowed down recently," I said. "Including Diggs' father."

"What do you want me to do about it?" Cameron asked, still prickly. "Would you like me to go after her? Take a boat and return to the mainland to track her down, or stay here and try to protect us from the real threat?"

"You don't have to get pissy about it," I said, my own temper rising. "But considering what your daughter's been up to lately, you can't expect us not to be leery when she comes sniffing around this island."

"Look, as much as I'd love to fight about Cameron's psychotic daughter," Diggs said, "I think there are some other issues we need to address. Namely, what the hell is our next move? Jenny's already killed three people, and she obviously hasn't left town yet. Tomorrow's New Year's Eve... Do you think she has anyone else in her crosshairs?"

"It's possible," Cameron said.

"And you really think J. might show up here? Or at least the team leader who's supposed to be overseeing this next operation?" Diggs pressed.

"Again," Cameron said, "it's possible. I don't know anything with any degree of certainty."

"Perhaps we should sit," Carl said. "As far as I can tell, there is no plan—no strategy for what we are doing. I would feel better to have some strategy."

"Strategy is good," Diggs agreed.

"I'll get tea," Jamie said.

"Coffee would be better," I said.

"Not for people who've slept less than five hours in the past forty-eight," she corrected me. I'd almost forgotten, running so long on adrenaline and pure fear. "Whatever else you people do tonight, you need to sleep." She exited to the kitchen without waiting for anyone to fight her on it.

"It doesn't seem like staying out here is doing anyone any good," Jack said when she had gone. The others settled around the table. "I'm going back to the mainland tomorrow. At least there I can do some surveillance, talk to others in town to try and figure out what's happening."

"Actually, we were talking about that," I said. "Earlier. And Cameron and I decided—" Cameron started to interrupt, which was bad because I knew he was about to blame the whole idea on me, so I just kept talking over him. "—that the best plan would actually be for all of us to come out of hiding tomorrow, and get back on the mainland for a while."

"You and Cameron decided that, huh?" Diggs said.

"It's possible the idea was originally mine," I said. "But he went along with it."

"I said it wasn't out of the question," Cameron said. "There's a difference."

"Not in Solomon's world," Diggs said.

"And what is this plan, exactly?" Jack asked.

"We stop hiding," I said simply. "We go to the mainland, and we do our thing. Talk to people—including Laurie Smith, that girl Diggs' dad was…friendly with. Try to get some investigation done in the daylight hours for a change."

To my surprise, Diggs didn't argue. "Personally, I'd feel

a lot better if we weren't trapped out here during the storm of the century," he conceded. "Jenny may be running loose on the mainland, but as far as we know she's not out for our blood. At least back in Littlehope, we have access to cops and roads and hospitals. If J. did decide to come out here, I don't care how many cameras we've got set up I don't see us having a lot of success fending them off. Especially not in a blizzard."

"And you don't think this is a terrible idea?" Jack asked Cameron.

"I don't have a better one," Cameron admitted. "We have a limited amount of time to do anything at this point, and the reality is that I think the police have better things to do right now than look for fugitives in Littlehope, Maine, particularly with the storm. Erin and Diggs are still wanted for questioning, but there's no arrest warrant out for them, to my knowledge. Consequently, the police are the smaller issue here. The larger issue is J."

"And you don't think they'll show up now?" I said.

"Not in the next few days, no," Cameron said. "If anything, I believe this is your best window to conduct an investigation safely. Despite what Jenny's done, J. won't risk coming to Littlehope in this kind of weather—particularly when their mission isn't scheduled until April."

"And it's not like you'll be alone," Monty said. "Carl and I'll be over there, along with Juarez here. I think we can handle it. Like you said, I feel better about our chances over there than I do out here."

Jamie returned bearing tea. I thought about her and Carl, suddenly, and of Urenna and Bear. They were somewhere in Northern Maine by now, presumably waiting for their parents.

"Maybe it would be a better idea for you guys to stick together," I said. Diggs looked at me quizzically. "Jamie, Carl, and Monty, I mean. Cameron said there's not a lot of danger, right? And we're all armed. You guys have a good thing going here—you've got kids and families and lives."

"No way in hell I'm leaving all the fun to go up to Northern Maine and run around in the snow with a bunch of dogs on New Year's Eve," Monty said. "Sorry, princess. You're not getting rid of me."

I noticed a look between Jamie and Carl. This time, Carl didn't jump in to argue with me. "How old is Urenna?" I asked.

"Seventeen."

"And her mother?"

He looked down for a second. "Her mother passed. It is just the two of us."

"Urenna," Diggs said. He seemed to be turning the name over. "That's Nigerian, isn't it?"

"It means 'father's pride,'" Carl said. "She was our third born—we had two boys already."

"And where are they?" I asked, my voice low. It was obvious from his expression what the answer would be.

"It's just us, now."

I looked at him evenly. The debate was already over, as far as I was concerned. "I'd like it if you left with Jamie tomorrow. Sit this out, please. Right now, we think things are all right—that we're safe. That can change on a dime with these people."

He frowned, and looked at Monty. Monty shrugged. "No shame in taking care of your own blood, brother."

"I'd feel better if you were with me, personally," Jamie said to him. "In case anything does go wrong and for some reason J. targets us, it would be good to know I've got someone with military training. Plus, you can keep me company on that snowy drive."

I caught just a hint of light when he looked at her, before he lowered his eyes. I wondered whether Jack had seen it, too.

"We're agreed, then?" I said. "If Monty wants to stay, that's one thing… But you and Jamie head up north at first light, so you can beat the storm." I knew I was being pushy about the whole thing, but I was too tired to be subtle. To be fair, though, I'm usually too tired for subtlety.

"We're agreed," Carl said.

I thought for d hoped to avoid since we returned here. I looked at Jamie. "Would you mind taking Einstein with you again?" I said. My voice shook. Jesus—I can handle any number of horrible things, but dog-related catastrophes are way beyond my scope. "Just until things are clear again. I just don't want him to be in the path of destruction if something happens."

"Of course," Jamie said. "I was going to offer, anyway. It's not a problem."

"Thanks," I said. One more second of breathing, and I was back on track. "And in the meantime, the five of us will head for the mainland. Diggs, Cameron, Jack, Monty, and me… Our own private army."

"What do you think?" Cameron asked Diggs.

Diggs frowned. "I assume catching the first flight to Jamaica still isn't on the table?" he asked me.

I just looked at him. "This is our shot to figure this out—to figure out what J. has planned, who they're working with, and maybe find a way to stop it before it happens. You really want to spend the next four months stuck on this island, skulking around the mainland at night trying to find the next nut job about to go postal? I say we just go in and get it done. And the sooner we do it and get the hell out, the less likely it is that J. will find out we're here."

"It's scary how you make a plan like this sound so reasonable," Jack said.

"It's a gift," I said.

I noticed that Diggs didn't jump in to agree with me.

Miraculously, Diggs and I managed to hit the hay by eleven o'clock that night. I'd been watching him for a while as the hours wore on—the way his eyes closed in the middle of conversations; the way his mind seemed to drift mid-sentence. If I'd gotten less than five hours of sleep in the past forty-eight, Diggs was lucky if he'd gotten two.

When we got through the bedroom door, I went to the bed and turned the lantern on which he shucked his jeans and sweatshirt. Our bed was an antique four poster, the sheets mismatched, the quilt a hideous maroon thing most pay-by-the-hour hotels would look down their noses at. Tonight, I wasn't about to complain. I pulled off ski pants and jeans until I eventually found a bottom layer under there. I stood shivering in long johns and a long-sleeved t-shirt, the same outfit Diggs wore now.

"I miss sexy sleep gear," Diggs said. I went to him, and he wrapped his arms around me and pulled me close.

"Sexy sleep gear? Did I ever wear that?" I asked.

"There was that thing in Paris—remember that?"

We'd been in Paris in 2004, covering the Tour de France—posing as husband and wife because of some French filly Diggs was trying to give the slip. I smiled at the memory.

"The black thing?" I said.

"The black thing," he agreed. His voice was low when he said it. Whatever tension there had been between us earlier vanished. Diggs held me for a while, swaying slightly.

"This is nice," I said into his chest, after a couple of minutes had passed. It was getting hard to breathe in there. "Are you still awake?"

"No," he said. He leaned down and nuzzled my ear. Behind me, I heard Einstein hop up on the bed and circle, pawing the comforter until he'd gotten it the way he wanted.

I found the hem of Diggs' shirt and rested my hands on his broad back. He jumped.

"Jesus, woman. Your hands are freezing."

"Why do you think I put them there? Now come on—get in bed."

"I think I'm too tired to move."

"All you have to do is fall sideways. I'll do the rest." He still didn't move. "Diggs?"

"I'm sorry I was a dick earlier—about you remembering. I should have realized the headache thing."

"You've been under a little stress—I understood. "

"There's still something you're holding back from me, though." He let me go then, and sat at the edge of the bed looking up at me. Gauging my reaction. "I know you well enough to know you're not telling me everything. I don't doubt there are things you can't remember… But there are things you can, too. And you're not telling me, for some reason."

Because apparently the Laura Ingalls Wilder childhood I thought I lived was closer to some sci-fi horror flick came to mind, but I kept it to myself. Which, I knew, was the problem.

"Anyway," Diggs said when I didn't say anything, "you should have told me about the headaches. I wouldn't have pushed so hard."

"You can push," I said. "It's not like a little old headache will stop me." I pulled the covers back. All it took was my index finger on his chest to push Diggs into bed. "We don't need to talk about this right now. Just sleep."

I turned off the lantern and went to the other side of the bed. Einstein grudgingly made room, and I curled into Diggs' chest when he pulled me to him.

"I'd ravage you if I could move," he said in my ear.

"You can ravage me another time."

He kissed my head and pulled me in closer. "Maybe you could just get on top and wriggle around a little."

I laughed. "Oh, that's sexy."

"Anything for you, baby." His voice was drifting, getting heavier. Just before he was fully under, he jerked awake again. "What do you think of Cameron?" he asked.

"Right now? Very little."

"I don't trust him."

I thought about the way Cameron had reacted to my questions; the lies we'd already caught him in. First he didn't know the team leaders, then he did. And Monty had said Jenny was looking for something on the island—not someone. Cameron had downplayed that, but I was sure it meant something. And the bit about Jack just randomly ending up in Littlehope at fifteen with Matt Perkins was a bullshit story if I'd ever smelled one. What else wasn't he telling us?

"You're wondering if he's giving us the whole story?" I guessed.

"Good to know we're still on the same page. Yeah. You

should check in with Kat, see if she knows anything."

"I'll think about it," I said. As with Cameron, all I needed to do to get in touch with Kat was place a Craigslist ad—something we'd only done three times since running last year.

It was strange to be in a position where I actually wanted to defend Cameron. How long had he been the specter in my dreams? Diggs was right, though: I'd be an idiot to believe the guy was suddenly completely trustworthy.

"I think you're right, though," I said. "So, we keep an eye on Cameron and his psycho daughter. And the rest of the town. And the weather," I added. He'd loosened his grip around me, but I could tell he wasn't asleep—his body tenser now, while he thought about whatever it was we were up against.

"The storm sounds bad tomorrow, you know. Possibly a record breaker."

"I wouldn't expect any less. What fun would it be for us to do any of this in nice weather?" I paused, and shifted to look at him. "You're supposed to be sleeping. Close your eyes." I swept the back of my hand over his forehead.

He didn't, though—just kept his eyes wide open, studying me. "They want you gone, Sol. For real. I know there's a storm tomorrow…but look at what these people have done over the years. You really think a little snow could stop them if they thought they had you in their sights again?" He kept going, gathering steam. "We're banking on Jenny and Cameron having nothing to do with J. anymore—but what if we're wrong? They could tip someone off."

"They're both running from J.," I argued. "They're both invested in taking them down. Cameron's sacrificed a hell of a lot to keep me safe over the years. Why would either of them tip off the organization now?"

"I don't know." His voice was ragged with frustration and fatigue. I took his face in my hands and kissed him firmly, fixing him with my sternest glare.

"No more thinking. No more talking. Close your eyes."

He didn't. I arched an eyebrow, which he may or may not have been able to see in the dark. He must have gotten the message, though, because I could just make out his features when he let his lids drift shut.

"Take a breath," I said. I laid down beside him again. This was something he'd started with me, when I was having trouble sleeping in Australia. He took a breath. "Let it out, nice and slow." He did.

Einstein shifted by my feet; I braved the cold and snuck one hand out from the blankets to scratch his ears, and tried not to think about the fact that I was sending him away in the morning.

"I love you," Diggs said, half asleep now. I kissed him one more time, and resettled in his arms.

"I love you, too," I said.

I closed my eyes.

Diggs slept.

I did not.

An hour passed.

I shifted positions. Einstein shifted positions. Diggs groaned.

"What are you doing?" he asked eventually. Not nicely.

"Nothing—go back to sleep."

He was snoring again within seconds. I put the pillow over my face. Einstein snuggled in under my arm. The dog generates heat like a freaking furnace—between him and Diggs it was like sleeping without A/C on the sun.

I opened my eyes and stared at the ceiling.

Allie made no appearance.

I listened to the house moan. They seemed like your usual old-house moans, but it still freaked me out. Overhead, floorboards creaked.

"Allie?" I whispered.

I waited five seconds. Nothing happened. I teetered between relief and disappointment. A stiff wind could have blown me in either direction.

Something else creaked above me—or rattled more than creaked, I decided after some thought. To the untrained ear, it sounded like a drawer being opened on the floor above.

No one was staying above us, though. The only people who had ever lived there, to my knowledge, were Isaac Payson and his family. My stomach tightened. It was bad enough having Allie rattling around in my subconscious, but if Isaac was going to take up residence there too, I might need to invest in a good shrink. Or some very strong medication.

I closed my eyes again, and listened. Whatever I'd heard above, it seemed to be gone now.

I tried counting sheep.

Then ghosts.

Eventually, I fell asleep.

I remained that way for a few hours before something woke me.

A hand, brushing against my cheek.

I opened my eyes to darkness…

And Allie Tate.

"Make it through the Crack and you live forever," she said.

My heart shimmied up my throat. I closed my eyes. "Jesus Christ, Allie. It's bad enough I'm talking to a ghost. Do we have to do the riddles, too?"

"It's where we kept our secrets. If you want to end this, you need those secrets."

I opened my eyes again. She still stared at me through broken Coke-bottle lenses, her own eyes wide.

"We kept our secrets at the Crack," I said, to clarify. She looked at me like I was an idiot. "Well, I'm sorry, Al—I've never dealt with a ghost before. Could you be a little less cryptic?"

"Who are you talking to?" Diggs mumbled next to me. Einstein was sleeping between us now, but Diggs reached across him and sort of patted/thumped my head. "Are you dreaming?"

"Yeah," I said. "Go back to sleep."

Allie was gone when I turned back, though. I lay there for a few minutes in the dark, thinking. *It's where we kept our secrets.* The Crack. What the hell did that even mean? I thought back to the memory I'd had the day before: Will leading us through the Crack, that narrow crevice up on the mountain. The headache started again, toward the back of my brain this time. *If you get stuck in the Crack, you'll die there. Make it through, and you live forever.*

"Shit," I said aloud.

Diggs mumbled something to me. I stayed still until he'd gone back to sleep, then got up. One of us should get a few hours of REM-time, at least. He didn't stir when I got out of bed. I hesitated all the same—he'd be beyond pissed, I knew, if he found out I'd left in the middle of the night. Would want to know why I hadn't at least woken him up and brought him along, particularly considering the fact that I knew Jenny had been wandering the island not so long ago.

I thought of Allie. Will.

The closet, where my father had kept me.

Diggs didn't know any of it—not really. I'd told him all the planted memories, all the things I thought were real before. For eighteen years now, I'd been telling him the same stories.

I didn't know how to tell him what was really there, now that the fantasy was gone.

"C'mon, Stein," I whispered. Einstein's ears perked up. Sweet boy that he is, he didn't hesitate.

I pulled my clothes on and used a back staircase I remembered from life on Payson Isle way back when, so Cameron didn't catch me leaving. I closed the door behind me when I reached the ground floor, then waited without breathing for a count of ten.

No Cameron.

No anyone.

There was a half-moon overhead. Still no snow on the ground, but by this time tomorrow I was guessing that wouldn't be an issue anymore. The smell of pine and salt were on the air. It was cold, too, which of course is to be expected from Maine in December. I pulled my hat down over my ears and plunged my gloved hands deep into my pockets.

I set out, alone.

16

MAKE IT THROUGH THE CRACK and you'll live forever, Will and Allie had said. I pushed past the walls of my own thick skull, trying to remember. Will Colby was handsome—or at least I'd thought he was, back then. Skinny, but pretty brown eyes and a rebellious streak that apparently made an impression, because it's the same one I love Diggs for.

I'm not allowed to talk to you anymore, I remembered saying to him. I remembered sunshine. An early morning. I hadn't known he would be there.

"What'd they do to you?" he asks. He doesn't look good—he looks wild. Angry. There's a purple bruise on his cheek.

"Nothing," I say. "Nobody did anything. Leave me alone."

"You were gone. For a week, you've been gone. I thought Isaac got you like he got Allie."

I shake my head. "You need to go." I start to turn, but he grabs my arm. Turns me around. I spin and look at him. He looks like maybe he's been crying. I try to remember what Daddy said. Will is the enemy. Allie's okay, she's waiting for me. And Will is the devil.

"Please leave me alone," I whisper.

"I won't let them hurt you again," he says. He means it,

too—I can see it in his eyes. "I'll take you away from here. My Uncle Jed has a boat. We can get it. Before they hurt you again, before they make you forget, let me take you away."

I stumbled on a tree root and righted myself just before I face planted on the trail. *Let me take you away.*

Einstein stopped when I did, and eyed me curiously. "Sorry, buddy. Come on. Let's keep going."

There were island deer out on the trail. Half a dozen of them stood with heads up and ears tipped forward, alert as Einstein and I came over the hill.

"Stay," I said. Einstein didn't move. Jamie and Bear were miracle workers.

The deer turned toward us. Stood for a moment, frozen in the moonlight, before they turned and bounded away. I remained where I was for a few seconds, listening to their hooves pound across frozen ground.

We resumed our trek.

My fingers ached with cold, and my toes and the tip of my nose had gone numb. We were on the last leg of the trail headed to the peak when I paused again. Einstein turned back. I heard rustling on the path behind us. Footsteps. Just a couple, before the sound stopped. Had it been an echo of my own feet, my own clumsy movements, or was someone following? My fingers curled around the pistol grip of the Ruger in my pocket.

"Hello?" I said, voice barely a whisper.

No response. Einstein looked at me again and whimpered. I reached down and scratched his ears, as much for my sake as his.

"We're almost there. Then I promise, we'll go home and get something warm and delicious. You game to go a little farther?"

The beautiful thing about dogs: they're always game. We set back out, but this time I kept my hand on my pistol the entire time.

There was a ring around the moon that night—a sign of snow, my father used to say. The sky was a deep, dark blue. Trees, stripped naked for winter, provided a skeletal canopy overhead as I reached the peak...

And the Crack.

"You're going to sit this one out, okay bud?" I said to Stein. He whined, then barked in protest when I tied him to a tree. I couldn't run the risk of him either following me in and getting stuck, or—worse—falling off the cliff on the other side. "Sorry, buddy. I won't be long."

It was maybe eighteen inches wide at the opening of the Crack. It would get narrower as I got farther in, I knew. If we'd had trouble passing through this thing as kids, I couldn't imagine how I would squeeze through now that I was working with a little T&A. Not a lot, mind you, but a little.

I took a breath. Straightened the headlamp.

Make it through the Crack...

"And you'll live forever," I finished. "Yeah. Thanks, guys. I've got it."

I turned sideways and shimmied inside. The crevice stretched fifteen, maybe twenty feet up, and a good twenty yards ahead of me. There was no light visible on the other side or above. The thing had seemed endless when we were kids; it didn't seem much less so now. When I disappeared, swallowed by the rock, Einstein barked after me.

"It's okay," I called back. "I'm good."

I wasn't really, though. My head was killing me—I imagined it splitting much the same way this rock had. I inched forward regardless.

"We keep our secrets here," Will Colby said. *"That way someone will know. Someday, they'll find this. And they'll know."*

"I'll take you away from here, Erin. I'll save you."

"We keep our secrets here."

Where?

Halfway through the Crack, it got so narrow I couldn't breathe. The rock was ice cold against my body, granite digging into my breasts—which were definitely not helpful in this situation. I was still sideways. I inched my right foot forward, and paused.

Something wedged at the base of the Crack barred the way. It reached my hip, making it impossible to continue unless I climbed.

I shimmied up. Found a toehold. Braced myself with knees and hands. Behind me, Einstein started barking again—louder now. More serious. With deadly intent.

Shit.

My breath wouldn't come.

I managed to get up high enough to get over the rock in my way. I could just barely see light up ahead, but it was distant. There was still a ways to go.

Where the hell were the secrets we'd kept here?

What did that even mean?

When I was past the rock in my way, it got narrow again. Einstein was still barking. It was so cold that I'd lost all feeling in my toes. My hands. I stopped for a second. Bile climbed my throat.

And suddenly, like some unexpected, drenching rain, the memories came.

"You don't have to be afraid," Will says. "It's just a little farther. You're so little, it won't be hard. Just follow me."

"I'm not afraid," I lie. We're already in the rock. It's light

enough that I can see him, just a foot or so in front of me. He's taller than me, skinny and brown-eyed and serious. The camera his uncle gave him—the one Isaac says he's not supposed to have—is on a string around his neck.

"What are we doing?" Allie hisses. She's behind me. "We're supposed to be in bed."

"It's not even dark out," I say back. "Only babies go to bed when it's still light. You can go back if you want. I'm staying with Will."

"How much further?" she asks.

"Not far," Will says. "Hang on—this is the hard part. I'll help you. Just wait a sec."

I hold still. I can feel Allie crowding in behind me. Will stops walking ahead, and climbs up instead. He mashes his butt against one rock, his feet against the other, and pushes himself up. Uses his hands to pull himself. He goes up and up, the camera bouncing every time he shoves himself up another foot.

"What are you doing?"

"I'm showing you," he says. "Just come. This is where we keep everything. Everything we don't want them to know."

"It's wrong to keep secrets," Allie says.

"So go," I whisper to her. "If you're so afraid, just go back to the house. I'll come in a minute."

"But Will—" she starts.

"We'll be okay, Al," I assure her. Will is waiting for me.

I wait till she goes before I start to climb.

Einstein stopped barking abruptly. His silence was more unnerving, by far. I angled my arm up and cast the flashlight beam around as best I could, trying to orient myself.

The light hit something solid about ten feet above me: another boulder like the one blocking my path below. This one, I remembered.

It was a couple of feet across, blocking the light in that one spot.

I approached it a little differently than Will had shown me that day—instead of using my ass, I straddled the Crack and pulled myself with my hands, holding steady and pushing myself up with my feet.

"That's it," Will says. "You're almost there."

My heart hammered loud enough to echo in the stillness. I was ten feet up, closing in on my destination. I climbed another five feet. The space was wider here, which meant I needed to work harder to span the distance between the two rock faces—one foot on either side as I scrabbled for a handhold, a toehold.

"How often do you come here?" I say.

"All the time. You can't tell Isaac about it—this is where I keep everything. No matter what happens, my stuff will still be here after I'm gone. You make it through the Crack, and you live forever. Nobody erases this."

"God makes sure we live forever," I hear Allie say below us.

"What are you still doing here?" I say.

"I want to see it, too."

Will looks at me. He rolls his eyes. I giggle. He points his camera at me. I stick out my tongue when he snaps the picture, and the flash blinds me. A second later, the picture comes out the front. He hands me the picture and the camera, and then he goes back down and helps Allie up. She's slower than me, not as good a climber. Will doesn't make fun of her, though. Dad doesn't like me spending time with him, but I don't understand why. He's nicer than any other boy here.

She finally makes it. All three of us are far up, holding tight to the rock. Will's camera is heavy, so I hand it back to him when he's close enough. I hang on to the picture, though. Will is closest to the rock—the thing that he says will make us live forever. I can't wait to see what he means.

He reaches inside the rock.

That's when Isaac calls for us.

The memory was enough to rattle me a hell of a lot more than the situation I was in now. A headache roared in my ears, something living, breathing, burrowing into my skull.

I was close enough now to see what I'd been looking for. Einstein hadn't made a sound in too long. I struggled to stay in the present, straining to hear the world around me. Were those footsteps above me, or some distant echo of the life I'd lived before?

"Allie!" Isaac says. "Will! Erin Solomon! Your family is looking for you!" He shouts it from somewhere in the forest, not far from us. My heart thumps in my chest. Allie gasps. Falls, a little way. Will grabs her arm.

"Stay quiet!" he whispers to us. "He won't find us here."

Isaac comes closer, though. He's angry—I can hear it in his voice. Daddy says Isaac will never get angry with me the way he does everybody else, but I don't know if that's true right now.

We all stay there, holding tight to the rock. Allie starts to cry.

I rested my head back against the cool rock, and forced myself back to the present. That was over—the whole thing was behind me now.

But, finally, I knew what I was looking for. Remembered what my father had made me forget.

Fifteen feet up, wedged between two granite rock faces with a scant beam of moonlight shining down, I angled myself closer to my goal:

Another rock. It was wedged in tight, maybe two feet wide, forming a shelf suspended in mid-air. I remembered Will's face. The triumph, before Isaac came.

This is where we keep our secrets.

I had no doubt that this was where I would find my answers.

I listened again. The footsteps weren't a memory, I realized now—I heard them clearly on the rock above me. Light, but distinct. I wasn't alone.

"Erin," someone called from above me. A woman. I recognized the voice instantly. "I've been looking for you."

Jenny—Cameron's daughter. The one born and bred for psychopathy. The one who had just run down Diggs' father and blown up a compound, with little regard for the lives inside. Memories faded; the here-and-now was suddenly just as terrifying.

"I think we're on the same team now," I said. "Trying to take J. down, I mean. So there's really no reason to sneak around like this." I was level with the rock now, just a few feet from open air above me. The light from my headlamp perfectly illuminated what I was looking at.

The rock was granite, but it wasn't whole. There was a cavern inside—big enough for me to reach inside easily.

"Somehow I doubt that," she said. "You're still not willing to do what it takes."

"You mean running down sick old men or blowing up little kids? Yeah, you've got me there. Is Einstein still out there?" I asked. The question made my heart hurt, just slightly.

"He's right where you left him, gnawing on a ham bone. Don't worry—I've spilled a lot of blood, but nothing with fur. He's safe."

That was a marginal relief—with the exception of the havoc a ham bone would wreak on my mutt's digestive system. It was better than the alternative, though. I tried taking a breath. "Okay. Good. So…what is it you want, exactly? I'm assuming this isn't a social call."

"Definitely not." I heard her shuffling around up there. When she spoke again, it sounded like she was practically on top of me. I looked up. She must have laid down on the rock, because her face was directly in the crack above me. She blinked in the glare of my headlamp.

"I've wanted to talk to you for a while, actually," she said conversationally. She was armed—I could see a gun peering into the Crack at me alongside her beady brown eyes. "And then you came out here and I figured…there we go. Kill two birds with one stone. So to speak."

I paused. My right leg was cramping. "I get that I'm the first bird. What's the second one?"

"This place, of course. Or I assume it is—I wasn't sure. I know they're looking for something out here, but I really had no clue where to come."

I could hear her breathing above me, just a few feet at this point—five, maybe six. I shifted enough to reach for the gun in my pocket.

"They?" I asked. My breath wouldn't come anymore, body shaking with adrenaline and fear and the tension of hanging like Spiderman fifteen feet above the earth. Jenny didn't answer. I eased my hand from my pocket, gun clenched in my frozen fingers. "Jenny? Who's they? Why would anyone be searching here?"

She laughed, completely unexpectedly. "My father didn't tell you, then?" she asked. "Hmm. I guess you guys aren't as chummy as I thought. I figured after your old man offed himself in front of you, Dad would take you under his wing. He always did love a feisty damsel in distress. But he's still keeping secrets, huh?"

"Why don't you enlighten me, then? Are we talking about J? Lilah Waters? Is she the one who would be out here looking for…whatever it is they're looking for?"

"Ehhhh," Jenny said, making the sound of a game-show buzzer. "Sorry, wrong answer. Right team, wrong player. And it turns out this game isn't as fun as I'd thought. So how about you haul whatever it is you were fetching out of there, and come on out?"

I maneuvered the gun towar dthe sky, and aimed it at the pale beam of light from Jenny's flashlight. Before I could even adjust my grip, a shot rang out. In the enclosed space, the sound alone was almost enough to split my skull open. I dropped my gun. I could just barely hear Jenny talking to me, a voice on the far end of a wind tunnel. In the process of trying to recover my gun, my foot slipped on the rocks. I fell a few feet, scrambling to find another foothold.

It was a few minutes before I could hear anything again. Jenny was right where I'd left her, staring down at me with her gun trained on my falling form.

"Sorry," she called to me, with no trace of remorse. "I'll aim for something more valuable than your hearing next time, though. Get whatever's in there, and bring it to me."

"No. You want it so much, you can come get it." She took aim again. My ears were still ringing. I definitely didn't want to go through that again. "Wait, wait. Fine. Just a second."

I shimmied back up and reached my hand in. A plastic container about the size of a shoebox was concealed inside the hollow. *"You can't tell anyone, Erin," Will whispers. "But you bring your secrets to the Crack, and we'll live forever."*

Why did J. care about the secrets of a kid dead twenty-five years, though? About a church led by a madman, him and his congregation long gone? I fumbled with the box for a few seconds, all too aware of the gun following my every move.

"I've got it," I said. My voice shook. "What do you want me to do now?"

"Climb up," she said. "Come to me."

"What am I, a freaking mountain goat? I can't climb that high."

"'Can't.' That's a terrible word. Come on, Erin. You're built of stronger stuff than that, right? I saw you try to stuff your dad's brains back in his head when you were half-dead yourself in Mexico. Heard all about you in those woods in Black Falls. Show me what you've got."

I shouldn't let her get to me, I knew. I was cold and tired and cursing my own stupidity, and the thought of my father… I shook it off. Tried to control my own fury. Started climbing.

My wrist still wasn't right after I'd broken it in Black Falls, even after more than a year and a handful of surgeries. It throbbed like a son of a bitch in the cold; just then, all I could feel was the ache. I clawed the rest of the way up, using my legs as much as possible. When my head cleared the top, Jenny was sitting up there waiting for me. She smiled brightly.

"See. I told you you'd make it."

She set the gun down, reached for my hand, and pulled me up.

I didn't even wait until I had my legs under me before I made my move. With my left hand still in her right, I summoned all the strength I had and swung the box I'd taken from the rock straight into her side. If nothing else, it caught her off balance enough to buy me some time. She went down—unfortunately, she still hadn't let go of my hand, so I went down with her.

On the ground and half on top of Jenny, Einstein barking furiously below, I dropped the box and let fly with a flailing right hook that caught her in the side of the head. The rage in her eyes told me I'd done little more than piss her off—I needed to find some way to get the upper hand, and fast. My gun was at the bottom of the Crack; hers was just a few feet away. I did the math, and went for it.

Jenny grabbed me by the back of the coast as I made for the gun and pulled me backward with little effort. She flipped me over so I was on my back withthe rough granite beneath me, and straddle me. She wasn't a big woman, but she was definitely bigger than me. And stronger. And trained.

Poised above me, she got one good punch in, just about knocking my tooth out, before I bucked up and caught her enough to tag her again myself. I was about to make my comeback—possibly—when I heard the ratched of a gun's safety in the darkness.

"I don't know whether to break this up or charge admission," Monty said from the shadows.

"I'm not ready to date a UFC champion yet," Diggs said. "Get off her, Jenny."

Jenny raised her hands, stood, and stepped away from me. I staggered to my feet and spit blood on the rocks. I wiped my mouth with the back of my sleeve. Below us, Einstein continued to bark with rabid intensity.

"You okay, champ?" Monty asked. Diggs remained conspicuously silent.

"Fine," I said. "I was just about to finish her off."

"Keep telling yourself that," Jenny said. I went in for a second round, but Diggs stopped me with an arm around my stomach. Meanwhile, Monty waved the gun toward Jenny and nodded her back another step.

The plastic container I'd taken from the rock had fallen to the ground, still sealed tight. I stooped to pick it up.

I'm not sure exactly what happened next. I heard Monty shout, and a second later Jenny shoved me aside, grabbed the container, and bolted for the woods. I started to run after her but Diggs grabbed my arm before I'd gotten two steps, nearly wrenching my shoulder out of its socket in the process.

"What are you doing? She's getting away!"

Monty ran past us, gun still in hand, moving at an impressive clip considering the darkness and the fact that we were twenty feet up on a hunk of granite.

"Let him go after her," Diggs said. "You've done enough tonight."

"The hell I have. She has the box."

"What box?" he asked. "What in hell are you doing out here?"

I thought of everything I'd remembered tonight, everything I'd seen…everything I suddenly knew about my past. Instead of answering, I pulled my arm from Diggs' grasp and stalked toward the edge of the rock, mouth still bleeding, and half limped and half slid back down the steep face to the ground below. I untied Einstein and knelt to reassure him I was alive. Diggs was a few steps behind me, still quiet.

Monty returned a minute or two later, gasping for breath. I wasn't surprised to see that he was empty handed—no box, no Jenny.

"She got away," he said. "Sorry. The bitch is fast."

"It's all right," I said numbly. "I wouldn't have done any

better. How did you guys find me?"

"Monty saw you on the monitor," Diggs said. "He came up and woke me. Imagine my surprise."

"Sorry," I said. Diggs kind of grunted.

"We should head back," Monty said. "That run warmed me up, but it looks like you could use a medic, princess."

He started back on the path. I hesitated. "Can you just give me a second?" I asked Diggs.

I didn't wait for him to answer before I dove back into the Crack. This time, I knew what I was looking for: I climbed up to the rock shelf, shoved my hand in, and retrieved a bundle of plastic-wrapped papers I'd pulled from the box before I handed the thing over to Jenny.

Diggs didn't say a word when I emerged this time.

He went in ahead of me when we got back to the house. I found him in the kitchen, putting water on the stove for tea. Cameron was with him. Monty was nowhere in sight.

"What the hell were you thinking?" Cameron demanded. I'd stuffed the bundle from the Crack down the back of my ski pants. I made no move to take it out.

"I went for a walk," I said.

"And you didn't think to wake someone? To tell *someone* where you were going?"

"It's been a rough few days. I figured they could use the sleep." The cold had frozen the blood on my mouth, and my lip had already swollen impressively. I wiggled each of my teeth with my tongue; none were loose. Always a silver lining.

Cameron shook his head and walked away. Diggs stood at the stove waiting for the water to boil. I considered telling the whole watched-pot deal, but figured I'd be bludgeoned for it so I kept quiet.

After Cameron had paced around the kitchen a couple times, he pulled up a chair and sat across from me. "What happened?" he asked.

"I ran into your daughter," I said. "We had a nice chat."

"Can you be serious for a moment, please?" he said. "What the hell were you doing out there? Did you remember something?"

I hesitated. The tea kettle whistled; Diggs removed it from the stove.

"You went to that crevice in the rocks, didn't you? That's where Monty said he saw you on the monitors. What were you doing there?"

Another second of hesitation. Cameron was as tens as I'd ever seen him. He leaned in toward me. For a second, I thought he might grab me. I flashed on my father, inexplicably—his hand digging into the wound in my side that last night in Coba. I shifted my chair away from him.

"Back off," Diggs said. Cameron looked up, like he'd forgotten Diggs was even there. "It was a stupid move, but she's hurt. She'll tell you everything after I get her cleaned up."

"We don't have time for games," Cameron said. He didn't move.

"We have five minutes for me to make sure she's still got all her teeth and she's not about to lose anything to frostbite," Diggs said, intractable. "Take five. Or better yet, go find your lunatic of a daughter before she kills anybody else."

To my surprise, Cameron stood. He brushed past Diggs, seething, and paused at the door. "When she ran, it looked like Jenny had something with her. She took that from you? From that rock?"

"No," I lied, no longer sure who to trust. Jenny had said he wasn't telling me everything. Why? "I don't know what she had. I told you, I went to get some air. I remembered how we used to go through there as kids; I just wanted to check it out."

It was obvious he knew I was lying. "If you're going to pull something like that again, I'd appreciate it if you told one of us," Cameron said. "I don't care who. But take someone other than the dog with you, if you decide you have to roam this island in the middle of the night again."

"Don't worry," I said. "It won't happen again."

"Excellent." He redirected his focus to Diggs. "Patch her up. Then I'd like to ask a few more questions."

Diggs acknowledged the comment with a nod. He sat down in the seat Cameron had vacated, while Cameron shrugged on his jacket and went out the backdoor, leaving us alone.

Diggs dipped a rag in hot water and handed it to me. Sort of shoved it at me, actually. No playing doctor tonight, then.

"I know you're pissed," I said.

He went to the backdoor and locked it, then stalked to the door leading from the kitchen to the corridor and blocked it with a chair.

"Pissed doesn't begin to cover it," he said. He came back, started to sit, then stood again. He paced the room.

I dabbed at my lip, winced, and set the cloth back down. I was still in my ski pants and parka, shivering beneath all the layers. The sides of the bundle I'd retrieved from the Crack dug into my back.

"I don't know why I didn't tell you," I said.

"Neither do I." He was on the opposite end of the

room. "Do you have any idea how stupid what you did out there is? Going out there in the middle of the night? Even without J., it would be an idiotic move this time of year. With them, though… Jesus, Solomon. What the hell were you thinking?"

"I wasn't, all right?" I said, my own temper flaring. "I just want to figure this out. I couldn't get to sleep, and I knew… I just knew there was something there."

"That bundle you took from the rock," he said. "Are you planning on showing me what it is, or am I not in on the big secret, either?"

I reached behind me and awkwardly extracted the bundle—a stack of letters, photos, and cards in a disintegrating plastic bag. I set them on the table. Diggs just stood there, watching me. Waiting for an invitation I couldn't bring myself to extend.

Finally, he came to the table and reached for the letter at the top of the stack.

Without thinking, I lay my hand over it. Pulled everything back toward me.

Diggs just stood there. He was angry, without question—I don't know if I'd ever seen him so angry. The hurt was the killer, though.

"Fine. Fuck it. You want to do this alone? Do it alone. Give a shout when you're ready to actually talk to me."

He walked out without another word. The door slammed behind him. I was alone with my ghosts once more.

17

DEAR ERIN,

I know you won't ever get this. Or maybe someday you will—maybe someday you'll remember. You just come to the Crack, and it'll all be here waiting for you. Make it through the Crack, and I'll live forever. Allie will live forever. No matter what happens, we'll be right here. Nobody else knows—Isaac hasn't found out about our spot. He still tries to get me to tell him. I think the only reason I'm still alive is he's too afraid of what I have out here. If I die before he finds this, he's screwed.

He'll kill me one day, though, just like he did Allie. I'm glad you got away. I don't know what they told you. I tried to find you—I really did. I would have saved you, if I could. I'm sorry I let them hurt you.

Turns out I can't save anybody. Not you. Not Allie. Not me. I try to get my mom to listen. This isn't the way it's supposed to be. You got away. Allie did too, in a way. Sometimes I wish he'd just kill me too. Get it over with.

I have to go, somebody's coming. I miss you. I hope I'll see you again someday.

Your friend,
Will

The letter was dated October, 1989—a month after my mother took me away from Payson Isle. There were more than a dozen letters here, all addressed to me, dated all the way up to a day before the fire. That wasn't all that was there, though. Will had documented everything. Photos of Isaac, notes from the other kids, descriptions of Isaac's conversations that Will had overheard. The kid was an investigative reporter waiting to happen—he didn't miss anything. He wrote about Zion Ashmont coming out to the island; about how obsessed Isaac got with him.

The new kid is crazy. He keeps telling us he's Jesus—that we're all going to die, and he's going to live. Him and Isaac. I shoved him down the other day and beat the snot out of him. I know it was wrong. I'm just so tired of all of it. Then Isaac let Zion beat me till my back was bloody. Took that stupid puppet Isaac gave me. I hate them all. I'm so glad you got away, Erin. I just wish I had too.

It was the photos that brought it all home, though.

Every memory locked in my head came spilling out as I looked through them.

I was in bed, Einstein beside me. The lights were low, the darkness outside very, very dark. It was four a.m. My lip was swollen, and I'd been too intent on reading the letters to worry about cleaning the blood on my face. I'd deal with it all tomorrow—or today. New Year's Eve. I had no clue what to expect anymore; no clue what Jenny might have gotten away with in that plastic container.

The door to the bedroom opened. Diggs came in. As far as I knew, Jack was asleep. Cameron still wasn't talking to me. And Diggs looked…lost. Hopeless, in a way I'd never seen him before.

"Hey," I said.

"Hey."

I set the letters down and looked at my hand, tracing patterns on my palm. "We should probably talk."

"Probably so." He sat down on the edge of the bed with a sigh, and shook his head. "Honestly, kid? I don't know what to do. I've tried listening; I've tried steamrolling you; I've tried being patient and just waiting for you to come to me. I'm here, Erin. I'm not going anywhere. But we keep coming back to this same brick wall with you."

"I'm trying."

"You keep saying that, and then you keep pulling the same shit." His voice was surprisingly even, like at this point he was more baffled than pissed off. "Why would you not wake me, if you were going out there tonight? How the hell does that make an ounce of sense? At the very least, you knew Jenny was out there earlier."

"I wasn't thinking." My voice broke. I hated how cool he was, how totally unreachable. At least when he was angry, I knew what to do. Lacking any other possible solution, I pushed the pile I'd pulled from the Crack toward him. "These are it. Read them. These are my childhood, apparently. Whatever the hell that means."

My eyes watered. I took a second to get on an even keel before I spoke again, wiping my eyes with my sleeve. I bumped my lip in the process, and my eyes watered that much more. "Ow. Shit." I sort of laughed and sort of cried and tried to find at least some semblance of dignity.

Diggs shook his head at me. "God, you're a mess," he said. He pushed everything aside for the moment and scooted closer to me. Gently pushed my hair back behind my ears and held my cheek in his cool, soothing hand. "What the hell am I gonna do with you, Solomon?"

A couple of tears broke loose and tracked down my cheeks. "I trust you more than anyone in my life. More than anyone I've ever known," I said. "It scares the shit out of me, how much I trust you. I'm not holding out on you because of that."

"Then *why*?"

He sat back, giving me space. I scratched the back of my head and tried to figure out how to explain the cluster fuck that was my past. "I spent so many years telling you the fairytale version—what I thought was real. And now I've got this brain-meld thing in my head, scrambling everything. But if I tell you the whole truth…" I stopped again. My vision blurred.

Diggs slid his hand over mine.

"What?" he asked. "You think what happened changes who you are now? I know you, kid. I know you better than myself—every flaw, every hair trigger, every obsession. This," he nodded to the letters, "doesn't change a goddamn thing. The only thing that changes any of it is if you keep shutting me out."

"I still don't know how to talk about it," I said.

"That's okay."

I hesitated. Swallowed past the heart-sized lump in my throat. "But I'll try. You want to know what happened to my friend? What Isaac did?" I kept myself carefully apart from him as I settled in bed. Diggs took off his shoes and his sweatshirt, and got under the covers beside me. "This is what I remember."

•

"He's getting closer," Will whispers to me.

I don't know how long we've been hiding in the Crack, but it's getting dark outside. Isaac keeps talking to us, standing out there somewhere, waiting for us. He quotes Bible verses to us. Tells us how families don't keep secrets from each other. My legs are numb from holding myself up so long, while we stay suspended toward the top of the rocks. Allie is leaning on Will—he's practically holding her up, to keep her from falling down that long stretch to the bottom of the Crack. She's stopped crying, but I can hear her sniffle when it gets quiet.

It's been quiet too long now.

"I think he left," Allie says.

"Sssh," Will says. "He didn't. He's still out there, I can tell. He's waiting for us."

"We can't stay here forever," she whispers.

"Allie, be quiet," I hiss. "We'll go when it's safe."

"If we just tell him…"

Will takes hold of her arm. "We can't tell him anything, Al," he whispers. I've never seen him so serious. "He can't find out. This is our place, not his. You have to promise."

I'm surprised when she doesn't start to cry again. Instead, she nods. She's serious, too. "I won't tell. I promise."

We wait forever. It's dark before Will finally agrees that we're safe, Isaac must have given up. We shimmy back down the rock. My legs have never hurt so bad. I have scrapes on my knees, scrapes on my elbows. I don't know what I'm going to tell my dad when he sees.

When we get to the bottom, Allie's the first one out. She's been quiet for a while now. I know Will thinks she'll go off and tell her mom or Isaac where we've been, but I know better. She might be a pain sometimes, but Allie never breaks a promise. If she said she won't tell, I know our secret's safe. Allie runs ahead on the path, but I stay behind and walk with Will. He slips his hand into mine.

A second later, he pulls me back from the path.

"We've been looking for you, Allie," I hear Isaac say. He's using his friendly voice—the one that makes you think you're his best friend. "Come on along. You missed dinner."

Will holds me back.

"Where are your friends?" Isaac asks.

"I was out here alone," Allie lies. She's the worst liar I've ever met. Her voice shakes, and she won't look you in the eye when she's lying. I think that's part of the reason she doesn't do it much.

"Oh, come on," Isaac says. He's still using his friendly voice. "I saw you leave with Will and Erin a little earlier. Where've you been all this time? You're getting so grown up these days—spending time with boys. Keeping secrets. What will I do with you, Alison Tate?"

She giggles when he uses her whole name. There's a lump in my stomach. Will won't let go of my hand.

"I was with Erin," Allie finally confesses. "And Will, for a little while. We were just taking a walk."

"I'm not comfortable with you two being alone with Will," Isaac says. "He's a troubled boy. There are things I haven't told you about him."

"Like what?" Allie asks.

Will's hand tightens around mine.

"I don't know if I should say," Isaac says. I don't like him talking about Will like this, but I can't help but want to hear what Isaac's saying. "Tell you what," he continues. "How about I tell you a secret, and you tell me your secret."

"I don't have a secret," Allie says immediately.

"I think you do," Isaac says. His voice is more dangerous now. Not so friendly. "The secret of where Will disappears sometimes. I think he took you there today."

"We just played in the woods."

"I don't believe you, Alison. You know it's not right to lie. God doesn't save liars—no matter how pretty they might be."

Will and I creep forward, getting closer and closer. My heart is pounding. Will's hand is still in mine, holding me back.

"I'm not lying," Allie whispers.

We can see them through the trees. It's nighttime, but the moon is so full that it shines almost like sunlight. Allie and Isaac look white in the glow. They're in a clearing with trees all around them. Isaac has his hand on Allie's arm. She looks up at him. Her glasses sparkle in the moonlight.

"Allie," Isaac says. He kneels down in front of her, so they're face to face. He still has hold of her arm. He whispers something that I can't hear. She shakes her head. Whimpers. Isaac touches her chin. Allie flinches.

I start to say something, but Will puts his hand over my mouth. He shakes his head at me. Puts a finger to his lips. We have to stay quiet.

"Please," Isaac says, like he's asking a favor. Like he wants more dessert, or to stay up past his bedtime. "Alison… Aren't we friends? Good friends?"

She shakes her head again, and I can see her start to cry. I look at Will. He's shaking, his fingers digging into my hand.

"Don't cry," Isaac soothes. He pulls Allie closer, and wraps her in his arms. She tries to get away, but he just pulls her tighter.

I start to say something, but Will puts his hand over my mouth again. Allie squirms, then she fights. She kicks Isaac in the shin and tries to run.

Isaac roars. I fight Will, trying to make him let me go so I can do something, but he won't let go. Isaac is a lion come to life—I know he'll eat all of us, every one, if we try to stop him. Still, I fight.

"Ssh," Will says in my ear. "Please, Erin. Stop. He'll kill us." He's crying. I nod. We keep hiding.

Isaac grabs Allie by her braid and pulls her back to him. She falls, hard, and I can tell that she sees us when she hits the ground. She screams. Her leg is hurt. I can feel Will shivering beside me, his arms wrapped around me tight.

Isaac puts his hand over Allie's mouth.

Will stays beside me. We don't move. We just lay in the bushes, quiet, and we see everything.

We stay there until Isaac goes away.

Isaac leaves, but Allie doesn't move again.

•

I spread the Polaroids across the bedspread for Diggs to see: me at eight years old, blurry and out of focus, tongue out. Smiling.

Will, making funny faces on the rock.

Allie, giggling, her eyes crossed behind her glasses and her tongue out.

Church services. Isaac with a whip in his hand. A woman on her knees in front of him.

Allie, on the ground.

Will had pictures of everything.

I got up and left the room. I coud hear Diggs behind me, but he didn't say anything. Einstein followed me down the stairs and out the front door. The vice tightened at my temples, until it felt like my head would pop. My blood had frozen in my veins.

"Isaac loves us, Erin," my father says. "He loves you. We've never been so safe, so loved, as we are out here."

I found a nearby shrub, got on my knees, and threw up. I kept going until my stomach was empty. When I stood, Diggs was waiting for me. He wrapped me in his arms and held me for a long time, swaying, his hand cradling the back of my head.

"You ready to go inside?" he asked, finally. "I think if you don't lose your toes to frostbite tonight, you must be made of stainless steel."

I nodded.

We walked in with his arm draped over my shoulder, Einstein beside us. Cameron was waiting when we got inside. A look passed between him and Diggs.

"We're going to bed for a couple hours," Diggs said to him. "But in the morning, we need to talk."

Cameron barred the way. "I'm sorry. It can't wait any longer—I've been as patient as I can be, but there's more to consider than whatever's going on between the two of you."

"Forget it," Diggs said. "We've got our plan. Everything else waits till morning."

He kept his arm around me and pushed past Cameron.

When we got back to the bedroom, I rinsed out my mouth while Diggs packed everything up and cleared it off the bed. It took some serious effort before I was able to pull myself back, for any number of reasons—not the least of which was that it felt like my skull was caving in. Diggs was doing his best not to look completely freaked out, but it was a hard sell. I smiled. Sort of.

"You still say this doesn't change anything?" I said.

Her didn't say anything. Instead, he pulled back the covers and nodded for me to get in. I did. He turned off the light and got in after me. It was 5:30 a.m. on the last day of the year. Diggs pulled me into his arms once we were under the blankets.

"Are you sorry I told you?" I asked.

He pulled back so he could look at me. "I'm sorry it happened. I'm sorry you had to see it. I'll never be sorry when you talk to me."

"I don't know what to do with it now," I said. "All the images. The story. It just keeps replaying in my head. Why didn't we do something?"

"Because he would have killed you, too," Diggs said. He brushed the hair back from my forehead. I was so tired. Tired to the ninetieth power. Cubed. "You were a little kid, Sol. You couldn't have saved her. You couldn't have saved Will. You couldn't have saved any of them."

My eyes watered. "I could have tried, though. Or Will could have. Why didn't he ever tell his uncle? When I talked to Jed a couple of years ago, he said Will was always angry, never quite right after his dad died. Jed saw both Will and his mom—"

Diggs put his finger to my lips. "Solomon," he whispered. "Stop."

"If you were smart, you'd run. Far," I whispered back.

He moved his finger, and kissed me gently on my bruised lips. "Then I'm an idiot, because I'm not running. I love you." He wrapped me up in his arms.

I thought of Will Colby—the boy I remembered

perfectly now. A fiery, cocky kid who kept me safe—who kept our secrets, all that time. A kid who died waiting for me to remember him.

"What are we going to do about tomorrow?" I asked. The words came out muffled by Diggs' chest. "Or today, I guess."

"I don't know yet."

"Do you still think Cameron's lying to us?"

"I don't know," he said again. I started to speak one more time. He leaned in and kissed the tip of my nose. Then, he kissed my right eyelid. My left.

"Solomon," he said. "Close your eyes. You've done enough, for now."

I closed my eyes.

Make it through the Crack and we'll live forever, Allie and Will whispered to me.

18

JACK WOKE FROM MORE DREAMS that morning, these more vivid than he'd had before. He lay in bed in the dark afterward, his heart beating hard, and tried to sort through everything he'd seen. Everything he remembered.

Guyana was clear now—too clear. He remembered the heat, the smells, the feel of his mother lying on top of him among a mass of bodies. Despite how young he'd been, the memories came rushing back.

It was the rest of his childhood that eluded him. The family in Guyana who took him in. Dexter Mandrake, raising him. That was all just blank space, with the occasional nonsensical image or soundbyte to interrupt a timeline that otherwise remained a mystery.

Why couldn't he remember anything about Mandrake? Those were the years that should be the most vivid, especially as he got older.

You have a home here, Jackie. You'll always have a home here.

He remembered a woman's voice. A kind voice. Whoever she was, he had liked her. Mandrake's wife? Had he thought of that woman as his mother?

It was five-thirty, still dark outside. New Year's Eve. He thought he'd heard voices and slamming doors in the night, but he had been too tired to rouse himself. Now, the house was quiet, his room cold. His bladder full to bursting. That was enough to motivate him to get up, but if it hadn't been, he knew he also had a six a.m. shift to watch the monitors for Cameron.

Despite the thermal long underwear he'd borrowed from Bear, it was cold outside the covers. Shivering, he pulled on a second layer and headed for the stairs. Even as he reached the first floor, thoughts of his past continued: a jungle in Guyana. A dark-skinned woman who had been his mother. And then, the family he didn't remember. Plural—families. All of them dead now.

At the bottom of the stairs, he paused to peer into the alcove where Cameron had set up his security equipment.

"I'll be ready in ten minutes," Jack said. "Let me just freshen up, get some coffee."

"No need," Cameron said. "I've got this."

The man's eyes were bloodshot, his face gaunt.

"You should sleep," Jack argued.

"Not today," Cameron said with a shake of his head. "Go on. I think the woman's up—Jamie. Find out if she needs anything before she leaves."

Jack went out the front for a pit stop in the outhouse—not his favorite part of island living—and then went around the side and back in through the kitchen. The room was still dark, barely lit by a lantern on the small kitchen table. Jamie was seated there alone. For the first time since he'd met her, she looked unwell. Pale. Vulnerable—a word he didn't readily associate with Jamie Flint.

She looked up when he came through the door, but she didn't appear surprised. "Up and out already?" she asked.

"The facilities were calling," he said. "Such as they are."

She grimaced. "We'll get plumbing out here this spring, I hope. One of my top priorities."

"No more sun showers?"

"Not if I can help it." She shrugged. "Not that it's that bad. It could always be worse, right?"

"It could," he agreed. He stepped farther into the room. Jamie wore a sweater and fleece pajama pants. A notebook and pen were set in front of her, beside a steaming mug of what looked like tea, from where he was standing.

She closed the notebook when he took a step closer.

"I can heat up some more water," she said, following his gaze. She started to stand, but he lay his hand on her shoulder, gently keeping her in place. He felt the muscle beneath his hand, the strength. It was surprising just how much he didn't want to remove his hand, after that scant contact had been made.

"Stay," he said. "I can do it."

He got water on the stove, and poured himself a bowl of granola cereal from the cupboard. He found a mug with a grinning pit bull on it, emblazoned with the words *Every Day is a Bully Day,* and set a tea bag inside.

All the while, he felt Jamie's eyes on him.

"Did you sleep all night?" she asked when he sat down.

"I did, actually. For the first time in a while." He took in her appearance, the shadows beneath her eyes. "I'm guessing you can't say the same."

"We had some activity in the night," she agreed. "Everyone's fine, but we were concerned for a while there."

"What happened?"

She smiled faintly. "I'll let Diggs and Erin explain. I only have part of the story."

At the fatigue in her eyes, he let it go.

Jamie finished her own cereal while Jack ate his. They sat in companionable silence, Jack still sorting through the images from his past.

"When are you leaving?" he finally asked, pulling himself back to the woman beside him.

"Shortly—another hour or so. Carl's packing the boat now." The way she said it made him curious, though he didn't ask the question that came to mind. Jamie smiled. "We're not together."

"I didn't say anything," Jack said.

"I know. But you wondered… Carl and I are friends. That's all."

"And he's okay with that?"

"He's fine with it," she said. It was clear the subject was closed to further discussion. "So, when will you head to the mainland with the others?"

He considered pursuing his previous question, but Jamie clearly had no intention of discussing it. "That depends on the others—and how long it takes them to recover from whatever it is that happened last night."

Jamie sipped her tea and leaned back in her chair, considering this. Outside, it was still black as night. Jack wondered what the hell Erin and Diggs had gotten themselves into this time. He felt a twinge of guilt for not being there to help them.

When Jamie had finished her breakfast, she stood and took her dishes to the sink. She took the boiling water from the tea kettle and filled the basin with it, adding dish liquid from a small, clear glass pitcher on the windowsill. Jack watched her for a moment before he got up to join her, bringing his own bowl and plate with him. He took the dishcloth from her, and nudged her gently out of the way with his hip. She nudged him back, hanging on to the dishcloth.

"You don't need to help," she said.

"I'm a guest—of course I need to help. Consider it payment for the haircut."

She glanced at him, working to suppress a grin. "You wash, I'll dry?"

"That's fair."

They worked in silence for a long time before Jamie glanced at him again. "What will you do?" Jack had been lost in thought, considering all the mysteries locked in his head. He pulled himself back again. "When this is all over," Jamie clarified. "After you've taken down the organization? Will you go back to the FBI?"

He considered the question. "I'm not sure they'll take me back—that's assuming I survive."

"God forbid you approach this mission with a little optimism but, yes… Yeah, Jack. Assuming you live."

Seconds passed, while he contemplated his life without J. The sink was empty, the water only lukewarm now. "I don't know what I'll do," he finally admitted. "I haven't really given it much thought."

When he looked at her, Jamie was studying him. He couldn't read her expression. "Maybe you should start thinking," she said. "There's a whole wide world out there, Jack. If you start considering what you could have rather than what you've lost, you might be surprised how much incentive it'll give you to actually come out of this thing alive. And move on, one of these days."

She dried the last of the dishes and put them neatly in the cupboard, her back to him. Jack stood at the sink and watched her; tried to imagine the world she spoke of, with J. behind him. The picture was even hazier than the dreamlike visions of his past.

At seven o'clock, Jamie went up to Diggs' and Erin's room while Jack remained in the meeting room. A few minutes later, Jamie returned with Einstein. Neither Diggs nor Erin were in sight.

"Erin's not coming down?" Jack asked, surprised.

"She said goodbye upstairs. It was a rough night—I don't think she's up for public…anything, right now. You mind walking us to the boat?"

"Of course. The fresh air would be nice."

"Even if it's freezing fresh air?"

"Better than staying in." To his surprise, he meant it. Being trapped in the old house was starting to get to him—right now, anything seemed better than four walls in a drafty house with too many secrets.

With the sun up and the sky gray behind it, Jack walked Jamie to the boat, a very unhappy Einstein alongside. The dog whimpered unhappily, straining at the leash to get back to Erin. Jamie murmured sympathetically, scratching the dog's ears as they continued the trek.

When they reached the dock, Jack helped load the last remaining luggage and gear onto the boat while the engine idled.

"So, it looks like this is goodbye again," Jamie said.

For reasons he preferred not to explore, Jack disliked the idea more than he should. "It does."

She hesitated for a moment before she spoke again, her eyes holding his through the silence. "Do me a favor? Just keep an eye on Cameron, please. I can't shake the feeling that there's something going on with him—something he's not telling you."

"I think he truly wants to destroy J.," Jack said, surprised at the request. "And the number of times over the years that he's saved my life…"

"I know," she agreed. "It's not that. I can't explain it. I just… There's something not right."

He frowned. They stood a foot apart on the dock, the black sea choppy around them. He thought again of her lips on his cheek in Coba.

"We'll be careful," he promised. "You do the same. When's the storm supposed to blow in?"

"Sometime this afternoon. I should be outrunning it, though. I'll be safe in Caribou by the time it hits that area. Keep watch on the weather yourselves—you'll need to figure out whether you want to be on the mainland or the island, probably by four or five this afternoon. You won't be able to travel safely back and forth after that."

"We'll figure it out."

"I'm sure you will." She glanced back at the boat. "Well—I should go. Be safe, Jack."

"You too."

There was no kiss this time. No hug. She didn't touch him at all, as a matter of fact. Jack stood on the dock and watched as Carl helped her load the dog into the boat, then hold her hand as she stepped over the rail easily herself. Einstein followed them into the pilothouse, still whining unhappily.

Jack remained at the dock, cold wind buffeting around him, until they were just an indiscernible spot on a darkening horizon.

It was after eight a.m. when Jack returned to the house, refreshed after a full night's sleep and some time alone in the fresh air. He found Monty seated at the kitchen table nursing his coffee, his head down. He looked like hell.

"Am I the only one who got any sleep last night?" Jack asked. He took a seat across from him at the table.

"It's a safe bet," Monty said. "Carl and Jamie gone?" Jack nodded. "Did Cameron fill you in on what went down?"

"No. And Jamie said I should wait for Diggs' and Erin's version."

"No need," Monty said. "I was there for the whole damned thing. Our favorite little leprechaun pulled quite a stunt." Usually easygoing, it was clear this time that he didn't approve. He took a sip of coffee before he elaborated. "Erin took off in the middle of the night—it was my shift at the monitors. Next thing I know, I see her headed off into the woods with her mutt. Then the hot blond shows up—Diggs and I got there just in time to interrupt a pretty severe beat-down. Though the redhead was holding her own, I'll give her that."

"Wait," Jack said. He sorted through the information. "Jenny showed up again?"

"Damn right she did," Monty said. "And I don't care how sweet that piece of tail looks, that bitch is dangerous. And nuts to boot. She took off with something, and didn't seem too keen to let it go anytime soon."

"What?" Jack asked.

Before they could answer, the kitchen door opened and Diggs came in with Cameron. If the others looked like they hadn't slept the night, Diggs looked like he hadn't slept in a week. Which, Jack reflected, was probably true.

Diggs closed the door behind him. "I assume we're talking about last night," he said.

"What in hell was Erin doing?" Jack asked. "Or thinking, for that matter?"

"Excellent question," Cameron muttered. He poured himself some coffee from the pot, then leaned back against the sideboard rather than join the others.

Diggs scrubbed a hand over his eyes and sat. "You know her—she got an idea in her head, and she decided it would be best for her to follow it through on her own. It's a long story. Epic, actually. But the gist is that she's remembering some things." He looked at Cameron.

"What things?" Cameron asked.

"Things about the Payson Church. And, specifically, Isaac Payson."

"She found something last night, didn't she?" Cameron said.

Diggs didn't answer, his gaze still level with Cameron's. Instead, he had his own questions.

"What the hell is going on? Why are we here? Why are *you* here? You might care about Solomon, but you don't give a rat's ass about Littlehope or this island. Why does J.? What possible role could Payson Isle play in anything they're doing now?"

"I told you," Cameron said. "It plays no role. I came here because I saw Erin's message and surmised from there that you had come here. And that you, in all likelihood, could use some help."

Diggs frowned. Jack tried to read Cameron, to try and determine whether he was lying. He seemed sincere, though. And how many times had the man saved his life over the years? And saved Diggs and Erin, on top of that?

"Let's say that is true," Jack said. "What's this about Erin finding something on the island? What is she remembering?"

"It's up to her to tell you that," Diggs said, his face a grim mask. "All I'll say is that there was a reason her father buried her memories of this place, and Isaac Payson was a hell of a lot darker than she remembered until last night."

"And what she found was proof of that?" Cameron asked.

The kitchen door opened again. Erin limped in, clearly in pain. She had what appeared to be a small stack of photos in her hand.

"Gang's all here, I see," Erin said. "Let's head for the meeting room—I can brief you there, where there's more room to spread out."

Diggs got up, poured another mug of coffee, and handed it to Erin. "You should have slept in," Jack heard him say.

"I'll sleep when I'm dead," she replied. "Which, considering how things are going, might not be too far from now."

After he'd had a moment to take in her appearance, Jack relaxed incrementally. Compared with battles Erin had had in the past, it appeared the damage was minor—all he could see was a slight bruising at her jaw, her upper lip a little swollen. So the physical damage was minimal, at least. Based on the way Diggs was watching her, Jack assumed the emotional toll had been far greater.

They filed into the meeting room after Erin, and the five of them settled in at the table.

"Shouldn't someone be watching the monitors?" Jack asked.

Cameron frowned.

"I'll go," Monty volunteered. "Just give me the bullets later."

He left for the alcove, while the others waited for someone

to begin. Finally, Erin started by laying the Polaroids out on the table between them.

"I found these in a hiding spot an old friend of mine had when we were kids," Erin said.

Cameron stood and leaned in to get a better view of the photos. "These are from the Payson Church," he said.

"They are."

Jack paused at sight of a photo of a silver-haired man with a switch in one hand. A woman, naked from the waist up, was on her knees in front of him.

"This is Isaac Payson?" he asked.

"Yeah," Erin said. She looked profoundly uncomfortable. "Nice, right? Clearly, my memories up till now have been a little off."

"You remember everything now, then?" Cameron asked.

"Not everything, I don't think. But the highlights."

"Such as?" Cameron prompted. It seemed to Jack that the man was fishing for something specific.

"I'll get to that in a minute," Erin said. "First, Jenny said something that I'm having a hard time getting out of my head. Something about you not telling me the whole truth—that I was looking for the right team, but the wrong players. What's she talking about?"

Jack thought he detected a flicker of annoyance as it crossed Cameron's face, but it vanished too quickly to be certain.

"She's lying," Cameron said. "Plain and simple."

"That's it?" Erin said doubtfully. "Your kid's full of shit—that's your story?"

"She said it to drive a wedge between you and me," Cameron said, his focus still on Erin. "She's always been jealous of you and your mother. In her mind, you are the reason our family fell apart—which is absurd, I realize. She told you I was keeping secrets because she knew it would make you distrust me." He paused, studying her for a moment. "Clearly, she succeeded."

Jack went over the information he'd already gleaned while Erin processed what Cameron had said.

"Diggs asked earlier why you're here," Jack said, interrupting what appeared to be a standoff between Erin and Cameron. "I agree. Why is this mission in Maine so important to J.? And what difference could these photos from the Payson Church possibly make to them? The preacher and the entire congregation are dead, except for Erin." He paused. "Right?"

"Of course," Cameron said tersely. "You've seen the coroner's reports. I was here for the event—believe me, I know the extent of the damage. Honestly, these photos have no bearing on anything. But if Erin is remembering her past, then she might remember something her father said that could lead us to J. now."

"He wasn't even in J. when I was here," Erin insisted. "So why the hell would he have been talking about future plans with the organization? It was over twenty years ago."

"It's a long shot," Cameron admitted. He studied Erin with what Jack thought appeared to be a trace of guilt. "Just keep thinking about it. If something occurs, let me know. And in the meantime…"

"In the meantime, what?" Jack said. "We still honestly have no idea what J.'s next move will be. And we don't have a clue where Jenny will strike next."

Cameron took a moment before he spoke again. He stood, and walked away from the table. By the time he'd returned, the conflict Jack had seen earlier in his eyes seemed to have resolved itself. For the first time, the man seemed utterly clear on his next step.

"Which is why it's best you leave now," he said. "I've given this a great deal of thought over the course of the past few hours. I want you to go. Leave the island. Leave Littlehope. Stay clear of here until I can talk to Jenny. Enjoy New Year's Eve—just do it somewhere else."

"Wait just a minute," Erin said, her temper flaring. "You can't send us away now. You said last night this was our window to figure things out. Why would we leave town now? We could actually make some progress."

"Or you could get yourself killed," Cameron said. "It's a wonder you didn't when you pulled that idiotic stunt in the middle of the night. Jenny will be furious when she realizes she doesn't have everything she was after—"

"Who says she'll even *know* she doesn't have everything?" Erin countered. "She didn't know where the box was—it didn't seem like she had a clue what the hell was in it."

"She'll know," he said. "I don't want to argue with you about this, Erin. You need to go."

"How has what happened last night changed anything?" she asked. "We had a plan. Why do we have to change that now?"

"Because Jenny will be looking for you," he said unequivocally. "She'll be after what you have. And with everything she's set in motion here, I'm not sure my assumption that J. will stay away was completely accurate."

"You seriously think they'd come here now?" Diggs said. He'd been curiously quiet up to this point. Now, there was fathomless dread in his tone.

"There's a possibility that they would do more than that..." Cameron said. He stopped. Jack waited impatiently for him to complete his thought. He thought again of all the voices in his head; all those memories he couldn't access. Everything Cameron had taken.

"Do more than what?" Jack prompted. "Jenny has killed their operatives. There's a blizzard coming in a few hours. They aren't scheduled to do anything until April—why would they risk coming here now?"

Cameron didn't speak, his gaze fixed on the table.

"The timetable we have is right though, isn't it?" Erin said. The same tension had crept into her voice. "I mean, the whole bit about them doing something in April. That's what we have on the list—so far, they've been pretty freaking devoted to that thing."

"They may need to reevaluate, this time," Cameron said finally.

"Reevaluate meaning what?" Erin said.

Whole seconds rolled past with no answer, while Cameron continued to stare pointedly at the table.

"Answer her, damn it!" Jack said. Frustration rose in his blood.

Cameron turned cool blue eyes on him. "Knowing J. as I do, they'll want to send a message," he said. "To make it clear that trying to disrupt their plans will come to no good—that it, in fact, will only make things worse."

"How would they do that?" Diggs asked.

Cameron looked at Erin. "If I were them, I would choose a date when I could make the most impact, and I would do it when those going up against me least expected it."

"New Year's Eve," Jack said.

"What?" Erin said. "What do you mean, New Year's Eve? You're saying they'll hit tonight? But we still don't have a target. And there's a blizzard. And their gunmen are dead."

"I've told you before," Cameron said. "J. plans for contingencies. If the gunmen are dead, either they'll have someone else in place, or the team leader is responsible for seeing the plan through themselves."

"Meaning Lilah Waters could come here," Jack said. "The woman in charge of this mission: LW." The same woman who had murdered Lucia.

"It's possible," Cameron said. "You see now why I want you gone?"

"I'm not leaving," Erin said. "Especially not if J.'s hitting Maine to potentially blow up my hometown. Screw that. We came this far to do something—now we finally have a plan, I'm not about to scrap it now. Anyone else who wants to go, I wouldn't blame you in the slightest." She looked at Diggs. Her voice quieted; Jack detected a near-apology in her tone, or as close as Erin ever came. "But I'm not leaving until I see this thing through. I can't."

Jack didn't hesitate. "I feel the same way. I'm here until the end."

Diggs thought for a moment. He looked at Erin, and Jack felt certain he was contemplating what they could face in the next several hours—everything that could go wrong. He took a long, deep breath before he nodded. "Yeah. I'm staying."

"That's the plan, then?" Cameron said. He didn't look happy. "You stay to face J.—whatever they may have in store."

"That's the plan," Diggs said. "We'll go to the mainland just like we'd planned, and see what we can do to figure things out. We'll chat up the locals, ask some questions—which just happens to be what Solomon and I do best."

Silence fell over the table. Jack thought of Lucia again—

liquid brown eyes watching him, the infectious laughter that had transported him from the time they first met. And then, he considered the fact that the woman behind her death could be this near, after all this time. There was nothing that would keep him from following through on this now.

"All right, then," Jack said. "It seems we have a plan. I say we get it done."

Before they could rise, Erin stayed them with a wave of her hand. "I just—I'm not going to make a big speech or anything, but I did want to say thanks for watching my back through all this…" She looked at Cameron. "I still don't understand exactly what role you've played all these years, and I know you've got secrets you're not sharing, but you've saved every one of us more than once. That has to count for something." She looked at Jack, then Diggs, and took a long, slow breath. "And… Hell, I don't know. If you guys would consider an alternative lifestyle, I think the three of us would make the perfect couple, so…" She looked away, eyes tearing, and cleared her throat. "Thanks. That's all. And, you know—don't die today. Or anytime soon."

Her cheeks were flaming by the time she'd finished. Jack went to her after Cameron had filed out and only she and Diggs remained. He tipped her chin up and tilted her face to the side, as much for the contact as the illusion that he was checking her injuries.

"Are you all right?" he asked.

She rolled her eyes. "What do you think?" There was less bite than usual in the tone, the words edged with profound fatigue. "I'm alive, though. That's something. What about you? Are you remembering anything else?"

"Not really," Jack said. He frowned. "What was it like? All of it rushing back like that?"

"Honestly?" she said. "It really sucked."

19

IT WAS ALMOST THREE O'CLOCK by the time Jack, Monty, Diggs, and I reached the mainland that New Year's Eve. No flakes were flying yet, but the sky was pure gray and the wind was already up. Eighteen to twenty-four inches of fluffy white stuff were predicted for the night, combined with high winds and record low temperatures. Cameron had insisted he'd take his own boat and meet us on the mainland within a couple of hours, but it made me nervous being separated from him that late in the game. I was grateful to be off the island, but there was no way in hell we'd get back to Cameron if it turned out he needed us.

Despite the fact that Diggs and I had managed to fit in a mid-morning nap, I was feeling far from daisy fresh. Beyond the exhaustion and the residual ches and pains from my run-in with Jenny, I kept getting little flashes of my past on Payson Isle. The hit list included Allie's death and my father locking me in that closet, but I was also remembering a whole lot more about my interactions with Isaac Payson. I'd said all along that I didn't think my father had ever allowed Isaac to do anything to me, and I actually still stood by that. But I got the feeling that the interactions Isaac and

I did have over the years were far from harmless.

Add to that the fact that I'd had to say goodbye to Einstein again that morning, and Morrissey could have been mistaken for a Mouseketeer next to me.

"You're quiet," Diggs said as we approached Bennett's Lobster Shanty. "You okay?"

"I'm tired," I said. "And my head hurts. And my childhood was a horrifying sham filled with bloodshed and violent death. Plus, my dog's gone again."

"So that's a no, then?"

I leaned into him and closed my eyes with a semi-tortured laugh. "I will be, I think. Assuming we survive the next twenty-four hours."

He kissed my temple. "That's the assumption I'm going with."

The parking lot at Bennett's had already started to fill. Diggs and I came in alone—Jack and Monty were pursuing their own leads and would join us later, since Diggs and I would most likely get more information about the goings-on around town if we were on our own.

Though it was late afternoon, the lighting was dim inside the Shanty, smoked-glass windows obscured by red pepper lights twined around a heavy fishing net suspended from the ceiling. A woman I recognized as Mimi Bennett, matriarch of the Bennett clan, was behind the bar when we came through the door. She just gave me the hairy eyeball, but she broke into a grin the second she caught sight of Diggs.

"Oh my gawd," she said, that rich Maine rhythm present in even those three words. She came out from behind the bar and pulled Diggs into a hug, though she barely reached his broad shoulders, then pushed him away and slapped him on the chest. "Where in blazes have you been? You blow up Kat's house, steal Mel's truck—she's still pissed about that, by the way, so you might want to keep your head down round here—and just leave that house of yours to rot."

She drew up short, as though suddenly remembering. "I'm sorry about your dad, hon. 'Course, I always thought he was an uptight prick—never did understand how swimmers from a man like that could turn into a boy like you."

She stood back and looked him up and down, as though to illustrate the point. "You look good. Beat as hell, but I guess that's to be expected. But tan. Buff. Like you been working out, living the good life. You finally come back here to make an honest woman of me?"

He laughed. "I've told you before, Mimi. You're too much woman for me." He draped his arm around my shoulders and pulled me into the space Mimi was dominating at the moment.

She looked at me for the first time, taking in my puffy lip and the fist-sized bruise on my jaw with a single keen glance. "Jesus, Erin. Who'd you get on the wrong side of this time, girl?"

"It's a long story," I said.

"What'd you do with your mother, anyway? Her house blows up, her girlfriend, partner, whatever you want to call it, up and leaves town, Diggs disappears… And last time you spent too much time around here, Matt Perkins and Joe Ashmont wound up dead. Seems like maybe you're a dangerous woman to keep around."

"Easy, Mimi," Diggs cautioned. "She'll put a hex on you, too."

I glared at him. He grinned back at me. It felt good—almost normal.

"So what's going on with your mum?" Mimi persisted. "Her and Maya kept this place afloat last winter, coming in for dinners half the week. Both of 'em were shit drinkers, but Maya was about the best tipper we ever had in this town. She still swings by every now and then, does a check-in at the clinic. I ain't seen hide nor hair of Kat, though."

"She's fine," I said. "She's on vacation."

The woman eyed me wisely. "Sure she is. All right, set down over in the corner there. You eat meat, or are you some damned veggie-tarian like Diggs?"

"No, I'm a carnivore. But I'm not—"

"Crabmeat," she announced. "I made a crabmeat quiche, just come out of the oven. Should I get you a basket of carrots to munch on or what, hon?" she asked Diggs.

"You still have those veggie burgers back there for me?"

"They might be a little freezer burned, but I've got 'em."

"Good. Basket of curly fries to share, and a veggie burger. Crabmeat quiche for my girl here."

"To drink?" she asked, not bothering to write anything down.

Diggs ordered his usual Coke, and I did the same on the assumption that if J. blew into town in hte next few hours, I would want to be moderately sober. Then, we obeyed Mimi's order—it sure as hell hadn't been a suggestion—and started for a table in the corner. At the last second, Diggs nodded toward a booth farther down. I caught sight of an older man in the booth next to it, though Diggs didn't say hello.

Diggs sank back on the bench opposite me. I took a second to study him, something I hadn't done enough of these past few days. Mimi was right: he did look tired, the usual spark in his blue eyes fallen flat. Diggs adapts well, can blend anywhere, but on the beaches of Australia, under the sun, able to stay in motion and escape those slow-killing daily strictures other men seem to handle so well… That's when he shined. He didn't look nearly so shiny now.

"So, enough about me," I said before he could ask for the thousandth time how I was doing. "How are you holding up in all this?"

"I'm okay," he said.

"Are you?"

He leaned forward and reached across the table to take my hand. "I've got you, my health, and a cold Coke and a freezer-burned veggie burger on the way. What else could I possibly need?"

"Jesus. Same old sweet talker," a gruff voice said from the next booth. Diggs smiled. He didn't look concerned, never loosening his grip on my hand.

"That's what I hate about this place, Sol," he said, raising his voice only slightly. "You try to have a private conversation with your girl, and you've got jaded old farts listening in everywhere you turn."

He let go of me and stood. "Are you coming over here, or are you just gonna stay there and eavesdrop?"

And older man, white-haired and sunworn, stood. I guessed him in his seventies, but still vital, rugged. I expected he'd been a real knockout back in the day; the years had done little to alleviate the appeal. Diggs ignored the hand he proffered and pulled him into a hug.

"I'm sorry about the reverend," the man said as they parted. "Godless son of a bitch that I am, I never had much use for him—but it's never easy to lose your folks."

"No," Diggs said. He looked uncomfortable for a second before he not-so-subtly changed the subject. "Bill, this is Erin Solomon. Erin, Bill Slater. Bill runs the smokehouse up the road, and about a dozen others around the country."

"Half a dozen," Bill corrected.

"Eleven," Diggs countered. Bill didn't argue. "Join us?"

"I don't want to intrude."

Diggs rolled his eyes. "Sit down, Bill. You already order?"

"Mimi knows what I'm having. It'll be here soon." Diggs returned to his seat and Bill slid in beside him. He looked at both of us with the kind of shrewd gaze that I expected missed little. "You here to put your old man to rest?"

"We were already in town," Diggs said. "Staying out on Payson Isle."

He looked surprised. "Been keeping a low profile, I guess."

"Trying to," Diggs said.

"Still, I'm surprised I didn't hear something, though— Lucy's tangled up with those dog people out on the island. She said she heard something about a pretty girl and a big blond oaf being in town. I should've done the math."

"Lucy's Bill's wife," Diggs explained. "It's hard to get much past her."

"You can't get anything past her," Bill corrected him. "I gave up trying a long time ago. So, what gives? What's the real reason you decided to brave the old port?"

"It's a long story," Diggs said. He hesitated, but only for a few seconds. "I was wondering something, though."

Bill raised his eyebrows when a couple of seconds had passed. "You plan on spitting it out, or wait till I die of suspense. Time's getting on—you probably won't have to wait long."

"Are you still active with the gun club?"

"Sure. What the hell else are you going to do around here if you can't shoot? And with the drug trade coming up the way it is, I figure it's best to keep on my game. Damn meth dealers keep creeping around our place. Why?"

"You know anyone around here who's a little...*too* into the guns? A little too enthusiastic?"

"It's a gun club, Diggs. We don't sit around and play bridge, for Christ's sake. Everybody's pretty into 'em."

"Then is there anybody around here who isn't in the gun club, but you'd think twice if you found out they were locked and loaded?" I asked.

He thought for a second, more reserved now that I was asking the questions. Scratched his beard. Adjusted his glasses. "Other than Mike Reynolds? Nobody who comes to mind."

"What happened out at his place the other day wasn't a surprise then," Diggs said.

"You kidding me? Everybody knew it was only a matter of time with that son of a bitch. I'm just grateful the kids got out of there safe."

"You knew him," I said.

"Sure. Small town, you know how it goes. He came to the range every so often. Knew his guns, and he was a hell of a marksman." He paused, studying us both. "I guess I'm not supposed to ask what the hell's going on with you two."

"Long story," Diggs and I said at the same time. A flicker of a smile crossed Bill's face.

"Lucy and I do that all the time—you'll want to watch it. You won't have a thought safe from her," he said to Diggs, nodding to me.

"That ship sailed years ago," Diggs said.

Mimi brought us our food and stood by expectantly, arms crossed over her chest and head at a slight tilt—waiting to be proven right. I tried the crabmeat quiche, since it appeared I had no choice.

And then I tried it again.

"Oh my god."

"Told you," she said. "You thought I was kidding. Best crabmeat in the state."

"You're such a loser for being a vegetarian right now," I said to Diggs, in between bites.

He bit into his freezer-burned veggie burger without argument.

Things were quiet around the table for a while after Mimi left us. I'd devoured most of my quiche and half the curly fries before Bill spoke again.

"Official word is your old man was a hit and run," he said.

Diggs nodded, immediately serious. Nothing like vehicular manslaughter to kill the mood. "That's right. You know anything about it?"

The older man looked uncomfortable.

"It's all right," Diggs said. The way he looked, you'd almost think he was telling the truth. "I know he'd gone round the bend. Did you talk to him at all, these past few months?"

"No," Bill said with a shake of his head. "I told you, I was never much for the godly set."

Another couple of seconds passed before Diggs finally got around to the question I knew he'd wanted to ask all along.

"I don't suppose you know anything about this girl my father supposedly..." He trailed off awkwardly.

Bill looked down, his jaw hard. "I might know a thing or two. Laurie—that's the girl—is my oldest's goddaughter. Whole family's spent some time at our place over the years."

"What do you know about what happened?" Diggs asked.

"Not much. But there's more to the story than most people are telling, I know that. Something funny'd been going on with Laurie for a lot of years. Don't know that the reverend was at the root of it, but the girl was never quite..." He shifted uncomfortably.

"Never quite what?" Diggs pressed.

Bill met his eye. "She was always pretty damned... forward. With men, I mean. Couldn't have been more than twelve or so and she was at our place playing one day. She came over to me and I just...got this feeling." He shook his head. "I didn't like her playing with the other grandkids, after that. Especially the boys. She was precocious, maybe you could say. I don't think it was her fault, of course—Lucy tried to talk to Jake and Alice, but Jake's a stubborn son of a bitch. He built that company of his from the ground up, trucks his traps all over the goddamn country—now he thinks he's the man with all the answers. You ask me, most likely he was at the bottom of it from the get-go anyway."

"Are they in town now?" Diggs said.

Bill frowned. "I don't know."

I didn't even know the man, and I could still tell he was lying. Diggs just raised his eyebrows, waiting.

"You don't think they've seen enough trouble from Diggins men?" Bill said.

"I just want to talk to Laurie. I won't cause any trouble, I promise. But I need to know if my father said anything to her." He reached into his back pocket for his wallet. Bill waved him off.

"I've got it."

"That's all right," Diggs said.

"I've got it," Bill repeated, more firmly. "You really gonna fight with an old man? Just take care of yourselves. Let me know if there's anything I can do."

"Thanks, Bill," Diggs said sincerely. He clapped the man on the shoulder, then looked at me. "Ready?"

So much for dessert. "Aren't I always?"

Diggs didn't even smile, that weight fully returned to his shoulders. We said goodbye to Mimi and stepped into the cold air and gathering clouds of New Year's Eve in Littlehope.

We decided against the rental we'd gotten the other day, and instead Diggs and I walked the scant half mile it took to reach the Smiths' little ranch-style home, on a dead-end street off Littlehope's main strip. There were no cars in the driveway, though a Christmas tree still sparkled in the window. We paused at the end of the walk. I looked at Diggs.

"So, what's the plan? You just go up, knock, say 'I know my father was accused of diddling your little girl, but I was hoping you wouldn't mind if I spoke with her alone.'"

"You don't think that would work?"

I just tipped my head and waited for him to get serious.

Before he could, the Smiths' front door opened.

If there had been any ambiguity in Bill Slater's comment about Laurie Smith, his meaning was pretty clear the second I laid eyes on the girl.

With big blue eyes and a generous mouth, lush curves and thick dark lashes, Laurie Smith was a vision. Bill wasn't talking about her looks, though—the moment she sashayed out the door, barefoot, that was obvious. She wore torn jeans and a soft-pink camisole that showed…a lot. Including, but not limited to, a sizable hickey at her collarbone. She crooked her finger at Diggs, turned, switched her hair over her shoulder, and walked back inside.

Diggs glanced at me. He looked worried.

"I'd like to remind you, your daddy already tapped that," I said.

"Feeling insecure, are we?"

"Just making sure you keep thinking with the right head."

He smiled. "That head being yours?"

"Damn straight, sweet pea," I said. I hip checked him into motion.

The front door was still open when we got there. Laurie was nowhere in sight. I arched an eyebrow at Diggs. He shrugged. We crossed the threshold. Music—Otis Redding, actually—was playing down the hall. We followed the tune and eventually found Laurie swaying to the music, standing in front of a giant Christmas tree. She had a glass of wine in her hand. Or I guess it could have been grape juice, but I wouldn't bet the farm on it.

"My name's—" Diggs started when we got through the door.

"I know who you are," Laurie said. "You're Daniel. The bastard." She turned to face us. Her eyes were bright. Borderline manic.

"My father told you that?" Diggs said.

"Among other things," she said. She bridged the distance between herself and Diggs, and ran a long finger along his chest. "He didn't say how hot you were, though."

Diggs carefully removed her hand and took a step back. "I wanted to ask some questions about…what happened between you and my father."

"Sex," she said simply. "I mean…you have heard of it, haven't you? He was nice to me. Sometimes. Liked me on my knees—"

"Okay," I interrupted. I stepped in between her and Diggs before things got messy. "That's not really what we're after, but thanks for searing that visual into my brain. What we're asking is more about what the reverend might have talked to you about. And…how things got started."

"I liked him," she said. "He was always so sad. And lonely. And I started thinking one day—like, how long since he'd actually *done* anything, you know? A decade? Longer? What would it be like, to have him touch me? So, I stayed after one day—told him and my parents I was having a spiritual crisis."

"So it happened more than once," Diggs said.

"Sure," she said. "Every Tuesday and Saturday, starting last May."

Holy shit. I tried to get my head around that one. "And did you two ever…talk, at all?" I was almost afraid of the answer.

"What kind of question is that?" She flopped back in an easy chair in the corner, stretching her long legs over the arm. Closer now, in addition to the hickey I could see what looked like a handprint on her upper right arm, like someone had grabbed her—and not nicely. "We fucked twice a week for months. Of course we talked—what do you think I am?"

So, so many responses came to mind. I nearly bit my tongue off to keep quiet.

"When was the last time you spoke with him?" Diggs asked.

"We stopped after my parents freaked out. I sent him a couple of letters, but he never wrote back." I thought I glimpsed a trace of sadness, which she quickly stuffed away. "After the stroke, though, I didn't try again. I figured he probably had enough problems. I sent him a card, though."

She stopped and drained her wine, then studied the glass for a few seconds. "I didn't mean for it all to get so screwed up afterward, you know? I just… I didn't think my parents would find out."

"Sure," I said. "Because when you're getting boned by a preacher four times your age twice a week in a town of thirteen hundred people, what are the chances that kind of thing will get out?"

Diggs shot me a look that told me clearly I needed to work harder on the whole biting-my-tongue thing. Laurie was shooting daggers at me with her eyes. Against my better judgment, I gave her and Diggs some space.

"Did you ever meet at my father's house?" he asked.

"No—he didn't like me going there. We always met at the church. I thought that was hotter, anyway."

"Did he ever mention my brother when you were together?"

Laurie studied him. There was an unexpected glimmer of intelligence reflected in her eyes. "Yeah, he did. He talked about him a lot, actually. And I know he felt guilty about what we were doing, even when I tried to convince him it was okay… He always said his son and his wife dying were his punishment. God testing the flesh—and he kept failing."

"Did he say anything that made you think he might be violent?" I asked.

She laughed. "Are you kidding? He was the most violent man I ever met—that was part of what I liked about him. He was so intense. His eyes had blood in them, you know? Guys my age don't know what to do, they're all freaked out by what they want and what they think they should want. And guys your age—" she looked at Diggs, "act like it's your God-given right. A man like the reverend… He was grateful, and passionate, and twisted, and everything was so…big. Every kiss, every touch, every decision meant something."

Diggs turned away. I stayed with it, though. "So you say you two talked," I said. "And he was definitely aggressive. Did you get any sense that he was thinking of inflicting violence—hurting people?"

"You mean other than me?" Diggs' flinched at the words, his back still to her. She smiled at his reaction, her eyes following his every move. "He'd go on rants sometimes. But the only one he ever really wanted to hurt, so far as I could tell, was you."

"He told you he wanted to hurt me?" he said. He turned to face her.

I thought of that stupid picture again—Diggs at four, big blue eyes and white-blond hair, clinging to his mom's skirt. Barely part of their story.

"I know what it's like," she said to Diggs. She barely acknowledged me at all now. "Having parents who think you're Satan's spawn—like it never dawns on them that maybe the reason you're so screwed up has something to do with them. I knew when he talked about you that I wasn't getting the whole story."

"What did he say?" Diggs asked.

She shrugged. "Just your standard reverend talk, you know? He sinned, the devil punished him by sending you—a reminder of his wife whoring around or whatever."

"He told you he wasn't my father," Diggs clarified.

"Of course. Wait—you didn't know that?" Diggs shook his head silently. A storm settled in the girl's eyes. She looked genuinely troubled. "Sorry. But…yeah."

"What about the later months? After you guys stopped talking," I said, to get us back on track. "Do you know if he was in touch with anyone else?"

She thought for a minute. "I saw him around Mike a few times—like, we'd meet at the church, and Mike would show up. Or I'd get there and they'd be hanging out. Your dad always got worked up then—I actually thought a couple times he was on something, the way he acted after Mike left."

"Mike. Mike Reynolds, you mean?" I asked.

"Yeah, that's right."

"Did Mike know what was going on between you and my father?" Diggs asked.

"He caught us doing it in your dad's office once." She made a face. "The dickhead tried to blackmail your dad into getting me to have sex with him to keep quiet, but the reverend just got pissed. He got Mike to back down. Not very many people got to see just how much power your dad had, you know? How much passion."

"So you saw Mike and the reverend together," I said, once again steering the conversation back on track. "Were they ever with anyone else?"

"A woman," she said immediately. "A couple times when I wasn't there, and I got *pissed*, because I thought maybe Mike brought her so they could do the deed—like all three of them or something. And it's not like I would have said no if they just asked me—"

"Was that why she was there?" I interrupted, before we got into something I would never, ever unsee.

"Nope. At least, the reverend said it wasn't—anyway, she was old. No way your dad would have gone for her."

"How old?" Diggs asked. "Did you know her?"

"Never saw her before. And *old,* old. I don't know—it's hard to judge after a certain point. Like, at least forty."

That made me feel great about my thirty-three years on the planet. Laurie looked at me like she knew exactly what I was thinking. "A lot older than you. Black hair. Really dark eyes. Maybe Spanish, I think."

"Did he ever say her name?" I asked. "Or tell you what she was doing there?"

"Lilah," Laurie said. I made an effort not to react to the name, thinking of the J. team leader Cameron had talked about: Lilah Waters. "I remember because of the whole Samson and Delilah story, you know? And I overheard them, the only other time I saw her here—talking about revolutions and the end of the world and all that shit. It didn't make a lot of sense."

"That's all right," Diggs said. "It might make more sense to us. Just tell us what you remember."

"They mostly just talked about how godless Littlehope was. And how people needed to understand what was coming, you know? Your dad was really into the godless angle. I got the feeling Mike just wanted to blow some shit up. Talk about anger issues."

"Was there anywhere in particular it seemed like they thought was more godless than others?" I asked. I'd been wondering what the reverend's target would have been, if he'd lived. Or Mike's, for that matter.

"Bennett's," she said immediately. "And the paper. He *hated* that paper—the *Trib?* He used to go on these crazy tirades."

"Anywhere else?" I asked.

She thought for a minute. "That island over there—the Payson place where all those church people died. He hated that place, too. And McDonalds."

"Wait—what did he say?" I said.

"It's making the country fat."

It took some effort not to strangle her. "No—not McDonalds. Payson Isle. What did he say about the island?"

"The usual: it was filled with evil, and if he could just wipe it off the map, he'd do it."

"Do you think he'd ever actually do something like that?" I said.

She looked at Diggs knowingly. "Uh—yeah. Definitely. Like I said, he was a violent guy. I mean, I like that kind of thing, so it wasn't a big deal. But yeah. Not too much would have surprised me where he was concerned." Her gaze fell to my swollen lip, then back to Diggs. "Did you do that to her?" she asked.

"No," he said tonelessly. "That was the reverend's thing. It's never been mine."

She looked disappointed. "Yeah. I figured. Listen, hang on just a second, okay? I've got something I want to give you."

She ran up the stairs. Diggs and I didn't say anything while we listened to drawers open and close; a door slam. Then, she hurried back down a minute later. She held a white jewel box in her hand. She pushed it toward Diggs awkwardly, a little out of breath.

"This is yours. Your dad gave it to me, but…" she faded.

Diggs looked stunned. "He gave it to you?"

"What is it?" I asked.

"He asked you to marry him, then," Diggs said.

She looked offended. "I told you: we had something, okay? But I felt bad when he gave that to me. He said he wanted to have a family again. Start over. And it's not like I didn't care about him, but no way do I want to get stuck in Littlehope, knocked up and married to some crazy old preacher. He wouldn't take it back, though."

I thought of the chaos in Diggs' house—the graffiti on the walls, the Bible verse. All that damage. The reverend had done it all.

"Is that what you were looking for at your place?" I asked Diggs.

He stared at the box for a minute before he nodded. "Yeah. That's it." He shoved it into his pocket without looking at what was inside. "Thanks," he said to Laurie. "I was looking for that, actually."

"I figured. You'll get more use out of it than me, anyway."

The way she said it sent a shiver of foreboding through me. I studied her. That manic light was still in her eyes, but there was a hollowness beneath it. I thought of what Bill had said back at Bennett's—about something having been off about her for a long time. We didn't have time to take on every horrible story in Littlehope right now, though, so I pushed the feeling aside.

"Just one more question, if you don't mind," I said. "This Lilah person. When was the last time you saw her?"

"Last night," she said. If I'd been eating anything, I would have spit it clear across the room.

"What? Where?"

"Edie Woolwich's place. My mom works there, volunteering with the crazies. Doing her civic duty, she says. I had the car, so I had to pick her up."

"You're saying this Lilah person is one of Edie's residents?"

She laughed. "It would make sense, right? Considering what happened to Mike and the reverend? But no, I think she's a friend of Edie's. They were going out to dinner."

Edie Woolwich was a little old lady who used to work for my mom at the medical clinic. Now, she ran a residential house for the mentally ill. I never had a grandmother, but if I could choose one out of any woman in the world, Edie would be in the top two—second only to Blanche Dubois on the *Golden Girls*. For very different reasons, obviously.

"You're sure?" I said.

"Pretty sure, yeah," she said with a shrug. She glanced at the clock. "Listen, I don't want to be rude or anything, but my father will be home soon. If he finds you here, he'll definitely lose his shit. He wasn't crazy about everything that went down with the reverend."

"Go figure," I said.

20

WHEN DIGGS AND I LEFT LAURIE'S, the sun was gone, the sky a pure washed-out gray. A few flurries were already flying, though the storm wasn't supposed to start in earnest until evening.

"So…the thing missing from your house was a ring."

He didn't look at me when he answered. "It belonged to my mother."

"Ah."

"I'm not even sure why she gave it to me. I mean, obviously she wasn't my biggest fan. But it was the only thing she left me in her will—her wedding ring."

I had no clue how to respond to that. "Well… Three wives later, at least she knows you got some use out of it, right?" I winced as soon as the words were out, but Diggs didn't look offended. He just shook his head at me.

"You're such an idiot," he said fondly. "That thing's been traveling with me or locked up from the day I got it. There was only one person I could ever imagine giving it to—and I couldn't figure out how the hell to make that happen."

I blinked somewhat stupidly. "You're not…"

"Proposing?" he supplied. He looked surprisingly calm.

A little amused, even. "What would you say if I was?"

"You've been married before," I pointed out.

"So have you."

"All the more reason we shouldn't be having this conversation." I was dangerously close to hyperventilating. Diggs and I weren't the kind of people who were supposed to get married. And if we *were* going to get married, I really didn't want him to propose outside his dead father's teenage lover's house just before a blizzard on New Year's Eve, when the evil organization infesting my brain could materialize at any moment and murder us both.

"So the answer would be no, then?" Diggs said. He was still the picture of calm.

I had to think before I answered. "No. I mean—I don't think so. But it would definitely be, not right now. Why would you even want to marry me, anyway? I'm a mess. You *know* I'm a mess."

He didn't argue. We just stood there for another couple of seconds, not speaking. I shivered when a gust of icy wind blew through me.

"Come on," he said, getting us moving. "Let's get out of here."

"I forgot how cold it gets here," I said, since a subtle change of subject was in order.

"After all the months I had to listen to you bitch about the heat in Australia, you better not be complaining about the weather."

"Not complaining. Just…noting." I glanced sideways at him, switching topics again. "So, that was a pretty horrifying glimpse into your old man's psyche. Are you ready to bleach your brain yet?"

"Pretty much. The good news? Apparently, he wasn't my old man after all."

"Maybe," I corrected. "So far, we don't have the most reliable witnesses backing up that story." My attention was diverted by a car idling in a driveway two doors down from Laurie Smith's place, in the opposite direction that we were headed. A navy-blue sedan, the engine running. I grabbed Diggs' arm.

"What are the chances Jenny's still looking for more J. operatives to murder?" I asked.

He followed my gaze, his jaw tense. "Better than average, I'd say."

He turned around and started toward the car without waiting for me, his hand already going for his gun. The car pulled out about two seconds before he got there. The way he ran after it told me Jenny had definitely been behind the wheel. By the time he'd returned to me, I was calling Cameron. He answered immediately.

"What have you found out?"

"Just a second. First, have you heard from Jenny?"

"No. Why, have you seen her?"

"She's apparently on the same trail we are, but she has that unfortunate habit of blowing people up first and asking questions later. And we're really trying to avoid that."

"Damn it," he said. "Did you talk to her?"

"No, we just spotted her outside the house of one of the people we were interviewing."

"You spotted her?" he asked.

"She was pretty obvious about it."

"Then she wants you to know she's there—she's not that sloppy."

"Are you still on the island? When are you getting over here?"

"Soon. I just want to do one more thing here. What did you do with the information you found last night?"

Diggs frowned at the expression on my face, which I was guessing wasn't a good one. I'd had a huge inner debate that morning before I finally decided to keep Will Colby's letters and photos close today.

"I have them," I said.

"Damn it," Cameron murmured under his breath. "You should have left everything with me. That means she'll be after you to get to them."

"That makes no sense," I said, frustration mounting. "You said Payson Isle doesn't have anything to do with anything, and the only reason Jenny was there was to come after me. What the hell does she want with any of the leftover shit from my childhood with the Payson Church?"

"Obviously, she thinks you have something that will help her get to J.—I have no idea why. Jenny's logic usually eludes me. You'll need to be careful, regardless. What else have you found out?"

"The biggest thing? Lilah's apparently in town—she was seen at Edie Woolwich's place last night. Do you know who that is?"

"I have no idea," Cameron said briefly. "It doesn't matter, though. If Lilah is in town, you need to leave. There's no question that something's about to happen."

"We already talked about this," I said. "We're not going anywhere—"

"Listen to me—"

"No," I said. "You listen to me. We're not going, and there's no time to keep having the same discussion. If Lilah was at Edie's place, what does that mean? What's our next step?

There was a long, seething silence on the other end of the line. Finally, Cameron spoke.

"Is it possible this Edie woman is another of J.'s operatives?" he asked. "That Lilah programmed her as the next alternate?"

"Edie Woolwich? Unless things have changed drastically since I was here a couple years ago, I seriously doubt it," I said.

"Will you check? *Carefully*.. I don't expect that you'll run into trouble there as long as you keep a low profile. Jenny will keep her distance, at the very least. And you won't find Lilah there," he said. "If she's still in town at all, she knows something's up. She'll be staying under the radar. If you could just talk to this Edie woman, get a sense of her state of mind… If she is another alternate and we're able to get a fix on her early, we may be able to stop this once and for all."

"Let's go hog wild and say your theory's right," I said, "and Edie Woolwich goes psycho killer on our asses? I mean, this is Diggs and me we're talking about. We tend to bring that out in people."

"Just tread carefully," he said. "I need to go. Call me as soon as you learn anything else."

He hung up on me.

"He wants us to talk to Edie?" Diggs asked.

"That's what he said." A red BMW convertible rolled toward Laurie's house with an attractive man about Diggs' age at the wheel. Laurie's dad, presumably. I nodded toward the sidewalk, and we got moving.

"Call Jack. Let's see what he says," Diggs said.

"Do I mention Lilah? Because let's not forget that she's ostensibly the woman responsible for his wife's death. It could get messy if he decides to come with us, and Lilah's actually there."

"You don't think it's going to get messy anyway?"

"Right."

We kept walking while I dialed, headed in the direction of Edie's rooming house. Jack took longer to answer the phone, and honestly wasn't that much more pleasant to talk to than Cameron.

"What's happening?" he asked.

"Any number of things," I said. "The most pressing at the moment is that we think someone from J. was at Edie Woolwich's place last night. Cameron wants Diggs and me to check it out."

"Someone from J.," he repeated. "Lilah?"

I thought of the look I'd seen in his eye that morning when we were talking about all this. Thought of what Diggs would do if someone did to me what J. did to his wife. The mental picture that came up wasn't a good one.

"Erin," he prompted.

"We think so," I said. "Yes."

"When was she seen last?" he asked.

"Last night."

"You're headed there now?"

"Yeah, but we're on foot."

"I just need to tie a few things up here. I'll meet you at Edie's."

And he hung up on me. I was sensing a trend.

"What did he say?" Diggs asked.

"Not goodbye. He'll meet us at Edie's."

"Good. At least we're not going in alone—that makes me feel a little better."

Since I figured neither of us had it in us to go over any more of what we'd learned from Laurie, and I definitely wasn't prepared to talk about that ring again, I settled for slipping my hand into Diggs' so he at least knew I was in his corner. He squeezed my fingers. We picked up our pace. Whether Lilah was at Edie's now or had simply been there recently, I really didn't want Jack to get there first.

Edie's place was close to the Littlehope wharf, which was conveniently located on the other side of town from Laurie's house. Diggs and I walked the mile there in silence, both of us hunched against the wind and snow, which was coming down harder now. The roads were already covered with a light dusting, but it did nothing to slow the pickups that sped past.

When we reached the end of the lane leading to Edie's, I searched the roads both ahead and behind. So far, we'd seen no sign of Jenny since we'd left Laurie's.

The Littlehope Residential Home for the Mentally Ill was a rambling old Victorian situated on a hill at the end of Seaside Lane. It housed at least half a dozen people with afflictions ranging from borderline personality to schizophrenia to bipolar disorder, and any number of combinations thereof. As we walked up the hill to Edie's place, I tried to ignore a mounting sense of dread.

A hinged wooden sign mounted on a post on the front lawn swung violently in the wind, the hinges creaking so loudly that I could hear them even after we were long past the thing. There was a wraparound deck at the front of the house, where a woman and two men were smoking. At a glance I could see that the woman was most likely not Lilah—Laurie had pegged her age as over forty, but had said she was dark-haired and Spanish. The woman on the deck had black hair tinged with silver, and looked closer to sixty. The thought that I was putting this much faith in Laurie's vague description was not comforting.

Diggs and I took the three steps onto the deck slowly, making sure to make eye contact and smile nicely. If we could avoid disturbing the natives, it would be a nice change of pace. The woman kept her eyes on the ground as she continued to smoke. One of the men ground out his cigarette as soon as he spotted me and hurried toward us, however. I glanced at Diggs.

"Hi," the man said, his voice low and tinged with a kind of aggressive pleasantness. I guessed his age at somewhere between forty and fifty. Good looking, with shaggy hair and baggy jeans. He stuck his hand out toward me. "Hi. I'm Walt. What's your name?"

I shook his hand. "I'm Erin. This is Diggs. We're looking for Edie."

He let go of my hand and shook Diggs' hand vigorously. "Hi, Diggs. I'm Walt. This is your girlfriend?"

Diggs smiled easily. "She is. You think you could find Edie for us, Walt?"

"Sure. Yeah, I can do that," he said. "I'll find anybody you need, Diggs. Just follow me, okay? You just follow me."

He strode past the others without acknowledging them, a sense of self-importance in his gait. A man on a mission. Diggs glanced at me, shrugged, and together we followed Walt inside.

"Wait here, okay?" Walt said as soon as we got through the door. "I'll bring her to you. Don't go anywhere."

"Thanks, Walt," Diggs said.

"Sure, Diggs," the man said. "Sure. Just wait here, Diggs."

Diggs and I waited. The house opened on a small foyer, with what looked like a large sitting room just off to our left and another one straight ahead. In the one to our left, an episode of *CHiPs* played on a giant old TV set. I couldn't tell if anyone was in the room, but a man stood in the doorway with his hands in his pockets, watching. He turned when we came in, but didn't say anything. He wore sunglasses despite the dim interior.

A minute later, Walt returned with Edie in tow.

"Here she is," he announced to us both.

Edie was five feet tall, and a little rounder than she'd been when I'd seen her last. Her gray hair was curled in a tight home-perm over her visibly pink scalp. Though she didn't appear visibly homicidal, she did seem harried when Walt led her through the door. At sight of Diggs and me, she brightened.

"It is you!" she said. She wiped her hands on her apron.

"I told you," Walt said. "Edie, this is Diggs. And this is his girlfriend, Erin. They're just visiting."

"Thank you, Walt," she said. "Walt's been working on introductions this week."

"Nice job," I said.

"Thanks, Erin." He took a step into my personal bubble. "Now you say you're welcome."

"You're welcome," I said. I fought the urge to step back.

•

We settled in a dining room off the kitchen, a bowl of fruit at the center of the table beside a pitcher of water. Walt wandered off on another mission, but three other residents—all men—stood watching from the doorway. They weren't exactly in the conversation, but they weren't quite out of it, either.

We'd already been through pleasantries, caught up on family, traded condolences… My head ached, my lip hurt, and I was beyond ready to move things along. Jack, thankfully, hadn't arrived yet.

"Lilah?" Edie asked, when we finally got to the point. "Of course. She's a friend of mine."

"From where, exactly?" Diggs asked.

"We met a couple months ago," Edie said. "We struck up a conversation over to Wallace's—it was pizza night, so I was there with a couple of the boys, picking up dinner. She's a real nice lady. Helps out here every so often."

Diggs and I exchanged a look. "With the residents?" Diggs said. "One on one?"

"Not really, no," Edie said. "But she'll take Nate over there out sometimes—to the store, that kind of thing. They've kind of taken to each other."

If her nod was any indication, Nate was the youngest of the three men watching us—the one we'd seen in the foyer. His eyes were still hidden behind dark sunglasses. He was dark complected, with curly black hair and a goatee.

"Why do you ask?" Edie said.

"Do you know how we can get in touch with this woman?" I asked, rather than responding. "Do you have a phone number? An address?"

"We usually just do e-mail, to be honest," Edie said. "We'll Facebook each other."

"She has a Facebook page?" Diggs said.

"Of course," Edie said. Like it was one of the dumber questions she'd been asked today.

"Would you mind showing us?" I asked.

Edie nodded warily. "Sure. Just let me get my laptop."

A minute or two later, she returned with an older Compaq

laptop. The three men who'd been watching us—two of them older, one with thinning gray hair and suspenders that barely covered a substantial gut, the other well over six feet tall and nearly as wide as that—went back into the living room and turned on the television. Edie had just succeeded in getting online when Nate came over to join us.

His sunglasses were still in place. His hands remained in his pockets.

"Hey," he said with a casual nod.

"You know how we feel about sunglasses inside," Edie chided. There was a tiny tic in Nate's jawline before he took the sunglasses off.

"Sorry. Forgot," he said. He had startling, electrified green eyes set in an undeniably handsome face. "What are you doing there?" he asked. He nodded toward the computer.

"Just looking something up," I said. "We're reporters. I'm Erin. This is Diggs." I started to offer my hand, but he took a step back. I let it drop.

"You're from around here?" he asked.

I told him we were. He took in the information with a nod, then asked a few more questions, listening with keen attention to every answer I gave.

"Here it is," Edie interrupted. "Lilah Salvator." Diggs and I joined her at the computer. Nate followed, standing beside me but well away.

"Lilah," Nate said. "What are you looking at her for?"

"I think I know her," I lied. "I'm just trying to figure out where from."

I looked at the screen.

It's not like I expected her to have a roster of Facebook friends who also happened to be J. operatives, but an update on her timeline indicating what she was planning to blow up in the next few months would have made things so much easier. It looked like Lilah rarely used her page, though. She didn't even have a profile picture.

"She's not much for online stuff, huh?" I said.

"Lilah's too private for that," Nate said. He looked like he was getting uneasy with our fixation on his friend.

"You guys know each other pretty well, then?" Diggs asked.

Nate tensed. He'd avoided any interaction with Diggs up until that point, focused more on Edie and me. Now, he shot Diggs a glare that could have disintegrated a lesser man.

"Why are you asking about Lilah?" he said. "She's a private person. We're both private people. You come in here, start snooping on her personal internet space, start asking questions that aren't relevant." He shoved his sunglasses back on. He wasn't shouting, but the intensity of his words was unnerving. "You know, people nowadays feel like they can just find out about anyone they want to. They put eyes in the sky that can see everything. You know that? You know there are satellites that can listen in on every single thing we say?"

"Nate," Edie said gently. "There's no one watching you. There's no one listening to you. You're safe here. You know we respect your privacy."

He nodded vigorously and took a step back. "I know. I know. I know. Sometimes I just forget. I'm going for a walk. Grab a smoke. Sorry."

He walked away mumbling to himself, his hands still in his pockets.

"Sorry about that," Edie said. "He's a good boy. It's hard on him, being here—most everyone else started out in tough circumstances, doesn't know much other than this. For most of them, this is the best their life's ever been. But Nate grew up in a good family, got good grades, led a pretty normal life. Smart, smart man. Then when he was about twenty-two, he got into drugs. That triggered his first big episode. Before that, he got a good glimpse of what he could have—what he thought he *would* have one day. It's been hard for him."

"Would you say he's an angry guy?" Diggs asked. I knew exactly what he was thinking.

"No more than most, really," she said. She hesitated. I knew then that she was holding back—she would have to, both legally and morally, for the sake of her residents. I also knew there was a damned good possibility she could pay with her life if we didn't get more information from her.

"You were about to say something," I said. "Diggs asked that question, and something occurred to you. What is it?"

"Nothing," she said. The two men who'd been watching us before returned. Neither of them came in, but both lingered in the doorway and continued watching our every move.

"Bert, Stan, why don't you go in and decide what you want for dinner tonight. And we've got movie night, too, so if you want to pick out snacks, that's fine."

"I already know what I want," the bigger of the two said. "I got two bags of chips stored away for tonight. Been saving them all year long."

"We'll talk about it later," Edie said. "But you know you're not allowed to eat two bags of chips in a night."

I saw a little flash of fire in his eyes. The man was a mountain. He looked at me. "Beautiful tits," he said. That was it. He turned and left with his friend.

"I'm sorry about that," Edie said.

"Don't worry about it," I assured her. "A compliment's a

compliment, right? I'm more worried about Nate."

"What kind of precautions do you have in place here if something goes wrong?" Diggs asked. "If someone does become violent? There must be a protocol in place."

"We call the police. They come in, and we'll usually take the resident to the psych unit at the hospital, where they'll stay overnight. A lot of times it's just a medication issue. If it's more serious, they'll go to Augusta and be admitted to the facility there until they're stabilized."

"So I assume no one has access to weapons here," I said.

She laughed outright. "Contrary to what it might look like, I don't have a death wish. Fred has guns, but he doesn't keep 'em on the property."

Fed was Edie's husband. "Where does he keep them?" Diggs asked.

"He's got a fishing shack over by the water."

"Do the guys know where that is?" I asked. "Does Nate know?"

She pulled up short, staring at us both. "I'd appreciate it if one of you would give me a straight answer. What in the name of Johnny's blue underthings are you talking about?"

"You just have to trust us, okay?" I said. She looked far from convinced. Time was marching on, though, and I knew we were onto something. I glanced in the direction Nate had just gone, and lowered my voice.

"Listen, do you ever do room searches?"

"Erin—"

"It's important," I stressed. "Please. I swear, I wouldn't be asking if it wasn't. Do you ever search the residents' rooms? Could you do something like that now?"

"These people trust me," she said. "I've set it up so they can come here and feel safe—like they're human beings with rights, something more than just the label society gives them."

"We're not trying to destroy that," Diggs said. "But this is serious. We have some concerns about Lilah—what her motives might be. If she was alone with Nate, it's possible she could have planted some…ideas."

"Just look in his room," I pleaded.

"I'll ask," she said after a few seconds' deliberation. "I'll ask him if I can go in there. If he says no, I won't push it."

"But—" I started. Diggs shot me a warning look. I shut up.

"That's fine," he said. "Whatever you can do."

We heard footsteps in the hallway. A second later, Walt reappeared in the doorway. His face was flushed.

"Jack's here," he announced. "Just visiting. He's a good guy. Jack. He said he's a friend of yours, Diggs. He can't stay for dinner."

Edie looked at Diggs and me like we were termites in danger of infestation. It stung, but I was guessing she wouldn't be so snippy if we ended up saving her life.

We met Jack back in the foyer. On Edie's advice—which felt more like insistence from where I was standing—we decided to wait outside while she and another aid talked to the residents. And, hopefully, checked their rooms.

The only problem was that Nate refused to even talk to her. Instead, we found him smoking outside when we stepped onto the porch. The wind had picked up, as had the snow. Nate stood and moved away from us, his back to us and his shoulders hunched. Everyone else had gone inside.

I went over and stood beside him, while Jack and Diggs kept their distance. "Can I bum a smoke?" I asked. Addiction: the universal tie that binds. He glanced at me, then dug into his pockets and came out with a pack of Camels. He handed me a lighter.

It was my first cigarette in a year; I was relieved to find with that first inhale that I'd pretty much lost my taste for it. I smoked it anyway.

"Are you from around here, Nate?" I asked.

"Grew up here," he said. "A couple streets over, on Sunset. You know where that is?"

"Sure. I grew up in a place on Main Street. So you graduated from Medomak?" He nodded. "What year?"

"Class of '96," he said. "You went there too, right? Erin? Graduated a couple years after me, I think."

"That's right," I said, surprised. We talked a little more about high school. He'd been more popular than me. Played sports. Had a band. I watched out of the corner of my eye as Jack and Diggs left the porch and headed for the car, giving us some space.

"Listen, Nate," I said after a while, once he'd relaxed. "I wanted to ask you a couple of things about Lilah."

He was on his third cigarette. I'd declined a second, vaguely nauseated by the time I was halfway into the first. At mention of Lilah's name, Nate closed himself off again.

"I don't want to talk about her."

"Why not?"

"There are people like me everywhere, you know. People who need to pay for their sins, and some who never sinned at all who deserve to be set free. No one should be stuck in a cage. Lilah knows that."

"And that's why you don't want to talk about her," I clarified. "Because she understands you."

"Because she's a friend. And she knew people would talk about her—ask questions about her. Want to define her."

"Define her?" I said. "I'm not sure I know what you mean."

He turned to face me. His sunglasses reflected a distorted image of my bruised face. I hated that I couldn't see his eyes.

"Define her," he repeated. "Who she is. What she stands for. People always want to define you. I'm Nate. Schizophrenic. That's all."

"But you're not," I said. I kept my tone easy. "I just met you and I already know that. You're Nate. Great taste in music. Chain smoker." He smiled at that. "Left handed. Former Medomak track all-star. A man who has schizophrenia." I paused. I had his attention, but I didn't know if I was getting through. "You see what I mean? I'm not looking to define anyone. But I would like to know about Lilah."

Seconds ticked by, while snow continued to fall around us. He shrugged. "I don't know. She's Lilah. She's pretty. Older than us, though. She speaks Spanish. Knows about politics and governments. Doesn't like cats. Knows how to swim." He paused, and looked away from me. "And she can read my mind."

I stayed cool, despite what I was thinking. "Can you explain what you mean by that?"

"She knows what I'm thinking. And sometimes, it's like…" He frowned. "She has the radio frequency inside my head. Before, only my father had that. My father, and John."

I looked at him blankly. He clamped his mouth shut. "John who?" I said.

"John Booth," he finally said. "John Wilkes Booth. He could speak to me—inside my head. He had the frequency."

"And now Lilah has the same frequency," I said.

"I'm not defining her," he said.

"No," I agreed, beyond serious. "That would be a bad idea."

Not unexpectedly, Nate had strong objections to Edie going through his room. He had some choice words for me when he learned I was behind the request, then locked himself in his room and turned up the Beatles on his stereo as loud as it would go. It was a nice stereo, too—it went pretty damned loud.

The rest of the residents were on edge by this time. Walt was no longer affable and pleasant—a storm had descended. He eyed me and muttered under his breath, his fists clenching and unclenching, his face scarlet with rage about to ignite.

Edie wouldn't let us back in the house, instead blocking the entrance.

"It might be a good idea to get some help out here," I said.

"Ya think?" she said. "Thanks to you, you're right. It's not that I don't like you, hon, but you've got a hell of a mess going on in here now. Sheriff Finnegan's on his way. If I can get Nate to turn that bleeping stereo of his down, everyone else will settle down. But as long as that's going, this place is full of ticking time bombs."

Great J. hadn't needed to send Lilah—apparently, I could bring out the homicidal rage in people just as effectively.

"Is there anything else you can tell me about Lilah?" I asked before I left. "Where she lives? What does she do for work?"

"She lives on the peninsula," I think," she said. "Over by the Olson House."

The Olson House is an old saltbox farmhouse in Cushing now owned by the Farnsworth Museum, made famous in a series of paintings done by Andrew Wyeth over the years. It's an easy reference point if people are talking about the tiny fishing village, but I would bet money Lilah didn't live anywhere near there. I made a note of it anyway, though, just in case.

"What about work?" I prompted.

"She doesn't work—retired, I think." She frowned. "Though come to think of it she's a little young to be retired, can't be more than fifty. Maybe she comes from money. She volunteers, though—that's how she spends most of her time. Churches, the prison, hospitals, a couple of local schools."

My stomach bottomed out. How many people had she accessed during her time in the area? "How long would you say she lived here?"

"When we met, she said she'd been here a few months. I don't know how long, exactly."

"Okay. One last question. I don't suppose you have a picture of her, do you?"

"As a matter of fact, I do," Edie whispered conspiratorially. "I knew Lilah would have a fit—she's pretty, but she's awful camera shy—but I snapped a pic of her and Nate one day. Hang on."

After she'd retrieved the picture from her phone and e-mailed it to me, I felt a brief surge of triumph. I didn't have a clue what J. had planned, but at least now I had a face to put to Lilah's name. Edie was right: Lilah was pretty, with dark hair and dark eyes and a quiet intensity about her that seemed menacing, even in a picture.

As I was leaving I reminded Edie to be careful, and from there got in the back of Jack's Honda Civic. We drove off just as Sheriff Finnegan was driving in, Diggs and I both ducking down as Jack drove past.

"I've got a picture of Lilah," I said to the guys. "But she's been here almost a year—which means she's talked to a hell of a lot of people. Nate, Mike Reynolds, and the reverend could just be the tip of the iceberg. Any sign of Jenny while I was in there?"

"I haven't seen her," Diggs said. "But that doesn't mean she's not here somewhere."

My mind was reeling. There were way too many things for us to keep track of alone. "Look, it seems like we're a little over our heads at this point. Or a lot. I mean, where do we even begin from here? Especially if something is really about to happen tonight, like Cameron has suggested."

"So, you want to pack up and head home?" Diggs said. "Ready to call it a day?"

"No, smartass," I said. I rolled my eyes. "But I think it's time to bring in reinforcements. At the very least, we could let Sheriff Finnegan know about Lilah and Jenny."

"Already done," Jack said. He glanced back at me over his shoulder. It was four o'clock, the snow flying in earnest now, the sky already dark. Jack drove us back toward Littlehope's main drag at a crawl, windshield wipers on high.

"Excuse me?" I said. "What do you mean?"

"I just finished with him," Jack said. "Just left Sheriff Finnegan's office. That's why it took me so long to get here."

"What did you tell him?" I asked.

"I told him the FBI has some evidence that there may be some trouble in Littlehope tonight, and it could be tied to the deaths of Reverend Diggins and Mike Reynolds and his girlfriend. Then, I gave him the description of Jenny. I'll send him the photo of Lilah next."

"What did he say?" Diggs asked.

"He'd already gotten word from someone else, actually," Jack said. He pulled into the parking lot at Bennett's. The place was filling fast.

"What do you mean?" I asked. "Who?"

Jack put the car in park and turned to look at both of us. "Trent Willett contacted him yesterday. Said he's on his way into town, but in the meantime the sheriff should be on high alert."

"Trent Willett, the douche bag who shot my dog?" I demanded.

"And you," Jack and Diggs reminded me at the same time. Like I'd forgotten that part.

"Finnegan also asked me if I'd heard anything from either of you," Jack said. "Willett was apparently asking."

Shit. Like there weren't enough things to worry about, now we had a government spook headed to town.

"Did he say when he'd get here?"

"Sometime today," Jack said. "Which means it might be a good idea for you to follow Cameron's suggestion and get the hell out of town."

"We'll keep a low profile," I said. "But I want to stay here a little longer, at least—especially if Lilah's around here somewhere. Getting to her is the best chance we have of actually reaching whoever leads the organization."

Jack didn't say anything, but the look on his face was damned unnerving. I kept going. "Jack… That means if we are able to find Lilah, you have to keep her alive," I said. "You can't just off her, no matter how much you might want to."

"I know that," he said. At the look in his eye, I wasn't so sure of that.

"Just as long as you do."

"What about targets?" Diggs said. "If we can't figure out who the actual operatives are at this point, maybe we can figure out what their target will be."

"We're talking county wide, then?" I asked. "From here all the way to Boothbay Harbor and Bath? You've got city New Year's celebrations, schools, hospitals, churches… Where do you suggest we start?"

"It seems like Lilah's been focused primarily on Littlehope—that's where Diggs' father was based, and so was Mike Reynolds. With the storm, it seems unlikely that they'd be traveling too far from here," Jack said.

"So you think they're actually going for something here in town?" I said doubtfully. "The only place where anyone will really be is Bennett's, and with the storm it won't exactly be Times Square there tonight."

"But they've had plenty of small targets before," Diggs said. "Two or three victims at a time. Bennett's would still mean a higher body count than that."

I hedged. "It's not much to go on."

"It's the best we've got right now, though," Jack said. "Bennett's is pretty much the only place open at this point—there were some other school dances, that kind of thing, but everything's shut down for the storm."

"Okay," Diggs said. "So, we've got Bennett's. The *Trib.* The island, though that's pretty much evacuated so I don't know what the point would be. Edie's place. There are no schools in session. Church services?"

I shook my head. "New Year's Eve isn't really a God holiday."

Diggs sighed. "Let's focus on what we've got so far, then. Come on. I want to go in and have a quick chat with Mimi, show her the picture we got. If nothing else, she might have some idea how to find Lilah."

Jack looked out at the blowing snow distastefully before he shut off the car. "It's coming down fast," he said.

"Finnegan said most people will stay in tonight, anyway. He doesn't think many cars will be on the road."

"Maybe, but we can't just count on that," I said. "People are pretty hearty around here. A little snow won't get between them and their favorite brew on New Year's Eve."

"A little snow?" Jack said as he slammed his car door. He leaned into the wind and put the hood up on his jacket.

"Okay, more than a little snow," I conceded as a gust of ice-cold wind took my breath away. Australia really was looking better and better.

21

JACK WENT INTO MIMI'S before Diggs and me, to scope things out and make sure Trent Willett wasn't lurking in the corner ready to gun me down again. When he was sure it was clear, he waved us in.

The place had livened up significantly, so I was guessing Mimi hadn't gotten the bad news from Sheriff Finnegan yet. Or maybe she had, and was just ignoring it. Diggs and I approached the bar while Jack went to a cell-friendly corner to send Lilah's picture to the sheriff.

Mimi took one look at Diggs and me, and shook her head. "You hear Finnegan's trying to shut me down?" she said. "This is my best day of the year next to St. Paddy's, and I got two new knees to pay for. No way in hell I'm closing down."

"Are you sure about that?" I said. "If the sheriff thinks it would be a good idea, maybe he's right. I mean, the weather's getting bad out there."

"There's nobody in this damn town who doesn't live within walking distance of this bar. Everybody who comes in tonight turns their keys in, and they don't get 'em back till I give them the go-ahead. Problem solved."

Only if our only problem really was the weather, but I was thinking that ranked low on the list of things we needed to worry about.

"What did Sheriff Finnegan tell you?" I asked.

"That the storm was coming in and it looks like it'll be bad. And he had some horseshit about somebody making a bomb threat. Honest to god, somebody looks at you cross-eyed these days and the whole state shuts down. I hope to hell I've got more spine than that."

"I don't think it's a matter of spine," Diggs argued. "I think it's a matter of being smart."

"Well, I never claimed to be a genius, hon, but I can do basic math. And I shut down tonight and the numbers don't add up."

Diggs looked at me helplessly. Mimi held up her hand before he could argue any further. "I'm done, Diggs. Gotta get back to work. And you…" She leveled a look at me, then jerked her head in the direction of a booth in the corner. "You got company. Bring this over, would you?" She handed me a tall fizzy drink and gave me a little shove. "Now, go on."

I looked at Diggs, who appeared as wary as me. With extreme caution, I made my way through the growing crowd. It was eight o'clock, the band—Storm Warning, Mimi announced at the top of her considerable voice—just getting started. Between the music and the growing masses, I could barely think straight.

When the booth was in sight, I stopped dead. Diggs grinned. He nodded toward the table. "Go on."

"You knew?" I hissed at him.

"Jack saw when he came in looking for Willett," he said.

"Now, don't just stand there."

I took a couple of steps closer. "You ordered this," I said.

My mother looked up from the table. She looked good—like, really good. Tanned, rested, toned. Well groomed. Totally sober. She gave me a kind of awkward half smile when she realized who it was, taking in my bruises and puffy lip in a glance. I started to hand her the drink, then took it back and tasted it. Sweet and syrupy, but definitely alcohol-free. Classic Coke, straight up. I set it in front of her, then sat down on the bench across from her. Diggs slid in beside me.

"You know, if you'd stop being such a smartass, maybe people would stop beating you up," she said.

"I'll take that under advisement," I said. "Hi, Mom. You look good."

I'd never called her mom before. It felt good, though, and she didn't look like she wanted to kick my teeth in for using the dreaded word. I figured maybe I'd stick with it for a while, see what happened.

"I wish I could say the same," she said to me. She eyeballed me, head to toe. "What did you do to your hair?"

"Dyed it. We're fugitives," I reminded her.

"Right. Well, it doesn't look good. You're a redhead. You should just stick with that."

"Okay," I agreed readily. I was too glad to see her to even be annoyed. I hadn't realized just how much I'd missed her, all these months away. I used to go long stretches without seeing Kat, but somehow all the death and mayhem over the past two years made me appreciate her more. She was prickly bordering on downright mean a lot of the time, but at least I knew what to expect from her.

"Hey," I said, as if it was a thought that had just occurred to me. "So here's a question: What the hell are you doing here?"

"I got word there was a reunion. I just figured my invitation got lost in the mail."

"We thought about getting in touch," Diggs said, "but given what may be about to happen here, we were trying to keep people we care about out of harm's way."

"Sucking up doesn't suit you, Diggs," she said. She paused, and got a little more serious. "Cameron wanted to keep me away from here, too. But if the town's going up, I'd like to at least try and help put it back together again afterward, if I can. If we can't stop it from happening, that is."

"Does that mean you're back to stay?" I asked.

"Not sure. It gets old on the run, though—how many cabana girls can a woman possibly seduce? I'd rather just take these sons of bitches down, and get back to my life."

"And Maya?" I said. "Are you going to call and let her know you're back?"

"Whether I do or don't doesn't have a damn thing to do with you," she said shortly. "So don't start playing matchmaker."

"I heard she still comes around here regularly. She's even asked Mimi if anyone's seen you around."

Kat looked at Diggs. "I don't know how you've put up with this one all these years."

"It's a mystery to me, too," Diggs said. He stood, then leaned in and kissed the top of my head. "You two catch up. I'm just going to talk to Mimi for a second. Can I see your phone?" he asked me.

I handed it to him. He squeezed my shoulder, and left us.

"So," Kat said when Diggs was gone. "You two are still together?"

"Seems like it," I said.

"And he's still sober."

"Yeah. Five years now."

She shook her head. "I'll tell you, I never envisioned this when you were following him around while you were still in high school. I figured you'd get knocked up, he'd disappear in the night…"

"We were friends. He didn't touch me back then. Not that way."

"So you've said. I think I'm actually starting to believe it." She paused. "Turns out he's a pretty good man." For Kat, this was tantamount to calling Diggs Christ himself.

"He is." I paused. "Did you know Reverend Diggins wasn't his father?"

She didn't look surprised. "I had my suspicions. I didn't know Ethan or the family when Diggs was growing up, though—I was, what, nine when he was born?" I stifled an inward groan at the reminder. It's one of the disadvantages of dating an older man when your mother was a teenage bride—the age gap between Diggs and me is only slightly less than the one between him and Kat. "Who the reverend's wife three towns over was screwing wasn't exactly on my radar."

"Yeah, I guess not. Any idea who his real dad might be?"

"No clue. It's kind of a relief he doesn't have that son of a bitch's blood running through his veins though, isn't it?"

I laughed. "Kind of," I admitted. I let the subject drop and moved on to more pressing matters. "We're still not sure what the town's in for tonight."

"What does Cameron have to say about it?"

"He doesn't seem to know any more than we do."

"Where is he?"

"Out on the island—I thought he was coming back to the mainland, but now I'm not so sure. He may end up stuck out there."

"Alone?" she asked.

"Yeah. He wanted to keep an eye out." She didn't say anything. "Why?"

"It just seems strange to me—him just sending you all out here, knowing what's at risk. All the people after you right now."

"It wasn't his preference," I admitted. "He tried to get us to leave town. We're staying to see this thing through, though."

"Stubborn idiots," she murmured. Her eyes shifted from mine. "What about Jenny?"

"She's out there, skulking around." I motioned to my lip. "She's the one who did this, actually. I think I tagged her once, but she's tough. She's been killing people left and right since she got here. I don't see her stopping anytime soon."

"But she's not working for this…what are you all calling it? J.?"

"No. She's trying to take them down—basically, by murdering anyone they come in contact with. Not a lot of finesse in the plan, but to be honest it's better than anything we've come up with so far."

The band kicked into a song I'd never heard before, about a cowboy whose buddies refused to party it up with him. He seemed pretty upbeat about the dilemma, and the lead singer was good—lean, goateed, and a total monster on the guitar. I watched for a second, letting my thoughts settle, until I pulled myself back to Kat. I considered asking her about what I'd remembered the night before, but couldn't imagine doing it without having some kind of emotional breakdown so figured it could wait.

"Did Dad ever say anything to you about the organization?" I asked. "Or maybe Isaac let something drop?"

Her eyes darkened when I mentioned Isaac's name, a reaction I'd seen from her before. "Isaac and I didn't have a lot to do with each other. And your father never really talked about his past. He told me about his sister, and a few things about Jonestown. But I knew very little about the organization until I talked to Cameron."

Before I could respond, Diggs appeared by my side. "Hey—sorry to interrupt, but we have to go."

"What's up?"

"Willett just pulled in."

I got to my feet. Kat started to rise as well, but I shook my head. "I think maybe you should stay here for now."

I'm sure she would have argued, but just then something caught her attention at the bar. I followed her gaze, and smiled. A tall, lean woman with curly gray-white hair sat talking to Mimi: Maya. She must have come in while I was talking to Kat.

"We'll come back for you," I promised. "Just stay out of trouble."

"Yeah," Kat said. "Because I'm the one who needs to be told that. Be careful out there."

I nodded as Diggs took my arm and swept me toward the back door, back into the storm.

Jack stayed inside to figure out what was going with

Willett, but Monty met us out back. He was covered in snow and hunched in his winter jacket, looking more ruffled than I'd ever seen him.

"What's going on?" I asked.

"I'm going bugshit is what's going on," Monty said. "On top of the storm, trying to keep track of Jenny, Lilah, and now this government guy, not to mention the local cops and this guy from the crazy house that Lilah may or may not have worked her mental magic on..."

"It's a lot," I agreed. "But Finnegan has his eye out for Lilah and Jenny now, and I'm assuming Willett will as well, unless he really is convinced that Diggs and I are mad bombers at the heart of the conspiracy."

"So what do you want my focus to be, then?" Monty asked.

I went over the whole thing in my head before I spoke. "The issue at hand is keeping people safe, right? Which means figuring out where J. is most likely to strike, and finding Lilah. Those are the priorities."

"If we can get access to a computer," Diggs said, "I can tap some online sources and see if I can find any record of where Lilah might be living around here. If she's been here for a year, she must have left some kind of trail."

"Did you have a particular computer in mind?" I asked, knowing full well what his answer would be.

"Let's hit the *Trib.*" He looked at Monty. "You think you could focus on keeping an eye out for Jenny right now? I have a feeling she might show up at Edie's place, so maybe swing by there."

Jack emerged from the bar. The music swelled for a second before he shut the door again. "Do we have a plan?"

"Diggs and I are going to the *Trib* to try and find some

record of Lilah. Monty will patrol the area and keep an eye out for Lilah or Jenny."

"Sounds good," Jack said. "I'm going to stay here for now, and work on Willett and Finnegan—try to get them to shut this place down for the night."

"Talk to Mimi," Diggs said. "I started working the guilt angle; how bad she'd feel if something happened to anyone because she wouldn't close for the night."

"Were you making progress?"

"I think so," Diggs said. "Right now, this bar is definitely the most populated place in the town. As long as that's the case and there's a possibility J. really is working in Littlehope, I can't imagine they'd choose any other target."

I hadn't actually thought of it in quite those terms up till that point. "I should go in and tell Kat and Maya to get out of there," I said.

"You're not going anywhere near there," Diggs said. "Jack can relay the message. You're with me, ace."

"Just make sure you tell them," I said to Jack. "Actually, tell them to go to the clinic. They should be safe there. I'll get a message to them as soon as I can."

"Got it. Now, go. Text me as soon as you have anything."

"Should we plan on meeting back up?" I asked.

"I think it's smarter if we stay split up," Jack said, "with you two out of sight. At least for now—the less attention you can call to yourselves, the better it'll be." He shifted his focus to Diggs. "You're armed?"

"Locked and loaded," Diggs said.

"Good," Jack said. "We'll do check-ins every half hour to make sure everyone's still okay. You two, don't leave the *Trib* without either Monty or me. There are too many psychopaths running loose in town right now. Extreme caution is the rule of thumb."

"Agreed," Diggs said seriously. "So, we'll see you in an hour."

Monty agreed. Jack nodded, but the intensity in his eyes made a fresh wave of concern run through me. He might be invested in keeping the rest of us safe, but right now caution was definitely not his first priority.

22

JACK WAITED UNTIL THE OTHERS HAD GONE before he ducked back into the bar. The music was too loud, and the snow seemed to have convinced everyone that New Year's Eve celebrations should start earlier than they might otherwise. At just past eight o'clock, it was wall-to-wall locals. He surveyed the masses grimly before he went to the bar and managed to clear a spot next to Erin's mother.

She was deep in conversation with Maya—the woman who had been her partner, up until last year. It looked like it was a good conversation, their heads tipped toward each other as they spoke. Jack tapped Kat's shoulder awkwardly. She glanced over her shoulder at him, frowned, and twisted on her barstool to see him better.

"What's the problem?" she said.

"Erin wants you two to get out of here," he said, shouting to be heard over the noise. Trent Willett was talking to the bartender, who didn't look at all receptive to his message—presumably, that she needed to close the bar for the night.

"Did she have some suggestion about where we should go?"

"The clinic," Jack said. He leaned in self-consciously.

"She said you'll be safe there."

Willett's gaze drifted to them. Since Mexico, Jack had had dealings with the agent more than once—primarily when Willett was questioning him about Erin and Diggs' whereabouts. Now, the man looked from Jack directly to Kat. He stood and headed toward them. If they left now, Willett would undoubtedly follow.

Jack shook his head. Kat followed his gaze and settled on the short, bespectacled man headed for them.

"A friend of yours?" she asked Jack.

"Trent Willett," Willett said before Jack could answer. He extended his hand, and nodded to Jack. Kat didn't shake. Instead, she looked at the man like he'd proposed something indecent rather than simply offering his name.

"Trent Willett," Kat said. "Now where do I know that name?" Jack didn't care for the look in her eye. The band started in with another number. Willett frowned. He nodded toward the door.

"Come outside with me," he said. Neither Kat nor Maya budged. Willett took his badge from his inside pocket and flashed it at them. "Please."

Kat hopped off her barstool. Maya started to follow, but Kat stopped her with a shake of her head. "Please—wait here. I promise, I won't be long."

At the look in her eye, Jack thought the woman would refuse. After a moment, however, Maya nodded. "I'll be here. But then, I'd really like an explanation."

Kat nodded, chastened for the first time since Jack had met her, and followed him outside.

A cluster of local men stood smokking in the parking lot when they got outside, their shoulders hunched against the gusting wind. It was impossible to tell how much snow had fallen, the ground bare in spots while snowdrifts a few feet away reached the wheel wells of the countless 4 x 4's that filled the lot. Jack felt only a moment's relief from the assault of the noise in the bar before the bitter wind had him longing to go back inside.

"What are you doing here?" he asked Willett, once they'd found a spot on the leeside of the building, safe from the wind.

"I was about to ask you the same thing," Willett said. "I've got reason to believe some shit's about to go down here. Interesting that you all just happen to have shown up here now."

"I'm from here," Kat said. "So I didn't just show up—it's the holidays, I figured it was a good time to come home. But you never answered my question back there. You said your name's Willett? That wouldn't be the same gun-toting moron who shot my daughter, would it?"

"I'm with the FBI," Willett said. Snow had gathered on his glasses. He took them off and blinked owlishly as he wiped them with his jacket sleeve. "And your daughter was fleeing when I was in pursuit." She took a step toward him. Surprisingly, Willett stood his ground. "You're Katherine Everett, then? I've actually been looking for your daughter for some time."

"And you expect me to help?" Kat said. "Erin and I aren't exactly close—I have no idea where she is. And considering what you did to her the last time you crossed paths, I'm pretty damn sure I wouldn't tell you if I did know."

"Spare me," Willett said, dismissing the statement. "The fact is, I already know she's in town. At the moment I don't give a rat's ass—right now, I'm more interested in talking to you."

"About?" Kat said. The amount of acid she managed to inject in the single word was impressive.

"Your husband, and a man by the name of Mitch Cameron."

"My *ex*-husband is dead," she said coolly, "and I don't know anyone named Mitch Cameron."

"No? Because I have some fairly intimate photos of you and Mr. Cameron taken over the past few months that would suggest otherwise."

"You must be a wizard with Photoshop then, because I don't know the man," Kat shot back, not at all flustered.

The color rose in Willett's cheeks. His eyes flashed with anger. "Look, this doesn't have to go badly. Ask Mr. Juarez here: I can be a reasonable man. But I'm working on a severely limited time table at the moment. I don't have time for games. If you ever want your daughter to be able to safely come out of hiding, you'll talk to me."

Kat's jaw tensed. After a few seconds, she reluctantly nodded. "Fine—go ahead. What do you want?"

"Do you know where Mitch Cameron is right now?"

"No," she said immediately.

Frustration was rapidly reaching a boiling point for the man. "Do you know a woman named Lilah Waters?"

"Never heard of her. Is that it?"

Willett took a step toward her. Jack had no doubt the man could—and would—do damage, but in this case he wasn't sure he would bet against Kat. Willett seemingly came to the same conclusion, because he reined himself in. "If you speak with Cameron or your daughter, this is my number," he said to Kat. He handed her his business card. Kat slipped it into her pocket without glancing at it.

"Is there anything else?" she asked.

He frowned. "Not at the moment."

"Good. Happy New Year, Agent Willett." She turned to the door, but paused to look at Jack before she disappeared inside again. "I think Maya and I will be leaving soon. You know where to find us?"

He thought of Erin's message, and nodded. "I do. I'll be in touch."

After she'd gone, Jack remained beside Willett. The snow had gathered around his collar, melting down the back of his neck until he was chilled to the bone.

"I know what you're thinking," Willett said when they were alone. "I'm the guy who shot your friend."

"And her dog," Jack pointed out. "She's actually more pissed about that."

"She ran—I gave her every opportunity to stop. And the dog…" He stopped with a frown. "I've been looking for these people for the better part of more than twenty years. That's my career, in a nutshell. I've watched them murder schoolrooms full of kids, whole families. I've watched them twist people's minds until all that's left is hate. So…yeah. I shot the damn dog. I shot Erin. Chances are pretty good that I'd do both again without a second thought, if it got me closer to shutting this organization down."

Jack didn't say anything. He turned the information over in his head, thinking again of Lucia. Always Lucia. Lucia, dying alone with their unborn child inside her—raped and tortured, terrified in those final moments. What would he do to put an end to J.?

"I'm just trying to stop them," Willett concluded, his tone suddenly weary.

"Then stop focusing on Erin and Mitch Cameron," Jack said. "Erin isn't behind any of it, and right now Cameron's accounted for. This Lilah Waters—what do you know about her?"

"She's a homicidal psychopath who gets off on inflicting pain more than anyone I've ever met." Jack didn't miss the significance of the statement. Willett didn't say more, but he didn't have to: Jack could tell that he knew what had happened to Lucia. And that Lilah and J. were behind her death. Willett hesitated.

"Do me a favor," Willett said. "Give me a second—I need to talk to the sheriff, and get him to shut this place down before something happens. Then, will you come with me?"

"Where?"

He indicated the general store a few houses down. "I'm renting a place over that store. I figured if the town went up in flames tonight, maybe I'd get a couple of nights comp'd. I've got files up there. I'll show you everything I have. Okay?"

"Yeah," Jack agreed after a moment's thought. "Okay. After we get the bar shut down."

Sheriff Finnegan arrived fifteen minutes after Willett called him, looking harassed and not at all pleased to be summoned by a federal agent when he clearly already had several other fires he was trying to put out.

"Willett," Finnegan said shortly, nodding as he approached the two men. "Jack."

They were inside the bar once more, the band still going full-bore. Kate and Maya had gone, but by Jack's count they were the only ones—the place was standing room only.

"I've got my men looking for those women whose descriptions you gave me. But that's not why you called me out here, is it?"

"This intelligence we have is good," Jack said. He led the

sheriff to a darkened corner that was only slightly quieter than the rest of the bar.

"Then why can't I get anyone but you to tell me about it?" the sheriff countered. It had been a mistake to underestimate him, Jack realized. "I've got a few contacts in DC myself, believe it or not. I gave them a call—and it turns out, they don't know what the hell either of you are talking about. From everything I can gather, you were fired six months ago." He directed the statement at Jack. "And you're one mistake from being shoved out the door yourself," he said to Willett. "And no one seems to know why the hell you would be in Littlehope, Maine, right now, running around screaming about the sky falling."

"Everything that's happened the last couple of years here," Jack began. "The showdown out on Payson Isle the spring before last; everything Diggs and Erin went through up north a few months later… Someone bombing Kat's house last winter. Do I really need to go on? You're a smart man. You really think this much bloodshed is standard for a town of less than fifteen hundred people?"

"Only if it's in a warzone," Finnegan returned evenly. "Don't talk down to me, of course I know something's not right. But if you know something—hopefully, something a little more concrete than the fact that there are two crazy women out there somewhere intent on doing some damage—I'd really appreciate being in the loop."

"As soon as I find out anything more, I'll let you know," Jack promised. "But please—clear this place out. It could be a huge mistake if you don't."

"It would have to be to make up for the stink Mimi's gonna put up when I tell her she has to call it a night." Jack didn't waver. Finally, the sheriff nodded. "Right. Shut it down."

"Is there anywhere else in town that you can think of where people would gather?" Willett asked. "If these people are targeting anything tonight, they're going for maximum carnage."

"In Littlehope? Bennett's is pretty much it. Everything else is closed tonight. The only other thing I can think of is Edie's place, and I already sent guys over there to keep an eye out."

"Good," Willett said. "Now all we need to do is find Jenny and Lilah and get them locked up, and maybe we can keep this thing from happening."

The sheriff took a breath and nodded toward the bar. "All right—if I'm doing this, I might as well do it now. You boys got my back? My guess is if any violence gets done tonight, it'll be when I tell everyone they need to call it a night at eight-thirty on New Year's Eve."

23

THE *TRIB* WAS LOCKED UP TIGHT when we got there, thanks to the weather and the holiday. Though the bar was only a couple of doors down, snow coated my eyelashes and froze my cheeks. The wind rattled signage along Main Street and whipped ice-coated branches off the trees. Eight clock on New Year's Eve, and—with the exception of Bennett's—the whole town was locked down tight.

"After you," Diggs said when he'd opened the door, and nodded me inside. I stomped my boots on the welcome mat at the door. Diggs did the same.

We didn't turn the lights on inside, but instead followed the red glow of fire doors and exit signs down the long linoleum hall. Like the rest of the town, the building was cold and utterly deserted. Somehow, it still managed to evoke the best memories I have of my teen years in Littlehope.

Diggs had gotten quiet again. Instead of heading for the newsroom at the very end of the hall, he stopped at a pale wooden door and fished a key from his pocket.

"What are you doing? I thought we were here to work." I asked as he unlocked the door.

"We are—but I'd rather work in here, away from all the

windows in the newsroom. Okay?"

Not the worst idea he'd ever had. Inside, Diggs closed the door behind us and flipped the light switch on the wall. The old florescent bulb overhead flickered a few times before it came on, bathing the room in an overly bright wash of white light. Together, Diggs and I surveyed our old domain.

The former storeroom hadn't changed much from the days when Diggs and I used to work together out of the space, back when I was in high school. Same hulking metal desk and same mini fridge, though someone had replaced the ancient plaid sofa that had been there before. A soft leather one was in its place.

Diggs draped his arm over my shoulders, warming me with that single move. I nodded toward the dinosaur of a computer on the desk.

"Can you even get the internet on that thing?"

"Can, do, and will," he said. "I think." He went over and started it up. It whirred with aged determination. Diggs grinned at me. "See?"

He sat down in a musty wooden chair, while I hopped up on the desk beside him. Against all odds, he got us online. Diggs typed with one hand, his other on my leg.

"Lilah Salvator," I said to Diggs. "That's what she's been going by here, according to Edie."

He typed it in. His other hand slid under the snowy cuff of my jeans. I saw him frown when he found thermal underwear instead of bare skin. Undeterred, he moved beyond the second layer. My eyes sank shut when he grazed my naked calf.

"You shaved," he murmured, his eyes still on the computer.

"It's New Year's Eve," I said. "I thought I might get lucky."

"Here it is," he said.

"What?"

I opened my eyes to find him smirking at me.

"Work, remember? Saving the town? I've got a Cushing address for Lilah Salvator."

"Oh. Right." I tried to move my leg. Diggs tightened his grip around my ankle, eyes back on the computer screen.

"Stay there," he said.

"Yes, sir. What's the address for Lilah?"

He frowned. "5 Hathorne Point Road."

"Edie said Lilah told her she lives near the Olson House."

"Well, according to this, she lives *in* the Olson House." He typed in something else. Meanwhile, his hand continued its path under my long johns, fast approaching the sensitive spot behind my knee that Diggs knows makes me crazy.

My phone buzzed. I reluctantly removed my leg from Diggs' reach and got off the desk, while he continued googling.

"Yeah," I said into the phone.

"I just spotted Jenny," Monty said. "Or her car, anyway. I'm still at Edie's place, but there's a navy-blue sedan parked on a back road out behind there."

"No sign of her?" I said.

"Nope."

"Crap. Check in with Jack, see if he has a line on where Sheriff Finnegan is. I'll give Cameron a call, see if he's heard anything."

"Sounds good. You two holding up all right?"

"Fine," I assured him. He said something about servicing me himself if Diggs didn't do his rightful duty soon, and I told him we had it covered. Then, I hung up on him.

"Everything all right?" Diggs asked.

"Jenny's car is out behind Edie's place," I said. I dialed Cameron. He didn't answer. Doom and gloom settled, just like that.

"Other than the phony address and the Facebook page Edie showed us, I'm not getting anything for a Lilah Salvator," Diggs said. I settled back on the edge of the desk. Diggs picked up where he'd left off, his fingers homing in on my knee.

"Try Waters," I suggested. I slid a little bit closer. Diggs eyes flicked toward me for a second. He smiled.

"Yes, ma'am." He typed in *Lilah Waters*. We got more hits for this one, but they were all just social media profiles for people who definitely didn't appear to be Lilah Waters, CEO of Misery at J. Enterprises.

When my jeans kept him from getting any higher up my leg, he slid his hand out entirely and leaned in to kiss my ankle. And then my calf.

"I think we should take a break," he said.

"We're supposed to be working," I reminded him.

"We'll be more productive if we do this first."

"This being…?"

He got up. I stayed on the desk. When our lips met, I winced.

"Ow—lip."

"Sorry." He kissed me again, very gently, then refocused on my ear. Always a good move. He lifted me off the desk and back to the floor, then pushed me back toward the couch, his mouth moving along my jaw and down to my neck. One hand snuck under my shirt and made its way to my left breast, while Diggs unbuttoned my jeans with the other. Tension—the good kind—coiled in my belly.

"No sweet talking tonight?"

"Right now I can think of better things to do with my mouth."

The backs of my knees hit the couch. I nearly fell, but Diggs steadied me. He pushed my shirt up over my head without another word, then slid the left bra strap off my shoulder.

"If I'd known at fifteen that we'd be back in this office with you doing that—" I gasped when he nipped my neck.

"Oh yeah?" Diggs said. "Come on. You would have been completely freaked out."

"At fifteen, we both would have been pretty damn freaked out. By eighteen, I definitely would've been on board."

Diggs took a step back. He pulled off his own shirt and I just lay there for a second, not even remotely decent, and took in his muscles and his scars, his barrel chest, not to mention the very exciting things happening farther south. I'd gone liquid in record time. His eyes were dark when he looked at me, no room anymore for regret or sadness. Now, all I saw was want.

"Come here," I said, when he just stood there.

"Not yet. Jeans off," he ordered. "And whatever you've got underneath them."

"You're bossy tonight."

He grinned. "I've missed you too much to wait. Come on, sweetheart—show me what you've got."

I pulled off my jeans while he watched. Then my long underwear. I kept my panties on. He shook his head.

"Everything."

Okay—yes, there was a blizzard, and homicidal lunatics, and we were in our old office with both said blizzard and lunatics just outside the door. But this was Diggs...and it really had been far too long. I ignored the blush rising in my cheeks, and teased my panties down my freshly shaven legs.

"That's my girl," he said.

When he finally came to me, he knelt beside the sofa and pulled me closer. Nuzzled my knee. I rested my hand on his head, twisting my fingers in his short hair. He kissed my thigh. I waited for him to speak—Diggs is usually a talker, and once you hit the bedroom he knows all the right things to say. Tonight, he was silent. His big hands were warm on my thighs; his scruff abraded sensitive skin as he nipped, kissed, tongued his way farther up.

I ran one hand alone his back, my nails lightly scoring corded muscle while my ohter hand remained on his head. Befre long, I stopped thinking about all he wasn't saying. I whispered his name and a dozen other things I don't really remember, that tension spiraling as he worshiped every inch of me.

When I came apart, there was barely time to recover before Diggs' jeans were off and he was inside me, my legs wrapped around his waist and not a centimeter of space between us. His mouth at my ear, he whispered just three words before we both tripped over the edge.

"I adore you."

•

"Are you okay?" I asked, an indeterminate amount of time later. I was still getting my breath back. We were crowded together on the couch, his arms around me. I kissed his jaw, despite my puffy lip.

"I think so," he said.

"You can talk to me if you need to," I said.

"I know."

He didn't talk, though. Neither did I. Time passed. It got chilly.

"We should get back to work," I finally said.

"I know," he agreed.

I started to move. He didn't. I shifted to look at him. "You're not moving."

"Two more minutes," he said.

I nodded. Things went quiet, the seconds ticking past. If he wasn't going to bring it up, someone really should. "Listen, the stuff Laurie said, about the reverend wanting to hurt you—the things he thought about you… None of this is your fault. Nothing you did could have changed any of this."

"I know that," he said. I wondered, though, if he really did.

I shifted to look at him. His eyes were the intense, stormy blue I love, his forehead furrowed. I smoothed the wrinkles with my index finger. "You know, even in the worst of it, somehow life with you really beats life without you."

He kissed me, somehow managing to get my mouth without hurting my bruised lip. Diggs is magic that way. He wrapped his arms around me and held me tight, laying his head at my breast. "I love you," he mumbled into my chest.

"Is that directed at me or the girls?"

"All three of you," he assured me.

I ran my fingers through his hair, his head still pillowed on my breast. Thought of all the shit we'd been through over the years—the divorces and the marriages and the drugs and the endless fighting. And, of course, Payson Isle and my father and Diggs' father, J. and Kat and whatever we were on the cusp of here in Littlehope. And then, I thought of the people we'd been. Me, at ten, fifteen, nineteen… Now. Diggs had been there, every step of the way.

"It was always you," I said. His hand stilled. He waited for me to finish, or at least explain myself. It wasn't an easy thing for me—I really hate talking about this kind of crap. Somehow, it's always worth trying, for him. "I saw who you were—when you weren't high as a kite, I mean. Or nailing everything with tits in a hundred-mile radius. And even at the worst, you were always…careful. Of my heart. I knew that first summer we were together, I'd never find someone else. It wouldn't ever be the same."

He held me closer, his ear pressed to my heart. Diggs isn't the kind of man who asks for comfort. He'll ask for sex; he'll hold me when I need it. But this… It was the first time I could remember when it felt like the only thing I could give him, the only thing he needed, was this—the two of us, quiet, knowing that there was no one else on the planet I would rather have in my arms.

"Does that mean you'll marry me?" he said.

I tensed. I would have gotten up, I think, but he still seemed very much opposed to the idea. "I'm thinking about it."

"What are you thinking?"

I rolled my eyes. "Whether or not it would be a good idea."

"Why wouldn't it be?"

"Diggs." I pulled him up, so I could look him in the eye. "We don't even know what we're going to do after this—after we take J. down. I mean…have you even thought about that? You and me together when we're on the run is one thing. But when we're just normal people living a normal life, how well do you think we'll do? How well do you think *you'll* do?"

"You're saying I can't do normal, and you can?" That was a challenge in his eyes if ever I'd seen one.

"I was a respected journalist married to a respectable professor for six years," I reminded him.

"A respectable professor who was twenty years older than you. And an asshole. I was a semi-respected reporter married to a very respectable accountant for three years. What's your point?"

I had to think about it, since I'd kind of lost track. I decided to abandon any conventional arguments, and go with the question I was most curious about at the moment.

"What *do* you want to do when this is all over?"

"Be with you," he said, without a moment's hesitation.

I slapped his naked chest. "Besides that. Where do you want to go? What do you want to do for work? I'm assuming if we survive this, we won't suddenly be independently wealthy."

"You don't think Cameron would be willing to support us for the rest of our days?" He got serious when I arched my eyebrow at him. "Okay. Honestly? I don't know. I know I want to be with you. I don't think I want to move to the suburbs, and I know I never want to be an editor again. At least, not an editor with a dozen reporters I have to manage. What do you want to do?"

Secretly, I'd actually been giving this a lot of thought. When I wasn't thinking about taking down J., of course. Or what horrors my past contained. Or whether or not Diggs and I would even survive all this madness.

"Do you remember that first summer we worked together?" I asked. "Running Buzz's paper? Late nights doing research, checking sources…"

"Making love…" Diggs finished for me. "Making love some more."

I warmed at the look in his eye. "Well, yeah… That was

a key part of that summer. But the rest of it was fun too, wasn't it? Just the two of us, accountable to no one else."

"You're saying you want to start a paper. I just said I don't want to be an editor again."

"Not a regular paper that covers a dozen stories, and no employees. Just the two of us, and one story at a time. We could have our own website. Do a regular podcast. Travel wherever we want. You said you hate this town—so let's not stay here. We pack up—with Einstein—and we go."

"Are we married in this scenario?"

"Is it a deal breaker if we're not?"

He frowned. I was genuinely surprised to realize he was serious about this. "Is that a no?" he said.

I shook my head, but before I could answer, my phone buzzed again. I held up my hand. "Hang on, it's Cameron. Hold that thought."

I reached for my clothes and flipped my phone open. "What's up?" I asked, pulling my long underwear on at the same time. It was creepy talking to Cameron when I was naked, even if he couldn't see me. Somehow, it felt like he'd just…know.

"Have you heard anything from Jenny yet?" he asked.

"No—I actually called to ask you the same thing a while ago, but you didn't answer. Monty found her car parked out near Edie Woolwich's place. Why? Have you heard anything else?"

I put the phone on speaker so Diggs could listen in, and set it on the desk. "Jenny hasn't contacted me," he said. "What else is going on?"

I figured he didn't mean Diggs' and me canoodling on the *Trib* sofa or Diggs' sudden interest in another trip down the aisle, so I stuck with the headlines. "The last I knew, Jack was trying to get Bennett's Shanty shut down for the night. Oh—and Trent Willett just showed up." Dead silence. "Cameron?"

"Trent Willett?"

"The FBI agent—the guy who shot me last year, and followed—"

"I know who he is. How did he find out?"

"How the hell should I know?" I said. "We didn't do a lot of chatting the last time I saw him." I could almost hear Cameron frowning through the phone. "What do you want us to do?"

"Stay away from him," Cameron said without hesitation. "He's dangerous—and given his past actions, he obviously doesn't care what happens to you."

"But if he wants to take down J.," Diggs interrupted, "doesn't that technically make him someone on our side? Maybe we should just pull him in."

"No," Cameron said unequivocally. "We don't know what other interests Willett might have—I'm not convinced he isn't working with J. himself. Stay away from him."

Another call came in from Monty while Cameron was still ordering us around. I cut him off.

"Okay, got it—no talking to Willett. Is there anything else, Mein Kommandant?"

"That's it," he said. He hesitated. "You're safe there? Keeping a low profile?"

"We are," I said. "We're checking in with Jack and Monty periodically, though. Trying to figure out what happens next."

"Good. Just stay out of sight, as much as possible. Where are you now?"

"The *Trib.* We're just doing some research." Diggs smirked at me.

"Good," Cameron murmured, almost inaudible through a wave of static. "Contact me if anything changes—in particular, if you get some idea of where Willett is headed next."

"Wait," I said. "Does that mean you're not leaving the island?"

He hung up without answering. Diggs was already redressed and back at the computer typing away. I settled at my former spot at the edge of the desk. His hand immediately found my ankle again.

"About that ring," I said.

He smiled. It seemed genuine. "Don't worry about it right now. I just wanted you to know I'm serious."

I leaned in and kissed his cheek. "You've made that pretty clear. Now…what are you looking at?"

"Call Monty back," he reminded me. "Something could be up."

Monty answered on the first ring. "Tell me I interrupted something good," he said.

"I will not," I said. "What's going on?"

There were voices in the background—several of them, it sounded like. "I'm at Edie's place. I was taking a look around and noticed one of the windows open on the second floor, and footprints in the snow. I went in just to let them know something might be up. Turns out that guy you were worried about earlier is running loose."

"Nate?"

"Yeah—that's the one. I know I was supposed to be keeping an eye on Jenny, but that car's still out there under about six inches of snow now. I don't know where the hell she is, but I'll keep looking."

"Okay," I agreed, uneasy now. "Be careful, all right?"

"Now what fun would that be?"

"I'm serious," I said.

Diggs looked up, frowning. "What's up?" he mouthed.

I held up a finger for him to wait. "Monty—careful, all right? With a capital K."

"Yes, ma'am. I'll check in again shortly."

I hung up. Diggs raised his eyebrows and waited for the story. "Nate's missing—I think he climbed out his bedroom window. Monty's over there now."

"And Jenny?" Diggs asked.

"He hasn't seen her, but he says her car is there. I don't like it. Something's happening, I can feel it."

I returned to the desk, where I looked over Diggs' shoulder at the computer. "What are you looking at now?"

"The coordinates. I'm just trying to figure out what they could be targeting, if they're based here and they're really considering hitting tonight."

"Honestly?" I said. "It doesn't make sense to me why they would, you know? Why wouldn't they at least wait for the storm to blow over?"

"Maybe they're planning to use the storm to their advantage—emergency vehicles crippled, the cops out of range… It would be the perfect way to send a message to Jenny to stop screwing with them."

"Where else do you think they'd strike?"

"I don't know," he said. "I'm just saying it might be smart to expand our search."

That headache I'd finally gotten rid of returned with a vengeance. "How are we supposed to do that? We're in the middle of a blizzard—what are we supposed to do, just start cruising the countryside?"

"Would you relax, woman?" he said. "I'm not saying I think it's far from here. I'm just saying, maybe the target itself isn't in Littlehope. It could be Cushing, Rockland, Thomaston, Warren…"

I put my head in my hands.

"Sorry. Why don't you give Jack a call," Diggs suggested. "See what he thinks."

I did, then waited uneasily for him to answer. Things were quiet now, but I couldn't shake the feeling that this brief respite was about to end—and none of us would like whatever came in its place.

24

IT TOOK SHERIFF FINNEGAN, two deputies, Jack, and Willett to keep the peace as Bennett's cleared out that night. It was nine-thirty by the time everyone was out and Jack watched Mimi grudgingly lock the place up and head home. By that time, the snow was raging and the wind was roaring, and the only ones braving the icy roads were snowplows—and those were few and far between.

With that mission accomplished, Willett led Jack up to the room he'd rented above Wallace's General Store. It consisted of bedroom, bath, and a small kitchenette. Everything was neatly appointed throughout—including a box of files set on an old wooden desk in the corner of the bedroom. Jack eyed them curiously as Willett pulled two Sea Dog Ales from the refrigerator.

"How did you get this assignment, anyway?" he asked. "Going after this organization?"

Willett cracked open one of the beers and handed it to Jack, then opened his own. Jack took a chair at the desk. Willett remained standing.

"I was assigned after the murder of a man by the name of Dexter Mandrake," Willett said. Jack tried to remain impassive, but he knew he'd failed at the look in Willett's eyes. "You know that name?"

"I've heard it before," Jack confirmed. "Were you at the scene, then? You saw what happened there?"

"One of the worst crime scenes I've ever been to. And considering that I've been following J. all this time, that's saying something."

Willett went to the window and looked out onto the street, frowning at the blustering snow. He let the curtain fall back into place, and returned to the topic at hand.

"We don't have time to go into all the details," the agent continued. "But you know these people—it's obvious you do. You know Mitch Cameron. He came up in this organization, and I can tell you firsthand: no one with J. gives a damn about how much blood is shed. Human life doesn't mean a thing compared with the goal—whatever that goal might be at the time."

"Considering your treatment of Erin Solomon last spring, I'd say you share that philosophy," Jack noted evenly.

"I told you what that was about," Willett said. His eyes hardened. "She ran. And this is the daughter of Adam Solomon—a man I'd been tracking for a lot of years. If she could get me closer to him—"

"She couldn't, though," Jack interrupted. "She knew almost nothing about him. And now he's dead, so there's no reason to keep pursuing her."

"Let's just agree to disagree when it comes to Erin," Willett said.

"That might be for the best," Jack agreed. He thought of Cameron, out on the island alone right now. Of Jenny—still a loose cannon, clearly intent on taking more lives before this was over and done.

"You mentioned Lilah Waters earlier," Jack said.

"I'm looking for her myself. And a woman named Jenny Cameron." Willett looked at him blankly. "Mitch Cameron's daughter."

"Went by Jenny Burkett for a while?" Willett asked.

Jack thought of the woman they had pursued in Kentucky, back before they knew anything about Project J. "She's the one. You heard about the deaths here lately—the hit and run of the preacher; the explosion at that meth place?"

"I did."

"Jenny was behind those. She's still out there. If you have any resources behind you, I'd say one of our best moves would be to sic some guys on her."

Willett's gaze slipped. He moved the curtain back again to look out the window, then let it fall back into place. "I can't. You heard the sheriff back there: they're ready to boot me out of the Bureau. They closed the investigation three months ago; I'm not even supposed to be here. Trust me when I say I'm the only resource I have right now."

"They closed the investigation into J-932? Why would they do that now, of all times?"

"I don't know." Willett took a long pull from his beer, and came closer. He sat at the edge of the bed, his gaze drawn to the files on the desk. "They said they couldn't waste any more energy or resources, but you look at the things that have happened in the past two years and tell me how shutting these people down would be a waste."

"You think someone higher up was putting on pressure?"

"I'm sure of it," Willett said. "Look—something is about to go down here. You know that. Cameron is here. Lilah is here. Adam Solomon's wife and daughter are here. Something is about to happen—something big. If we can prevent that, don't you think we should at least try?"

Jack hesitated, but only for a few seconds. He saw another flash from beyond; heard that voice that he believed had meant something to him once—this time, raised in a scream.

"That scene," Jack said, rather than answering the man. "The Mandrake murders. How many dead were there?"

"Five," Willett said. "Three from the Willett family, and two J. operatives. In the family, it was Dex Mandrake, his wife—Betty—and a six-year-old girl. Betty raped, the little girl tortured; Mandrake forced to watch the whole thing. Neighbors said there was a boy, too, but we never found any sign of him. We figured they must have taken him."

Jack didn't look up at that, digesting the information. "And do you know who orchestrated the murders? Mandrake was the leader of the organization at that time, wasn't he?"

"He was," Willett confirmed. "I never knew for sure who put the whole plan in motion, but my guess was always Mitch Cameron. He'd kind of left the organization by then, but he was still on the perimeter. The other two dead on the scene were fairly high up in the organization—one of them was Susan Stargill. Cameron's wife. I figure maybe he recruited her for a coup, and something went wrong."

Jack thought of the story Cameron had told the day before—about how he'd gone off the rails after Payson Isle. *I managed to take out two of the team members.* Was that what had actually happened? Cameron had tried to protect Mandrake, and inadvertently wound up killing his own wife in the process? Jack recalled the look on Cameron's face when he'd recounted the story, and was convinced: that was exactly what had happened.

"So what happened then?" Jack asked. "You really think Mitch Cameron took over the organization at that point?"

"No—he was never management material, but he did go back to them after Mandrake's death. His kid was seven, eight years old by then, and she was already indoctrinated. So, he went back under. But I know he was never at the helm."

"And you have no idea who is," Jack said.

Willett frowned. "No. I'm telling you, the organization is impenetrable. Some of the names associated, though… They'd blow your mind. Carl Wright. Allen Phippsburg. Andrew Bellows…."

"The US Attorney General and a Supreme Court judge…and Bellows," Jack repeated, turning the name over. "Where do I know that name?"

"He's a congressman out in Washington State—from a political family. His sister was Jane Bellows."

"The senator who was murdered in 2012," Jack said. Shortly after Erin had learned her father had been staying with the woman.

"That's right," Willett confirmed. It was apparent by the look on his face that he was aware of the significance.

Before Jack could reply, his phone rang. He checked the number briefly before answering.

"Have you heard about Nate?" Erin asked.

"Hang on," he said. In the distance, he heard a siren. Willett returned to the window "Can you see what's happening?" he asked Willett.

"We don't have any windows," Erin said.

"Not you. I'm with—" He stopped, frowning. Something indefinable raised the hair at the back of his neck. "Willett, move back from the window."

"You're with Willett?" Erin said.

"I'll call you back." He hung up before she could protest.

"Willett!"

The man turned. "Just a minute, for Christ's sake. I'm trying to figure out what's going on out there."

"What is it?"

"The snow's too bad to see much, but there are flashing lights—blue and red—across town."

"Well, just do me a favor and stay away from the—"

The shot came before he could finish the sentence, shattering glass in every direction. A gust of wind and snow came with it. The bullet hit Willett in the center of his forehead; a second shot a split second later caught him in the shoulder as he went down, spinning him sideways.

Jack hit the floor. He scrambled toward Willett, already well aware that the man was dead. His phone rang. He ignored it.

Willett's files were on the table. An entire career's worth of information on Project J. Outside, though, Lilah could be out there—getting away. He dove to the window and peered over the ledge into the driving snow outside. Across the street, he could just make out a figure in black. It was impossible to tell whether it was a man or woman, but he had no doubt that this was the shooter.

Could it be Lilah?

He didn't waste time debating the question before he ran for the door, tore it open, and, gun drawn, dashed headlong down the stairs. Once outside, he was hit by a face full of snow and a fresh gust of wind. Jacketless, head down, he ran for the corner where he'd seen the figure. Footprints in the snow told him it hadn't been his imagination. He scanned the darkened street until he saw someone climb into a pickup. She turned back to look at him and he saw her face moments before she slammed the door and peeled away, sliding briefly before the tires caught.

Jenny.

Breathing hard, adrenaline still on high, Jack returned to the apartment and trudged back up the stairs. With frozen fingers, he fumbled his phone out of his pocket and called Erin.

"Are you all right?" he asked the moment she answered.

"I was just about to ask you the same thing. Yeah, we're fine," she said. "Just checking in. Nate's missing. What's happening?"

"I can't really talk right now, but I need you and Diggs to lock yourselves in, wherever you are. Stay down. Jenny just killed Willett."

"What do you mean—"

He returned to the apartment and looked around, at the shattered glass, the dead body, and the files waiting on the table. "I can't really go into details right now. Just stay where you are. I'll be there as soon as I can."

He hung up. Blood had pooled beneath Willett's still frame. Twenty minutes had passed since Jenny had fired through the window. Now, all was still.

His phone rang. Sheriff Finnegan's name came up on the ID. Jack answered immediately, recalling the sirens he'd heard just before the shot was fired.

"What's happening?" he asked as he flipped the phone open.

"You wanted an update if there were any new developments," the sheriff said. "We just found Jake Smith dead in his home. Stabbed multiple times with a kitchen knife. Wife's out of town. Daughter's missing."

Jasck ran through the long list of names in his head. "Who the hell is Jake Smith?"

"Father of Laurie Smith," the sheriff said. "The girl who

had the affair with Reverend Diggins."

"Okay," Jack said. His mind was racing. "Any other developments?"

"Just one," the sheriff said. "You wanted me to keep an eye on Edie Woolwich's place. I just got word: Nate Simpson is missing."

"How long?" he asked immediately.

"They're not sure. He had his music up, but I guess Edie had been trying to get him to turn it down and talk to him all night. One of your people was going by and saw the window open, so he went in there to have them check it out. Nate must've gone out the window. No idea when, but I talked to Fred—Edie's husband. The tracks are pretty well buried, so he's been gone a while.

"Do you know if he's armed?"

"Fred said no, but it wouldn't take much to come up with something." He paused. "Jake Smith had a gun safe at his place, too. It's open. If Nate had anything to do with this, he's got everything he needs."

"I have a problem on my side, too," he said.

"What's that?" Finnegan asked.

"Someone just killed Willett. That first woman I told you to be on the lookout for—the blond. I'm pretty sure it was her."

"Shit," Finnegan said.

"Still doubting it was a good idea to shut down Bennett's?"

"Don't get smug, smartass. I'll be over there as soon as I can, but I've got this scene to process and a three-car pile-up on Route 1 I'm supposed to be at, with more calls coming in all the time. It's all hands on deck, at least until this storm is over and we figure out what in hell is going on. I did make a call to the Feebs, though. The scope of this is looking like something way beyond my guys."

"What was their response?"

"They're sending someone as soon as they can. The storm's hanging things up, though."

Jack nodded grimly. "That's what I figured. What can I do for you in the meantime?"

"Find the crazy bitch who just took out Willett," Finnegan said.

"Got it. I'll see what I can do," Jack promised.

He hung up and surveyed the scene one more time before he retrieved Willett's files, turned out the light, closed the door, and left the building.

25

"WHAT'S GOING ON?" Diggs asked as Jack and I hung up.

"Jenny just gunned down Willett. Why the hell would she do that?" I went to the door and checked to make sure it was locked; it was. "Aren't we all supposed to be on the same side?"

"Cameron thought Willett might be working for J.," Diggs reminded me. "Maybe Jenny thought the same thing. What did Jack say?"

"Not much—just that we should stay put and he'd come for us."

The phone buzzed again. I jumped, completely on edge when I answered. It was Jack again.

"What now?" I asked.

He gave me the lowdown on every terrible thing happening in Littlehope at the moment: Nate Simpson had given Edie the slip, which we of course already knew; Laurie Smith was missing; her father was dead, left to bleed out in the living room Diggs and I had been in just that afternoon.

I thought of the man in the cherry-red BMW we'd seen earlier. My stomach soured. "I'd say it's safe to say whatever plan J. has, it's fully in motion at this point, then," I said. "We need to figure out what the hell their target is."

"I have no more ideas than you do," he said. I put the phone on speaker at Diggs' glance.

"Are you okay?" he asked Jack, when we were all on the line.

"I'm fine," he said. "I was completely clear when the bullet hit Willett."

"That's not what he meant," I said.

"I know," Jack said flatly. "Look, I need to go. But if you could do a little more research, see what you can maybe figure out about the target, I think that would be the most helpful thing anyone can do right now."

He hung up again. Diggs and I kind of stared at each other for a few seconds. My stomach was churning.

"We need to talk to someone who knew Laurie and her father," Diggs said. "And Nate, ideally." I picked up the phone. "Who are you calling?"

"Who would know the most intimate details of everyone in town?" I asked. "Who's sleeping with who, what medications they're taking, what obsessions they might have…" Diggs looked clueless. "The town doctor," I answered for him.

I called Kat and gave her a super-condensed version of everything happening. To my surprise, she put me on speaker about halfway through my explanation.

"Maya's here too," she said. "She should hear this—she's the one who's been here for the past year."

"Did you know about the affair between Laurie Smith and Reverend Diggins?" I asked. There was no answer. I heard Kat and Maya murmuring about patient confidentiality, until Kat tugged Maya over to the dark side with the rest of us.

"I was aware, yes," Maya said. "Laurie had been coming

to me for birth control and routine exams for the past year or so."

"What about Nate Simpson?" I asked. "Do you have any idea what might be going on with him?" I thought of the look on Nate's face that afternoon when I'd left him. How angry he'd been when he realized I'd been the one to suggest Edie search his room. *People always want to define you. I'm Nate. Schizophrenic. That's all.*

Lilah had preyed on that belief. Exploited his desire to be something beyond just that label. And now, in all likelihood, Nate Simpson would pay with his life, just like so many had before him.

"I'm not sure," Maya said. "But you said Nate and Laurie are both missing."

"They are," I said. "Laurie mentioned earlier when we were there that her mother volunteers at Edie's place, so the guys there would know her. If Laurie's father was stabbed to death, it's possible that Nate did it."

"I'd say it's more than possible," Maya said. Another pause ensued. I waited impatiently for her to come out with whatever she was getting to. "Though if Laurie and Nate are together, I don't think she went unwillingly."

I stared at her. Down the hall, I thought I heard a door slam. I tensed.

Diggs touched my arm and put his finger to his lips. I ended the call.

We waited thirty seconds. A minute. Two. Five. Ten.

Nothing happened.

"Should we go out there?" I whispered to Diggs.

"Not in this lifetime," he whispered back. "Are you sure you heard something? It could have been the wind."

I made a face. "When in the history of movies has it ever been the wind?"

"Except this isn't a movie. In real life, sweetheart, there are plenty of times when it's just the wind."

I wasn't sure where he'd been for the past two years, but clearly he hadn't been paying attention. "There's no other way out of this room, is there?"

He pointed to a stack of boxes at the back of the room. "There's a door behind there. I don't think anyone's coming in that way." Which left the door in front of us, which opened directly into the hallway. Diggs had his Glock, and I had my Ruger—if someone tried to come through that door, there was no way in hell they'd get far.

My phone buzzed again. This time I didn't put it on speaker, but Diggs leaned in to listen alongside me.

"What the hell happened—I was getting ready to go over there," Kat said.

"Ignore that impulse," I hissed, "no matter what happens. I think we're running out of time, so let's get back to what we were talking about before. Laurie and Nate… Maya, why do you think there was something between them?"

"You're sure you're all right?" Maya said.

"Not even close," I said. "But that's completely beside the point right now. Please…"

"Fine. As I said, Laurie came to the clinic for birth control. The last time I saw her, it actually seemed like she was doing better. Bruises and other signs of…abuse, were common with her—which is obviously cause for concern. This time, though, there were very few. She said she was seeing someone new—someone different from anyone she'd ever been with before."

"How do you get Nate Simpson from that?" I asked.

"She talked about college—which I'd never heard her do before. She asked me what I thought about psychiatry;

whether I thought it might be a good field for her. Then she said her boyfriend had been heavily medicated most of his life, and she wished she could help him… That he didn't like what the medications did to him. And then, she asked some fairly specific questions about schizophrenia and schizo-effective disorder, which I believe are Nate's diagnoses."

"And you didn't report this?" I asked.

"I had no real evidence, and Laurie's eighteen. And Nate… Despite being in the residential home, he's his own guardian. And to be honest, I had never heard her more… eloquent. More clearly concerned about someone else's welfare." She paused. "But if they killed Laurie's father…"

"We don't know that," I said. "We don't really know anything. Which brings us back to the beginning: what's the target? If we can just figure out where Nate would head next… How surprised are we about Laurie's father?"

"We're not," Kat said flatly. "She'd never say, but I'm sure Jake had been molesting her for years." Which was certainly consistent with her behavior.

It seemed like we had everything we'd get from the dual doctors, so Diggs and I told them both to lay low and I hung up. Diggs looked at me, following the same line of logic we'd gotten tangled in on the phone.

"So if Nate killed him, he was targeting someone who hurt the woman he loves," he said. "Or the girl, in this case. What did Nate say when you talked to him today?"

I thought back. "I don't know—a lot. Nothing. He talked about how much he hates being defined by his illness. How he feels like he's behind bars, locked out." *There are people like me everywhere. No one should be in a cage.* I shook my head. "I don't really know how any of what we talked about gets us to J.'s target."

"Whatever's happening, they're going for maximum carnage," Diggs said. "J. is planning something significant. Cameron has said as much."

"What are the local towns where something could happen?" I said.

"The ones most likely as far as I'm concerned would be Littlehope, Friendship… Cushing, Warren, and Thomaston don't technically fall within the coordinates given, but these are desperate times."

"Warren," I said. Nate's words came to me again. *There are people like me everywhere… People who need to pay for their sins, and some who never sinned at all who deserve to be set free. No one should be stuck in a cage.*

Diggs got there the same time I did. "The State Prison."

That was it—I was sure of it. I called Jack back. I'd barely gotten the information out before he decided I was on the right track, and hung up to get Monty and Sheriff Finnegan up to speed. Meanwhile, I called Cameron. He sounded tense, which wasn't exactly a surprise. He sounded even more tense when I told him Jenny had just taken out Trent Willett.

When I mentioned that Kat was back in town, however, I thought he might have flatlined on the other end of the phone.

"Cameron?" I prompted.

"Where is she?" he demanded.

"She and—" I stopped, recalling the look he got whenever he mentioned my mother. "She's at the clinic. I told her to stay low, keep out of the way."

I heard him mutter something about impossible women under his breath.

"What's the problem?" I said. "Jenny's going after J.,

right? Kat doesn't have anything to do with them."

"Do you think Jenny has any idea where Katherine is right now?" Cameron asked. "Does she know your mother is in town?"

"I don't know," I said. "Cameron, why would Jenny care? Kat doesn't have anything to do with J." I felt myself starting to panic. "*Right?*"

"You need to get to her," Cameron said, without answering my question. "Call her. Talk to her. Tell her to stay out of sight until this is over. Both you and her need to stay away from Jenny."

I started to question him again, but he interrupted me.

"I have to go. But damn it, listen to me: get Katherine somewhere safe. Jenny will look at the clinic—trust me, if she knows your mother is in town, then she's looking for her. That's one of the places she'll go."

"Okay," I agreed. "We'll get to her. Call me if you hear anything, please."

"I will." There was a pause on the line. "Tell your mother that I said she's a pain in the ass...and to please be careful. I'll speak with you soon."

As soon as I was off the phone, I went for my jacket. "We need to get to them," I said.

Diggs stood in front of the door. "Not on your life. She's gunning for you too—you heard Cameron. Call Kat. Tell her what he told you, and let her do the math. She can find a hiding spot; there's no reason you need to hold her hand."

"So I'm just supposed to sit here, locked in this friggin' box until the whole thing blows over?"

"Call Kat," Diggs said. His arms were crossed in front of his chest, his jaw set. I made the call.

Before it went through, I heard the door open out front.

This time, it was unmistakable.

"Get the computer," Diggs whispered. A light came on in the hallway, a strip of yellow spilling under the storeroom door. I went over and turned off the monitor. We were plunged into darkness. I waved my arms in front of me, using the scant light from the hall to guide me back to Diggs. He took my hand and leaned in to whisper in my ear. Footsteps—heavy, definitely someone in thick boots—echoed in the hallway.

"It's probably someone who works at the paper," he said. I nodded, but didn't speak.

The footsteps paused farther up the hall. Then, there was a loud crack that it took a second for me to identify. A second followed.

A boot, hitting the door. It slammed open.

"Aiiiii-rin," Jenny sang out. "Time to go, bitch."

I texted a desperate message to Jack. Boots echoed in the hallway once more. Two more cracks, her steel-toed foot against another wooden door.

"The back door," I whispered to Diggs.

"Go," he said.

The light from my phone provided just enough illumination to ensure I didn't trip over my own feet and give us away. I reached the far wall. Stacks of boxed files barred our only other exit. Diggs' hand settled at the small of my back. I could hear Jenny getting closer.

"Wait," he whispered.

He drew his Glock and got in front of me.

"Don't be an idiot," I hissed. "You don't have to do that."

"Sssh," he whispered back.

The footsteps stopped just outside the door. My heart pounded, my palms slick with sweat. I rubbed them on my jeans and held my breath.

Her boot hit the door. It cracked, but held. Diggs and I were in the farthest corner of the room, Diggs in front of me, gun drawn—pointed directly at the door.

She kicked it again.

Again, it held. One more, though, and I knew it wouldn't.

A split second passed.

And then, a phone rang.

I nearly passed out, until I realized it didn't belong to Diggs or me.

"What?" Jenny answered.

Her footsteps faded as she moved away from the door. Diggs and I made for the back door, silently moving boxes out of the way while I listened to Jenny's conversation in the hallway.

"I'm not negotiating this," she said. "We can't do this without that bitch. You knew this when we started—you agreed. If we're doing this, Erin needs to be on the island with us. Whatever it takes."

I grabbed another box, my muscles tensed from the effort of trying to be quiet.

"Willett would have ruined this," Jenny continued. "You know that. We couldn't risk it, not now. When did you get so soft, Daddy? When you gunned down my mother, I don't remember you showing so much mercy."

Diggs took the box from me. I reached for another. I didn't get a good grip, though—in the process of setting it back down, it slipped from my hand. The sound that it made when it landed couldn't possibly have been loud; it fell no more than an inch to the ground. It felt as deafening as the gunshot I was certain would follow.

Jenny paused, for just an instant. Diggs and I both froze.

Then:

"Explain to me how we're supposed to do this without Erin?" she asked. "We have a trap, but you know we need more for bait than that goddamn box."

Incredibly, her voice was getting more distant.

"Fine. You want to do it this way, I'll try it," I heard her say. "I'll get to the island as fast as I can."

I heard the door to the outside open, then clamber closed. My knees were shaking. Diggs' hand had found my arm at some point, though I couldn't remember when. He squeezed lightly.

"Holy shit," he whispered.

"My thoughts exactly."

We waited in the dark for ten minutes. Twenty. Half an hour. There wasn't another sound in the hallway.

Jack finally texted back.

What's happening? RU OK?

I texted back, hands still shaking. *Close call. Where RU?* Diggs would be appalled that I'd resorted to text-speak, but I figured if any situation excused the degradation of the English language, this would be it.

Prison w/ sheriff. Meet us? Finnegan won't turn you in but we need to talk.

"What do you think?" I asked Diggs, showing him the text. He frowned, but eventually nodded.

"We're probably safer with them than anywhere else. We'll need a ride, though."

"Kat's car," I said. Which would conveniently give me a chance to check in and make sure Jenny hadn't eviscerated my mother on her way out to the island.

I texted Jack back and told him we were on our way. Diggs and I straightened from the awkward crouch we'd been frozen in.

"Should we take the back door?" I asked.

There were still about ten boxes blocking the way. Diggs shook his head. "You heard her: Cameron told her to move along."

"What the hell do you think they were talking about?"

Diggs went to the door. He still had his gun drawn, tension simmering. "I don't know. But it sounds like Cameron's been in on the plan from the start – "

"You think he and Jenny worked together to kill the J. operatives?" I asked.

"That's my guess. Hang on a second, okay?" He pushed the door open, but remained inside the room with me. I waited for gunfire to erupt.

Nothing.

Diggs stuck his head out the door. No one shot it off. He looked back and forth. Jenny didn't appear from the recesses of the hallway.

"Okay," he whispered, still scanning the empty hallway. "Let's go. Quickly."

We stepped into the hallway together, staying close to the wall. There were three other doors in the hallway—all of them open. I saw a boot print on one, the wood cracked. The front door was twenty feet down the cavernous corridor. It seemed like miles. I took the first step.

That was when I saw the shadow in the office directly across the hall from us. Diggs saw it at the same time.

"Go back!" Diggs shouted. He grabbed me, spun me around, pushed me forward. I flinched as a gunshot sounded. It took me a second before I realized Diggs was the one who had fired. Jenny cried out. A second gunshot went off. Diggs' hand returned to my back, pushing me through the door and back into the safety of the storeroom.

He slammed the door shut.

"I think I got her," he said, the words clipped, his breathing ragged.

"It sounded like it," I agreed.

We both moved deeper into the room, toward the back door. There was no time to waste on consultation—without a word, we flung boxes aside. Jenny's footsteps approached again. I could almost feel her fury when she called to us.

"You think you're getting away?" she shouted. "Did you hear that phone call? Daddy Dearest, begging for your life yet again? Like you're his flesh and blood, when we both know that's not true. We know your dad was never a quarter of the man my father is. I saw his fingers digging into your side."

I shut out her words and stayed focused. The last box was on the floor. Diggs leaned down and grabbed it. He stumbled on the way back up.

"Sol—" he said. He dropped the box.

Jenny's boot landed at the center of the door. I shoved the box out of the way. Reached for the door. Diggs leaned against the wall.

"What are you doing?" I said. "Go."

He nodded, but the way he moved—suddenly sluggish, heavy—told me that something was wrong. I opened the double doors. Wind and freezing snow gusted in, so cold it felt like I'd been plunged into a world of ice water. I pushed Diggs forward and grabbed a lug wrench that had been standing by the exit. I closed the doors again, then shoved the wrench through the handles. I didn't care how hard Jenny kicked, she wasn't getting out this way. Diggs stumbled again when we were outside. He fell to his knees. Lit by a world of blinding white snow, I finally saw why:

There was a hole in the front of his parka—in the upper chest. Blood blossomed in a wide, perfect circle. He looked at me, his eyes round. I read panic there, unlike anything I'd ever seen before.

"Hang on," I said, blinking back tears and snow and terror. "You'll be all right." I couldn't think. "I'll make sure you're all right."

Behind us, I could hear Jenny getting closer.

26

IT WAS TEN-THIRTY when Jack saw the text from Erin. Monty had joined him when they realized Jenny had switched cars and wasn't likely to come near Edie's again that night. Now, he and Monty left were in Jack's Honda Civic, idling outside the prison while they waited for the sheriff to confer with the warden inside. The storm and the location had ensured that cell service was spotty up to that point. By the time he'd learned that Erin and Diggs were fine, a fresh wave of anxiety had run up and over him. Sometimes, he thought Erin might kill him sooner than J. ever did.

"They're all right?" Monty asked, equally concerned.

"For now," Jack said. "They're on their way here. I'll feel better if I can keep them in sight."

Monty grunted, which Jack took as an exhausted assent.

The sheriff emerged from the prison, clearly harried and out of patience. Not that Jack could blame him.

"They're on lockdown—no one goes in or out. Same with the prison farm down the road—I gave everyone the word. They've got extra personnel coming in, just in case. But the bottom line is, even if Nate Simpson is crazy enough to try it, there's no way in hell he'll get through here."

Jack looked up as a pair of headlights swung up the snowy drive toward the prison security gate. The sheriff's hand went to the gun at his belt.

"What the hell?" Monty said, frowning in the direction of the vehicle. "Hold your fire, sheriff. Goddamn it."

He left them without explanation, jogging toward the car. Jack ran with him, squinting against the blowing ice and snow. "Who is it?"

Monty didn't have to answer, though—Jack saw the *Flint K-9* on the side of the snowy vehicle. A moment later, Jamie stuck her blond head out the window.

"What the hell are you doing here?" Jack and Monty asked at the same time.

She smiled. "I don't like running from a fight."

Moments later, they were assembled together with the sheriff as he resumed his debriefing, reiterating his belief that there was no way anyone could breach the prison.

"What if he had explosives of some kind, in a vehicle?" Jack pressed. "Could he drive something into the side of either this facility or the prison farm next door?"

Finnegan looked uneasy for a moment. "Not unless he's got some kind of big rig—that's the only way he could get through the front security gate. And there's no way in hell he's driving something like that in a storm like this."

"If he was, though," Jack pressed, "where would he get something like that? Is there somewhere local where they keep big rigs?"

"There are usually at least a couple of rigs parked at the Littlehope Trap Co.," Finnegan said. "But—"

"The Littlehope Lobster Trap Company?" Jamie said. Finnegan nodded. "The place owned by Jake Smith?"

The sheriff blanched. "I'll make the call."

•

Wind buffeted Jamie's SUV, snow blowing hard enough to make visibility nearly impossible. Jack gripped the dashboard as Jamie expertly navigated over unplowed roads and patches of bare ice.

"You know where we're going?" he asked. The sheriff was sending someone out, but staff was spread thin and his priority was making sure that if, on the off chance that Nate actually got a truck all the way to the prison, he had the personnel on hand on that end to deal with it.

"It's at the end of the peninsula. Another ten miles, maybe," she said without looking at him. "You really think this is what he's planning?"

"I do," he said without question. It was the first certainty he'd felt since this whole thing began. "If Laurie's father owned the place, she would have access to the trucks. Nate would know that. It's the only thing that makes sense."

"As much as any of this makes sense," Jamie murmured.

They hit a patch of ice; the SUV shimmied to the right. Jamie just barely touched the wheel, no tension visible on her face as she maneuvered. A split second later, they were moving forward again. Jack noted that her hands clenched a little more tightly around the steering wheel when they were on their way again, though.

"Can I ask you a question?" he asked.

"Go ahead."

"Why are you here?"

She smiled, just barely. "Here with you, you mean." It wasn't a question.

"Yes. Here with me. You risked your life for me in Coba.

Allowed us to stay on the island here with you. And now, you've come back here in a blizzard to… I don't understand."

"I told you: I don't like running from a fight. And these are bad people."

"They are bad people," he agreed. "But there are other bad people in the world. Coming back here makes no sense to me. We barely know each other."

"No," she said. Her mouth tightened. Her knuckles flexed. She said nothing more. Up ahead, he could just make out headlights headed toward them. He curled his fingers around the handle above the door.

"I see it," Jamie said. She edged the SUV over to the side infinitesimally as the headlights neared. Her windshield wipers beat faster, trying to keep the snow at bay. The wind roared outside as snow pelted the steel body that separated them from the elements.

Jamie's hands were clenched around the wheel. If it was Nate and Laurie driving a tractor trailer, Jack wondered what the hell he and Jamie were supposed to do. It wasn't like they could stop him in this thing.

The headlights drew closer.

"It's just a car," Jamie said two seconds later. He took in a breath, and watched the vehicle creep past. There was a moment when he wondered if the car could still belong to Nate, but then he saw the headlights turn into a driveway they had just passed.

Jamie released a long, slow breath.

"You okay?" he asked.

"Somehow I feel like I age faster around you. I don't think that's a good thing."

"Which begs the question…" he said.

She glanced in the rearview, then up ahead again. "We've

got another five minutes before we get there, probably. You want to call Finnegan?"

"He said he'll call if anything's happening," Jack said. "He has enough going on without having to update me every two minutes."

"Right," she said.

He studied her profile as they drove on in silence. *Sometimes when a woman is quiet, she's just quiet,* he remembered Lucia telling him once. That wasn't the case here, though. Jamie was quiet, certainly, but there was something she wasn't saying.

"Look…" he began.

She glanced at him. He could just see the intensity in her eyes.

"Let it go," she said. Something else Lucia used to say to him, often. He'd never been very good at letting things go, though.

"Whatever it is…" he began.

"Oh, for crying out loud, Jack," she said. "It's not something I can explain, okay? It's just a…feeling I got, when we met in Black Falls. And then somehow you keep showing up, and the feeling gets stronger."

He wasn't a man prone to blushing, but he felt his cheeks heat regardless. "Oh." Silence fell. He tried again. "It's not that I don't find you attractive—"

"Not that feeling!" she said. He couldn't tell if she was embarrassed herself, or laughing at him. "God, Jack. I just… I get feelings sometimes—you know that, right? Not emotions, but…"

"Premonitions," he said.

"You said it, not me," she said.

"And you had a premonition about me," he clarified.

With someone else, he would be skeptical. Jamie wasn't a woman who invited skepticism, however.

Up ahead, headlights appeared on the horizon again. He tensed, recalling why they were here.

"What is the premonition?" he asked.

"Hang on," she said, her voice suddenly tight. "This is it—those aren't a car's headlights. This is a truck. A big one."

It was clear as the lights drew closer that she was right. It was likewise clear that whoever was driving the vehicle wasn't completely in control. It barreled toward them, driving straight across the center line. The massive trailer behind the cab swayed dangerously in the wind.

"Jamie—" Jack warned.

"I know." She eased as far to the side as she could. Just as she'd gotten to the far right, her tires hit another ice patch. The truck tore closer, faster, seeming to gain speed with every second, while Jamie's SUV careened toward it. Locked in the skid, Jamie fought to regain control of the SUV as the truck's horn blared.

At the last second, the SUV's tires once more hit bare road. Jamie spun the wheel to the right, out of harm's way. The truck barreled past.

When they were clear, she stopped the car. They sat there for a split second of silence, both regaining their breath.

"You should call the sheriff," she said.

Jack already had his phone out. Jamie put the SUV in drive again, and pulled a U-turn in the road.

Finnegan didn't answer when Jack called. Jack left a voicemail message, then tried Monty. It took five rings before he finally picked up, static making it nearly impossible to understand him. Jack gave him the latest, and advised him of what was on the way toward them.

"Any news there?" he asked. "Are the others there yet?"

"No," Monty said. A pause followed. "But we've got a problem."

"Of course we do," Jack said. Up ahead, the truck appeared once again on the horizon. Jamie got closer. Jack watched with every muscle tensed as the trailer swayed with every reckless weave of the truck's tires. "What is it?" he pressed Monty.

"Diggs and Erin never showed up here." More static. Jack had to have him repeat the rest of the story. Finally, he got the gist of it: They weren't answering their texts. And gunshots had been reported coming from the *Trib.*

A wave of nausea ran through him. "Can you go there?" Jack asked. "I'll get there as fast as I can. We have to take care of this first."

"I'll meet you there," Monty said. He hung up. Jamie didn't ask for details, her focus entirely on the road ahead—and the truck now in clear view of them.

Another half mile down the road, Jack remembered a hairpin turn they'd barely cleared on the way here. Jamie tapped the brake. Clearly, she remembered it too.

He waited to see brake lights flash on the truck. None did.

"He's going to—"

"I know," Jamie cut him off. She slowed further. There was a house directly on the left-hand side of the curve. Jack could see the lights on. A white picket fence out front. A decorated Christmas tree in the yard.

There was no doubt this time: the driver wouldn't be able to recover from this. Jack got on the phone a millisecond before the truck lost control.

There were no screeching brakes, no blaring horns. The whole event was strangely silent—surreal, with the blowing snow and the darkness and the Christmas lights in the distance. Jack saw the moment the truck's tires hit the ice: the driver must have panicked, because the vehicle jerked to the right only briefly before they lost control completely. The trailer swayed so far to the left that for a moment it was traveling at a forty-five degree angle.

"Where are we?" Jack shouted to Jamie as 911 dispatch answered.

"Route 97," she said. "Just past Cross Road."

He repeated the address to the 911 operator just as the truck briefly, miraculously, righted itself. The skid was too severe, though, the ice too thick, the driver far too erratic. An instant later, still trying to navigate the sharp curve, the vehicle jerked to the right. The trailer swayed. Picked up speed. Sparks flew up off the road.

Both truck and trailer up-ended and hit the snowy pavement, then continued moving. The sound of metal on ice was a primal scream that tore the night in two.

Jamie stopped the SUV. She and Jack sat there frozen for the next horrifying seconds as the vehicle hurtled forward. It mowed through the picket fence, wood flying like shrapnel. The truck kept going, headed directly for the farmhouse.

Jack got out, head ducked against the wind. Jamie did the same, the two of them standing together—waiting, impotent, for the final impact.

27

I HEARD THE WORD "NO" trip off my tongue half a dozen times as I pulled Diggs up, back to his feet.

"You have to keep going," I said.

"It's bad, isn't it?" he said. I hated the fear on his face—it was terrifying. I shook my head, but I could feel the tears in my eyes. I brushed them away.

"You're okay. We're going next door. We'll go to the clinic. Kat will fix you—she'll fix this."

Behind us, Jenny was still trying to knock the door down. She would come to her senses in a second and come out the front door. I steered Diggs toward the street. He staggered. Leaned on me more heavily. I'd never known panic like this. Fear gripped me in a steel-plated fist.

Halfway across the road, Diggs' legs buckled. He almost took me down with him.

"You have to keep going," I said. "Please."

Somehow, he managed to stay on his feet. I felt him draw from whatever well it is that has kept Diggs going through shit that would have dropped other men years ago. He pushed himself forward.

We crossed the street.

Jenny still hadn't emerged from the *Trib.*

We reached the wheelchair ramp into the clinic. Diggs' blood drenched my jacket. This time when he sagged, there was no getting him back up. He fell to his knees. I looked back across the street, squinting through the snow and the darkness.

I could see no sign of Jenny.

I eased Diggs back so he was leaning against the railing of the wheelchair ramp. "'ll be right back," I said. There was no time for pep talks—I ran the last few feet to the clinic and pounded on the front door.

No one answered.

I reached into my pocket so I could call Kat, but my phone must have fallen out of my pocket when we were running.

I pounded harder on the door.

Across the street, I saw Jenny emerge from the *Trib.* I kicked the door. Screamed for Kat to open up.

At last, she opened the door.

"What the hell—"

She stopped at sight of the blood drenching the front of my jacket.

"It's Diggs," I said. "I need help."

She looked down at the bottom of the ramp. Called for Maya.

Jenny limped across the street toward us, moving slowly. Diggs had gotten her—she was obviously hurt. It was impossible to tell how badly from here, though.

Kat and I got Diggs back on his feet. We half dragged him up the ramp. Through the door.

I saw Jenny watching from the curb just before I slammed the door behind us.

We got Diggs into an exam room, and hefted him onto a table. His fingers were tight around my bicep, digging into me. His eyes were dark with fear, his breath coming hard.

"You're okay," I said. I smoothed his hair back while Kat cut away his jacket and shirt.

"This isn't the way it's supposed to happen," he whispered to me. His breath rattled in his chest.

"I think she nicked his lung," I said.

"You need to get out of the way," Kat said.

Diggs hand tightened around my arm. "Don't go."

At the front of the clinic, someone pounded on the front door. We'd locked it; I knew that wouldn't help, though.

"I called the police," Maya said.

By the time they got here, it would be too late.

Jenny kicked the front door. Maya looked almost as terrified as Diggs. She'd locked us in the exam room, a chair stuck under the doorknob as a barricade. There was no way in hell it was enough to stop Jenny. I was beginning to think the bitch wasn't human.

I heard the door burst open when Jenny got through.

Kat had gotten Diggs' shirt off. I fought to keep the terror from my own face at sight of the blood—or the bullet hole in his upper chest… If it had missed his heart, it would be nothing short of a miracle.

Jenny rapped lightly on the door. "Time to go, Erin."

Diggs still had my arm, his eyes locked on mine. He's been reading me since I was fifteen years old—the talent didn't fail him now. "Please don't," he whispered.

"You want answers, right?" Jenny said through the door. She didn't sound great herself, but her voice was still strong. "You want to know what happened that night, when the Payson Church went up. You want to know what your sniveling, weak-kneed daddy had to do with any of it."

"I know what happened that night," I said—loud enough for her to hear.

Kat was trying to stop Diggs from bleeding out. She and Maya turned him on his side to check the exit wound—he gasped at the pain, his face paler than I'd ever seen it.

The exit was clean, just below his right shoulder blade. It would leave a hell of a scar—another one—but at least the bullet wasn't still inside.

"You don't know shit about that night," Jenny said. "Why do you think they let your father live? Hmm? He and Isaac were both guilty of the same sin, weren't they? They both ran from J. So, why did they burn Isaac alive, and leave your dear old dad to wander around the island, mad as a hatter?"

Against my will, I found myself drawn into her words. "It was to punish him," I said, reciting the story I'd been told. "To show him what it would cost if he ran—after that, he worked for them again."

"My father told you that, did he?" Jenny asked. "What bullshit story did he tell you about that night?"

"You need to get out of the way," Kat said. I stepped aside—close enough to continue holding Diggs' hand, but my mind was wrapped up in the story. The *real* story.

I sifted through the muddled accounts I'd gotten of that night, from Matt Perkins, Joe Ashmont, my mother, Noel Hammond… Cameron himself. "A boy was killed," I said. "Zion Ashmont. And Isaac was shot. Matt Perkins killed them…" Did I really know that, though? The fact was, after all this time I didn't really know what the hell happened that night. "Cameron let Zion's mother live, but he locked the rest of the congregation in the church and lit the match."

Jenny scoffed. "And he had them drink something, right? He gave everybody a special batch of magic Kool-Aid?"

My blood chilled. "Scopolamine," I said. "From henbane—they grew it in the greenhouse."

I heard Jenny shift on the other side of the door. "You don't think it's weird that my father—a man who barely knew the island or anyone on it—would take time to mix up a batch of herbs? How did he get everyone to drink it? How did he even find it? And how did he get that entire congregation into the church in the first place? Thirty-four people he'd never met just drank some concoction and followed him to the chapel?"

I thought of that night in the motel room with my father. The phone call that came in the middle of the night. My father's disappearance, late that night until almost eleven the following morning.

He tended the garden.

He knew henbane.

Cameron had said my father was supposed to do it, but he backed out at the last minute.

Why would he lie about that?

What the hell really happened that night?

"Damn it, Erin," Kat said. "Stop listening to her—"

"You still really don't get it, do you?" Jenny said through the door. "Jesus Christ, Erin. It's right in front of you. Come on out here, and I'll make sure you get all the answers you can handle. And if the two of us team up, I promise you: J. is going down today."

"Don't even think about it," Kat interrupted. "We need to get Diggs to a hospital. I might be able to stabilize him, but I can't do much more than that here."

"You have two choices," Jenny said. "You can stay in

that room—in which case, I'll burn this place down, come in there, and pull you out by your flaming fucking hair. Or, you and Kat can come out to the island with me, and leave your mom's carpet-munching BFF to take care of your boyfriend."

Kat and Maya were working in tandem, moving easily around each other as they got bandages, checked Diggs' vitals, did what they do. There was no way in hell Maya could do it alone—no one could.

The truth was within my grasp, after all this time. I could get that…and save the people I loved at the same time. I swallowed past my fear.

"You can't have Kat," I shouted through the door.

"Solomon," Diggs said. His eyes found mine, and held. "Don't." Already three steps ahead of me.

"I'll be okay," I said. I blinked back a sudden rush of tears and fought to keep my voice steady. "You will too, okay? Maya and Kat will take care of you. You'll be fine. And I'll come back to you." I leaned down and rested my forehead against his. "Please, Diggs."

"Don't do this," he whispered.

"We need to work, Erin," Kat said. She was focused on the job at hand, but I knew her well enough to know she was fully aware of what was about to happen.

"Just a second," I said. I refocused on Diggs, shutting everything else out. I looked him in the eye. "Do you know how many times you've saved me?" I couldn't stop the tears now. I brushed them aside. "A thousand times, a thousand ways, you've saved my life. Give me a chance to return the favor."

I kissed him fiercely, my heart shattered in that way you don't realize a heart can shatter until it already has. "I love you."

"Then stay," he said. "Marry me." His eyes drifted shut, his breathing suddenly shallow. Jenny rapped on the door again. I heard her ratchet the safety off her gun.

I wasn't coming back from this—I was suddenly certain of it. Whatever Jenny had in store, wherever she planned to take me, there was no way I could survive. But if I could save Diggs…

"I'll marry you," I said to Diggs. I turned off the waterworks and forced myself to be calm. "Just stay alive. Just live, for me. Okay?"

"You've got till three," Jenny said. "Then I start shooting. One."

Diggs opened his eyes. The pain there was endless. He held tightly to my arm. "You don't have to do this."

"I do," I said. I ran my hand down the side of his face, my voice even now. "This is always the way it had to end. If I can come back to you, I will. I always have. I won't stop now, if I can help it."

I pried my arm from his grip. "I'm coming out," I called to Jenny, then looked at Kat. "You two stay. Save him, okay?"

"I'm not letting you—" Kat began. I shook my head, more certain than I'd ever been about anything in my life.

"Stay here, damn it," I said. "Save him. If there's any way in hell I can come back, I will."

I went to the door, where I knew Jenny was waiting just outside. I glanced back at Kat, Maya, and Diggs.

And opened the door.

28

THE SECOND THE TRUCK came to a complete stop, Jack was in motion. It had come to rest in the front yard of the farmhouse, demolishing the fence and the Christmas tree but miraculously leaving the house itself unscathed.

"Go get whoever's inside the house out," he instructed Jamie. "If there are explosives, we need everyone out of here."

"But—"

"Go!"

She nodded and ran, flat-out. Meanwhile, Jack approached the truck with more caution, his gun drawn. The truck had landed on the passenger's side, and the impact had smashed the truck's grill, and cracked the windshield, but otherwise it seemed intact.

"Help me!" a girl called to him. Her body was angled half-in, half-out of the driver's side window, above him. She was dressed in a camisole and blue jeans, nothing more, her face and shirt blooded.

"Please," she cried. Her voice bordered on hysteria.

"Where's Nate?" Jack asked.

"He's here," she said, sobbing now. "He's hurt."

"Can you get out?"

"I don't want to leave Nate."

"I'll go in and get him," Jack promised. "But I need you out of the way and safe first." He took a step forward, waiting until he had her eye. "Trust me, okay? Just come on out. Can you do that?"

She nodded, still crying. He climbed up on one of the wheels and held out his hand. The girl leaned out. Jack could smell leaking fuel. He noted the gash in her forehead, the blood drenching the front of her thin top. She was shivering, ice cold, when he finally held her hand.

Jack reached for her waist and helped her down. He noted that she wasn't armed—not something difficult to ascertain, since she was wearing so little.

"I didn't know," she said. There was a glaze of shock on her tear-stained face. "I thought I could help him."

Jack shrugged off his jacket and wrapped it around her.

"What's in the back of the truck?" he asked.

"I don't know—Nate wouldn't tell me. Just that we were leaving, but we had to set everybody free first. He killed—" she sobbed again. "Did you see? Did you see my father? I thought—"

Jack gently took hold of her shoulders, forcing her to look at him. "We'll deal with all of that, okay? But right now, it's just important that you're safe. Someone is getting people out of the house—I want you to go over there, all right? Stand over there with them."

She nodded, still weeping as she walked away. Jack brushed the snow and sweat from his face with his sleeve and used the wheel to hoist himself up and into the trailer. It was slippery going, the wind crippling him further, but eventually he was on top of the truck, peering into the cab.

Nate Simpson was dead—there was no question of that,

as soon as Jack saw him. What concerned him more was the man's obvious cause of death:

He sat slumped in the passenger's seat, his throat slashed.

Nate hadn't been driving—which meant only one person could have been.

He climbed back down from the truck and scanned the horizon. The fuel smell was getting stronger; beneath it, for the first time, he smelled smoke. Through the snow, he could just make out Laurie as she reached a cluster of other forms—presumably, Jamie and the residents of the home.

His head spun. Laurie, the truck potentially filled with explosives, or Erin and Diggs currently in a fight for their lives.

He texted Jamie: *Laurie did it. Keep her away frm family.*

If there were explosives in the truck, they were about to blow—there was nothing he could do about that. Out of ideas, he turned and ran headlong toward the farm. The smell of fuel permeated the air. The good news was that there were no other houses in the immediate area. If the truck did go up, the farmhouse would be destroyed, but it looked like that would be the extent of the damage.

Jamie had herded the family toward her SUV. Not far from them, Jack heard sirens headed their way. He continued looking in all directions, searching for some sign of the girl. When he reached Jamie, he pulled her aside.

"Did you get my text?" he asked.

She nodded. "Laurie never came to me, though—I don't know where she is. Where she went. What do you want to do?"

"This is everyone in the house?" Two young children and a woman were crowded into the SUV. The smaller of the kids—a little boy—was crying, while the mother and the sister tried in vain to quiet him. Jamie nodded.

"The husband's away on business. They just moved in—there's no livestock yet, no pets."

"Well, that's something, I guess." He looked back toward the truck. It was still smoking, but he saw no flames. If there were explosives, they should have gone up by now.

"What do you want to do?" Jamie asked.

A fire truck pulled in, followed by two police cruisers. Sheriff Finnegan emerged from one.

Before Jack could answer Jamie's question, his cell rang again. The number wasn't familiar.

"Agent Juarez?" a woman said. "It's Kat Everett—Erin's mother."

"What's happening?" he asked immediately, stepping away from Jamie.

"I'm at the clinic—I'm hoping to get Diggs airlifted out of here, but I don't think it'll happen in this weather. He's stable, though. But Jenny took Erin."

"Took her?" He blinked snow out of his eyes. Refocused. "Took her where?"

"Back out to the island, I think," Kat said. She sounded rushed. Harried. Afraid. "Goddamn Erin decided today was the day to become a martyr for the cause—she made Jenny promise to leave the rest of us, and she headed out there alone. In this weather, her odds of even getting out there are slim to nil. I tried the Coast Guard, but they can't send anybody out in this; they have to wait for the storm to clear."

She hesitated. "I didn't know who else to call. Cameron's already out there…"

He closed his eyes. It would take twenty minutes to get back to the wharf. Another hour to get out to the island, at least. There was chaos all around him, but it seemed like a safe harbor compared to what he would find on the water tonight.

"Why do you think they went to the island?"

"Jenny said that's where they were going—God knows why. I think she and Cameron set a trap out there." There was another moment's pause. "Look, I don't want to be rude, but I can't go out there—I promised Erin I'd stay with Diggs, see him through this thing. I'm not going to break another goddamn promise. Not to mention, I couldn't do a thing once I did get out there. But you—"

He nodded, the decision made. "I know. I'm going. I'll call you as soon as I know anything."

"If you need a boat…" she began. Jack glanced toward Jamie. She'd gotten the woman who owned the farmhouse out of the SUV along with her kids, and was walking the three of them over to the police.

"No," he said. "I've got it covered."

"Good. Jack…" This time, the pause was endless. "Just… thanks, all right? Whatever you can do…"

"I'll try," he said.

He ended the call, then jogged over to meet Jamie and Sheriff Finnegan. Jamie watched him as he approached, keen awareness on her face.

"I need to go," Jack said as soon as they were close. "I just got word that Erin's been taken—it looks like they're headed back out to Payson Isle."

"In this storm?" Finnegan said. "Jesus, is anyone sane on this goddamn mission? I can try and get in touch with someone in the Coast Guard, but I'll tell you right now there's no way in hell they're sending anyone out."

"I know," Jack said. He hesitated. "It's all right. Send

someone as soon as you can. I'm going over now."

A firefighter in full gear approached the group, gesturing Finnegan over to him. The sheriff didn't move, clearly torn.

"Go," Jack said. "Take care of this. I'll report back as soon as I can." When the sheriff had gone, he and the firefighter gesturing toward the smoldering truck several yards from them, Jack turned to Jamie. "Can I borrow your car?" he asked.

"I'll give you a lift," she said. "I'm used to the weather—I'll get us there faster."

There was no time to argue.

They drove too fast through the driving snow, the road barely plowed from the latest onslaught of fluffy white powder—the kind of snow that drifted and blew to near-white-out conditions in the bitter cold. Jack thought of Erin. Lucia. The child J. had taken from him, when they murdered his wife. Why? How had he ended up back in J.'s clutches after Cameron had worked so hard to extract him? Why were they so intent on destroying his life? Making his loved ones suffer?

"You asked why I keep coming back," Jamie said.

He pulled himself from his thoughts. When he looked out the windshield at the snow coming at them, it gave the illusion that they were floating—flying. Completely apart from the car, and the road beneath.

"I did," he said.

Jamie didn't look at him, her hands tight on the steering wheel. He got the sense that whatever she was about to say, admitting it wasn't an easy thing.

"It sounds ridiculous," she said.

"More ridiculous than a seventy-year-old national conspiracy coming to a head on a deserted Maine island in the middle of a blizzard?"

"Probably not," she said with a laugh. "It's not like we have some deep connection or something—I didn't know you before that first meeting up in Black Falls. But when we met..." she trailed off.

"You got a feeling," he supplied.

She nodded. He wasn't sure how far they were from the Littlehope wharf, but it felt like they had to be getting close. He hoped to hell they were, anyway.

"I'm supposed to save your life," Jamie said.

He looked at her sharply. Studied her serious profile in the darkly lit car. "What?"

"I told you—it's just a feeling. Sometimes there are flashes that come with it, but... There it is. I'm supposed to save your life."

He fell silent. How did someone respond to something so ridiculous, proposed by someone as earnest, as grounded, as Jamie Flint?

In his marriage, Lucia was the believer of the two. Jack had his faith: he went to church, took confession, accepted many of the more extraordinary miracles the church set forth as gospel. Lucia, however, *believed.* She believed in the nature of good and evil; the notion that there was a plan... That God always had his reasons for the pain they suffered.

Jack didn't know what he believed anymore. Lately, he wondered if it was anything at all.

Neither he nor Jamie spoke again until she half drove and half slid down the steep grade to the Littlehope wharf.

It was deserted, nearly every boat pulled out of the harbor. Jack got out of the SUV before Jamie had turned off her engine. "I need to borrow your boat," he said, shouting over the wind.

"I'll drive," she shouted back.

He shook his head. "Not this time."

"Jack—"

"You're supposed to save my life," he finished for her. "I know." He took a step closer. Set his hands at her arms, lost for the briefest moment in the serious blue eyes that gazed back at him. "Not tonight. Whatever is supposed to happen between us, it doesn't happen tonight. Please? Stay here."

For a few seconds, she didn't respond. He wondered what she was thinking—what rarely spoken thoughts, feelings, ran through her head in that moment. At last, she nodded. She reached into her pocket and pulled out a key.

"This is a suicide mission, you know," she said.

He imagined Lucia's wide eyes, dark with terror. Heard her crying his name until the very last. He shook his head and stepped away from Jamie, breaking their tenuous contact.

"It's not. It's just what has to be done."

He turned and left her standing on the wharf, watching him go.

29

I DON'T REMEMBER MUCH about the ride back to Payson Isle that night—just that it was terrifying. I kept flashing back through the highlight reel of my life with Diggs:

That first interview when I was fifteen; the fights and the stories and the drama and the laughter; that first kiss, in a crowded Portland bar when something just…slipped into place. Running for our lives in Black Falls—when it became so painfully, brutally clear that we could never just walk away from each other.

Jenny almost wrecked the boat a couple of times, barely avoiding the shoals while the storm raged and the wind buffeted the boat perilously close to the granite shore. The waves were black, but the rest of the world was pure white—a wall of blowing snow that seemed to determine to keep us back. Jenny was more determined.

Somehow, we made it.

There was another boat near the dock—this one wrecked, the hull splintered. There was no sign of anyone on board, and I didn't see a soul when Jenny and I set foot on the island.

I kept my head low. I'd stopped crying ages ago; now

I was just numb. Numb, frozen, and ready to end this. Jenny grabbed my arm and pushed me forward roughly. Apparently, she was just as ready.

"So, this is what you've been after, all this time," Jenny shouted above the wind. "You wanted the truth, right? Well, here you go."

The trip up the steep incline from the dock was slick, wind howling in my ears all the while. A foot of snow had fallen since Diggs and I had left that afternoon—powdery light stuff that I plowed through with my head down, not even sure any longer where I was.

Eventually, we reached the Payson House. Snow had blown up to the doorstep and beyond, reaching nearly to the doorknob. I looked at Jenny blankly. She waved the gun at me.

"Go ahead," she said. "Open it."

There was a feverish intensity in her eyes. She didn't have long, I realized—her face pale, her speech slurred. Diggs had done that. This woman would die, and when she did, it would be because he had killed her, protecting me.

And might well have killed himself, in the process.

I opened the front door.

Jenny gestured me inside, keeping her distance. I stumbled up and over the threshold, into the Payson meeting room.

Cameron was at the table. He stood as soon as we opened the door.

"Erin—I told you to stay away."

Jenny followed me inside, and he paled. "What the hell did you do?" he demanded of her.

"I sweetened the pot," Jenny said, "just like I said I would." Finally inside, she leaned back against the wall. Her hand fell to her side. The gun just hung there. If I wanted it, I could take it now. I didn't think Cameron would stop me.

"What do you mean, you sweetened the pot?" I asked.

"Dad wanted him to come," Jenny said. "But he wouldn't admit that this was what it would take to get him here."

She scanned the room at about the same rate I did. My eyes fell to a painting above the blazing fire: Christ on the cross, a thousand warriors in flame around him. Isaac's old painting. It hadn't been here before.

"I tried to get your perfect Katherine, too," Jenny said. Her eyes burned with hate. "But Erin was the best I could do. You think she'll be enough to draw him out, though? Knowing what else we have?"

The plastic container I'd taken from the Crack—the one Jenny had stolen from me—was on the meeting room table. I looked at Cameron.

"You were working together," I said. "All the people who died—Reverend Diggins, Mike Reynolds…"

"They would have killed," Cameron said. He sounded so reasonable. "That's what J. makes: killers. They made me. The least I can do is kill the other killers they've made."

"And draw them out," Jenny said. "Right, Dad? We kill the killers, find J.'s secrets, remind them that Payson Isle holds the key…and make them come to us."

"You weren't supposed to come back," Cameron said to me. He shook his head. "I did everything I could to keep you and Diggs out of this when the time came. But I have to admit, I never would have found everything your friend had been hiding, without you. You did what you were supposed to do." He paused and looked at Jenny again, suddenly stern. A father who lived by the sword. "I told you to keep them away from here tonight."

"And I told you—this is the way to bring him out. If I brought her, he can't stay away. You're here. I'm here. The magical Erin Solomon is here. And all his secrets are here."

I went to the table. No one tried to stop me.

In the kitchen, I heard the door open and shut again. Cameron closed his eyes, but he didn't move. Jenny looked toward the sound. I'd never seen her afraid before, but she was afraid now. Deathly so. For a minute or more, nothing happened. There was no other sound from the kitchen, and neither Jenny nor Cameron made a move to investigate.

I returned my attention to the table, and opened the plastic box. There was a small, old stuffed bear that used to be mine. A blue-eyed angel, its blonde hair pulled back in a tattered braid—Allie's angel. The rest were odds and ends that meant nothing to me, but would have been treasured by a twelve-year-old boy.

I removed everything, thinking again of Will Colby.

I would have saved you, if I could. But I can't save anybody.

At the bottom of the box, stuffed there as though Will had known these would be the key one day, I found what I was looking for: three more photos, weathered and worn.

Isaac, handing a paper cup to a woman. The light was dim, the image itself barely discernible. I could see candlelight in the background. They were inside the church. A second photo showed a cluster of women with glazed eyes and serene smiles, seated together. The third photo was another of Isaac.

He stood beside Rebecca Ashmont and a much-younger Cameron, as Cameron struck a match outside the chapel.

My hand shook. I got snow on the side of the Polaroid, and tried to wipe it away.

"He was dead," I said. My voice was hoarse. "You said Isaac died."

"That was the story we told," Cameron said. "And we told it so many times, it became the truth. Reality is all about perception. And perception is malleable—that's what J. taught me, years ago. You know, now, just how malleable it is."

"But Will," I said. I thought back to the police reports. Thirty-four bodies recovered, only thirty identified conclusively. Will Colby's name hadn't been on the roster of the dead. Neither had Allie Tate's. Now I knew, that was because Allie had already been dead for a year. And Will… "He wasn't in the church?" I asked Cameron.

"He was hiding," someone said from just outside the room.

The voice sent me back twenty-five years. Eight years old, hiding with Will. Trembling in fear.

Isaac Payson entered slowly. At the same time, the door opened beside Jenny, and an attractive dark-haired woman came in with her gun up. I recognized her immediately from the photo Edie Woolwich had shown me.

"Guns down," she said to Jenny, Cameron, and me.

Cameron set his down.

Jenny didn't.

Instead, she aimed at Isaac. Lilah shot her where she stood. Cameron uttered a cry that was more animal than human, part surprise and part horror, as Jenny fell. Lilah's gun shifted to me in an instant.

"I know you don't want to lose her, too," Lilah said. "Give me the gun."

She stepped over Jenny's now-limp form without looking at her. Isaac took another couple of steps, but he still remained apart. His hair was silver, his eyes bright. He had aged well—he had to be in his early seventies, but he still stood tall, with broad shoulders and a lean frame.

When he took in the room, his gaze fell to the painting above the mantle. "One of my favorites. How thoughtful, Cameron."

He came into the room fully, and Isaac's familiar eyes found me. It was like the blizzard had found its way inside; the world went cold.

"Erin. I'd imagined this moment differently, I have to say." I remembered that friendly, affable tone. How powerfully he used to weave his spell. He took a step closer. I could see Cameron tensed, poised to make a move, but I couldn't imagine how he could with Lilah's gun pointed directly at him.

"What happened that day?" I asked. "What the hell did you do?"

"Is it story time, then? After all these years, all the lives lost, all the bloodshed, you still want to know?" He smiled at me. "Very well then, Erin Solomon. I'll give you your truth."

•

"But you got shot," I argued, thinking of Matt Perkins' account of that night.

"Illusions are a beautiful thing, Erin. Magicians make entire buildings vanish—surely I can make three people already blind with grief believe that I am dead. I wasn't shot. Zion was." He looked genuinely saddened at the thought. "The boy was remarkable. Losing him was a blow. Matt showing up that night was never part of the plan. Cameron's intent had always been for Adam to strike the final blow, but of course your father went into hiding and left us to do it ourselves."

"So, Zion was dead," I said. "What about Rebecca, Matt Perkins, and Joe Ashmont? You still had to deal with them, didn't you?"

"Matt and Joe returned to the mainland. Cameron left me with Rebecca. By that time, I already had the congregation up in the chapel—they were more than happy to drink the henbane your father left for me, though they of course had no idea. I ministered to Rebecca. She was understandably bereft. And, again…so malleable. I planted a few suggestions, Cameron returned, and from that point on she believed that Cameron had done the whole thing alone… That I, like Zion, was dead."

"What about my father?" I asked. "Did he know by then what was going on?"

"He did," Isaac confirmed. "I left the island after that and went underground once more. Cameron very kindly kept my secret—as far as J. was concerned, he had done his job. Adam and I had paid for our betrayal. Me with my life, Adam with…his life, essentially. And Cameron, meanwhile, had a little bit of a breakdown around that time, didn't you? A crisis of conscience. I'd been counting on him to help me on the frontlines, give me some inroads into the organization, but he was really no help at all."

I thought of the story Cameron had told me before—about coming to Kat after the fire. About how she'd helped him. How he'd saved us both.

"He fell off the radar for a while," Isaac continued. "But by then Adam was back in with Dexter Mandrake again, so I had an in."

"Wait," I said. "My father… I don't understand. He hid from J. until the fire, when Rebecca outed him and Cameron came here. But then he stayed on the island for ten years, until he faked his death. He was working for J. that entire time?"

"He was—it was easy enough for him to get off the island when he was needed, and he was well above suspicion as far as the rest of the world was concerned. So, while he continued to work with J., I took a step back. For three years, I planned. Organized. Infiltrated the organization, one operative at a time. And then, I orchestrated the coup."

Cameron looked up for the first time. The hate in his eyes was so deep, so black, that I half expected Isaac to drop from that alone. But he just smiled.

"My second-in-command on that mission, funnily enough, was a woman named Susan Stargill. Did Cameron ever tell you about her?" He looked at me. I didn't answer one way or the other. "No, I don't suppose he did. Susan was Cam's lovely wife. Jenny's mother. Jenny was…what, seven years old by then? And Susan had been raising her primarily on her own for those three years, while you nursed your grief. Watched over your *other* family. We went into the Mandrake home late that night. I took Mandrake's wife—a pretty thing. Weak, but pretty. Killed his daughter. And Mandrake watched, every step of the way. And then, I killed him."

It looked like Cameron had checked out of the conversation. I could understand that—I was getting a little woozy from the whole thing myself. Isaac's gaze locked on Cameron.

"My own Judas," he said softly. Almost admiring. "You sat at my right hand all those years after Mandrake was gone. Operation after operation, building it all up… But you still had Katherine. Still had Erin. Tucked away, gently tugging the strings to keep them safe."

His eyes fell on me again. "Do you know all he did over the years to keep you from me?" He closed the distance between us. His damp hand came to my face, and he cupped my cheek. "Do you know how many have stood between us all these years? What is it about you, Erin, that inspires men and women alike—even a young, angry boy like Will Colby—to risk everything to keep you safe?"

I stiffened at his touch. Cameron had frozen across the table. I moved my head back and thought of Diggs, waiting for me.

"Did you ever think maybe all that betrayal, all those shady deals, don't have anything to do with what a great catch I am—and everything to do with what a creepy fucking monster you are?" I said.

He grinned. "You are a fighter. So was your mother, you know. I took her—the great Katherine Everett, begging for her life. On her knees before me." His hand slipped from my cheek to my hair; he tightened the grip painfully, pulling my head back.

"I've imagined you—this—for a very long time, Erin."

"You know I'm in my thirties now," I ground out. "Isn't that a little old for you?" Despite the awkward angle and the fact that terror burned through me, I found his gaze. Held it. For the first time, I saw real anger there. I didn't look away. "Allie Tate," I said. "She was nine years old. I saw you, rutting on her like—"

Isaac backhanded me, and my head snapped back. If he hadn't been holding onto me, I would have fallen. "Shut up."

"You looked all this time, didn't you?" I forged ahead, pushing beyond the blood in my mouth, my throbbing cheek. "Trying to find whatever Will had on you. Because we saw you that night."

His hand slipped to my throat. He squeezed, moving closer to me. I could see Cameron behind him. Jenny, on the floor. Lilah, with her gun on us. I clawed at his fingers—thinking again of that night. The frenzy in his eyes when he murdered Allie.

Isaac didn't lose control—

But he had that day. And I had the proof.

"Let her go!" Cameron shouted. He got to his feet. Lilah didn't look exactly clear on what was happening.

"Isaac," she said, her tone cool now. "We're here for a reason."

After another second, he nodded. "Of course." He loosened his grip on my throat. I tried to cough and gulp air at the same time. He shook his finger at me like I was a naughty child. "You've always tested my patience, Erin," he said. "We'll work on that later. First—I need you to show me where you put it."

I stared at him blankly, honestly puzzled for a minute.

"That wasn't everything that was in the container," he said. "There was something else. I want all of it. I need everything."

"I don't know what you're talking about," I lied. He closed the distance between us again, his hand once more fisted in my hair, his lips at my ear now.

"No more lies," he whispered, spittle wetting my cheek. I cringed away when he nuzzled my ear with his mouth. His teeth grazed my earlobe. "Tell me where you keep your secrets, Erin." I felt him, his hand sliding to my breast…

I brought my knee up, hard, and caught him in the groin.

When he hit me this time, it sent me flying. The edge of the table caught the small of my back and I gasped at the pain before I folded. As soon as I hit the ground, Isaac was on me—straddling me, his hands around my neck.

"It's upstairs!" Cameron shouted. "Goddamn it, Isaac, it's upstairs. She put it up in that room on the top floor."

Isaac looked from me to Cameron and back again. I had no idea what Cameron was playing at, but I nodded.

"He's right. That's where I put it."

Isaac stood, jerking me up by my hair. "Where?" he demanded. That frenzy I remembered from my childhood came rushing back to me—the inhumanity. The monster, ready to be unleashed on me the way it had been unleashed on Allie. I fought tears. Pure terror. I looked at Cameron.

"Your old space," Cameron said again. "On the third floor. I'm telling you, it's there."

He was lying, I knew. Everything I'd taken from the Crack was on the mainland, tucked away in the only safe place I'd been able to think of at the time: the *Trib.*

"Go!" Isaac shouted.

"Wait!" Cameron said. "I'll go. I'll show you where it is." He approached me, Lilah's gun trained on him all the while, and stood close.

"Thank you, but no," Isaac said. "I've been hoping for some time alone with Ms. Solomon, anyway. We have a lot to talk about."

Cameron kept coming toward us. Isaac had hold of me, but I saw his eyes bounce from me to Cameron and back again, not clear on what was happening.

"Let me..." Cameron said awkwardly, eyes begging Isaac. "Let me say goodbye, at least."

There was no mistaking his suspicion, but Isaac still took a step back. Cameron pulled me into a hug, holding me tight against his thin frame. It said something about the situation that hugging Cameron was the most normal thing happening just then.

"I'm sorry," he said. "It wasn't supposed to be you."

I nodded, still forcing those tears back, but I knew he was wrong. From the day I watched Allie die; the day I was chosen to survive the Payson fire; the day I watched my father take his own life because of these people...

It was always going to be me.

Cameron let me go. Isaac pulled me back to him and shoved me forward. I tripped on the stairs. Fell. Picked myself up again. At the top of the stairs, I saw a little girl with glasses. A brown-eyed boy beside her, the two hand in hand. Isaac gave no indication that he saw anything at all.

They watched, silent, as Isaac pushed me forward. Cameron and Lilah stayed downstairs. Isaac and I moved further into the house, until we reached the narrow stairwell to his family's old apartment. What the hell was I supposed to do when I got there? There was no doubt in my mind what would happen when he had me alone.

And then, I remembered the other night—lying in bed before Allie woke me. Listening to the creak of floorboards above. A drawer, sliding open.

Cameron had planned this.

It wasn't supposed to be you.

He brought Isaac here.

I kept walking. A small, quiet certainty took hold of me. I looked back over my shoulder.

Will and Allie stood at the bottom of the steps. Waiting for me, it seemed.

I opened the door to Isaac's old apartment. Outside, I could hear the wind screaming—like it would tear the roof off, shred the house from the rafters to the floorboards.

Forget the dark spots, Erin, I remembered my father telling me.

Now, those dark spots were all I could think of.

I stepped into the room. Flower-printed wallpaper hung in strips from the sloped walls. It was dank and dark and it felt like bad things had happened here—ages ago, maybe, but I couldn't shake the feeling that the house hadn't forgotten.

Isaac shined the flashlight into the room. "Where?" he demanded.

I thought of the noise I'd heard the other night, and followed the beam of light as he scanned the room. An antique bureau stood against one wall. I went to it.

"Can I have the light?" I asked.

"No." He liked the word—it was obvious in his voice. "You're fine."

He moved a little closer, but stayed far enough back that I couldn't try any Ninja moves to take him down. I was left with a little bit of space, and a lot of shadows.

I opened the top drawer.

There was nothing there.

I wet my lips. Looked back over my shoulder. "Sorry. I'm nervous."

I closed the drawer, and opened the next one.

Nothing.

"What are you doing?" Isaac asked me. "I have games in mind for us, Erin, but this isn't one of them."

I slid the next door closed. The third drawer was missing an ornate gold handle. I swallowed hard, and reached for the other handle. The drawer opened hard—I remembered the rattling noise again. This was it.

I moved my body to ensure Isaac couldn't see. My hands were shaking. I blinked uncertainly at what stared back at me, nestled in the shadows of the ancient drawer.

There were no fancy digital numbers...but there were lots of wires.

And lots of explosives.

Fear chewed at me, but I pushed it back. I thought of Diggs, waiting for me. Allie and Will, at the foot of the stairs. Cameron, downstairs. The feel of his arms around me.

"No more games, Erin," Isaac said. "Give it to me, damn it."

I put my hand in my pocket. Found what I now realized Cameron had put there just moments ago.

The faces of all the people Isaac had killed flashed through my mind—everyone who had ever suffered at his hand. At the hands of this organization. Isaac had raped Kat. Terrorized Will. Murdered Allie.

"Erin," he said. His voice was low. Threatening.

"You want it?" I said. I stepped away from the drawer. "Get it yourself."

I stepped back. Hate, vitriol, burned black in his eyes. But he weighed torturing me now versus torturing me later. I saw the moment when he made the decision—the one that would cost him his life.

He pushed past me. Opened the drawer. I hurtled past him when he was still looking inside, trying to figure out what he was seeing. I reached the door, and slammed it shut behind me. Half ran but mostly fell down the darkened stairs, and then didn't wait.

"Cam! Get out!" I screamed. I was aware of Isaac, still in the room. Running for all I was worth down the hall, I thought of Diggs. Jack. Kat. Einstein. My father, ruined by these people.

I slammed my thumb down on the button of the detonator Cameron had put in my pocket.

31

THE HOUSE WAS CONSUMED by flames by the time Jack got there. Half dead, drenched in snow and icy ocean water, later he wouldn't even be able to say how he'd safely navigated the treacherous waters. Somehow, against all odds, he did.

He ran the steep slope from the dock, and trekked through the woods toward the blaze. Nearly there, the flames just up ahead, he ran headlong into a woman on the path. Dark hair, dark eyes. He read terror on her face.

Lilah.

"You can kill me or you can save them," she said. His gun came up. She stared down the barrel, and didn't waver.

"Or I can do both," he said. "Why did you kill my wife?"

"Those were my orders."

"Torturing her? Raping her? Those were your orders?"

She stared at him impassively. "Those were my orders," she repeated.

"Why?" He was aware of the house burning—seconds ticking past. Lilah stared at him for one more precious second before she spoke.

"Because you left. You have secrets the organization will

kill for—yet you left. You're the boy who wouldn't die, Jackie. Living happily ever after? It's not in the cards for you."

She continued to stare at the gun. There was no fear in her eyes. "You can kill me, or you can save them," she said again.

"I'm not killing you. Come with me." He waved the gun toward the path.

"I'm not going anywhere with you." The flames were burning hotter now—he could hear them, raging more loudly than the wind. "Erin's trapped in there right now. You're really going to do this with me?"

He could shoot her. Tie her. Force her to come with him.

There was no time.

In the end, she made the decision for him. Without a backward glance, she turned and broke into a run. Within seconds, she had vanished into the night.

He let her go, and ran for the fire.

Cameron was half dead when he found the man outside the house—still calling for Erin.

"Where is she?" Jack demanded.

"Inside. I can't find her."

"Wait here," Jack said. Cameron nodded. Jack went to the door, and backed off immediately when he was met by a wall of flames.

"Erin!" he shouted.

He put his shirt up over his mouth. Searched the night for some way in, some break in the flames.

"Erin!" he said again, the name ripped from somewhere deep.

The fire roared, drowning out everything else. For

seconds, minutes, it was all he could hear. And then, barely audible, he heard something else.

"Jack! I'm here. I'm here."

He found her in an alcove under the stairs, her lungs raw from the smoke, but barely touched by the flames. Together, they stumbled out the back door while the house burned, screamed, howled behind them.

Afterward, he sat with Erin and Cameron, no one speaking, as the flames roared toward the sky. The wind died down. The snow stopped.

The Payson House burned to the ground.

32

IT WAS DAYS before I was able to return to Payson Isle. Days in the hospital, mostly by Diggs' side while he battled through the pain and slowly inched toward recovery. He refused any painkillers beyond Tylenol, despite doctors' warnings that by doing so he was putting his body under more stress than it could potentially handle. Kat stood by him on that count, though, and the gratitude I saw in Diggs every time she took up the fight when he was too tired to continue was something I knew neither of us would ever be able to repay.

It was only when I started to see something other than pain in his eyes that I decided it was time to make the trek.

Nine days after Diggs had been shot and the Payson House went up in flames, I made the journey back to Payson Isle.

It was unseasonably warm, the sky blue, though the ocean was still the icy black of the Atlantic in January. Jack and Einstein were with me. Jamie and Bear met us at the dock.

"How goes the fight?" I asked.

Jamie smiled. Einstein greeted Bear ecstatically, circling

the boy and yapping wildly while we trekked back toward the house. Or the site where the house had once stood.

"I was trying to figure out how to get rid of that place, you know," she said. "Explosives hadn't even occurred to me."

"You spend enough time with us, you learn to think outside the box."

"So I've gathered."

Monty and Carl were at the boarding house with the rest of the crew, working to salvage lumber from the fire.

"I assume this means you're staying on the island," I said.

For the first time since I'd met her, Jamie looked guarded. "If you'll let us—or if you're really ready to sell, I can see what I can come up with to buy the place."

"I already sold it to you. Was I speaking Lebanese when we did that whole thing? The place is yours. If it'll make you feel better, let's draw up the papers. I don't want this place. You need it. It seems pretty straightforward to me."

Jamie's smile broadened to the widest grin I'd ever seen from her. "You're sure?"

"Abso-frakking-lutely. Change the name, knock shit down, build shit up… I don't care. It's yours. Do something good with it."

She nodded. "I think we can do that."

Monty joined us before things got awkward. "How's that man of yours?" he asked. "We could use another set of hands out here."

"He'll be laid up for a while, but he'll be all right."

He grinned. Unlike the rest of us, he seemed to have gotten through this whole thing unscathed. "If you need a pinch hitter till he's back in the game, you know where to find me."

"You'll be the first one I call."

He draped his arm over my shoulders. "See that you do, princess."

After that, I left the others to their work. I knew my destination:

The Crack, one more time.

Will Colby had taken pictures of the Payson fire—which meant he hadn't died with everyone else. But if he didn't die with everyone else, where the hell was he?

I had Einstein with me, and an oversized flashlight. I felt little of the fear I'd known before when I came here. I didn't see Allie Tate's ghost. I didn't hear any voices.

I had a feeling that the last of those voices had died out in the fire at the Payson House, for me. I'd come to after the first explosion with Isaac's burning body just a few feet away, and it seemed then that all I could hear were the dying cries of all those I'd lost—the families I'd known on Payson Isle, the kids I'd played with, Rebecca and Matt and Joe… My father. I'd crawled to a space under the stairs where Allie and I used to hide when I was little, and sat there as the screams and the heat and the flames intensified. I was almost out, almost faded to black, when I realized that one of those cries didn't come from the dead—it was from the boy who lived. The man who wouldn't die.

And Jack had saved me, one more time.

Now, I pulled myself from the flames one more time, back to the present, and crept through the darkness, the granite close on either side of me. I reached the hip-height rock I'd had to climb over the last time I was here. This time, though, I didn't keep climbing up the way I had before—I just climbed over it. I shined my flashlight on the other side of the rock, into a crevice just beneath it.

I found a Polaroid camera.

And the remains of Will Colby.

I cried for a long time that day, at the top of the Crack alone with Einstein. From our vantage high up on the rock, I could see everything: the island, the ocean, Littlehope, and most of Muscongus Bay. Will never got away. No one came to save him. I didn't know what happened to him—how he died out here. Even if he'd drunk the henbane Isaac had given him, it would only have been enough to make him woozy. It wouldn't have killed him. All I knew was that he'd been alone here. Terrified.

And it had taken me twenty-five years to even remember that we had been friends.

"But you remember now," Diggs reminded me gently, later that night. He was in his bed at the hospital, while I sat beside him. His pallor put a whole new spin on fifty shades of gray.

"I do remember now," I said. He brushed a tear from my cheek. "I just hate the idea of him being alone all this time."

He looked at me a little funny, but he didn't point out that Will Colby hadn't been alone all that time—because he'd been dead. He wet his lips instead. Closed his eyes. "He's not alone anymore," he said. "He's not lost now. You found him. You can't do any more than that."

"I know." I kissed his cheek. "You're tired. I'll go."

"Did you hear they found Laurie Smith?" he asked.

"No—where?"

"She was picked up hitchhiking in Newry. The woman who gave her a ride recognized her from the news, and led the police right to her."

"No more bloodshed?" I asked.

"Not a drop," he said. "The sheriff dropped by earlier. He said she's sticking to her story: that it was all Nate's idea, and she was there against her will."

"Did she explain how Nate got his throat slit?"

"Self-defense is her story," he said. Diggs shifted, then gasped at the pain.

"Easy," I said. "Do you want me to get the doctor?"

He shook his head. "No. They'll just try to give me something I can't take." He slipped his hand into mine, and squeezed hard. "Can you just stay a little longer?"

"I'll stay as long as you want."

"Just until I sleep," he said. He closed his eyes again. I lay my head on his shoulder, and stayed there until I could hear his breathing even out once more.

•

The next day, Jack, Kat, Maya, and I went to dinner at Bennett's. There was another snowstorm in the forecast for the overnight hours. Mimi was running a Cabin Fever Reliever special as a result: every entrée just $12.95—with the understanding, of course, that we would all spend six bucks a pint on beer and drink ourselves into a stupor.

"Gotta find some way to make up for you assholes shutting me down the other night," she said when she delivered our dinners. Maya raised her hands, the one innocent party in all this.

"Don't look at me. I was there to get sloshed with the rest of the town."

"Well, you'll just have to make up for it tonight," Mimi said. "So long as you got yourself a designated driver, of course."

Maya glanced at Kat with the faintest hint of a smile. "What do you think?"

Kat nodded. Slipped her hand over Maya's. "We can probably work something out."

Jack had been quiet since the events on Payson Isle—even more so than usual. I waited until Mimi had gone before I said anything.

"So, what are you going to do now?" I asked him.

He looked uncertain. "What do you mean?"

I laughed—probably more than I should have. He just looked so confused. "I mean… You don't have a job, right? And I know Lilah is still out there, but blood vengeance doesn't really pay the bills."

"No," he said. I did manage to get a smile out of him. "I suppose it doesn't. I'm not sure. Jamie actually offered… something."

"Something?" I raised my eyebrows.

"Helping with searches," he clarified. "On a case-by-case basis—not full time. I'm not sure what else I'll do."

"What about Lilah?" I asked. "Any word?"

The question killed his brief moment of good humor. "No. I've got a description out, but I haven't heard anything. Probably won't. I get the feeling she's used to keeping a low profile."

"Do you think that means J. will just rise again?" I said. "New leader, same mission? Whatever the hell that mission was."

"I've been thinking about that a lot, actually," Jack said. He took a second to bite into one of the biggest burgers I'd ever seen, chewed, and wiped his mouth after he'd swallowed. Then, he finally continued. It was good to see he had his appetite back, but I was on the edge of my seat waiting for his theory.

"I have Willett's files—they're exhaustive, actually. There's no question the organization was massive when Mandrake was manning it."

"You think that's changed over time?" I said.

"Think about it. He lost Cameron. Adam. And as much as we might not approve of Jenny's tactics, there's no question that they were effective in at least dealing a blow to the organization."

"Not to mention the fact that Isaac was a complete psychopath, all about taking what he wanted—it doesn't seem like he could see past his own needs or twisted desires to run an organization well," I said. I noticed that Kat remained quiet, her gaze off in the distance. Jack continued, oblivious.

"I think he was trying to change that—or at least give the impression that he was changing it. Willett's theory was that he'd be making a bid soon to expand his influence—gather new followers."

"Which he couldn't do if I showed up with evidence that he'd raped and murdered a nine-year-old girl," I summarized grimly. "People would have a hard time buying into a guru with that on his resume."

"Exactly," Jack said, equally grim.

Kat got up abruptly. "I'm just going out for some air."

"We can change the subject," I said.

"No—don't bother. I'll just be outside."

I looked at Maya after Kat had gone. "Has she talked to you at all about what happened on the island? When she was with my father?"

"No. She doesn't really do that." Before I could say anything, she added, "She is trying, though. It doesn't come naturally, but she's working at not shutting me out. That's something."

I shared the woman's genes; had lived under the same roof with her for eight years. Not shutting someone out wasn't just something—it was damned close to everything.

"I'm gonna go out for a minute," I said. I looked at Jack. "Don't eat my fries." He looked at me with wide eyes and a devil's grin. If it had been Diggs, my fries would be history before I hit the front door. Jack wouldn't steal a single one, I had no doubt.

When I found her, Kat stood off to the side of the parking lot staring in the direction of the clinic, her jacket pulled tight around her.

"We've stopped talking about it," I said. "You can come back in."

"Okay. Be right there." She didn't move.

"Have you heard anything from Cameron?" I asked.

"He called last night," she said, to my surprise. "He's on the run again."

"But he was working with Jenny on this, then? The two of them were killing the J. operatives? They planned to lure Isaac out together?"

"You knew he wasn't a saint," she reminded me. She turned to look at me, wide green eyes serious. I thought of everything I'd learned over the past two years—about her. My father. Me. I couldn't believe how wrong I'd had it, all these years.

"He's in love with you, you know," I said.

"I know," she agreed without argument. She seemed sad about it.

"So, this past few months when you were running…"

She rolled her eyes. "Jesus, Erin, can't you let anything go? He's a complicated man. And I'm in love with someone else."

I figured I shouldn't push any further, since I wasn't sure I really wanted to know all that had gone on between her and Cameron, anyway.

"Listen, everything that happened with Isaac..." I began.

Her eyes darkened. Flashed fire. And then, the deepest regret I'd ever seen. "Your father told me he would keep you safe. And if I hadn't left..."

"Isaac would have killed you," I said. I nodded. "Dad kept his promise, you know—or he tried, anyway. Isaac never touched me. Never came near me. I saw what he did to the others, but I was always off limits. At least, I was until I saw what he did to Allie."

"Your father did love you, you know," she said after a few seconds. She lowered her eyes. Seemed almost shy, suddenly, and I imagined who she had been, *what* she had been, at seventeen years old. Just venturing onto Payson Isle for the first time.

"He had more demons than anyone I've ever met," Kat said. "But he wanted to be a good man. He tried so many times to get away from them. It just never took."

Until his last resort had been a gun to his head, in a rainy jungle in Coba.

"I know," I said. "Or I think I do, anyway. I'm starting to."

Kat shook off the mood abruptly, with a hearty shiver. "All right. Enough talk about the psychotic mind fucker who was Isaac Payson. Next subject."

"That being?" The look in her eyes made me uneasy.

"Diggs," she said. I got the sense she'd been planning this. May have even lured me out here, for exactly this reason. Tricky bitch. "You need to stop putting the man in mortal danger."

"It's not always my fault." She leveled me with a glare. "Okay. A lot of times, it's my fault."

"He's got a serious addiction," she said, all trace of mirth gone. "And I'm not talking about you. Every time something like this happens, every time he ends up in the hospital again, you put his recovery at risk. So far, he's managed to do everything without anesthesia or pain meds, but if I hadn't been there this last time to advocate for him, that wouldn't have been the case. He's a strong man, but once you trigger those cravings, those behaviors, you run the risk of losing him down the rabbit hole again. You understand what I'm telling you?"

"No more mortal danger?" I said.

"Or at least start carting some Kevlar around with you. I know I didn't raise an idiot—just be smart."

"Okay." I was shivering now, arms over my chest, stomping my feet to keep the blood circulating. Kat didn't even look chilled. "I'll do my best."

"Good. Now, come on, let's get you back in. A few months in the wrong hemisphere and you've turned into a pansy."

"It's five below zero."

"Your point being?"

I shrugged. Clearly, there was no point at all. Just before I opened the door to go back in, Kat called after me.

"So, are you and Diggs getting hitched or what?"

I stopped and turned. "You do know we've both been down the aisle before, right? A multitude of times, actually."

"With idiots," she said briefly. "I'm just asking because Maya was wondering. She doesn't have any kids, you know."

The lack of segue had me stymied. Kat tipped her head and tried to lack cavalier. She didn't do a very good job.

"So?" I said. "What does Maya not having kids have to do with Diggs and me?"

"So…she wants grandkids. Nobody else can step up to the plate."

I ran my hand through my hair. "So you want me to start breeding now?"

"You've had worse ideas." She nodded toward the door. "Come on—get inside. It's freezing out here."

•

Later that night, I lay in Diggs' hospital bed with him—at his insistence, of course. He said if he couldn't take pain meds, at least I could get his endorphins running with a little physical contact. Very little, mind you, but I understood his point.

"So, Cameron's gone," he said.

"And Lilah. Jack's not happy about that."

"And the high-ups Willett thought were involved in this…. What about them?"

"My guess? Denial, across the board. There's no real evidence against any of them." I thought of Jane Bellows, the senator who had been killed in 2012. As usual, Diggs seemed to follow my line of thinking.

"Did you see the news tonight?" he asked. "Andrew Bellows was killed outside his home in Seattle."

I didn't say anything. Couldn't, really. Cameron was still out there. I got the sense that, whatever else happened in the coming months, he wouldn't rest until he'd ensured the people who ran J. paid for their sins. As long as he was still breathing, I doubted anyone would be able to reorganize the project.

"I didn't know," I said. "I've been thinking about Bellows' sister, though—the senator. I think maybe my father went to her for help. Maybe he was trying to take J. down…or maybe he was just trying to get away from them. And it got her killed."

"It's possible," Diggs said. His eyes drifted shut. I lay there beside him, not at all comfortable—hospital beds really aren't conducive to cuddling—and thought about everything Kat had said.

"You know how I was talking before about us hitting the road?" I said. "Doing our own thing—getting back to being reporters instead of crime fighters?"

I felt him tense beside me. Neither of us had mentioned his mom's wedding ring since we'd been reunited. Between the pain and the chaos and everything else swirling around us, somehow that conversation had eluded us.

"I remember," he said.

"Would you like that? Going somewhere warm? No bosses, our own deadlines, our own rules?"

He turned his head and studied me. "You really want to do that?"

"I think so. Once you're well, I mean." He didn't say anything. I shifted. He was making me nervous. "And…we could get married. If you still want, I mean. I understand if you don't, though—I mean, we were under a lot of pressure before, people about to murder and maim us and the blizzard and you bleeding out—"

"Sol," he interrupted. He shook his head, and groaned at the movement. "I still want to. If it was just the murder and maiming that prompted the proposal, I would have asked years ago. Probably should have. But…yeah." He stopped. Appeared to be turning it over in his head. "Let's get married."

"Okay, then," I said. I realized I was grinning—a little stupidly, as a matter of fact. Diggs caught the smile. Smiled back.

"Okay then," he echoed.

We lay there in silence for a long time after that. I felt Diggs drifting beside me. Found myself doing the same. An image popped into my head: Diggs and me, on a beach somewhere. Diggs tanned, healthy. A boy with curly white-blond hair, riding on his shoulders... A kid who would never stand at the edge of a family, looking for a way in.

It was a stupid idea—kids are a ton of work. They cry. They poop. I'd never really wanted one, to be honest. And now, wasn't even sure I could have one, after my failed pregnancy two years ago. One working fallopian tube. Terrible genes. A whole lot of demons.

What were the chances any of it could work?

Diggs shifted. His breathing evened out. I closed my eyes.

"You're thinking very loudly," Diggs murmured. "Care to share?"

"Just wondering what happens next," I said. I saw a slight smile touch his lips. "In a good way?" he said.

"Yeah." I took a breath. It was easier, somehow, than it had been. "In a very good way, I think."

THE END

Looking for more from Jen Blood?

Turn the page for a free excerpt from
the first novel in the brand new
Flint K-9 Search and Rescue Series,
THE DARKEST THREAD.

1

THE BRUSH WAS THICK and the air cool, and rain pelted my chilled skin. My shirt was drenched, and my ponytail had gotten snagged so many times I was debating cutting the damned thing off. Up ahead, I caught sight of a flash of white fur and cursed under my breath.

Casper is my son's dog, a rescued pit bull who'd been closer to death than life when Bear—my seventeen-year-old son—insisted we rescue him almost three years ago. By breed alone, he's not your typical search and rescue K-9. The fact that his temperament runs from high-energy to bouncing off the walls makes that doubly so, but Bear has been working with him since Casper was six months old. According to Bear, it's just a matter of time before we all see what the dog can do.

I was still waiting for that moment. This morning, it wasn't looking good.

"Caz!" Bear shouted. The dog continued on, heedless of my son's call. Bear glanced at me, and I could feel his frustration. "He's just looking for the scent."

"Well, he's doing a bang-up job," I said dryly. "Considering the scent was a good half-mile back."

Bear grimaced. This was our own version of a field trial, since Bear had been pushing for more autonomy with Casper when we were out on searches. My business, Flint K-9, is run from the mid-coast Maine island where I live with Bear, a small staff, and a whole slew of dogs and other assorted wild things. We decided to take a couple of days on the mainland with Casper, though, and see what he could do. The night before, I came out and set a scent trail that wound through a stretch of woods in Appleton, Maine, and then Bear and I returned first thing this morning with Casper. Now, an hour later, Casper was running wild and the scent was far behind us.

"You know we can 't just let him run loose like this, especially not on a search," I said. "What if he's running deer—"

"He's not," Bear said impatiently. "Casper! Damn it, come on!" he called. He returned his attention to me. "If he's doing this, there's a reason for it. He must have found something."

My guess was a squirrel or a flash of light that caught his eye; Casper is a sweet dog, but his enthusiasm makes it hard to gauge just how bright he actually is.

"Up ahead!" Bear said suddenly. I followed his gaze, but saw nothing. Not surprising—where wild things are concerned, Bear has a sixth sense I've never been able to top or tap into.

Sure enough, an instant later I heard Casper's telling, high-pitched double bark. *I found it!*

The question was, what exactly had he found.

My concern built as we followed the reckless trail Casper

had blazed, and saw a felled doe just to our left. I moved closer, and knelt next to the body. Based on decay, she'd been killed at least a day ago. I felt a surge of rage at sight of the wound, knowing she'd not only been shot off-season, but the asshole who had done it hadn't even cared enough to follow up, find her, and finish the job. I expected to find Casper with the deer, but the dog was nowhere to be seen.

"Well, I guess we know what scent he was following," Bear said soberly. His forehead was furrowed, his green eyes soft at sight of the find.

"Yeah," I said. "I'll call the ranger, let him know he's got a poacher out here." I looked around. "But if he found what he was looking for, where the hell is your dog now?"

Bear scanned the thick woods, rain dripping from his shaggy dark hair. I glanced at the doe one more time, and my anxiety returned and then spiked when I noted the swollen teats… Our victim had been a nursing mother.

"There!" Bear said. He pointed into a stand of spruce and pine, and I caught sight of a bright white tail whipping through the underbrush.

I moved forward, Bear beside me. The woods smelled of overripe berries and fresh earth, but there was a scent of blood beneath it that made my heart still. Bear's face was tense, his eyes no longer hopeful.

He'd been in this business long enough to know the likelihood of what we'd find.

Casper, scarred white body wriggling, lay down on the wet earth and crawled into the brush until his head and muzzle were no longer visible.

"Call him off," I said to Bear. "Now!"

"Just hang on," Bear said calmly.

Casper's head reappeared as he twisted to look at me, shining brown eyes meeting mine. He barked again, twice, just in case we hadn't heard him the first time. I always find any dog's second alert to be a little patronizing, as though he's suggesting I might be slow on the uptake for not getting there sooner.

He returned his focus to whatever was in the brush and crawled forward until he was half swallowed by the bushes himself. Bear and I lay down on our bellies beside him and inched in, ignoring the thorns that tore at our cheeks and hair or the mud that drenched our fronts.

"Well, hello there," Bear said quietly when we finally caught sight of her—a young fawn speckled with white, caught in blackberry brambles and too weak to struggle.

The fawn flailed at sight of me, letting out a pitiful bleat, then stilled when Casper whimpered and ran his tongue over the deer's tawny fur in long, leisurely strokes.

The fawn calmed. She turned wide brown eyes on me. I crept in further.

"Good boy, Casper," I said. "Good find."

Bear stayed where he was, petting his dog. Beaming.

●

It took just under twenty minutes to get the fawn untangled once we'd found her. In the meantime, we found her brother farther in the brush, also alive. Both were scraped up and plenty scared, but there were no broken bones. That didn't mean they were home free—I've seen plenty of animals succumb to shock after something like this, when it seemed at first they were fine. Still, it was a start.

Bear had offered Casper the knotted rope he typically earned after a successful search, but the pit bull ignored it, more concerned with his new charges. My opinion of the dog was growing by leaps and bounds.

From here, our destination was Payson Isle, an island ten miles off the coast of Maine, where Bear and a team of gypsies, tramps, and thieves assist me in running a wildlife rehabilitation center and Flint K-9, a business devoted to training working dogs for individuals, law enforcement, and search and rescue divisions around the world. The fawns would get the requisite care out on the island before they were ideally released back into the wild as soon as they were able.

We'd just gotten back to the Jeep when Monty, my second-in-command, called. I answered my cell while Bear was getting the fawns safely situated in one of the padded crates we always carry with us for just such emergencies, his voice low and soothing as he murmured reassurances to the animals.

"Funny story," I answered at sight of Monty's name on the call screen. "We hit the woods with one dog and a few strategically placed scent markers... We're coming back with a couple of injured fawns that should get a once-over. I need to get in touch with the warden, but will you let Therese know we're coming? We should be back on the island by nine, if she wants to meet us at the dock."

"I'll let her know," he said. Therese is our staff veterinarian, a necessity when you're on a remote island with a squadron of animals, many of whom have serious health issues when they first arrive. "And I'll meet you at the dock in Littlehope, actually," he added.

"No need. The boat's at the wharf, we can bring the fawns straight over."

There was a pause on the line. "Actually, I'm not sure you'll be back on the island for a few days yet."

I didn't like the sound of that, and said so. Monty gave me no details as to why I couldn't head home yet, but there was something about his voice that made me uneasy. The rain had cleared, but a lingering heaviness remained in the air. I've been called superstitious more than once in my life, but I've learned to listen to the chills that climb the base of my spine, the voices that ride the wind.

Right now, those voices were deafening.

2

TRUE TO HIS WORD, Monty met me at the town landing in Littlehope, a fishing village off Route 97 with a population of 753, including the team of seven I'd relocated with me to the island a year before. Two people stood beside him. One was a striking black woman who could have been anywhere from thirty-five to fifty, wearing a tailored business suit. Her dark hair was pulled back in a bun, her arms crossed over her chest. Despite her conservative dress, there was an athleticism and grace about her that was apparent even from a distance. I didn't know her.

I did know the man, however. He stood at the dock with sunglasses on, taller by several inches than the woman beside him, a grim expression on his face. It was, I noted despite circumstances, a very handsome face.

"Will you get the fawns aboard and ready for the trip?" I asked Monty, without greeting Special Agent Jack Juarez or the woman by his side. Bear and I carried the crate between us, careful not to jostle it. Monty—five-foot-nine and 190 pounds of pure muscle—took my end.

"Will do," he agreed. "Did you get in touch with the warden?"

"Yeah," I said. "I talked to him in the car—they already

caught the guy. Some asshole who got drunk the other night and decided going out in the dark off-season and shooting things was the perfect way to pass the time. The warden didn't know the doe had fawns, though."

"So they'll string the guy up by his balls till he rots?" Monty said, grim.

"Fingers crossed," Bear said, with just a hint of a smile.

"I told Therese to expect us. Any idea when you'll be back?"

"I don't even know I'm going anywhere," I said with a pointed look. "I still don't have a clue what this is about. Once I have some idea, I'll let you know."

Monty eyed Jack with a hint of distrust, but made no comment.

Monty and I have worked together for six years now, ever since he was first recommended to me—two days after being released from the Maine State Prison. There, he'd been part of a dog training program for inmates that was run by a friend of mine. Marie Finnegan's endorsement isn't one that comes easily. I hired Monty on the spot, and haven't had a moment of regret since.

He is, however, occasionally a little overprotective.

Once Monty and Bear were on the boat, I turned my attention to Jack Juarez. His dark hair was cut shorter and his suit hung looser than it had when I'd seen him last, almost nine months ago. Half circles shadowed his dark eyes. Though at five-foot-ten I'm taller than many women and a lot of the men I work with, Jack never fails to make me feel smaller. Petite, almost. He has broad shoulders and an athletic frame that easily tops six feet, his darker skin tone thanks to a Mexican mother who died when Jack was young and a Cuban father he never knew.

Those parents are just a few of the ghosts who haunt

Jack. Right now, he looked like they were doing a bang-up job.

"Monty tells me someone's been asking for me?" I said.

"I guess you could say that. There's a situation...of sorts." He looked uneasily at the woman beside him. Since I didn't know what he was talking about and he'd spent the past nine months dodging my calls, I folded my arms and waited. Maybe it was petty, but I refused to make things any easier for him. Jack cleared his throat.

"I'm Special Agent Allie Blaze," the woman said, stepping forward with her hand extended. She shot Jack a look, presumably for not being smoother about all this himself. "I've heard a lot about you. It's a pleasure."

I shook her hand, noting the iron grip that stopped just shy of bone crushing. "What can I do for you, Agent Blaze?" I asked.

She looked surprised for only a second at my unwillingness to make small talk before she got down to business. "We have a situation—two sisters who've gone missing."

I couldn't hide my surprise. "If you're looking to organize a search, all you needed to do was call. We've got—"

"It's not as simple as that," Jack interjected.

"Of course it is," Blaze said coolly. The tension between them was palpable.

"What isn't so simple about it?" I asked, directing the question to Jack.

"The girls went missing in Vermont. Up around Glastenbury Mountain, along the Long Trail."

"You're not working with Vermont K-9?" I asked. "That's their turf."

"They're out there," Jack said. "Police are there, forest service is there, reporters are there. It's a three-ring circus."

Blaze didn't look pleased with his assessment. The

moment he mentioned Glastenbury Mountain, though, I knew what he was talking about. Any time a search is organized around the country, it's my business to at least take notice. In this case, as I remembered it K-9 SAR teams were out looking for two girls in their early twenties who had been missing since the previous morning.

"VTK9 is good," I said. "They know that area well. I'm flattered that you think I'd be helpful, but I think you're better off with that crew. I've worked with them before, and I've always been impressed."

"We actually got a special request to bring you in," Blaze said with a shake of her head. "That's why I'm here. I know you and Juarez—uh, Jack—have worked together before, so I asked if he would make introductions."

"A special request by whom?"

"The father of the girls who went missing," she said. There was something about the way she said it, a look in her eyes, that implied I wasn't getting the full story. "He doesn't trust us, and we were the ones who brought in Vermont K-9. He's taken it into his head that the search and rescue team may be collaborating with the FBI."

"But Vermont K-9 has nothing to do with the FBI," I said.

"Trust me, we've told him that," Agent Blaze said, a bit wearily. "But we have a history with the family, which means they don't believe much that we say."

I considered the situation for a few seconds before I said, "Would you give Agent Juarez and me a few minutes? I'd like to ask him some questions."

She didn't look especially pleased at the request, but she nodded her agreement without protest. I waited until she was well out of earshot before I shifted my focus back to Jack.

"What exactly have you stepped in?" I asked him. "Why is the FBI even in on this thing? I'm sure it's already a jurisdictional nightmare between local, state, and forest service. What made your people throw their hats in the ring?"

"You don't know the story?" he asked.

"I know there's a search on Glastenbury Mountain. There's more of a story than that?"

"There's definitely more to it than that. I guess you probably don't have a lot of time for the news out on the island these days," Jack said.

"I've got seven people—two of them teenagers—helping me build a business and the buildings that will house that business, from the ground up. There's a lot I don't have time for these days."

He looked guilty at that, not without reason. Nine months before, I'd offered him a job when it seemed his tenure with the FBI was most likely up. I would have been fine with him saying no—hell, I was glad he'd been able to salvage what had seemed an unsalvageable career at the time. But he could have at least called to let me know what was happening.

"Right," he agreed. "You have a point. Dean Redfield is the patriarch of the family—the oldest of ten siblings. Well, six now. About a month ago, he and his family bought up land in an unincorporated town in southwestern Vermont called Glastenbury. There was no real fuss about it, but Dean's got a history with the FBI so we were keeping an eye on him."

"Agent Blaze mentioned that. What kind of history are we talking about, exactly?"

"He's been in and out of prison for tax evasion. And…" He hesitated. "Do you remember a case in Western Mass about seven years ago? Two sisters…"

I searched my memory. "Dean Redfield, you said? His sisters were murdered, weren't they? By…" I paused, realizing the implication for the first time. "By an FBI agent, wasn't it?"

"Exactly," Jack agreed, grim now. "Gordon Redfield was—is—Dean's brother. He was convicted of killing his sisters, twins a decade younger than him. Gordon, incidentally, has maintained his innocence since that time."

"But you guys don't buy that."

"No. Most of us don't," Jack said. There was something steely in his eyes when he said it, and I realized that this case had some deep roots for him. "Back in 2009, the government had taken over the Redfields' land after Dean refused to pay taxes for…well, ever. We'd just moved in on the place when the bodies were found. Two women, twenty-nine years old."

Hazy memories of barely recalled news reports surfaced. "Yeah, I think I remember that. It was a rough case, wasn't it?"

"You could say that," he agreed. He removed his sunglasses, and his dark eyes held mine for a second. I felt that inexplicable warming I always feel in Jack's presence, and resisted the urge to take a step back. "Their names were June and Katie Redfield, two of only three sisters in the Redfield clan. When they were found, both had been drugged, raped, and tortured. Both of them bound together through the whole experience."

Finally, the whole thing clicked into place. "Wait, I think I remember that. The victims were found with purity rings around their necks or something, weren't they?"

"That's the case," he said with a nod. "Genital mutilation of both bodies—while the women were still alive and conscious. All the victims were killed in pairs, strangled by chains holding antique purity rings."

"All the victims?" I echoed. "You said he was convicted of killing his sisters."

"There was never enough evidence to bring the other murders to trial. But eight other women had been killed in pairs around the U.S., strangled and found with purity rings. All prostitutes."

"This is why I prefer dogs," I said with a shiver.

"I'm not arguing with you." He paused. "There were some…extenuating circumstances with the case, made it kind of a nightmare around the office for a while."

"In what way?" I asked.

I caught something in his eyes, a hint of whatever story I wasn't being told, before he glanced back toward Agent Blaze and the look vanished. "It's not relevant here," he said with a wave, dismissing it out of hand. "The bottom line is that Gordon had all of us fooled, but ultimately the evidence put him away. Dean is a hard man, but he isn't heartless. The whole thing kind of broke him."

"I bet." I waited for him to continue. He didn't. "I'll agree, this all sounds tragic. I'm not sure I understand what any of it has to do with me, though."

He frowned. "Honestly, it doesn't have anything to do with you—at least not as far as I'm concerned. But, like Blaze said, Dean doesn't trust us. None of his family does. And now that his daughters are missing, they're convinced it's happening again."

"What's happening again? The murders? Gordon Redfield is behind bars, though."

"The Redfields always thought the FBI had more to do with it than we did," Jack said. "Dean was convinced there was a conspiracy. And now he's sure that we're somehow responsible for the other girls going missing."

"Well, whatever he might think, he should know that Vermont K-9 doesn't have anything to do with it. And they're the ones who should be running the search."

"No one's disputing that," Jack said. "But it wouldn't hurt to have another hand on deck, would it?"

Actually, if it was as much of a three-ring circus as Jack had said, it could well hurt things very much. I said as much to Jack, but he shook his head.

"I'm not saying you need to bring the whole team out there. Just you and your dog… You can coordinate with VTK9, explain the situation, tell them you're not there to step on anyone's toes. We're looking at a search area that could be as much as twenty thousand acres, all of it rough terrain, mountainous, with twelve peak stopping three thousand feet in elevation. You're seriously telling me they couldn't use the help?"

He was right there. I had a good relationship with the organization, had trained with many of the handlers there, so they wouldn't get territorial if I showed up and offered to lend a hand. Chances were good that other K-9 organizations had already been called in, so it wasn't really that much of a concern.

"They still haven't found any sign of either of the women?" I asked.

Jack shook his head. "Not a trace. Dean's been through this before with June and Katie—his sisters. Those two had taken off a week before and dropped out of sight from there. You can imagine what he's going through now that the girls missing are his own daughters."

I thought of what I'd be going through if this were Bear, and stifled a shiver. Torture was the only word for it.

Monty and Bear were back on the sidelines. I nodded them over, while Jack went to have a word with Blaze. They came as if they'd been waiting for the signal for a while.

"You need us to gear up?" Monty asked.

"No," I said. "Just me—I'll take Phantom, probably be gone no more than a couple of days. You think you can handle things without me?"

"You're going on a search?" Bear asked. "You sure you don't need a hand?"

"Positive—" I began.

"Because we could get geared up fast," he pressed. "You saw how good Casper was this morning—"

"He completely ignored the scent trail I laid and took off on his own, and you couldn't get him back."

"I could have if I really tried," he said. "But I could tell he was onto something. He has good instincts—"

"And no discipline."

"That's not fair," he said with a frown. "This would be good experience. I could come, maybe bring Minion. Three teams are better than one."

"Minion and Ren, you mean?" I asked.

My son, never much for subterfuge, blushed. Monty snickered beside him. Urenna—Ren—is the seventeen-year-old daughter of another of the staff with Flint K-9, Carl Mensah, a former Nigerian soldier who fled his homeland after his wife and sons were murdered. He and Ren have been with me since first immigrating to the U.S. in 2012. The growing bond between Ren and Bear—platonic, Bear insists—has been one he's denied for years, but there's no doubt in my mind that his feelings for the girl run far deeper than simple friendship.

"We don't really need more teams, Bear," I said. "This is just a quick operation for me. To be honest, I'm not even clear why I'm going, much less why I'd bring anyone else."

"It'd be a good road trip," Monty said, always helpful.

"Get the kids out there, show 'em how the Feebs do it."

I shot him a glare, but all he did was grin in return. "We'd do whatever you need—" Bear presed.

I sighed. "You really think Ren can handle things out there?"

Bear looked at me pityingly. "Seriously?"

"Yes, seriously," I said. "If we actually end up pitching in, we're talking cold temps, rough terrain, and two women who may well not even be found alive. Conditions don't get much tougher than that."

"Ren can handle it," he said unequivocally.

"Okay… Then here's the bigger question: Can Casper handle it?"

Bear bristled. "He'll never learn if you don't start giving him the chance to get out there. He just needs a chance."

I glanced at Monty, who shrugged.

"Trial by fire, right?" he said. "I say give 'em the call, see what happens."

I weighed the argument for a few seconds before I finally nodded. "Okay, fine. Gear up Casper, and call in Ren and Minion. I'll give VTK9 a call, clear it with them."

"Yes!" Bear said, half under his breath. I shot him a look, and he got his enthusiasm under wraps. "You won't regret it, I promise."

Famous last words. Blaze and Jack returned then, Blaze just ending a call. "I've got a plane on standby. You think you can be ready by ten hundred?"

Two hours to gear up and head out for what seemed, for all intents and purposes, like a fool's errand. I nodded. "We'll be there."

Agent Blaze said she had business to take care of and would meet us at the airport, but Jack joined us on the boat.

Monty got behind the wheel of our (?), piloting us across the harbor with the (?) engine at full throttle. The seas were calm and the sky had cleared, but there was a heaviness to the air that suggested we weren't through with the rain yet. We'd need to check the weather for Glastenbury, as well as the maps. Jack and I stood portside with the wind in our hair and watched as the island got closer.

"One question," I said. "Agent Blaze said Dean Redfield has heard of me. That's flattering, but I'm not exactly a household name."

"Apparently, Dean was friends with someone you used to work with—a Brock Campbell? I know Campbell died a few years ago, but I guess he spoke highly enough of you when he was alive that Dean had heard of you, too."

Jack watched me as he fed me the details, reading my expression. I kept it as clear as I could. He already knew the truth—he would have to. Or at least as much as the rest of the world did: that Brock Campbell had been my mentor, yes, but that he had also left his entire estate—including a thriving business and a barren mansion that I sold the second Brock was in the ground—to Bear and me.

"I've never met any of them," I said. "Apart from the stories I remember from the news, I've never heard of them."

"I know," Jack said. "And I hate to be the one to come here and ask you to get involved. The higher-ups knew that we'd worked together and there was potentially a…relationship there." He paused on "relationship." The air warmed between us. There has never been a relationship between Jack and me, though—not really. We've worked together a few times. Shared a hotel room one night, but separate beds. Once, when I was feeling particularly brave, I kissed him on the cheek.

That is the extent of our "relationship."

"So they thought they'd take advantage of that," I said.

"Blaze was pretty insistent," he said with a measure of guilt I still didn't understand. "And now that she's not here," I just want to make sure you know you can turn this down if you want. There's no pressure. You don't have to do this—I wouldn't blame you."

Silence fell between us. A shimmer of light caught the sun over Jack's right shoulder. I stared at it for a few seconds. A familiar tremor slid beneath my skin.

I'd seen that light before. It followed Jack; shone brighter the worse things got for him. Right now, it was blinding.

"Are you all right?" I asked him.

He looked surprised. I noted again how thin his face was. His complexion was a shade lighter than usual, as though he hadn't been in the sun much in recent months. Though he's only a few years older than my thirty-two years, right then Jack looked a decade beyond that.

"I'm fine," he said. His voice sounded weary, though. The professional guise he'd had in place from the time I'd stepped on the wharf this morning momentarily vanished. "I mean… I guess I'm fine. I get up every day. Put one foot in front of the other. Try to find answers."

"And?" I asked.

"And…none yet. But I'm still looking."

Jack's wife—that brilliant light shining forever in the distance for him—was raped and murdered in Nicaragua six years ago. He had some idea of who had done it, I thought, but no name; no one to actually pin it on. From what I could tell, it was eating him up.

I scratched the back of my neck, still wet from the rain, and considered the situation. "Is there something you're not telling me?" I asked. "Some reason I should turn this down rather than going with you to Vermont?"

He looked up ahead, forehead furrowed, as though searching for an answer on the horizon. Scrubbed his hand across his mouth. And, finally, shook his head.

"I can't make the decision for you. But if you don't want to come..."

"Unless you give me a reason why I shouldn't, I'm coming with you. We're always waiting for a call like this, it's what we train for. I'm not about to turn it down without a reason."

He didn't look happy with my choice, which confused me all the more. "Okay. Good, then. Decision made."

I nodded up ahead, where a darkened land mass stood looming above the water. "And now, if you can keep yourself out of trouble for twenty minutes, I'll get everything pulled together and we'll get out of here. We're used to gearing up fast."

He looked more uneasy the closer we got to the island, but he nodded. For a moment, our eyes caught. He managed a naked smile. "I really am glad to see you, Jamie. I should have called sooner, but it will be good to work together again."

I shrugged, but felt my cheeks warm at his words. "It's my job, Jack. This is what I do."

More Erin Solomon Mysteries

In Between Days
Diggs & Solomon Shorts
1990 - 2000

Midnight Lullaby
Prequel to
The Erin Solomon Mysteries

The Payson Pentalogy
The Critically Acclaimed 5-Book Set
Readers Can't Put Down!

Book I: All the Blue-Eyed Angels
Book II: Sins of the Father
Book III: Southern Cross
Book IV: Before the After
Book V: The Book of J

And the First Novel in the Jamie Flint K-9 Search and Rescue Mysteries

The Darkest Thread

ABOUT THE AUTHOR

Jen Blood is a freelance journalist and author of the bestselling Erin Solomon mystery series. She is also owner of Adian Editing, providing expert editing of plot-driven fiction for authors around the world. Jen holds an MFA in Creative Writing/Popular Fiction, with influences ranging from Emily Bronte to Joss Whedon and the whole spectrum in between. Today, Jen lives in Maine with her dog Killian, where the two are busy conquering snowbanks and penning the next Erin Solomon mystery.

For regular updates, free short stories, contests,
and giveaways between book releases,
visit http://jenblood.com/,
and like us on Facebook at
http://facebook.com/jenbloodauthor/

Made in the USA
Lexington, KY
29 July 2019